H. RIDER HAGGARD

MARIE

Illustrated by Hookway Cowles

MACDONALD · LONDON

First published 1912
First published in this series in 1959
This impression 1973

ISBN 0 356 01260 3

Published by
Macdonald & Co. (Publishers), Ltd,
St Giles House, 49 Poland Street, London, W.1
Printed in Great Britain by
Redwood Press Limited
Trowbridge, Wiltshire

DEDICATION

Ditchingham, 1912.

My dear Sir Henry,—

Nearly thirty-seven years have gone by, more than a generation, since first we saw the shores of Africa rising from the sea.
Since then how much has happened : the Annexation of the
Transvaal, the Zulu War, the first Boer War, the discovery of
the Rand, the taking of Rhodesia, the second Boer War, and
many other matters which in these quick-moving times are now
reckoned as ancient history.

Alas ! I fear that were we to re-visit that country we should
find but few faces which we knew. Yet of one thing we may be
glad. Those historical events, in some of which you, as the
ruler of Natal, played a great part, and I, as it chanced, a smaller
one, so far as we can foresee, have at length brought a period
of peace to Southern Africa. To-day the flag of England flies
from the Zambesi to the Cape. Beneath its shadow may all
ancient feuds and blood jealousies be forgotten. May the natives
prosper also and be justly ruled, for after all in the beginning the
land was theirs. Such, I know, are your hopes, as they are mine.

It is, however, with an earlier Africa that this story deals. In
1836 hate and suspicion ran high between the Home Government and its Dutch subjects. Owing to the freeing of the slaves
and mutual misunderstandings, the Cape Colony was then in
tumult, almost in rebellion, and the Boers, by thousands, sought
new homes in the unknown, savage-peopled North. Of this
blood-stained time I have tried to tell ; of the Great Trek and its
tragedies, such as the massacre of the true-hearted Retief and his
companions at the hands of the Zulu king, Dingaan.

But you have read the tale and know its substance. What,
then, remains for me to say ? Only that in memory of long-
past days I dedicate it to you whose image ever springs to my

mind when I strive to picture an English gentleman as he should be. Your kindness I never shall forget; in memory of it, I offer you this book.

Ever sincerely yours,

H. RIDER HAGGARD.

To SIR HENRY BULWER, G.C.M.G.

PREFACE

THE Author hopes that the reader may find some historical interest in the tale set out in these pages of the massacre of the Boer general, Retief, and his companions at the hands of the Zulu king, Dingaan. Save for some added circumstances, he believes it to be accurate in its details.

The same may be said of the account given of the hideous sufferings of the trek-Boers who wandered into the fever veld, there to perish in the neighbourhood of Delagoa Bay. Of these sufferings, especially those that were endured by Triechard and his companions, a few brief contemporary records still exist, buried in scarce works of reference. It may be mentioned, also, that it was a common belief among the Boers of that generation that the cruel death of Retief and his companions, and other misfortunes which befell them, were due to the treacherous plottings of an Englishman, or of Englishmen, with the despot, Dingaan.

EDITOR'S NOTE

THE following extract explains how the manuscript of "Marie," and with it some others, one of which is named "Child of Storm," came into the hands of the Editor. It is from a letter, dated January 17th, 1910, and written by Mr. George Curtis, the brother of Sir Henry Curtis, Bart., who, it will be remembered, was one of the late Mr. Allan Quatermain's friends and companions in adventure when he discovered King Solomon's Mines, and who afterwards disappeared with him in Central Africa.

This extract runs as follows :

"You may recall that our mutual and dear friend, old Allan Quatermain, left me the sole executor of his will, which he signed before he set out with my brother Henry for Zuvendis, where he was killed. The Court, however, not being satisfied that there was any legal proof of his death, invested the capital funds in trustee securities, and by my advice let his place in Yorkshire to a tenant who has remained in occupation of it during the last two decades. Now that tenant is dead, and at the earnest prayer of the Charities which benefit under Quatermain's will, and of myself—for in my uncertain state of health I have for long been most anxious to wind up this executorship—about eight months ago the Court at last consented to the distribution of this large fund in accordance with the terms of the will.

"This, of course, involved the sale of the real property, and before it was put up to auction I went over the house in company of the solicitor appointed by the Court. On the top landing, in the room Quatermain used to occupy, we found a sealed cupboard that I opened. It proved to be full of various articles which evidently he had prized because of their associations with his early life. These I need not enumerate here, especially as I have reserved them as his residuary legatee and, in the event of my death, they will pass to you under my will.

"Among these relics, however, I found a stout box, made of some red foreign wood, that contained various documents and letters and a bundle of manuscripts. Under the tape which fastened these manuscripts together, as you will see, is a scrap of paper on which is written, in blue pencil, a direction signed 'Allan Quatermain,' that in the event of anything happening to him, these MSS. are to be sent to you (for whom, as you know, he had a high regard), and that at your sole discretion you are to burn or publish them as you may see fit.

"So, after all these years, as we both remain alive, I carry out our old friend's instructions and send you his bequest, which I trust may prove of interest and value. I have read the MS. called 'Marie,' and certainly am of opinion that it ought to be published, for I think it a strange and moving tale of a great love—full, moreover, of forgotten history.

"That named 'Child of Storm' also seems very interesting as a study of savage life, and the others may be the same; but my eyes are troubling me so much that I have not been able to decipher them. I hope, however, that I may be spared long enough to see them in print.

"Poor old Allan Quatermain. It is as though he had suddenly reappeared from the dead! So at least I thought as I perused these stories of a period of his life of which I do not remember his speaking to me.

"And now my responsibility in this matter is finished and yours begins. Do what you like about the manuscripts.

"GEORGE CURTIS."

As may be imagined, I, the Editor, was considerably astonished when I received this letter and the accompanying bundle of closely-written MSS. To me also it was as though my old friend had risen from the grave and once more stood before me, telling some history of his stormy and tragic past in that quiet, measured voice that I have never been able to forget.

The first manuscript I read was that entitled "Marie." It deals with Mr. Quatermain's strange experiences when as a very young man he accompanied the ill-fated Pieter Retief and the Boer Commission on an embassy to the Zulu despot, Dingaan. This, it will be remembered, ended in their massacre, Quatermain himself and his Hottentot servant Hans being the sole survivors of the slaughter. Also it deals with another matter more personal to himself, namely, his courtship of and marriage to his first wife, Marie Marais.

Of this Marie I never heard him speak, save once. I remember that on a certain occasion—it was that of a garden fête for a local charity—I was standing by Quatermain when some one introduced to him a young girl who was staying in the neighbourhood and had distinguished herself by singing very prettily at the fête. Her surname I forget, but her Christian name was Marie. He started when he heard it, and asked if she were French. The young lady answered No, but only of French extraction through her grandmother, who also was called Marie.

" Indeed ? " he said. " Once I knew a maiden not unlike you who was also of French extraction and called Marie. May you prove more fortunate in life than she was, though better or nobler you can never be," and he bowed to her in his simple, courtly fashion, then turned away. Afterwards, when we were alone, I asked him who was this Marie of whom he had spoken to the young lady. He paused a little, then answered :

" She was my first wife, but I beg you not to speak of her to me or to anyone else, for I cannot bear to hear her name. Perhaps you will learn all about her one day." Then, to my grief and astonishment, he broke into something like a sob and abruptly left the room.

After reading the record of this Marie I can well understand why he was so moved. I print it practically as it left his hands.

There are other MSS. also, one of which, headed " Child of Storm," relates the moving history of a beautiful and, I fear I must add, wicked Zulu girl named Mameena who did much evil in her day and went unrepentant from the world.

Another, amongst other things, tells the secret story of the causes of the defeat of Cetawayo and his armies by the English in 1879, which happened not long before Quatermain met Sir Henry Curtis and Captain Good.

These three narratives are, indeed, more or less connected with each other. At least, a certain aged dwarf, called Zikali, a witch-doctor and a terrible man, has to do with all of them, although in the first, " Marie," he is only vaguely mentioned in connection with the massacre of Retief, whereof he was doubtless the primary instigator. As " Marie " comes first in chronological order, and was placed on the top of the pile by its author, I publish it first. With the others I hope to deal later on, as I may find time and opportunity.

But the future must take care of itself. We cannot control it, and its events are not in our hand. Meanwhile, I hope that those who in their youth have read of King Solomon's Mines and Zuvendis, and perhaps some others who are younger, may find as much of interest in these new chapters of the autobiography of Allan Quatermain as I have done myself.

CONTENTS

LIST OF ILLUSTRATIONS

I

ALLAN LEARNS FRENCH

ALTHOUGH in my old age I, Allan Quatermain, have taken to writing—after a fashion—never yet have I set down a single word of the tale of my first love and of the adventures that are grouped around her beautiful and tragic history. I suppose this is because it has always seemed to me too holy and far-off a matter—as holy and far-off as is that heaven which holds the splendid spirit of Marie Marais. But now, in my age, that which was far-off draws near again ; and at night, in the depths between the stars, sometimes I seem to see the opening doors through which I must pass, and leaning earthwards across their threshold, with outstretched arms and dark and dewy eyes, a shadow long forgotten by all save me—the shadow of Marie Marais.

An old man's dream, doubtless, no more. Still, I will try to set down that history which ended in so great a sacrifice, and one so worthy of record, though I hope that no human eye will read it until I also am forgotten, or, at any rate, have grown dim in the gathering mists of oblivion. And I am glad that I have waited to make this attempt, for it seems to me that only of late have I come to understand and appreciate at its true value the character of her of whom I tell, and the passionate affection which was her bounteous offering to one so utterly unworthy as myself. What have I done, I wonder, that to me should have been decreed the love of two such women as Marie and of that Stella, also now long dead, to whom alone in the world I told all her tale ? I remember I feared lest she should take it ill, but this was not so. Indeed, during our brief married days, she thought and talked much of Marie, and some of her last words to me were that she was going to seek her, and that they would wait for me together in the land of love, pure and immortal.

17

So with Stella's death all that side of life came to an end for me, since during the long years which stretch between then and now I have never said another tender word to woman. I admit, however, that once, long afterwards, a certain little witch of a Zulu did say tender words to me, and for an hour or so almost turned my head, an art in which she had great skill. This I say because I wish to be quite honest, although it—I mean my head, for there was no heart involved in the matter—came straight again at once. Her name was Mameena, and I have set down her remarkable story elsewhere.

To return. As I have already written in another book, I passed my youth with my old father, a Church of England clergyman, in what is now the Cradock district of the Cape Colony.

Then it was a wild place enough, with a very small white population. Among our few neighbours was a Boer farmer of the name of Henri Marais, who lived about fifteen miles from our station, on a fine farm called Maraisfontein. I say he was a Boer, but, as may be guessed from both his Christian and sur-name, his origin was Huguenot, his forefather, who was also named Henri Marais—though I think the Marais was spelt rather differently then—having been one of the first of that faith who emigrated to South Africa to escape the cruelties of Louis XIV. at the time of the revocation of the Edict of Nantes.

Unlike most Boers of similar descent, these particular Marais —for, of course, there are many other families so called—never forgot their origin. Indeed, from father to son, they kept up some knowledge of the French tongue, and among themselves often spoke it after a fashion. At any rate, it was the habit of Henri Marais, who was excessively religious, to read his chapter of the Bible (which it is, or was, the custom of the Boers to spell out every morning, should their learning allow them to do so), not in the *taal* or *patois* Dutch, but in good old French. I have the very book from which he used to read now, for, curiously enough, in after years, when all these events had long been gathered to the past, I chanced to buy it among a parcel of other works at the weekly auction of odds and ends on the market square of Maritzburg. I remember that when I opened the great tome, bound over the original leather boards in buckskin, and discovered to whom it had belonged, I burst into tears. There was no doubt about it, for, as was customary in old days, this Bible had sundry fly-leaves sewn up with it for the purpose of the recording of events important to its owner.

The first entries were made by the original Henri Marais, and record how he and his compatriots were driven from France, his father having lost his life in the religious persecutions. After this comes a long list of births, marriages and deaths continued from generation to generation, and amongst them a few notes telling of such matters as the change of the dwelling-places of the family, always in French. Towards the end of the list appears the entry of the birth of the Henri Marais whom I knew, alas ! too well, and of his only sister. Then is written his marriage to Marie Labuschagne, also, be it noted, of the Huguenot stock. In the next year follows the birth of Marie Marais, my Marie, and, after a long interval, for no other children were born, the death of her mother. Immediately below appears the following curious passage :

" *Le 3 Janvier*, 1836. *Je quitte ce pays voulant me sauver du maudit gouvernement Britannique comme mes ancêtres se sont sauvés de ce diable—Louis XIV.*

" *A bas les rois et les ministres tyrannique ! Vive la liberté !* "

Which indicates very clearly the character and the opinions of Henri Marais, and the feeling among the trek-Boers at that time.

Thus the record closes and the story of the Marais ends— that is, so far as the writings in the Bible go, for that branch of the family is now extinct.

Their last chapter I will tell in due course.

There was nothing remarkable about my introduction to Marie Marais. I did not rescue her from any attack of a wild beast or pull her out of a raging river in a fashion suited to romance. Indeed, we interchanged our young ideas across a small and extremely massive table, which, in fact, had once done duty as a block for the chopping up of meat. To this hour I can see the hundreds of lines running criss-cross upon its surface, especially those opposite to where I used to sit.

One day, several years after my father had emigrated to the

Cape, the Heer Marais arrived at our house in search, I think, of some lost oxen. He was then a thin, bearded man with rather wild, dark eyes set close together, and a quick, nervous manner, not in the least like that of a Dutch Boer—or so I recall him. My father received him courteously and asked him to stop to dine, which he did.

They talked together in French, a tongue that my father knew well, although he had not used it for years ; Dutch he could not, or, rather, would not, speak if he could help it, and Mr. Marais preferred not to talk English. To meet someone who could converse in French delighted him, and although his version of the language was that of two centuries before and my father's was largely derived from reading, they got on very well together, if not too fast.

At length, after a pause, Mr. Marais, pointing to myself, a small and stubbly-haired youth with a sharp nose, asked my father whether he would like me to be instructed in the French tongue. The answer was that nothing would please him better.

" Although," he added severely, " to judge by my own experience where Latin and Greek are concerned, I doubt his capacity to learn anything."

So an arrangement was made that I should go over for two days in each week to Maraisfontein, sleeping there on the intervening night, and acquire a knowledge of the French tongue from a tutor whom Mr. Marais had hired to instruct his daughter in that language and other subjects. I remember that my father agreed to pay a certain proportion of this tutor's salary, a plan which suited the thrifty Boer very well indeed.

Thither, accordingly, I went in due course, nothing loth, for on the veld between our station and Maraisfontein many *pauw* and *koran*—that is, big and small bustards—were to be found, to say nothing of occasional buck, and I was allowed to carry a gun, which even in those days I could use fairly well. So to Maraisfontein I rode on the appointed day, attended by a Hottentot after-rider, a certain Hans, of whom I shall have a good deal to tell. I enjoyed very good sport on the road, arriving at the stead laden with one *pauw*, two *koran*, and a little *klip-springer* buck which I had been lucky enough to shoot as it bounded out of some rocks in front of me.

There was a peach orchard planted round Maraisfontein, which just then was a mass of lovely pink blossom, and as I rode through it slowly, not being sure of my way to the house, a lanky child appeared in front of me, clad in a frock which exactly matched the colour of the peach bloom. I can see her now, her dark hair hanging down her back, and her big, shy eyes staring at me from the shadow of the Dutch *kappie* which she wore. Indeed, she seemed to be all eyes, like a *dikkop* or thick-head plover ; at any rate, I noted little else about her.

I pulled up my pony and stared at her, feeling very shy and not knowing what to say. For a while she stared back at me, being afflicted, presumably, with the same complaint, then spoke with an effort, in a voice that was very soft and pleasant.

" Are you the little Allan Quatermain who is coming to learn French with me? " she asked in Dutch.

" Of course," I answered in the same tongue, which I knew well ; " but why do you call me little, missie ? I am taller than you," I added indignantly, for when I was young my lack of height was always a sore point with me.

" I think not," she replied. " But get off that horse, and we will measure here against this wall."

So I dismounted, and, having assured herself that I had no heels to my boots (I was wearing the kind of raw-hide slippers that the Boers call *veld-shoon*), she took the writing slate which she was carrying—it had no frame, I remember, being, in fact, but a piece of the material used for roofing—and, pressing it down tight on my stubbly hair, which stuck up then as now, made a deep mark in the soft sandstone of the wall with the hard pointed pencil.

" There," she said, " that is justly done. Now, little Allan, it is your turn to measure me."

So I measured her, and, behold ! she was the taller by a whole half-inch.

" You are standing on tiptoe," I said in my vexation.

" Little Allan," she replied, " to stand on tiptoe would be to lie before the good Lord, and when you come to know me better you will learn that, though I have a dreadful temper and many other sins, I do not lie."

I suppose that I looked snubbed and mortified, for she went

on in her grave, grown-up way : " Why are you angry because God made me taller than you ? especially as I am whole months older, for my father told me so. Come, let us write our names against these marks, so that in a year or two you may see how you outgrow me." Then with the slate pencil she scratched " Marie " against her mark very deeply, so that it might last, she said ; after which I wrote " Allan " against mine.

Alas ! Within the last dozen years chance took me past Maraisfontein once more. The house had long been rebuilt, but this particular wall yet stood. I rode to it and looked, and there faintly could still be seen the name Marie, against the little line, and by it the mark that I had made. My own name and with it subsequent measurements were gone, for in the intervening forty years or so the sandstone had flaked away in places. Only her autograph remained, and when I saw it I think that I felt even worse than I did on finding whose was the old Bible that I had bought upon the market square at Maritzburg.

I know that I rode away hurriedly without even stopping to inquire into whose hands the farm had passed. Through the peach orchard I rode, where the trees—perhaps the same, perhaps others—were once more in bloom, for the season of the year was that when Marie and I first met, nor did I draw rein for half a score of miles.

But here I may state that Marie always stayed just half an inch the taller in body, and how much taller in mind and spirit I cannot tell.

When we had finished our measuring match Marie turned to lead me to the house, and, pretending to observe for the first time the beautiful bustard and the two *koran* hanging from my saddle, also the *klipspringer* buck that Hans the Hottentot carried behind him on his horse, asked :

" Did you shoot all these, Allan Quatermain ? "

" Yes," I answered proudly ; " I killed them in four shots, and the *pauw* and *koran* were flying, not sitting, which is more than you could have done, although you are taller, Miss Marie."

" I do not know," she answered reflectively. " I can shoot very well with a rifle, for my father has taught me, but I never would shoot at living things unless I must because I was hungry, for I think that to kill is cruel. But, of course, it is different with men," she added hastily, " and no doubt you will be a great hunter one day, Allan Quatermain, since you can already aim so well."

" I hope so," I answered, blushing at the compliment, " for I love hunting, and when there are so many wild things it does not matter if we kill a few. I shot these for you and your father to eat."

" Come, then, and give them to him. He will thank you," and she led the way through the gate in the sandstone wall into the yard, where the outbuildings stood in which the riding horses and the best of the breeding cattle were kept at night, and so past the end of the long, one-storied house, that was stone-built and white-washed, to the stoep or veranda in front of it.

On this broad stoep, which commanded a pleasant view over rolling, park-like country, where mimosa and other trees grew in clumps, two men were seated, drinking strong coffee, although it was not yet ten o'clock in the morning.

Hearing the sound of the horses, one of these, Mynheer Marais, whom I already knew, rose from his hide-strung chair. He was, as I think I have said, not in the least like one of the phlegmatic Boers, either in person or in temperament, but, rather, a typical Frenchman, although no member of his race had set foot in France for a hundred and fifty years. At least, so I discovered afterwards, for, of course, in those days I knew nothing of Frenchmen.

His companion was also French, Leblanc by name, but of a very different stamp. In person he was short and stout. His large head was bald except for a fringe of curling, iron-grey hair which grew round it just above the ears and fell upon his shoulders, giving him the appearance of a tonsured but dis-hevelled priest. His eyes were blue and watery, his mouth was rather weak, and his cheeks were pale, full and flabby. When the Heer Marais rose, I, being an observant youth, noted that Monsieur Leblanc took the opportunity to stretch out a rather shaky hand and fill up his coffee cup out of a black bottle, which from the smell I judged to contain peach brandy.

In fact, it may as well be said at once that the poor man was a drunkard, which explains how he, with all his high education and great ability, came to hold the humble post of tutor on a remote Boer farm. Years before, when under the influence of drink, he had committed some crime in France—I don't know what it was, and never inquired—and fled to the Cape to avoid prosecution. Here he obtained a professorship at one of the colleges, but after a while appeared in the lecture-room quite drunk and lost his employment. The same thing happened in other towns, till at last he drifted to distant Maraisfontein, where his employer tolerated his weakness for the sake of the intellectual companionship for which something in his own nature seemed to crave. Also, he looked upon him as a compatriot in distress, and a great bond of union between them was their mutual and virulent hatred of England and the English, which in the case of Monsieur Leblanc, who in his youth had fought at Waterloo and been acquainted with the great Emperor, was not altogether unnatural.

Henri Marais's case was different, but of that I shall have more to say later.

"Ah, Marie," said her father, speaking in Dutch, "so you have found him at last," and he nodded towards me, adding : "You should be flattered, little man. Look you, this missie has been sitting for two hours in the sun waiting for you, although I told her you would not arrive much before ten o'clock, as your father the *prédicant* said you would breakfast before you started. Well, it is natural, for she is lonely here, and you are of an age, although of a different race "; and his face darkened as he spoke the words.

"Father," answered Marie, whose blushes I could see even in the shadow of her cap, "I was not sitting in the sun, but under the shade of a peach tree. Also, I was working out the sums that Monsieur Leblanc set me on my slate. See, here they are," and she held up the slate, which was covered with figures, somewhat smudged, it is true, by the rubbing of my stiff hair and of her cap.

Then Monsieur Leblanc broke in, speaking in French, of which, as it chanced, I understood the sense, for my father had grounded me in that tongue, and I am naturally quick at modern languages. At any rate, I made out that he was asking if I was the little "*cochon d'anglais*," or English pig, whom for his sins he had to teach. He added that he judged I must be, as my hair stuck up on my head—I had taken off my hat out of politeness—as it naturally would do on a pig's back.

This was too much for me, so, before either of the others could speak, I answered in Dutch, for rage made me eloquent and bold :

" Yes, I am he ; but, mynheer, if you are to be my master, I hope you will not call the English pigs any more to me."

" Indeed, *gamin* " (that is, little scamp), " and, pray, what will happen if I am so bold as to repeat that truth ? "

" I think, mynheer," I replied, growing white with rage at this new insult, " the same that has happened to yonder buck," and I pointed to the *klipspringer* behind Hans's saddle. "I mean that I shall shoot you."

" *Peste ! Au moins il a du courage, cet enfant* " (At least the child is plucky), exclaimed Monsieur Leblanc, astonished. From that moment, I may add, he respected me, and never again insulted my country to my face.

Then Marais broke out, speaking in Dutch that I might understand :

" It is you who should be called pig, Leblanc, not this boy, for, early as it is, you have been drinking. Look ! the brandy bottle is half empty. Is that the example you set to the young ? Speak so again and I turn you out to starve on the veld. Allan Quatermain, although, as you may have heard, I do not like the English, I beg your pardon. I hope you will forgive the words this sot spoke, thinking that you did not understand," and he took off his hat and bowed to me quite in a grand manner, as his ancestors might have done to a king of France.

Leblanc's face fell. Then he rose and walked away rather unsteadily ; as I learned afterwards, to plunge his head in a tub of cold water and swallow a pint of new milk, which were his favourite antidotes after too much strong drink. At any rate, when he appeared again, half an hour later, to begin our lesson, he was quite sober, and extremely polite.

When he had gone, my childish anger being appeased, I presented the Heer Marais with my father's compliments, also with the buck and the birds, whereof the latter seemed to please him more than the former. Then my saddle-bags were taken to my room, a little cupboard of a place next to that occupied by Monsieur Leblanc, and Hans was sent to turn the horses out with the others belonging to the farm, having first knee-haltered them tightly, so that they should not run away home.

This done, the Heer Marais showed me the room in which we were to have our lessons, one of the *sitkammer*, or sitting chambers, whereof, unlike most Boer steads, this house boasted two. I remember that the floor was made of *daga*, that is, ant-heap earth mixed with cow-dung, into which thousands of peach-stones had been thrown while it was still soft, in order to resist footwear—a rude but fairly efficient expedient, and one not unpleasing to the eye. For the rest, there was one window opening on to the veranda, which, in that bright climate, admitted a shaded but sufficient light, especially as it always stood open; the ceiling was of unplastered reeds; a large bookcase stood in the corner containing many French works, most of them the property of Monsieur Leblanc, and in the centre of the room was the strong, rough table made of native yellow-wood, that once had served as a butcher's block. I recollect also a coloured print of the great Napoleon commanding at some battle in which he was victorious, seated upon a white horse and waving a field-marshal's baton over piles of dead and wounded; and near the window, hanging to the reeds of the ceiling, the nest of a pair of red-tailed swallows, pretty creatures that, notwithstanding the mess they made, afforded to Marie and me endless amusement in the intervals of our work.

When, on that day, I shuffled shyly into this homely place, and, thinking myself alone there, fell to examining it, suddenly I was brought to a standstill by a curious choking sound which seemed to proceed from the shadows behind the bookcase. Wondering as to its cause, I advanced cautiously to discover a pink-clad shape standing in the corner like a naughty child, with her head resting against the wall, and sobbing slowly.

" Marie Marais, why do you cry ? " I asked.

She turned, tossing back the locks of long, black hair which hung about her face, and answered :

" Allan Quatermain, I cry because of the shame which has been put upon you and upon our house by that drunken French-man."

" What of that ? " I asked. " He only called me a pig, but I think I have shown him that even a pig has tusks."

" Yes," she replied, " but it was not you he meant ; it was all the English, whom he hates ; and the worst of it is that my father is of his mind. He, too, hates the English, and, oh ! I am sure that trouble will come of his hatred, trouble and death to many."

" Well, if so, we have nothing to do with it, have we ? " I replied with the cheerfulness of extreme youth.

" What makes you so sure ? " she said solemnly. " Hush ! here comes Monsieur Leblanc."

II

THE ATTACK ON MARAISFONTEIN

I DO not propose to set out the history of the years which I spent in acquiring a knowledge of French and various other subjects, under the tuition of the learned but prejudiced Monsieur Leblanc. Indeed, there is " none to tell, sir." When Monsieur Leblanc was sober, he was a most excellent and well-informed tutor, although one apt to digress into many side issues, which in themselves were not uninstructive. When tipsy, he grew excited and harangued us, generally upon politics and religion, or rather its reverse, for he was an advanced freethinker, although this was a side to his character which, however intoxicated he might be, he always managed to conceal from the Heer Marais. I may add that a certain childish code of honour prevented us from betraying his views on this and sundry other matters. When absolutely drunk, which on an average was not more than once a month, he simply slept, and we did what we pleased —a fact which our childish code of honour also prevented us from betraying.

But, on the whole, we got on very well together, for, after the incident of our first meeting, Monsieur Leblanc was always polite to me. Marie he adored, as did everyone about the place, from her father down to the meanest slave. Need I add that

I adored her more than all of them put together, first with the
love that some children have for each other, and afterwards, as
we became adult, with that wider love by which it is at once
transcended and made complete. Strange would it have been
if this were not so, seeing that we spent nearly half of every
week practically alone together, and that, from the first, Marie,
whose nature was as open as the clear noon, never concealed
her affection for me. True, it was a very discreet affection,
almost sisterly, or even motherly, in its outward and visible
aspects, as though she could never forget that extra half inch of
height or month or two of age.

Moreover, from a child she was a woman, as an Irishman
might say, for circumstances and character had shaped her thus.
Not much more than a year before we met, her mother, whose
only child she was, and whom she loved with all her strong
and passionate heart, died after a lingering illness, leaving her
in charge of her father and his house. I think it was this heavy
bereavement in early youth which coloured her nature with a
grey tinge of sadness and made her seem so much older than her
years.

So the time went on, I worshipping Marie in my secret thought,
but saying nothing about it, and Marie talking of and acting
towards me as though I were her dear younger brother. Nobody,
not even her father or mine, or Monsieur Leblanc, took the
slightest notice of this queer relationship, or seemed to dream
that it might lead to ultimate complications which, in fact, would
have been very distasteful to them all for reasons that I will
explain.

Needless to say, in due course, as they were bound to do,
those complications arose, and under pressure of great physical
and moral excitement the truth came out. It happened thus.

Every reader of the history of the Cape Colony has heard of
the great Kaffir War of 1835. That war took place for the most
part in the districts of Albany and Somerset, so that we inhabitants of Cradock, on the whole, suffered little. Therefore, with
the natural optimism and carelessness of danger of dwellers in
wild places, we began to think ourselves fairly safe from attack.
Indeed, so we should have been, had it not been for a foolish
action on the part of Monsieur Leblanc.

It seems that on a certain Sunday, a day that I always spent at home with my father, Monsieur Leblanc rode out alone to some hills about five miles distant from Maraisfontein. He had often been cautioned that this was an unsafe thing to do, but the truth is that the foolish man thought he had found a rich copper mine in these hills, and was anxious that no one should share his secret. Therefore, on Sundays, when there were no lessons, and the Heer Marais was in the habit of celebrating family prayers, which Leblanc disliked, it was customary for him to ride to these hills and there collect geological specimens and locate the strike of his copper vein. On this particular Sabbath, which was very hot, after he had done whatever he intended to do, he dismounted from his horse, a tame old beast. Leaving it loose, he partook of the meal he had brought with him, which seems to have included a bottle of peach brandy that induced slumber.

Waking up towards evening, he found that his horse had gone, and at once jumped to the conclusion that it had been stolen by Kaffirs, although in truth the animal had but strolled over a ridge in search of grass. Running hither and thither to seek it, he presently crossed this ridge and met the horse, apparently being led away by two of the Red Kaffirs, who, as was usual, were armed with assegais. As a matter of fact these men had found the beast, and, knowing well to whom it belonged, were seeking its owner, whom, earlier in the day, they had seen upon the hills, in order to restore it to him. This, however, never occurred to the mind of Monsieur Leblanc, excited as it was by the fumes of the peach brandy.

Lifting the double-barrelled gun he carried, he fired at the first Kaffir, a young man who chanced to be the eldest son and heir of the chief of the tribe, and, as the range was very close, shot him dead. Thereon his companion, leaving go of the horse, ran for his life. At him Leblanc fired also, wounding him slightly in the thigh, but no more, so that he escaped to tell the tale of what he and every other native for miles round considered a wanton and premeditated murder. The deed done, the fiery old Frenchman mounted his nag and rode quietly home. On the road, however, as the peach brandy evaporated from his brain, doubts entered it, with the result that he determined to say nothing of his adventure to Henri Marais, whom he knew was particularly anxious to avoid any cause of quarrel with the Kaffirs.

So he kept his own counsel and went to bed. Before he was up next morning the Heer Marais, suspecting neither trouble nor danger, had ridden off to a farm thirty miles or more away to pay its owner for some cattle which he had recently bought, leaving his home and his daughter quite unprotected, except by Leblanc and the few native servants, who were really slaves, that lived about the place.

Now on the Monday night I went to bed as usual, and slept, as I have always done through life, like a top, till about four in the morning, when I was awakened by someone tapping at the glass of my window. Slipping from the bed, I felt for my pistol, as it was quite dark, crept to the window, opened it, and keeping my head below the level of the sill, fearing lest its appearance should be greeted with an assegai, asked who was there.

" Me, baas," said the voice of Hans, our Hottentot servant, who, it will be remembered, had accompanied me as after-rider when first I went to Maraisfontein. " I have bad news. Listen. The baas knows that I have been out searching for the red cow which was lost. Well, I found her, and was sleeping by her side under a tree on the veld when, about two hours ago, a woman whom I know came up to my camp fire and woke me. I asked her what she was doing at that hour of the night, and she answered that she had come to tell me something. She said that some young men of the tribe of the chief Quabie, who lives in the hills yonder had been visiting at their kraal, and that a few hours before a messenger had arrived from the chief saying that they must return at once, as this morning at dawn he and all his men were going to attack Maraisfontein and kill everyone in it and take the cattle ! "

" Good God ! " I ejaculated. " Why ? "

" Because, young baas," drawled the Hottentot from the other side of the window, " because someone from Marais-fontein—I think it was the Vulture " (the natives gave this name to Leblanc on account of his bald head and hooked nose)— " shot Quabie's son on Sunday when he was holding his horse."

" Good God ! " I said again, " the old fool must have been drunk. When did you say the attack was to be—at dawn ? " and I glanced at the stars, adding, " Why, that will be within less than an hour, and the Baas Marais is away."

" Yes," croaked Hans ; " and Missie Marie—think of what the Red Kaffirs will do with Missie Marie when their blood is up."

I thrust my fist through the window and struck the Hottentot's toad-like face on which the starlight gleamed faintly.

" Dog ! " I said, " saddle my mare and the roan horse and get your gun. In two minutes I come. Be swift or I kill you."

" I go," he answered, and shot out into the night like a frightened snake.

Then I began to dress, shouting as I dressed, till my father and the Kaffirs ran into the room. As I threw on my things I told them all.

" Send out messengers," I said, " to Marais—he is at Botha's farm—and to all the neighbours. Send, for your lives ; gather up the friendly Kaffirs and ride like hell for Maraisfontein. Don't talk to me, father ; don't talk ! Go and do what I tell you. Stay ! Give me two guns, fill the saddle-bags with powder tins and *loopers*, and tie them to my mare. Oh ! be quick, be quick ! "

Now at length they understood, and flew this way and that with candles and lanterns. Two minutes later—it could scarcely have been more—I was in front of the stables just as Hans led out the bay mare, a famous beast that for two years I had saved all my money to buy. Someone strapped on the saddle-bags while I tested the girths ; someone else appeared with the stout roan stallion that I knew would follow the mare to the death. There was not time to saddle him, so Hans clambered on to his back like a monkey, holding two guns under his arm, for I carried but one and my double-barrelled pistol.

" Send off the messengers," I shouted to my father. " If you would see me again send them swiftly, and follow with every man you can raise."

Then we were away with fifteen miles to do and five-and-thirty minutes before the dawn.

" Softly up the slope," I said to Hans, " till the beasts get their wind, and then ride as you never rode before."

Those first two miles of rising ground! I thought we should never come to the end of them, and yet I dared not let the mare out lest she should bucket herself. Happily she and her companion, the stallion—a most enduring horse, though not so very swift—had stood idle for the last thirty hours, and, of course, had not eaten or drunk since sunset. Therefore, being in fine fettle, they were keen for the business; also we were light weights.

I held in the mare as she sported up the rise, and the horse kept his pace to hers. We reached its crest, and before us lay the great level plain, eleven miles of it, and then two miles down hill to Maraisfontein.

" Now," I said to Hans, shaking loose the reins, " keep up if you can ! "

Away sped the mare till the keen air of the night sung past my ears, and behind her strained the good roan horse with the Hottentot monkey on its back. Oh! what a ride was that !

Further I have gone for a like cause, but never at such speed, for I knew the strength of the beasts and how long it would last them. Half an hour of it they might endure; more, and at this pace they must founder or die.

And yet such was the agony of my fear, that it seemed to me as though I only crept along the ground like a tortoise.

The roan was left behind, the sound of his footbeats died away, and I was alone with the night and my fear. Mile added itself to mile, for now and again the starlight showed me a stone or the skeleton of some dead beast that I knew. Once I dashed into a herd of trekking game so suddenly, that a springbok, unable to stop itself, leapt right over me. Once the mare put her foot in an ant-bear hole and nearly fell, but recovered herself— thanks be to God, unharmed—and I worked myself back into the saddle whence I had been almost shaken. If I had fallen; oh ! if I had fallen !

We were near the end of the flat, and she began to fail. I had over-pressed her; the pace was too tremendous. Her speed lessened to an ordinary fast gallop as she faced the gentle rise that led to the brow. And now, behind me, once more I heard the sound of the hoofs of the roan. The tireless beast was coming up. By the time we reached the edge of the plateau he was quite near, not fifty yards behind, for I heard him whinny faintly.

Then began the descent. The morning star was setting, the east grew grey with light. Oh! could we get there before the dawn? Could we get there before the dawn? That is what my horse's hoofs beat out to me.

Now I could see the mass of the trees about the stead. And now I dashed into something, though until I was through it, I did not know that it was a line of men, for the faint light gleamed upon the spear of one of them who had been overthrown.

So it was no lie! The Kaffirs were there! As I thought it, a fresh horror filled my heart; perhaps their murdering work was already done and they were departing.

The minute of suspense—or was it but seconds?—seemed an eternity. But it ended at last. Now I was at the door in the high wall that enclosed the outbuildings at the back of the house, and there, by an inspiration, pulled up the mare—glad enough she was to stop, poor thing—for it occurred to me that if I rode to the front I should very probably be assegaied and of no further use. I tried the door, which was made of stout stinkwood planks. By design, or accident, it had been left unbolted. As I thrust it open Hans arrived with a rush, clinging to the roan with his face hidden in its mane. The beast pulled up by the side of the mare which it had been pursuing, and in the faint light I saw that an assegai was fixed in its flank.

Five seconds later we were in the yard and locking and barring the door behind us. Then, snatching the saddle-bags of ammunition from the horses, we left them standing there, and I ran for the back entrance of the house, bidding Hans rouse the natives, who slept in the outbuildings, and follow with them. If any one of them showed signs of treachery he was to shoot him at once. I remember that as I went I tore the spear out of the stallion's flank and brought it away with me.

Now I was hammering upon the back door of the house, which I could not open. After a pause that seemed long, a window was thrown wide, and a voice—it was Marie's—asked in frightened tones who was there.

"I, Allan Quatermain," I answered. "Open at once, Marie. You are in great danger; the Red Kaffirs are going to attack the house."

She flew to the door in her nightdress, and at length I was in the place.

" Thank God! you are still safe," I gasped. " Put on your clothes while I call Leblanc. No, stay, do you call him ; I must wait here for Hans and your slaves."

Away she sped without a word, and presently Hans arrived, bringing with him eight frightened men, who as yet scarcely knew whether they slept or woke.

" Is that all ? " I asked. " Then bar the door and follow me to the *sitkammer*, where the baas keeps his guns."

Just as we reached it, Leblanc entered, clad in his shirt and trousers, and was followed presently by Marie with a candle.

" What is it ? " he asked.

I took the candle from Marie's hand, and set it on the floor close to the wall, lest it should prove a target for an assegai or a bullet. Even in those days the Kaffirs had a few firearms, for the most part captured or stolen from white men. Then in a few words I told them all.

" And when did you learn all this ? " asked Leblanc in French.

" At the Mission Station a little more than half an hour ago," I answered, looking at my watch.

" At the station a little more than half an hour ago ! *Peste !* it is not possible. You dream or are drunken," he cried excitedly.

" All right, monsieur, we will argue afterwards," I answered. " Meanwhile the Kaffirs are here, for I rode through them ; and if you want to save your life, stop talking and act. Marie, how many guns are there ? "

" Four," she answered, " of my father's ; two *roers* and two smaller ones."

" And how many of these men "—and I pointed to the Kaffirs—" can shoot ? "

" Three well and one badly, Allan."

" Good," I said. " Let them load the guns with *loopers* "— that is, slugs, not bullets—" and let the rest stand in the passage with their assegais, in case the Quabies should try to force the back door."

Now, in this house there were in all but six windows, one to each sitting-room, one to each of the larger bedrooms, these four opening on to the veranda, and one at either end of the house, to give light and air to the two small bedrooms, which were approached through the larger bedrooms. At the back, fortunately, there were no windows, for the stead was but one room deep with a passage running from the front to the back door, a distance of little over fifteen feet.

As soon as the guns were loaded I divided up the men, a man with a gun at each window. The right-hand sitting-room window I took myself with two guns, Marie coming with me to load, which, like all girls in that wild country, she could do well enough. So we arranged ourselves in a rough-and-ready fashion, and while we were doing it felt quite cheerful—that is, all except Monsieur Leblanc, who, I noticed, seemed very much disturbed.

I do not for one moment mean to suggest that he was afraid, as he might well have been, for he was an extremely brave and even rash man ; but I think the knowledge that his drunken act had brought this terrible danger upon us all weighed on his mind. Also there may have been more ; some subtle foreknowledge of the approaching end to a life that, when all allowances were made, could scarcely be called well spent. At any rate he fidgeted at his window-place, cursing beneath his breath, and soon, as I saw out of the corner of my eye, began to have recourse to his favourite bottle of peach brandy, which he fetched out of a cupboard.

The slaves, too, were gloomy, as all natives are when suddenly awakened in the night ; but as the light grew they became more cheerful. It is a poor Kaffir that does not love fighting, especially when he has a gun and a white man or two to lead him.

Now that we had made such little preparations as we could, which, by the way, I supplemented by causing some furniture to be piled up against the front and back doors, there came a pause, which, speaking for my own part—being, after all, only a lad at the time—I found very trying to the nerves. There I stood at my window with the two guns, one a double-barrel and one a single *roer*, or elephant gun, that took a tremendous charge, but both, be it remembered, flint locks ; for, although percussion caps had been introduced, we were a little behind the

times in Cradock. There, too, crouched on the ground beside
me, holding the ammunition ready for re-loading, her long,
black hair flowing about her shoulders, was Marie Marais, now
a well-grown young woman. In the intense silence she whispered to me:

"Why did you come here, Allan? You were safe yonder,
and now you will probably be killed."

"To try to save you," I answered simply. "What would
you have had me do?"

"To try to save me? Oh! that is good of you, but you
should have thought of yourself."

"Then I should still have thought of you, Marie."

"Why, Allan?"

"Because you are myself and more than myself. If anything
happened to you, what would my life be to me?"

"I don't quite understand, Allan," she replied, staring down
at the floor. "Tell me, what do you mean?"

"Mean, you silly girl," I said; "what can I mean, except
that I love you, which I thought you knew long ago."

"Oh!" she said; "*now* I understand." Then she raised
herself upon her knees, and held up her face to me to kiss, adding,
"There, that's my answer, the first and perhaps the last. Thank
you, Allan dear; I am glad to have heard that, for you see one
or both of us may die soon."

As she spoke the words, an assegai flashed through the
window-place, passing just between our heads. So we gave
over love-making and turned our attention to war.

Now the light was beginning to grow, flowing out of the
pearly eastern sky; but no attack had yet been delivered,
although that one was imminent that spear fixed in the plaster
of the wall behind us showed clearly. Perhaps the Kaffirs had
been frightened by the galloping of horses through their line
in the dark, not knowing how many of them there might have
been. Or perhaps they were waiting to see better where to
deliver their onset. These were the ideas that occurred to me,
but both were wrong.

They were staying their hands until the mist lifted a little
from the hollow below the stead where the cattle kraals were
situated, for while the fog remained they could not see to get

the beasts out. These they wished to make sure of and drive away before the fight began, lest during its progress something should happen to rob them of their booty.

Presently, from these kraals, where the Heer Marais's horned beasts and sheep were penned at night, about one hundred and fifty of the former and some two thousand of the latter, to say nothing of the horses, for he was a large and prosperous farmer, there arose a sound of bellowing, neighing, and baaing, and with it that of the shouting of men.

" They are driving off the stock," said Marie. " Oh ! my poor father, he is ruined ; it will break his heart."

" Bad enough," I answered, " but there are things that might be worse. Hark ! "

As I spoke there came a sound of stamping feet and of a wild war chant. Then in the edge of the mist that hung above the hollow where the cattle kraals were, figures appeared, moving swiftly to and fro, looking ghostly and unreal. The Kaffirs were marshalling their men for the attack. A minute more and it had begun. On up the slope they came in long, wavering lines, several hundreds of them, whistling and screaming, shaking their spears, their war-plumes and hair trappings blown back by the breeze, the lust of slaughter in their rolling eyes. Two or three of them had guns, which they fired as they ran, but where the bullets went I do not know, over the house probably.

I called out to Leblanc and the Kaffirs not to shoot till I did, for I knew that they were poor marksmen and that much depended upon our first volley being effective. Then as the captain of this attack came within thirty yards of the stoep—for now the light, growing swiftly, was strong enough to enable me to distinguish him by his apparel and the rifle which he held—I loosed at him with the *roer* and shot him dead. Indeed the heavy bullet passing through his body mortally wounded another of the Quabies behind. These were the first men that I ever killed in war.

As they fell, Leblanc and the rest of our people fired also, the slugs from their guns doing great execution at that range, which was just long enough to allow them to scatter. When the smoke cleared a little I saw that nearly a dozen men were down, and that the rest, dismayed by this reception, had halted.

If they had come on then, while we were loading, doubtless they might have rushed the place ; but, being unused to the terrible effects of firearms, they paused, amazed. A number of them, twenty or thirty perhaps, clustered about the bodies of the fallen Kaffirs, and, seizing my second gun, I fired both barrels at these with such fearful effect that the whole regiment took to their heels and fled, leaving their dead and wounded on the ground. As they ran our servants cheered, but I called to them to be silent and load swiftly, knowing well that the enemy would soon return.

For a time, however, nothing happened, although we could hear them talking somewhere near the cattle kraal, about a hundred and fifty yards away. Marie took advantage of this pause, I remember, to fetch food and distribute it among us. I, for one, was glad enough to get it.

Now the sun was up, a sight for which I thanked Heaven, for, at any rate, we could no longer be surprised. Also, with the daylight, some of my fear passed away, since darkness always makes danger twice as terrible to man and beast. Whilst we were still eating and fortifying the window-places as best we could, so as to make them difficult to enter, a single Kaffir appeared, waving above his head a stick to which was tied a white ox-tail as a sign of truce. I ordered that no one should fire, and when the man, who was a bold fellow, had reached the spot where the dead captain lay, called to him, asking his business, for I could speak his language well.

He answered that he had come with a message from Quabie. This was the message : that Quabie's eldest son had been cruelly murdered by the fat white man called " Vulture " who lived with the Heer Marais, and that he, Quabie, would have blood for blood. Still he did not wish to kill the young white chieftainess (that was Marie) or the others in the house, with whom he had no quarrel. Therefore if we would give up the fat white man that he might make him " die slowly," Quabie would be content with his life and with the cattle that he had already taken by way of a fine, and leave us and the house unmolested.

Now, when Leblanc understood the nature of this offer he went perfectly mad with mingled fear and rage, and began to shout and swear in French.

"Be silent," I said; "we do not mean to surrender you, although you have brought all this trouble on us. Your chance of life is as good as ours. Are you not ashamed to act so before these black people?"

When at last he grew more or less quiet I called to the messenger that we white folk were not in the habit of abandoning each other, and that we would live or die together. Still, I bade him tell Quabie that if we did die, the vengeance taken on him and all his people would be to wipe them out till not one of them was left, and therefore that he would do well not to cause any of our blood to flow. Also, I added, that we had thirty men in the house (which, of course, was a lie) and plenty of ammunition and food, so that if he chose to continue the attack it would be the worse for him and his tribe.

On hearing this the herald shouted back that we should everyone of us be dead before noon if he had his way. Still, he would report my words faithfully to Quabie and bring his answer.

Then he turned and began to walk off. Just as he did so a shot was fired from the house, and the man pitched forward to the ground, then rose again and staggered back towards his people, with his right shoulder shattered and his arm swinging.

"Who did that?" I asked through the smoke, which prevented me from seeing.

"I, *parbleu!*" shouted Leblanc. "*Sapristi!* that black devil wanted to torture me, Leblanc, the friend of the great Napoleon. Well, at least I have tortured him whom I meant to kill."

"Yes, you fool," I answered; "and we, too, shall be tortured because of your wickedness. You have shot a messenger carrying a flag of truce, and that the Quabies will never forgive. Oh! I tell you that you have hit us as well as him, who had it not been for you might have been spared."

These words I said quite quietly and in Dutch, so that our Kaffirs might understand them, though really I was boiling with wrath.

But Leblanc did not answer quietly.

"Who are you," he shouted, "you wretched little Englishman, who dare to lecture me, Leblanc, the friend of the great Napoleon?"

Now I drew my pistol and walked up to the man.

" Be quiet, you drunken sot," I said, for I guessed that he had drunk more of the brandy in the darkness. " If you are not quiet and do not obey me, who am in command here, either I will blow your brains out, or I will give you to these men," and I pointed to Hans and the Kaffirs, who had gathered round him, muttering ominously. " Do you know what they will do with you ? They will throw you out of the house, and leave you to settle your quarrel with Quabie alone."

Leblanc looked first at the pistol, and next at the faces of the natives, and saw something in one or other of them, or in both, that caused him to change his note.

" Pardon, monsieur," he said ; " I was excited. I knew not what I said. If you are young you are brave and clever, and I will obey you," and he went to his station and began to re-load his gun.

As he did so a great shout of fury rose from the cattle kraal. The wounded herald had reached the Quabies and was telling them of the treachery of the white people.

III

THE RESCUE

THE second Quabie advance did not begin till about half-past seven. Even savages love their lives and appreciate the fact that wounds hurt very much, and these were no exception to the rule. Their first rush had taught them a bitter lesson, of which the fruit was evident in the crippled or dying men who rolled to and fro baked in the hot sun within a few yards of the stoep, not to speak of those who would never stir again. Now, the space around the house being quite open and bare of cover, it was obvious that it could not be stormed without further heavy losses. In order to avoid such losses a civilised people would have advanced by means of trenches, but of these the Quabies knew nothing ; moreover, digging tools were lacking to them.

So it came about that they hit upon another, and in the circumstances a not inefficient expedient. The cattle kraal was built of rough, unmortared stones. Those stones they took, each man carrying two or three, which, rushing forward, they piled up into scattered rough defences of about eighteen inches or two feet high. These defences were instantly occupied by as many warriors as could take shelter behind them, lying one on top of the other. Of course, those savages who carried the first stones were exposed to our fire, with the result that many of them fell, but there were always plenty more behind. As they were being built at a dozen different points, and we had but seven guns, before we could reload, a particular *schanz*, of which perhaps the first builders had fallen, would be raised so high that our slugs could no longer hurt those who lay behind it. Also, our supply of ammunition was limited, and the constant expenditure wasted it so much that at length only about six charges per man remained. At last, indeed, I was obliged to order the firing to cease, so that we might reserve ourselves for the great rush which could not now be much delayed.

Finding that they were no longer harassed by our bullets, the Quabies advanced more rapidly, directing their attack upon the south end of the house, where there was but one window, and thus avoiding the fire that might be poured upon them from the various openings under the veranda. At first I wondered why they selected this end, till Marie reminded me that this part of the dwelling was thatched with reeds, whereas the rest of the building, which had been erected more recently, was slated.

Their object was to fire the roof. So soon as their last wall was near enough (that is, about half-past ten of the clock), they began to throw into the thatch assegais to which were attached bunches of burning grass. Many of these went out, but at length, as we gathered from their shouts, one caught. Within ten minutes this part of the house was burning.

Now our state became desperate. We retreated across the central passage, fearing lest the blazing rafters should fall upon our natives, who were losing heart and would no longer stay beneath them. But the Quabies, more bold, clambered in through the south window, and attacked us in the doorway of the larger sitting-room.

Here the final fight began. As they rushed at us we shot, till they went down in heaps. Almost at our last charge they gave back, and just then the roof fell upon them.

Oh, what a terrible scene was that! The dense clouds of smoke, the screams of the trapped and burning men, the turmoil, the agony!

The front door was burst in by a flank onslaught.

Leblanc and a slave who was near him were seized by black, claw-like hands and dragged out. What became of the Frenchman I do not know, for the natives hauled him away, but I fear his end must have been dreadful, as he was taken alive. The servant I saw them assegai, so at least he died at once. I fired my last shot, killing a fellow who was flourishing a battle-axe, then dashed the butt of the gun into the face of the man behind him, felling him, and, seizing Marie by the hand, dragged her back into the northernmost room—that in which I was accustomed to sleep—and shut and barred the door.

" Allan," she gasped, " Allan dear, it is finished. I cannot fall into the hands of those men. Kill me, Allan."

" All right," I answered, " I will. I have my pistol. One barrel for you and one for me."

" No, no! Perhaps you might escape after all; but, you see, I am a woman, and dare not risk it. Come, now, I am ready," and she knelt down, opening her arms to receive the embrace of death, and looked up at me with her lovely, pitiful eyes.

" It doesn't do to kill one's love and live on oneself," I answered hoarsely. " We have got to go together," and I cocked both barrels of the pistol.

The Hottentot, Hans, who was in the place with us, saw and understood.

" It is right, it is best! " he said, and turning, he hid his eyes with his hands.

" Wait a little, Allan," she exclaimed; " it will be time when the door is down, and perhaps God may still help us."

" He may," I answered doubtfully; " but I would not count on it. Nothing can save us now unless the others come to rescue us, and that's too much to hope for."

Then a thought struck me, and I added with a dreadful laugh: " I wonder where we shall be in five minutes."

" Oh ! together, dear ; together for always in some new and beautiful world, for you do love me, don't you, as I love you ? Maybe that's better than living on here where we should be sure to have troubles and perhaps be separated at last."

I nodded my head, for though I loved life, I loved Marie more, and I felt that we were making a good end after a brave fight. They were battering at the door now, but, thank Heaven, Marais had made strong doors, and it held a while.

The wood began to give at last, an assegai appeared through a shattered plank, but Hans stabbed along the line of it with the spear he held, that which I had snatched from the flank of the horse, and it was dropped with a scream. Black hands were thrust through the hole, and the Hottentot hacked and cut at them with the spear. But others came, more than he could pierce, and the whole door-frame began to be dragged outwards.

" Now, Marie, be ready," I gasped lifting the pistol.

" Oh, Christ, receive me ! " she answered faintly. " It won't hurt much, will it, Allan ? "

" You will never feel anything," I whispered ; as with the cold sweat pouring from me I placed the muzzle within an inch of her forehead and began to press the trigger. My God ! yes, I actually began to press the trigger softly and steadily, for I wished to make no mistake.

It was at this very moment, above the dreadful turmoil of the roaring flames, the yells of the savages and the shrieks and groans of wounded and dying men, that I heard the sweetest sound which ever fell upon my ears—the sound of shots being fired, many shots, and quite close by.

" Great Heaven ! " I screamed ; " the Boers are here to save us. Marie, I will hold the door while I can. If I fall, scramble through the window—you can do it from the chest beneath— drop to the ground, and run towards the firing. There's a chance for you yet, a good chance."

" And you, you," she moaned. " I would rather die with you."

" Do what I bid you," I answered savagely, and bounded forward towards the rocking door.

It was falling outward, it fell, and on the top of it appeared two great savages waving broad spears. I lifted the pistol, and the bullet that had been meant for Marie's brain scattered that of the first of them, and the bullet which had been meant for my heart pierced that of the second. They both went down dead, there in the doorway.

I snatched up one of their spears and glanced behind me. Marie was climbing on to the chest; I could just see her through the thickening smoke. Another Quabie rushed on. Hans and I received him on the points of our assegais, but so fierce was his charge that they went through him as though he were nothing, and being but light, both of us were thrown backwards to the ground. I scrambled to my feet again, defenceless now, for the spear was broken in the Kaffir, and awaited the end. Looking back once more I saw that Marie had either failed to get through the window or abandoned the attempt. At any rate she was standing near the chest supporting herself by her right hand. In my despair I seized the blade end of the broken assegai and dragged it from the body of the Kaffir, thinking that it would serve to kill her, then turned to do the deed.

But even as I turned I heard a voice that I knew well shout: "Do you live, Marie?" and in the doorway appeared no savage, but Henri Marais.

Slowly I backed before him, for I could not speak, and the last dreadful effort of my will seemed to thrust me towards Marie. I reached her and threw my hand that still held the gory blade round her neck. Then as darkness came over me I heard her cry:

"Don't shoot, father. It is Allan, Allan who has saved my life!"

After that I remember no more. Nor did she for a while, for we both fell to the ground senseless.

When my senses returned to me I found myself lying on the floor of the wagon-house in the back yard. Glancing from my half-opened eyes, for I was still speechless, I saw Marie, white as a sheet, her hair all falling about her dishevelled dress. She was seated on one of those boxes that we put on the front of wagons to drive from, *voorkissies* they are called, and as her eyes were watching me I knew that she lived. By her stood a tall and dark young man whom I had never seen before. He was holding her hand and looking at her anxiously, and even then I felt angry with him. Also I saw other things; for instance, my old father leaning down and looking at *me* anxiously, and outside in the yard, for there were no doors to the wagon-house, a number of men with guns in their hands, some of whom I knew and others who were strangers. In the shadow, too, against the wall, stood my blood mare with her head hanging down and trembling all over. Not far from her the roan lay upon the ground, its flank quite red.

I tried to rise and could not, then feeling pain in my left thigh, looked and saw that it was red also. As a matter of fact an assegai had gone half through it and hit upon the bone. Although I never felt it at the time, this wound was dealt to me by that great Quabie whom Hans and I had received upon our spears, doubtless as he fell. Hans, by the way, was there also, an awful and yet a ludicrous spectacle, for the Quabie had fallen right on the top of him and lain so with results that may be imagined. There he sat upon the ground, looking upwards, gasping with his fish-like mouth. Each gasp, I remember, fashioned itself into the word " *Allemachte !* " that is " Almighty," a favourite Dutch expression.

Marie was the first to perceive that I had come to life again. Shaking herself free from the clasp of the young man, she staggered towards me and fell upon her knees at my side, muttering words that I could not catch, for they choked in her throat. Then Hans took in the situation, and wriggling his unpleasant self to my other side, lifted my hand and kissed it. Next my father spoke, saying:

" Praise be to God, he lives ! Allan, my son, I am proud of you ; you have done your duty as an Englishman should."

" Had to save my own skin if I could, thank you, father," I muttered.

" Why as an Englishman more than any other sort of man, Mynheer Predicant ? " asked the tall stranger, speaking in Dutch, although he evidently understood our language.

" The point is one that I will not argue now, sir," answered my father, drawing himself up. " But if what I hear is true,

there was a Frenchman in that house who did not do his duty ;
and if you belong to the same nation, I apologise to you."

" Thank you, sir ; as it happens, I do, half. The rest of me
is Portuguese, not English, thank God."

" God is thanked for many things that must surprise Him,"
replied my father in a suave voice.

At that moment this rather disagreeable conversation, which
even then both angered and amused me faintly, came to an end,
for the Heer Marais entered the place.

As might have been expected in so excitable a man, he was
in a terrible state of agitation. Thankfulness at the escape of his
only, beloved child, rage with the Kaffirs who had tried to kill
her, and extreme distress at the loss of most of his property—all
these conflicting emotions boiled together in his breast like
antagonistic elements in a crucible.

The resulting fumes were parti-coloured and overpowering.
He rushed up to me, blessed and thanked me (for he had learnt
something of the story of the defence), called me a young hero
and so forth, hoping that God would reward me. Here I may
remark that *he* never did, poor man. Then he began to rave at
Leblanc, who had brought all this dreadful disaster upon his
house, saying that it was a judgment on himself for having
sheltered an atheist and a drunkard for so many years, just
because he was French and a man of intellect. Someone, my father
as a matter of fact, who with all his prejudices possessed a great
sense of justice, reminded him that the poor Frenchman had
expiated, or perchance was now expiating any crimes that he
might have committed.

This turned the stream of his invective on to the Quabie
Kaffirs, who had burned part of his house and stolen nearly all
his stock, making him from a rich man into a poor one in a
single hour. He shouted for vengeance on the " black devils,"
and called on all there to help him to recover his beasts and kill
the thieves. Most of those present—they were about thirty in
all, not counting the Kaffir and Hottentot after-riders—answered
that they were willing to attack the Quabies. Being residents
in the district, they felt, and, indeed, said, that his case to-day
might and probably would be their case tomorrow. Therefore
they were prepared to ride at once.

Then it was that my father intervened.

"Heeren," he said, "it seems to me that before you seek vengeance, which, as the Book tells us, is the Lord's, it would be well, especially for the Heer Marais, to return thanks for what has been saved to him. I mean his daughter, who might now very easily have been dead or worse."

He added that goods came or went according to the chances of fortune, but a beloved human life, once lost, could not be restored. This precious life had been preserved to him, he would not say by man—here he glanced at me—but by the Ruler of the world acting through man. Perhaps those present did not quite understand what he (my father) had learned from Hans the Hottentot, that I, his son, had been about to blow out the brains of Marie Marais and my own when the sound of the shots of those who had been gathered through the warning which I left before I rode from the Mission Station, had stayed my hand. He called upon the said Hans and Marie herself to tell them the story, since I was too weak to do so.

Thus adjured, the little Hottentot, smothered as he was in blood, stood up. In the simple, dramatic style characteristic of his race, he narrated all that had happened since he met the woman on the veld but little over twelve hours before, till the arrival of the rescue party. Never have I seen a tale followed with deeper interest, and when at last Hans pointed to me lying on the ground and said, "There is he who did these things which it might be thought no man could do—he, but a boy," even from those phlegmatic Dutchmen there came a general cheer. But, lifting myself upon my hands, I called out:

"Whatever I did, this poor Hottentot did also, and had it not been for him I could not have done anything—for him and the two good horses."

Then they cheered again, and Marie, rising, said:

"Yes, father; to these two I owe my life."

After this, my father offered his prayer of thanksgiving in very bad Dutch—for, having begun to learn it late in life, he never could really master that language—and the stalwart Boers, kneeling round him, said "Amen." As the reader may imagine, the scene, with all its details, which I will not repeat, was both remarkable and impressive.

What followed this prayer I do not very well remember, for I became faint from exhaustion and the loss of blood. I believe, however, that, the fire having been extinguished, they removed the dead and wounded from the unburnt portion of the house and carried me into the little room where Marie and I had gone through that dreadful scene when I went within an ace of killing her. After this the Boers and Marais's Kaffirs, or rather slaves, whom he had collected from where they lived away from the house, to the number of thirty or forty, started to follow the defeated Quabie, leaving about ten of their number as a guard. Here I may mention that of the seven or eight men who slept in the outbuildings and had fought with us, two were killed in the fight and two wounded. The remainder, one way or another, managed to escape unhurt, so that in all this fearful struggle, in which we inflicted so terrible a punishment upon the Kaffirs, we lost only three slain, including the Frenchman, Leblanc.

As to the events of the next three days I know only what I have been told, for practically during all that time I was off my head from loss of blood, complicated with fever brought on by the fearful excitement and exertion I had undergone. All I can recall is a vision of Marie bending over me and making me take food of some sort—milk or soup, I suppose—for it seems I would touch it from no other hand. Also I had visions of the tall shape of my white-haired father, who, like most missionaries, understood something of surgery and medicine, attending to the bandages on my thigh. Afterwards he told me that the spear had actually cut the walls of the big artery, but, by good fortune, without going through them. Another fortieth of an inch and I should have bled to death in ten minutes!

On this third day my mind was brought back from its wanderings by the sound of a great noise about the house, above which I heard the voice of Marais storming and shouting, and that of my father trying to calm him. Presently Marie entered the room, drawing-to behind her a Kaffir kaross, which served as a curtain, for the door, it will be remembered, had been torn out. Seeing that I was awake and reasonable, she flew to my side with a little cry of joy, and, kneeling down, kissed me on the forehead.

" You have been very ill, Allan, but I know you will recover now. While we are alone, which," she added slowly and with meaning, " I dare say we shall not be much in future, I want to thank you from my heart for all that you did to save me. Had it not been for you, oh ! had it not been for you "—and she glanced at the blood stains on the earthen floor, put her hands before her eyes and shuddered.

" Nonsense, Marie," I answered, taking her hand feebly enough, for I was very weak. " Anyone else would have done as much, even if they did not love you as I do. Let us thank God that it was not in vain. But what is all that noise ? Have the Quabies come back ? "

She shook her head.

" No ; the Boers have come back from hunting them."

" And did they catch them and recover the cattle ? "

" Not so. They only found some wounded men, whom they shot, and the body of Monsieur Leblanc with his head cut off, taken away with other bits of him for medicine, they say to make the warriors brave. Quabie has burnt his kraal and fled with all his people to join the other Kaffirs in the Big Mountains. Not a cow or a sheep did they find, except a few that had fallen exhausted, and those had their throats cut. My father wanted to follow them and attack the Red Kaffirs in the mountains, but the others would not go. They said there are thousands of them, and that it would be a mad war, from which not one of them would return alive. He is wild with grief and rage, for, Allan dear, we are almost ruined, especially as the British Government are freeing the slaves and only going to give us a very small price, not a third of their value. But, hark ! he is calling me, and you must not talk much to excite yourself, lest you should be ill again. Now you have to sleep and eat and get strong. Afterwards, dear, you may talk ; " and, bending down once more, she blessed and kissed me, then rose and glided away.

IV

HERNANDO PEREIRA

SEVERAL more days passed before I was allowed out of that little war-stained room of which I grew to hate the very sight. I entreated my father to take me into the air, but he would not, saying that he feared lest any movement should cause the bleeding to begin again or even the cut artery to burst. Moreover, the wound was not healing very well, the spear that caused it having been dirty or perhaps used to skin dead animals, which caused some dread of gangrene, that in those days generally meant death. As it chanced, although I was treated only with cold water, for antiseptics were then unknown, my young and healthy blood triumphed and no gangrene appeared.

What made those days even duller was that during them I saw very little of Marie, who now only entered the place in the company of her father. Once I managed to ask her why she did not come oftener and alone. Her face grew troubled as she whispered back, "Because it is not allowed, Allan," and then without another word left the place.

Why, I wondered to myself, was it not allowed, and an answer sprang up in my mind. Doubtless it was because of that tall young man who had argued with my father in the wagon-house. Marie had never spoken to me concerning him and his business.

It appeared that he was the only child of Henry Marais's sister, who married a Portugese from Delagoa Bay of the name of Pereira, who had come to the Cape Colony to trade many years before and settled there. Both he and his wife were dead, and their son, Hernando, Marie's cousin, had inherited all their very considerable wealth.

Indeed, now I remembered having heard this Hernando, or Hernan, as the Boers called him for short, spoken of in past years by the Heer Marais as the heir to great riches, since his father had made a large fortune by trading in wine and spirits under some Government monopoly which he held. Often he had been invited to visit Maraisfontein, but his parents, who doted on him and lived in one of the settled districts not far from Cape Town, would never allow him to travel so far from them into these wild regions.

Since their death, however, things had changed. It appeared that on the decease of old Pereira the Governor of the Colony had withdrawn the wine and spirit monopoly, which he said was a job and a scandal, an act that made Hernando Pereira very angry, although he needed no more money, and had caused him to throw himself heart and soul into the schemes of the disaffected Boers. Indeed, he was now engaged as one of the organisers of the Great Trek which was in contemplation. In fact, it had already begun, into the partially explored land beyond the borders of the Colony, where the Dutch farmers proposed to set up dominions of their own.

That was the story of Hernando Pereria, who was to be—nay, who had already become—my rival for the hand of the sweet and beautiful Marie Marais.

One night when my father and I were alone in the little room where he slept with me, and he had finished reading his evening portion of Scripture aloud, I plucked up my courage to tell him that I loved Marie and wished to marry her, and that we had plighted our troth during the attack of the Kaffirs on the stead.

" Love and war indeed ! " he said, looking at me gravely, but showing no sign of surprise, for it appeared that he was already acquainted with our secret. This was not wonderful, for he informed me afterwards that during my delirium I had done nothing except rave of Marie in the most endearing terms. Also Marie herself, when I was at my worst, had burst into tears before him and told him straight out that she loved me.

" Love and war indeed ! " he repeated, adding kindly, " My poor boy, I fear that you have fallen into great trouble."

" Why, father ? " I asked. " Is it wrong that we should love each other ? "

" Not wrong, but, in the circumstances, quite natural—I should have foreseen that it was sure to happen. No, not wrong, but most unfortunate. To begin with, I do not wish to see you marry a foreigner and become mixed up with these disloyal Boers. I hoped that one day, a good many years hence, for you are only a boy, Allan, you would find an English wife, and I still hope it."

" Never ! " I ejaculated.

" Never is a long word, Allan, and I dare say that what you are so sure is impossible will happen after all," words that made me angry enough at the time, though in after years I often thought of them.

" But," he went on, " putting my own wishes, perhaps prejudices, aside, I think your suit hopeless. Although Henri Marais likes you well enough and is grateful to you just now because you have saved the daughter whom he loves, you must remember that he hates us English bitterly. I believe that he would almost as soon see his girl marry a half-caste as an Englishman, and especially a poor Englishman, as you are and, unless you can make money, must remain. I have little to leave you, Allan."

" I might make money, father, out of ivory, for instance. You know I am a good shot."

" Allan, I do not think you will ever make much money, it is not in your blood ; or, if you do, you will not keep it. We are an old race, and I know our record, up to the time of Henry VIII. at any rate. Not one of us was ever commercially successful. Let us suppose, however, that you should prove yourself the exception to the rule, it can't be done at once, can it ? Fortunes don't grow in a night like mushrooms."

" No, I suppose not, father. Still, one might have some luck."

" Possibly. But meanwhile you have to fight against a man who has the luck, or rather the money in his pocket."

" What do you mean ? " I asked, sitting up.

" I mean Hernando Pereira, Allan, Marais's nephew, who they say is one of the richest men in the Colony. I know that he wishes to marry Marie."

" How do you know it, father ? "

" Because Marais told me so this afternoon, probably with a purpose. He was struck with her beauty when he first saw her after your escape, which he had not done since she was a child, and as he stopped to guard the house while the rest went after the Quabies—well, you can guess. Such things go quickly with these Southern men."

I hid my face in the pillow, biting my lips to keep back the groan that was ready to burst from them, for I felt the hopelessness of the situation. How could I compete with this rich and fortunate man, who naturally would be favoured of my betrothed's father? Then on the blackness of my despair rose a star of hope. I could not, but perchance Marie might. She was very strong-natured and very faithful. She was not to be bought, and I doubted whether she could be frightened.

"Father," I said, "I may never marry Marie, but I don't think that Hernando Pereira ever will either."

"Why not, my boy?"

"Because she loves me, father, and she is not one to change. I believe that she would rather die."

"Then she must be a very unusual sort of woman. Still, it may be so; the future will tell to those who live to see it. I can only pray and trust that whatever happens will be for the best for both of you. She is a sweet girl and I like her well, although she may be Boer—or French. And now, Allan, we have talked enough, and you had better go to sleep. You must not excite yourself, you know, or it may set up new inflammation in the wound."

"Go to sleep. Must not excite yourself." I kept muttering those words for hours, serving them up in my mind with a spice of bitter thought. At last torpor, or weakness, overcame me, and I fell into a kind of net of bad dreams which, thank Heaven! I have now forgotten. Yet, when certain events happened subsequently I always thought, and indeed still think, that these or something like them, had been a part of those evil dreams.

On the morning following this conversation I was at length allowed to be carried to the stoep, where they laid me down, wrapped in a very dirty blanket, upon a rimpi-string bench or primitive sofa. When I had satisfied my first delight at seeing the sun and breathing the fresh air, I began to study my surroundings. In front of the house, or what remained of it, so arranged that the last of them at either end were made fast to the extremities of the stoep, was arranged an arc of wagons, placed as they are in a laager and protected underneath by earth thrown up in a mound and by boughs of the mimosa thorn. Evidently these wagons, in which the guard of Boers and armed natives who still remained on the place slept at night, were set thus as a defence against a possible attack by the Quabies or other Kaffirs.

During the daytime, however, the centre wagon was drawn a little on one side to leave a kind of gate. Through this opening I saw that a long wall, also semicircular, had been built outside of them, enclosing a space large enough to contain at night all the cattle and horses that were left to the Heer Marais, together with those of his friends, who evidently did not wish to see their oxen vanish into the depths of the mountains. In the middle of this extemporised kraal was a long, low mound, which, as I learned afterwards, contained the dead who fell in the attack on the house. The two slaves who had been killed in the defence were buried in the little garden that Marie had made, and the headless body of Leblanc in a small walled place to the right of the stead, where lay some of its former owners and one or two relatives of the Heer Marais, including his wife.

Whilst I was noting these things Marie appeared at the end of the veranda, having come round the burnt part of the house, followed by Hernan Pereira. Catching sight of me, she ran to the side of my couch with outstretched arms as though she intended to embrace me. Then seeming to remember, stopped suddenly at my side, coloured to her hair, and said in an embarrassed voice :

" Oh, Heer Allan "—she had never called me Heer in her life before—" I am so glad to find you out ! How have you been getting on ? "

" Pretty well, I thank you," I answered, biting my lips, " as you would have learnt, Marie, had you come to see me."

Next moment I was sorry for the words, for I saw her eyes fill with tears and her breast shake with something like a sob. However, it was Pereira and not Marie who answered, for at the moment I believe she could not speak.

" My good boy," he said in a pompous, patronising way and in English, which he knew perfectly. " I think that my cousin has had plenty to do caring for all these people during the last few days without running to look at the cut in your leg. However, I am glad to hear from your worthy father that it is almost well and that you will soon be able to play games again, like others of your age."

Now it was my turn to be unable to speak and to feel my eyes fill with tears, tears of rage, for remember that I was still very feeble. But Marie spoke for me.

" Yes, Cousin Hernan," she said in a cold voice, " thank God the Heer Allan Quatermain will soon be able to play games again, such bloody games as the defence of Maraisfontein with eight men against all the Quabie horde. Then Heaven help those who stand in front of his rifle," and she glanced at the mound that covered the dead Kaffirs, many of whom, as a matter of fact, I had killed.

" Oh ! no offence, no offence, Marie," said Pereira in his smooth, rich voice. " I did not want to laugh at your young friend, who doubtless is as brave as they say all Englishmen are, and who fought well when he was lucky enough to have the chance of protecting you, my dear cousin. But after all, you know, he is not the only one who can hold a gun straight, as you seem to think, which I shall be happy to prove to him in a friendly fashion when he is stronger."

Here he stepped forward a pace and looked down at me, then added with a laugh, " Allemachte ! I fear that won't be just at present. Why, the lad looks as though one might blow him away like a feather."

Still I said nothing, only glanced up at this tall and splendid man standing above me in his fine clothes, for he was richly dressed as the fashion of the time went, with his high colouring, broad shoulders, and face full of health and vigour. Mentally I compared him with myself, as I was after my fever and loss of blood, a poor, white-faced rat of a lad, with stubby brown hair on my head and only a little down on my chin, with arms like sticks, and a dirty blanket for raiment. How could I compare with him in any way ? What chance had I against this opulent bully who hated me and all my race, and in whose hands, even if I were well, I should be nothing but a child ?

And yet, and yet as I lay there humiliated and a mock, an answer came into my mind, and I felt that whatever might be the case with my outward form ; in spirit, in courage, in determination and in ability, in all, in short, that really makes a man, I was more than Pereira's equal. Yes, and that by the help of these qualities, poor as I was and frail as I seemed to be, I would beat him at the last and keep for myself what I had won, the prize of Marie's love.

Such were the thoughts which passed through me, and I think that something of the tenor of them communicated itself to Marie, who often could read my heart before my lips spoke. At any rate, her demeanour changed. She drew herself up. Her fine nostrils expanded and a proud look came into her dark eyes as she nodded her head and murmured in a voice so low that I think I alone caught her words :

"Yes, yes, have no fear."

Pereira was speaking again (he had turned aside to strike the steel of his tinder-box, and was now blowing the spark to a glow before lighting his big pipe).

"By the way, Heer Allan," he said, "that is a very good mare of yours. She seems to have done the distance between the Mission Station and Maraisfontein in wonderful time, as, for the matter of that, the roan did too. I have taken a fancy to her, after a gallop on her back yesterday just to give her some exercise, and although I don't know that she is quite up to my weight, I'll buy her."

"The mare is not for sale, Heer Pereira," I said, speaking for the first time, "and I do not remember giving anyone leave to exercise her."

"No, your father did, or was it that ugly little beast of a Hottentot ? I forget which. As for her not being for sale—why, in this world everything is for sale, at a price. I'll give you—let me see—oh, what does the money matter when one has plenty ? I'll give you a hundred English pounds for that mare ; and don't you think me a fool. I tell you I mean to get it back, and more, at the great races down in the south. Now what do you say ? "

"I say that the mare is not for sale, Heer Pereira." Then a thought struck me, or an inspiration, and, as had always been my fashion, I acted on it at once. "But," I added slowly, "if you like, when I am a bit stronger I'll shoot you a match for her, you staking your hundred pounds and I staking the mare."

Pereira burst out laughing.

"Here, friends," he called to some of the Boers who were strolling up to the house for their morning coffee. "This little

Englishman wants to shoot a match with me, staking that fine mare of his against a hundred pounds British; against me, Hernando Pereira, who have won every prize at shooting that ever I entered for. No, no, friend Allan, I am not a thief, I will not rob you of your mare."

Now among those Boers chanced to be the celebrated Heer Pieter Retief, a very fine man of high character, then in the prime of life, and of Huguenot descent like Heer Marais. He had been appointed by the Government one of the frontier commandants, but owing to some quarrel with the Lieutenant-Governor, Sir Andries Stockenstrom, had recently resigned that office, and at this date was engaged in organising the trek from the Colony. I now saw Retief for the first time, and ah! then little did I think how and where I should see him for the last. But all this is a matter of history, of which I shall have to tell later.

Now, while Pereira was mocking and bragging of his prowess, Pieter Retief looked at me, and our eyes met.

"Allemachte!" he exclaimed, "is that the young man who, with half a dozen miserable Hottentots and slaves, held this stead for five hours against all the Quabie tribe and kept them out?"

Somebody said that it was, remarking that I had been about to shoot Marie Marais and myself when help came.

"Then, Heer Allan Quatermain," said Retief, "give me your hand," and he took my poor wasted fingers in his big palm, adding. "Your father must be proud of you to-day, as I should be if I had such a son. God in Heaven! where will you stop if you can go so far while you are yet a boy? Friends, since I came here yesterday I have got the whole story for myself from the Kaffirs and from this *mooi meisje*" (pretty young lady), and he nodded towards Marie. "Also I have gone over the ground and the house, and have seen where each man fell—it is easy by the blood marks—most of them shot by yonder Englishman, except one of the last three, whom he killed with a spear. Well, I tell you that never in all my experience have I known a better arranged or a more finely carried out defence against huge odds. Perhaps the best part of it, too, was the way in which this young lion acted on the information he received and the splendid ride he made from the Mission Station. Again I say that his father should be proud of him."

" Well, if it comes to that, I am, mynheer," said my father, who just then joined us after his morning walk, " although I beg you to say no more lest the lad should grow vain."

" Bah ! " replied Retief, " fellows of his stamp are not vain ; it is your big talkers who are vain," and he glanced out of the corner of his shrewd eye at Pereira, " your turkey cocks with all their tails spread. I think this little chap must be such another as that great sailor of yours—what do you call him, Nelson ?— who beat the French into frothed eggs and died, to live for ever. He was small, too, they say, and weak in the stomach."

I must confess I do not think that praise ever sounded sweeter in my ears than did these words of the Commandant Retief, uttered as they were just when I felt crushed to the dirt. More-over, as I saw by Marie's and, I may add, by my father's face, there were other ears to which they were not ungrateful. The Boers also, brave and honest men enough, evidently appreciated them, for they said :

" *Ja ! ja ! das ist recht* " (That is right).

Only Pereira turned his broad back and busied himself with relighting his pipe, which had gone out.

Then Retief began again.

" What is it you were calling us to listen to, Mynheer Pereira ? That this Heer Allan Quatermain had offered to shoot you a match ? Well, why not ? If he can hit Kaffirs running at him with spears, as he has done, he may be able to hit other things also. You say that you won't rob him of his money—no, it was his beautiful horse—because you have taken so many prizes shooting at targets. But did *you* ever hit a Kaffir running at *you* with an assegai, mynheer, you who live down there where every-thing is safe ? If so, I never heard of it."

Pereira answered that he did not understand me to propose a shooting match at Kaffirs charging with assegais, but at some-thing else—he knew not what.

" Quite so," said Retief. " Well, Mynheer Allan, what is it that you do propose ? "

" That we should stand in the great kloof between the two *vleis* yonder—the Heer Marais knows the place—when the wild geese flight over an hour before sunset, and that he who brings down six of them in the fewest shots shall win the match."

" If our guns are loaded with loopers that will not be difficult," said Pereira.

" With loopers you would seldom kill a bird, mynheer," I replied, " for they come over from seventy to a hundred yards up. No, I mean with rifles."

" Allemachte ! " broke in a Boer; " you will want plenty of ammunition to hit a goose at that height with a bullet."

" That is my offer," I said, " to which I add this, that when twenty shots have been fired by each man, he who has killed the most birds wins, even if he has not brought down the full six. Does the Heer Pereira accept ? If so, I will venture to match myself against him, although he has won so many prizes."

The Heer Pereira seemed extremely doubtful; so doubtful, indeed, that the Boers began to laugh at him. In the end he grew rather angry, and said that he was willing to shoot me at bucks or swallows, or fireflies, or anything else I liked.

" Then let it be geese," I answered, " since it is likely to be some time before I am strong enough to ride after buck or other wild things."

So the terms of the match were formally written down by Marie, as my father, although he took a keen sporting interest in the result, would have nothing to do with what he called a " wager for money," and, except myself, there was no one else present with sufficient scholarship to pen a long document. Then we both signed them, Hernan Pereira not very willingly, I thought; and if my recovery was sufficiently rapid, the date was fixed for that day week. In case of any disagreement, the Heer Retief, who was staying at Maraisfontein, or in its neighbourhood, for a while, was appointed referee and stakeholder. It was also arranged that neither of us should visit the appointed place, or shoot at the geese before the match. Still we were at liberty to practise as much as we liked at anything else in the interval and to make use of any kind of rifle that suited us best.

By the time that these arrangements were finished, feeling quite tired with all the emotions of the morning, I was carried back to my room. Here my midday meal, cooked by Marie, was brought to me. As I finished eating it, for the fresh air had given me an appetite, my father came in, accompanied by the Heer Marais, and began to talk to me. Presently the latter asked me kindly enough if I thought I should be sufficiently strong to trek back to the station that afternoon in an ox-cart with springs to it and lying at full length upon a hide-strung *cartel* or mattress.

I answered, " Certainly," as I should have done had I been at the point of death, for I saw that he wished to be rid of me.

" The fact is, Allan," he said awkwardly, " I am not inhospitable as you may think, especially towards one to whom I owe so much. But you and my nephew, Hernan, do not seem to get on very well together, and, as you may guess, having just been almost beggared, I desire no unpleasantness with the only rich member of my family."

I replied I was sure I did not wish to be the cause of any. It seemed to me, however, that the Heer Pereira wished to make a mock of me and to bring it home to me what a poor creature I was compared to himself—I a mere sick boy who was worth nothing.

" I know," said Marais uneasily, " my nephew has been too fortunate in life, and is somewhat overbearing in his manner. He does not remember that the battle is not always to the strong or the race to the swift, he who is young and rich and handsome, a spoiled child from the first. I am sorry, but what I cannot help I must put up with. If I cannot have my mealies cooked, I must eat them green. Also, Allan, have you never heard that jealousy sometimes makes people rude and unjust ? " and he looked at me meaningly.

I made no answer, for when one does not quite know what to say it is often best to remain silent, and he went on :

" I am vexed to hear of this foolish shooting match which has been entered into without my knowledge or consent. If he wins he will only laugh at you the more, and if you win he will be angry."

" It was not my fault, mynheer," I answered. " He wanted to force me to sell the mare, which he had been riding without my leave, and kept bragging about his marksmanship. So at last I grew cross and challenged him."

" No wonder, Allan ; I do not blame you. Still, you are silly, for it will not matter to him if he loses his money ; but that beautiful mare is your ewe-lamb, and I should be sorry to see you parted from a beast which has done us so good a turn. Well, there it is ; perhaps circumstances may yet put an end to this trial ; I hope so."

" I hope they won't," I answered stubbornly.

" I dare say you do, being sore as a galled horse just now. But listen, Allan, and you, too, Predicant Quatermain ; there are other and more important reasons than this petty squabble why I should be glad if you could go away for a while. I must take counsel with my countrymen about certain secret matters which have to do with our welfare and future, and, of course, they would not like it if all the while there were two Englishmen on the place, whom they might think were spies."

" Say no more, Heer Marais," broke in my father hotly ; " still less should we like to be where we are not wanted or are looked upon with suspicion for the crime of being English. By God's blessing, my son has been able to do some service to you and yours, but now that is all finished and forgotten. Let the cart you are so kind as to lend us be inspanned. We will go at once."

Then Henri Marais, who was a gentleman at bottom, although, even in those early days, violent and foolish when excited or under the influence of his race prejudices, began to apologise quite humbly, assuring my father that he forgot nothing and meant no offence. So they patched the matter up, and an hour later we started.

All the Boers came to see us off, giving me many kind words and saying how much they looked forward to meeting me again on the following Thursday. Pereira, who was among them, was also very genial, begging me to be sure and get well, since he did not wish to beat one who was still crippled, even at a game of goose shooting. I answered that I would do my best ; as for my part, I did not like being beaten at any game which I had set my heart on winning, whether it were little or big. Then I turned my head, for I was lying on my back all this time, to bid good-bye to Marie, who had slipped out of the house into the yard where the cart was.

" Good-bye, Allan," she said, giving me her hand and a look from her eyes that I trusted was not seen. Then, under pretence of arranging the kaross which was over me, she bent down and whispered swiftly :

" Win that match if you love me. I shall pray God that you may every night, for it will be an omen."

I think the whisper was heard, though not the words, for I saw Pereira bite his lip and make a movement as though to interrupt her. But Pieter Retief thrust his big form in front of him rather rudely, and said with one of his hearty laughs :

" Allemachte ! friend, let the *missje* wish a good journey to the young fellow who saved her life."

Next moment Hans, the Hottentot, screamed at the oxen in the usual fashion, and we rolled away through the gate.

But oh ! if I had liked the Heer Retief before, now I loved him.

V

THE SHOOTING MATCH

My journey back to the Mission Station was a strange contrast to that which I had made thence a few days before. Then, the darkness, the swift mare beneath me rushing through it like a bird, the awful terror in my heart lest I should be too late, as with wild eyes I watched the paling stars and the first gathering grey of dawn. Now, the creaking of the ox-cart, the familiar veld, the bright glow of the peaceful sunlight, and in my heart a great thankfulness, and yet a new terror lest the pure and holy love which I had won should be stolen away from me by force or fraud.

Well, as the one matter had been in the hand of God, so was the other, and with that knowledge I must be content. The first trial had ended in death and victory. How would the second end ? I wondered, and those words seemed to jumble themselves up in my mind and shape a sentence that it did not conceive. It was : " In the victory that is death," which, when I came to think of it, of course, meant nothing. How victory could be death I did not understand—at any rate, at that time, I who was but a lad of small experience.

As we trekked along comfortably enough, for the road was good and the cart, being on springs, gave my leg no pain, I asked my father what he thought that the Heer Marais had meant when he told us that the Boers had business at Marais-fontein, during which our presence as Englishmen would not be agreeable to them.

" Meant, Allan ? He meant that these traitorous Dutchmen are plotting against their sovereign, and are afraid lest we should report their treason. Either they intend to rebel because of that most righteous act, the freeing of the slaves, and because we will not kill out all the Kaffirs with whom they chance to quarrel, or to trek from the Colony. For my part I think it will be the latter, for, as you have heard, some parties have already gone ; and, unless I am mistaken, many more mean to follow, Marais and Retief and that plotter, Pereira, among them. Let them go ; I say, the sooner the better, for I have no doubt that the English flag will follow them in due course."

" I hope that they won't," I answered with a nervous laugh ; " at any rate, until I have won back my mare." (I had left her in Retief's care as stakeholder, until the match should be shot off.)

For the rest of that two and a half hours' trek my father, looking very dignified and patriotic, declaimed to me loudly about the bad behaviour of the Boers, who hated and traduced missionaries, loathed and abominated British rule and per-manent officials, loved slavery and killed Kaffirs whenever they got the chance. I listened to him politely, for it was not wise to cross my parent when he was in that humour. Also, having mixed a great deal with the Dutch, I knew that there was another side to the question, namely, that the missionaries sometimes traduced them (as, in fact, they did), and that British rule, or, rather, party government, played strange tricks with the interests of distant dependencies. That permanent officials and im-per-manent ones too—such as governors full of a little brief authority—often misrepresented and oppressed them. That Kaffirs, encouraged by the variegated policy of these party governments and their servants, frequently stole their stock ; and if they found a chance, murdered them with their women and children, as they had tried to do at Maraisfontein ; though there, it is true, they had some provocation. That British virtue had liberated the slaves without paying their owners a fair price for them, and so forth.

But, to tell the truth, it was not of these matters of high policy, which were far enough away from a humble youth like myself, that I was thinking. What appealed to me and made my heart sick was the reflection that if Henri Marais and his friends trekked, Marie Marais must perforce trek with them; and that whereas I, an Englishman, could not be of that adventurous company, Hernando Pereira both could and would.

On the day following our arrival home, what between the fresh air, plenty of good food, for which I found I had an appetite, and liberal doses of Pontac—a generous Cape wine that is a kind of cross between port and Burgundy—I found myself so much better that I was able to hop about the place upon a pair of crutches which Hans improvised for me out of Kaffir sticks. Next morning, my improvement continuing at a rapid rate, I turned my attention seriously to the shooting match, for which I had but five days to prepare.

Now it chanced that some months before a young Englishman of good family—he was named the Honourable Vavasseur Smyth—who had accompanied an official relative to the Cape Colony, came our way in search of sport, of which I was able to show him a good deal of a humble kind. He had brought with him, amongst other weapons, what in those days was considered a very beautiful hair-triggered small-bore rifle fitted with a nipple for percussion caps, then quite a new invention. It was by a maker of the name of J. Purdey, of London, and had cost quite a large sum because of the perfection of its workmanship. When the Honourable V. Smyth—of whom I have never heard since—took his leave of us on his departure for England, being a generous-hearted young fellow, as a souvenir of himself, he kindly presented me with this rifle,[1] which I still have.

That was about six months earlier than the time of which I write, and during those months I had often used this rifle for

[1] This single-barrelled percussion-cap rifle described by Allan Quatermain, which figures so prominently in the history of this epoch of his life, has been sent to me by Mr. Curtis, and is before me as I write. It was made in the year 1835 by J. Purdey, of 314½, Oxford Street, London, and is a beautiful piece of workmanship of its kind. Without the ramrod, which is now

the shooting of game, such as blesbuck and also of bustards.
I found it to be a weapon of the most extraordinary accuracy
up to a range of about two hundred yards, though when I
rode off in that desperate hurry for Marajsfontein I did not
take it with me because it was a single barrel and too small in
the bore to load with *loopers* at a pinch. Still, in challenging
Pereira, it was this gun and no other that I determined to use;
indeed, had I not owned it I do not think that I should have
ventured on the match.

As it happened, Mr. Smyth had left me with the rifle a large
supply of specially cast bullets and of the new percussion caps,
to say nothing of some very fine imported powder. Therefore,
having ammunition in plenty, I set to work to practise. Seating
myself upon a chair in a deep kloof near the station, across which
rock pigeons and turtle doves were wont to fly in numbers at
a considerable height, I began to fire at them as they flashed
over me.

Now, in my age, I may say without fear of being set down a

---

missing, it weighs only 5 lbs. 3¾ oz. The barrel is octagonal, and the rifled
bore, designed to take a spherical bullet, is ½ in. in diameter. The hammer
can be set to safety on the half-cock by means of a catch behind it.

Another peculiarity of the weapon, one that I have never seen before,
is that by pressing on the back of the trigger the ordinary light pull of the
piece is so reduced that the merest touch suffices to fire it, thus rendering it
hair-triggered in the fullest sense of the word.

It has two flap-sights marked for 150 and 200 yards, in addition to the
fixed sight designed for firing at 100 yards.

On the lock are engraved a stag and a doe, the first lying down and the
second standing.

Of its sort and period, it is an extraordinarily well-made and handy gun,
finished with horn at the end of what is now called the tongue, and with
the stock cut away so as to leave a raised cushion against which the cheek
of the shooter rests.

What charge it took I do not know, but I should imagine from 2½ to 3
drachms of powder. It is easy to understand that in the hands of Allan
Quatermain this weapon, obsolete as it is to-day, was capable of great
things within the limits of its range, and that the faith he put in it at the
trial of skill at the Groote Kloof, and afterwards in the fearful ordeal of the
shooting of the vultures on the wing upon the Mount of Slaughter, when
the lives of many hung upon his markmanship, was well justified. This,
indeed, is shown by the results in both cases.

In writing of this rifle, Messrs. Purdey informed me that copper percussion
caps were experimented with by Colonel Forsyth in 1820, and that their firm
sold them in 1824, at a cost of £1 15s. per 1,000, although their use did not
become general until some years later.—THE EDITOR.

boaster, that I have one gift, that of marksmanship, which, I suppose, I owe to some curious combination of judgment, quickness of eye, and steadiness of hand. I can declare honestly that in my best days I never knew a man who could beat me in shooting at a living object; I say nothing of target work, of which I have little experience. Oddly enough, also, I believe that at this art, although then I lacked the practice which since has come to me in such plenty, I was as good as a youth as I have ever been in later days, and, of course, far better than I am now. This I soon proved upon the present occasion, for seated there in that kloof, after a few trials, I found that I could bring down quite a number of even the swift, straight-flying rock pigeons as they sped over me, and this, be it remembered, not with shot, but with a single bullet, a feat that many would hold to be incredible.

So the days passed, and I practised, every evening finding me a little better at this terribly difficult sport. For always I learned more as to the exact capacities of my rifle and the allowance that must be made according to the speed of the bird, its distance, and the complications of the wind and of the light. During those days, also, I recovered so rapidly that at the end of them I was almost in my normal condition, and could walk well with the aid of a single stick.

At length the eventful Thursday came, and about midday— for I lay in bed late that morning and did not shoot—I drove, or, rather, was driven, in a Cape cart with two horses to the place known as Groote Kloof or Great Gully. Over this gorge the wild geese flighted from their *pans* or feeding grounds on the high lands above, to other *pans* that lay some miles below, and thence, I suppose, straight out to the sea coast, whence they returned at dawn.

On arriving at the mouth of Groote Kloof about four o'clock in the afternoon, my father and I were astonished to see a great number of Boers assembled there, and among them a certain sprinkling of their younger womenkind, who had come on horseback or in carts.

" Good gracious ! " I said to my father ; " if I had known there was to be such a fuss as this about a shooting match, I don't think I could have faced it."

" Hum," he answered ; " I think there is more in the wind than your match. Unless I am much mistaken, it has been made the excuse of a public meeting in a secluded spot, so as to throw the Authorities off the scent."

As a matter of fact, my father was quite right. Before we arrived there that day the majority of those Boers, after full and long discussion, had arranged to shake the dust of the Colony off their feet, and find a home in new lands to the north.

Presently we were among them, and I noticed that, one and all, their faces were anxious and preoccupied. Pieter Retief caught sight of me being helped out of the cart by my father and Hans, whom I had brought to load, and for a moment looked puzzled. Evidently his thoughts were far away. Then he remembered and exclaimed in his jolly voice :

" Why ! here is our little Englishman come to shoot off his match like a man of his word. Friend Marais, stop talking about your losses "—this in a warning voice—" and give him good day."

So Marais came, and with him Marie, who blushed and smiled, but to my mind looked more of a grown woman than ever before ; one who had left girlhood behind her and found herself face to face with real life and all its troubles. Following her close, very close, as I was quick to notice, was Hernan Pereira. He was even more finely dressed than usual and carried in his hand a beautifully new, single-barrelled rifle, also fitted to take percussion caps, but, as I thought, of a very large bore for the purpose of goose shooting.

" So you have got well again," he said in a genial voice that yet did not ring true. Indeed, it suggested to me that he wished I had done nothing of the sort. " Well, Mynheer Allan, here you find me quite ready to shoot your head off." (He didn't mean that, though I dare say he was.) " I tell you that the mare is as good as mine, for I have been practising, haven't I, Marie ? as the *aasvogels* " (that is, vultures) " round the stead know to their cost."

" Yes, Cousin Hernan," said Marie, " you have been practising, but so, perhaps, has Allan."

By this time all the company of Boers had collected round us, and began to evince a great interest in the pending contest, as was natural among people who rarely had a gun out of their hands, and thought that fine shooting was the divinest of the arts. However, they were not allowed to stay long, as the Kaffirs said that the geese would begin their afternoon flight within about half an hour. So the spectators were all requested to arrange themselves under the sheer cliff of the kloof, where they could not be seen by the birds coming over them from behind, and there to keep silence. Then Pereira and I—I attended by my loader, but he alone, as he said a man at his elbow would bother him—and with us Retief, the referee, took our stations about a hundred and fifty yards from this face of cliff. Here we screened ourselves as well as we could from the keen sight of the birds behind some tall bushes which grew at this spot.

I seated myself on a camp-stool, which I had brought with me, for my leg was still too weak to allow me to stand long, and waited. Presently Pereira said through Retief that he had a favour to ask, namely, that I would allow him to take the first six shots, as the strain of waiting made him nervous. I answered, " Certainly," although I knew well that the object of the request was that he believed that the outpost geese—" spy-geese " we called them—which would be the first to arrive, would probably come over low down and slow, whereas those that followed, scenting danger, might fly high and fast. This, in fact, proved to be the case, for there is no bird more clever than the misnamed goose.

When we had waited about a quarter of an hour Hans said : " Hist ! Goose comes."

As he spoke, though as yet I could not see the bird, I heard its cry of " *Honk, honk* " and the swish of its strong wings.

Then it appeared, an old spur-winged gander, probably the king of the flock, flying so low that it only cleared the cliff edge by about twenty feet, and passed over not more than thirty yards up, an easy shot. Pereira fired, and down it came rather slowly, falling a hundred yards or so behind him, while Retief said : " One for our side."

Pereira loaded again, and just as he had capped his rifle three more geese, also flying low, came over, preceded by a number of ducks, passing straight above us, as they must do owing to the shape of the gap between the land waves of the veld above through which they flighted. Pereira shot, and, to my surprise, the second, not the first, bird fell, also a good way behind him.

" Did you shoot at that goose, or the other, nephew ? " asked Retief.

" At that one for sure," he answered with a laugh.

" He lies," muttered the Hottentot ; " he shot at the first and killed the second."

" Be silent," I answered. " Who would lie about such a thing ? "

Again Pereira loaded. By the time that he was ready more geese were approaching, this time in a triangle of seven birds, their leader being at the point of the triangle, which was flying higher than those that had gone before. He fired, and down came not one bird, but two, namely, the captain and the goose to the right of and a little behind it.

" Ah ! uncle," exclaimed Pereira, " did you see those birds cross each other as I pulled ? That was a lucky one for me, but I won't count the second if the Heer Allan objects."

" No, I did not, nephew," answered Retief, " but doubtless they must have done so, or the same bullet could not have pierced both."

But Hans and I only looked at each other and laughed. Still we said nothing.

From the spectators under the cliff there came a murmur of congratulation not unmixed with astonishment. Again Pereira loaded, aimed, and loosed at a rather high goose—it may have been about seventy yards in the air. He struck it right enough, for the feathers flew from its breast ; but to my astonishment the bird, after swooping down as though it were going to fall, recovered itself and flew away straight out of sight.

" Tough birds, these geese ! " exclaimed Pereira. " They can carry as much lead as a sea-cow."

" Very tough indeed," answered Retief doubtfully. " Never before did I see a bird fly away with an ounce ball through its middle."

" Oh ! he will drop dead somewhere," replied Pereira as he rammed his powder down.

Within four minutes more Pereira had fired his two remaining shots, selecting, as he was entitled to do, low and easy young geese that came over him slowly. He killed them both, although the last of them, after falling, waddled along the ground into a tuft of high grass.

Now murmurs of stifled applause broke from the audience, to which Pereira bowed in acknowledgment.

" You will have to shoot very well, Mynheer Allan," said Retief to me, " if you want to beat that. Even if I rule out one of the two birds that fell to a single shot, as I think I shall, Hernan has killed five out of six, which can scarcely be bettered."

" Yes," I answered ; " but, mynheer, be so good as to have those geese collected and put upon one side. I don't want them mixed up with mine, if I am lucky enough to bring any down."

He nodded, and some Kaffirs were sent to bring in the geese. Several of these, I noted, were still flapping and had to have their necks twisted, but at the time I did not go to look at them. While this was being done I called to Retief, and begged him to examine the powder and bullets I was about to use.

" What's the good ? " he asked, looking at me curiously. " Powder is powder, and a bullet is a bullet."

" None, I dare say. Still, oblige me by looking at them, my uncle."

Then at my bidding Hans took six bullets and placed them in his hand, begging him to return them to us as they were wanted.

" They must be a great deal smaller than Hernan's," said Retief, " who, being stronger, uses a heavier gun."

" Yes," I answered briefly, as Hans put the charge of powder into the rifle, and drove home the wad. Then, taking a bullet from Retief's hand, he rammed that down on to the top of it, capped the gun, and handed it to me.

By now the geese were coming thick, for the flight was at its full. Only, either because some of those that had already passed had sighted the Kaffirs collecting the fallen birds and risen— an example which the others noted from afar and followed—or because in an unknown way warning of their danger had been conveyed to them, they were flying higher and faster than the first arrivals.

" You will have the worst of it, Allan," said Retief. " It should have been shot and shot about."

" I had not long to wait, for presently over came a wedge
of geese . . . " (*See page* 71)

" Perhaps," I answered, " but that can't be helped now."

Then I rose from my stool, the rifle in my hand. I had not long to wait, for presently over came a wedge of geese nearly a hundred yards up. I aimed at the first fellow, holding about eight yards ahead of him to allow for his pace, and pressed. Next second I heard the clap of the bullet, but alas ! it had only struck the outstretched beak, of which a small portion fell to the ground. The bird itself, after wavering a second, resumed its place as leader of the squad and passed away apparently unharmed.

" Baas, baas," whispered Hans as he seized the rifle and began to reload, " you were too far in front. These big water-birds do not travel as fast as the rock pigeons."

I nodded, wishing to save my breath. Then, quivering with excitement, for if I missed the next shot the match appeared to be lost, presently I took the rifle from his hand.

Scarcely had I done so when a single goose came over quite as high as the others and travelling " as though the black devil had kicked it," as Retief said. This time I allowed the same space to compensate for the object's increased speed and pressed.

Down it came like a stone, falling but a little way behind me with its head knocked off.

" Baas, baas," whispered Hans, " still too far in front. Why aim at the eye when you have the whole body ? "

Again I nodded, and at the same time heaved a sigh of relief. At least the match was still alive. Soon a large flight came over, mixed up with mallard and widgeon. I took the right-hand angle bird, so that it could not be supposed I had " browned the lot," as here in England they say of one who fires at a covey and not at a particular partridge. Down he came, shot straight through the breast. Then I knew that I had got my nerve, and felt no more fear.

To cut a long story short, although two of them were extremely difficult and high, one being, I should say, quite a hundred and twenty yards above me, and the other by no means easy, I killed the next three birds one after the other, and I verily believe could have killed a dozen more without a miss, for now I was shooting as I had never shot before.

" Say, nephew Allan," asked Retief curiously in the pause between the fifth and sixth shots, " why do your geese fall so differently to Hernan's ? "

" Ask him ; don't talk to me," I answered, and next instant brought down number five, the finest shot of the lot.

A sound of wonder and applause came from all the audience, and I saw Marie wave a white handkerchief.

" That's the end," said the referee.

" One minute before you stir," I answered. " I want to shoot at something else that is not in the match, just to see if I can kill two birds with one bullet like the Heer Pereira."

He granted my request with a nod, holding up his hand to prevent the audience from moving, and bidding Pereira, who tried to interrupt, to be silent.

Now, while the match was in progress I had noticed two falcons about the size of the British peregrine wheeling round and round high over the kloof, in which doubtless they bred, apparently quite undisturbed by the shooting. Or, perhaps, they had their eyes upon some of the fallen geese. I took the rifle and waited for a long while, till at last my opportunity came. I saw that the larger hen falcon was about to cross directly over the circle of its mate, there being perhaps a distance of ten yards between them. I aimed ; I judged—for a second my mind was a kind of calculating machine—the different arcs and speeds of the birds must be allowed for, and the lowest was ninety yards away. Then, with something like a prayer upon my lips, I pressed while every eye stared upwards.

Down came the lower falcon ; a pause of half a second, and down came the higher one also, falling dead upon its dead mate !

Now, even from those Boers, who did not love to see an Englishman excel, there broke a shout of acclamation. Never had they beheld such a shot as this ; nor in truth had I.

" Mynheer Retief," I said, " I gave you notice that I intended to try to kill both of them, did I not ? "

" You did. Allemachte ! you did ! But tell me, Allan Quatermain, are your eye and hand quite human ? "

" You must ask my father," I answered with a shrug as I sat myself down upon my stool and mopped my brow.

The Boers came up with a rush, Marie flying ahead of them

like a swallow, and their stout womenfolk waddling behind, and formed a circle round us, all talking at once. I did not listen to their conversation, who was engaged in some eye-play with Marie, till I heard Pereira say in a loud voice :

" Yes, it was pretty, very pretty, but all the same, Uncle Retief, I claim the match, as I shot six geese against five."

" Hans," I said, " bring my geese," and they were brought, each with a neat hole through it, and laid down near those that Pereira had shot. " Now," I said to Retief, " examine the wounds in these birds, and then that on the second bird which the Heer Pereira killed when he brought down two at once. I think it will be found that his bullet must have splintered."

Retief went and studied all the birds, taking them up one by one. Then he threw down the last with a curse and cried in a great voice :

" Mynheer Pereira, why do you bring shame on us before these two Englishmen ? I say that you have been using *loopers*, or else bullets that were sawn in quarters and glued or tied with thread. Look, look ! " and he pointed to the wounds, of which in one case there were as many as three on a single bird.

" Why not ? " answered Pereira coolly. " The bargain was that we were to use bullets, but it was never said that they should not be cut. Doubtless the Heer Allan's were treated in the same way."

" No," I answered, " when I said that I would shoot with a bullet I meant a whole bullet, not one that had been sawn in pieces and fixed together again, so that after it left the muzzle it might spread out like shot. But I do not wish to talk about the matter. It is in the hands of the Heer Pieter Retief, who will give judgment as it pleases him."

Now, much excited argument ensued among the Boers, in the midst of which Marie managed to whisper to me unheard :

" Oh ! I am glad, Allan, for whatever they may decide, you won, and the omen is good."

" I don't see what geese have to do with omens, sweetheart," I answered—" that is, since the time of the ancient Romans. Anyhow, I should say that the omens are bad, for there is going to be a row presently."

Just then Retief put up his hand, calling out :

"Silence! I have decided. The writing of the match did not say that the bullets were not to be cut, and therefore Hernan Pereira's birds must count. But that writing does say that any bird accidentally killed should not count, and therefore one goose must be subtracted from Pereira's total, which leaves the two shooters equal. So either the match is dead or, since the geese have ceased to come, it must be shot off another day."

"Oh! if there is any question," said Pereira, who felt that public opinion was much against him, "let the Englishman take the money. I dare say that he needs it, as the sons of missionaries are not rich."

"There is no question," I said, "since, rich or poor, not for a thousand pounds would I shoot again against one who plays such tricks. Keep your money, Mynheer Pereira, and I will keep my mare. The umpire has said that the match is dead, so everything is finished."

"Not quite," interrupted Retief, "for I have a word to say. Friend Allan, you have played fair, and I believe that there is no one who can shoot like you in Africa."

"That is so," said the audience of Boers.

"Mynheer Pereira," went on Retief, "although you, too, are a fine shot, as is well known, I believe that had you played fair also you would have been beaten, but as it is you have saved your hundred pounds. Mynheer Pereira," he added in a great voice, "you are a cheat, who have brought disgrace upon us Boers, and for my part I never want to shake your hand again."

Now, at these outspoken words, for when his indignation was aroused Retief was no measurer of language, Pereira's high-coloured face went white as a sheet.

"*Mein Gott*, mynheer," he said, "I am minded to make you answer for such talk," and his hand went to the knife at his girdle.

"What!" shouted Retief, "do you want another shooting match? Well, if so I am ready with whole bullets or with split ones. None shall say that Pieter Retief was afraid of any man, and, least of all, of one who is not ashamed to try to steal a prize as a hyena steals a bone from a lion. Come on, Hernan Pereira, come on!"

Now, I am sure I cannot say what would have happened,

although I am quite certain that Pereira had no stomach for a duel with the redoubtable Retief, a man whose courage was as proverbial throughout the land as was his perfect uprightness of character. At any rate, seeing that things looked very black, Henri Marais, who had been listening to this altercation with evident annoyance, stepped forward and said :

" Mynheer Retief and nephew Hernan, you are both my guests, and I will not permit quarrelling over this foolishness, especially as I am sure that Hernan never intended to cheat, but only to do what he thought was allowed. Why should he, who is one of the finest shots in the Colony, though it may be that young Allan Quatermain here is even better ? Will you not say so, too, friend Retief, especially just now when it is necessary that we should all be as brothers ? " he added pleadingly.

" No," thundered Retief, " I will not tell a lie to please you or anyone."

Then, seeing that the commandant was utterly uncompromising, Marais went up to his nephew and whispered to him for a while. What he said I do not know. The result of it was, however, that after favouring both Retief and myself with an angry scowl, Pereira turned and walked to where his horse stood, mounted it, and rode off, followed by two Hottentot after-riders.

That was the last I saw of Hernan Pereira for a long while to come, and heartily do I wish that it had been the last I ever saw of him. But this was not to be.

VI

THE PARTING

THE Boers, who ostensibly had come to the kloof to see the shooting match, although, in fact, for a very different purpose, now began to disperse. Some of them rode straight away, while some went to wagons which they had outspanned at a distance, and trekked off to their separate homes. I am glad to say that before they left quite a number of the best of them came up and congratulated me both on the defence of Marais-fontein and on my shooting. Also not a few expressed their views concerning Pereira in very straightforward language.

Now, the arrangement was that my father and I were to sleep that night at Marais's stead, returning home on the following morning. But my father, who had been a silent but not unobservant witness of all this scene, coming to the conclusion that after what had happened we should scarcely be welcome there, and that the company of Pereira was to be avoided just now, went up to Marais and bade him farewell, saying that we would send for my mare.

" Not so, not so," he answered, " you are my guests to-night. Also, fear not, Hernan will be away. He has gone a journey upon some business."

As my father hesitated, Marais added : " Friend, I pray you to come, for I have some important words to say to you, which cannot be said here."

Then my father gave way, to my delight and relief. For if he had not, what chance would there have been of my getting some still more important words with Marie ? So having collected the geese and the two falcons, which I proposed to skin for Marie, I was helped into the cart, and we drove off, reaching Maraisfontein just as night set in.

That evening, after we had eaten, Heer Marais asked my father and myself to speak with him in the sitting-room. By an afterthought also, or so it seemed to me, he told his daughter, who had been clearing away the dishes and with whom as yet I had found no opportunity to talk, to come in with us and close the door behind her.

When all were seated and we men had lit our pipes, though apprehension of what was to follow quite took away my taste for smoking, Marais spoke in English, which he knew to a certain extent. This was for the benefit of my father, who made it a point of honour not to understand Dutch, although he would answer Marais in that language when *he* pretended not to understand English. To me he spoke in Dutch, and occasionally in French to Marie. It was a most curious and polyglot conversation.

" Young Allan," he said, " and you, daughter Marie, I have heard stories concerning you that, although I never gave you leave to *opsit* " (that is, to sit up alone at night with candles according to the Boer fashion between those who are courting), " you have been making love to each other."

" That is true, mynheer," I said. " I only waited an opportunity to tell you that we plighted our troth during the attack of the Quabies on this house."

" Allemachte ! Allan, a strange time to choose," answered Marais, pulling at his beard ; " the troth that is plighted in blood is apt to end in blood."

" A vain superstition to which I cannot consent," interrupted my father.

" Perhaps so," I answered. " I know not ; God alone knows. I only know that we plighted our troth when we thought ourselves about to die, and that we shall keep that troth till death ends it."

" Yes, my father," added Marie, leaning forward across the scored yellow-wood table, her chin resting on her hand and her dark, buck-like eyes looking him in the face. " Yes, my father, that is so, as I have told you already."

" And I tell you, Marie, what I have told you already, and you too, Allan, that this thing may not be," answered Marais, hitting the table with his fist. " I have nothing to say against you, Allan, indeed, I honour you, and you have done me a mighty service, but it may not be."

" Why not, mynheer ? " I asked.

" For three reasons, Allan, each of which is final. You are English, and I do not wish my daughter to marry an Englishman ; that is the first. You are poor, which is no discredit to you, and since I am now ruined my daughter cannot marry a poor man ; that is the second. You live here, and my daughter and I are leaving this country, therefore you cannot marry her ; that is the third," and he paused.

" Is there not a fourth," I asked, " which is the real reason ? Namely, that you wish your daughter to marry someone else."

" Yes, Allan ; since you force me to it, there is a fourth. I have affianced my daughter to her cousin, Hernando Pereira, a man of substance and full age; no lad, but one who knows his own mind and can support a wife."

"I understand," I answered calmly, although within my heart a very hell was raging. "But tell me, mynheer, has Marie affianced herself—or perhaps she will answer with her own lips?"

"Yes, Allan," replied Marie in her quiet fashion, "I have affianced myself—to you and no other man."

"You hear, mynheer," I said to Marais.

Then he broke out in his usual excitable manner. He stormed, he argued, he rated us both. He said that he would never allow it; that first he would see his daughter in her grave. That I had abused his confidence and violated his hospitality; that he would shoot me if I came near his girl. That she was a minor, and according to the law he could dispose of her in marriage. That she must accompany him whither he was going; that certainly I should not do so, and much more of the same sort.

When at last he had tired himself out and smashed his favourite pipe upon the table, Marie spoke, saying:

"My father, you know that I love you dearly, for since my mother's death we have been everything to each other, have we not?"

"Surely, Marie, you are my life, and more than my life."

"Very well, my father. That being so, I acknowledge your authority over me, whatever the law may say. I acknowledge that you have the right to forbid me to marry Allan, and if you do forbid me—while I am under age, at any rate—I shall not marry him because of my duty to you. But "—here she rose and looked him full in the eyes, and oh! how stately she seemed at that moment in her simple strength and youthful grace!— "there is one thing, my father, that I do not acknowledge— your right to force me to marry any other man. As a woman with power over herself, I deny that right; and much as it pains me, my father, to refuse you anything, I say that first I will die. To Allan here I have given myself for good or for evil, and if I may not marry Allan, I will go to the grave unwed. If my words hurt you, I pray you to pardon me, but at the same time to remember that they are my words, which cannot be altered."

Marais looked at his daughter, and his daughter looked at Marais. At first I thought that he was about to curse her; but if this were so, something in her eyes seemed to change his mind, for all he said was:

"Intractable, like the rest of your race! Well, Fate may lead those who cannot be driven, and this matter I leave in the hands of Fate. While you are under age—that is, for two years or more—you may not marry without my consent, and have just promised not to do so. Presently we trek from this country into far-off lands. Who knows what may happen there?"

"Yes," said my father in a solemn voice, speaking for the first time, "who knows except God, Who governs all things, and will settle these matters according to His will, Henri Marais? Listen," he went on after a pause, for Marais made no answer, but sat himself down and stared gloomily at the table. "You do not wish my son to marry your daughter for various reasons, of which one is that you think him poor and a richer suitor has offered himself after a reverse of fortune has made *you* poor. Another and a greater, the true reason, is his English blood, which you hate so much that, although by God's mercy he saved her life, you do not desire that he should share her life. Is it not true?"

"Yes, it is true, Mynheer Quatermain. You English are bullies and cheats," he answered excitedly.

"And so you would give your daughter to one who has shown himself humble and upright, to that good hater of the English and plotter against his King, Hernando Pereira, whom you love because he alone is left of your ancient race."

Remembering the incident of the afternoon, this sarcasm reduced Marais to silence.

"Well," went on my father, "although I am fond of Marie, and know her to be a sweet and noble-hearted girl, neither do I wish that she should marry my son. I would see him wed to some English woman, and not dragged into the net of the Boers and their plottings. Still, it is plain that these two love each other with heart and soul, as doubtless it has been decreed that they should love. This being so, I tell you that to separate them and force another marriage upon one of them is a crime before God, of which, I am sure, He will take note and pay it back to you. Strange things may happen in those lands whither you go, Henri Marais. Will you not, then, be content to leave your child in safe keeping ? "

" Never ! " shouted Marais. " She shall accompany me to a new home, which is not under the shadow of your accursed British flag."

" Then I have no more to say. On your head be it here and hereafter," replied my father solemnly.

Now unable to control myself any longer I broke in :

" But I have, mynheer. To separate Marie and myself is a sin, and one that will break her heart. As for my poverty, I have something, more perhaps than you think, and in this rich country wealth can be earned by those who work, as I would do for her sake. The man to whom you would give her showed his true nature this day, for he who can play so low a trick to win a wager, will play worse tricks to win greater things. Moreover, the scheme must fail since Marie will not marry him."

" I say she shall," replied Marais ; " and that whether she does or not, she shall accompany me and not stay here to be the wife of an English boy."

" Accompany you I will, father, and share your fortunes to the last. But marry Hernando Pereira I will not," said Marie quietly.

" Perhaps, mynheer," I added, " days may come when once again you will be glad of the help of an ' English boy.' "

The words were spoken at random, a kind of ejaculation from the heart, caused by the sting of Marais's cruelty and insults, like the cry of a beast beneath a blow. Little did I know how true they would prove, but at times it is thus that truth is mysteriously drawn from some well of secret knowledge hidden in our souls.

" When I want your help I will ask for it," raved Marais, who, knowing himself to be in the wrong, strove to cover up that wrong with violence.

" Asked or unasked, if I live it shall be given in the future as in the past, Mynheer Marais. God pardon you for the woe you are bringing on Marie and on me."

Now Marie began to weep a little, and, unable to bear that sight, I covered my eyes with my hand. Marais, who, when he was not under the influence of his prejudices or passion, had a kind heart, was moved also, but tried to hide his feelings in rough-ness. He swore at Marie, and told her to go to bed, and she obeyed, still weeping. Then my father rose and said :

" Henri Marais, we cannot leave here to-night because the horses are kraaled, and it would be difficult to find them in this darkness, so we must ask your hospitality till dawn."

" *I* do not ask it," I exclaimed. " I go to sleep in the cart," and I limped from the room and the house, leaving the two men together.

What passed afterwards between them I do not quite know. I gathered that my father, who, when roused, also had a temper and was mentally and intellectually the stronger man, told Marais his opinion of his wickedness and folly in language that he was not likely to forget. I believe he even drove him to confess that his acts seemed cruel, excusing them, however, by announcing that he had sworn before God that his daughter should never marry an Englishman. Also, he said that he had promised her solemnly to Pereira, his own nephew, whom he loved, and could not break his word.

" No," answered my father, " because, being mad with the madness that runs before destruction, you prefer to break Marie's heart and perhaps become guilty of her blood."

Then he left him.

The darkness was intense. Through it I groped my way to the cart, which stood where it had been outspanned on the veld at a little distance from the house, wishing heartily, so miserable was I, that the Kaffirs might choose that black night for another attack and make an end of me.

When I reached it and lit the lantern which we always carried, I was astonished to find that, in a rough fashion, it had been made ready to sleep in. The seats had been cleared out, the hind curtain fastened, and so forth. Also the pole was propped up with an ox-yoke so as to make the vehicle level to lie in. While I was wondering vaguely who could have done this, Hans climbed on to the step, carrying two karosses which he had borrowed or stolen, and asked if I was comfortable.

" Oh, yes ! " I answered; " but why were you going to sleep in the cart ? "

"Baas," he replied, "I was not; I prepared it for you. How did I know that you were coming? Oh, very simply. I sat on the stoep and listened to all the talk in the *sitkammer*. The window has never been mended, baas, since the Quabies broke it. God in Heaven! what a talk that was. I never knew that white people could have so much to say about a simple matter. You want to marry the Baas Marais's daughter; the baas wants her to marry another man who can pay more cattle. Well, among us it would soon have been settled, for the father would have taken a stick and beaten you out of the hut with the thick end. Then he would have beaten the girl with the thin end until she promised to take the other man, and all would have been settled nicely. But you Whites, you talk and talk, and nothing is settled. You still mean to marry the daughter, and the daughter still means not to marry the man of many cows. Moreover, the father has really gained nothing except a sick heart and much bad luck to come."

"Why much bad luck to come, Hans?" I asked idly, for his naïve summing up of the case interested me in a vague way.

"Oh! Baas Allan, for two reasons. First, your reverend father, who made me true Christian, told him so, and a prédicant so good as he, is one down whom the curse of God runs from Heaven like lightning runs down a tree. Well, the Heer Marais was sitting under that tree, and we all know what happens to him who is under a tree when the lightning strikes it. That my first Christian reason. My second black-man reason, about which there can be no mistake, for it has always been true since there was a black man, is that the girl is yours by blood. You saved her life with your blood," and he pointed to my leg, "and therefore bought her for ever, for blood is more than cattle. Therefore, too, he who would divide her from you brings blood on her and on the other man who tries to steal her, blood, blood! and on himself I know not what." And he waved his yellow arms, staring up at me with his little black eyes in a way that was most uncanny.

"Nonsense!" I said. "Why do you talk such bad words?"

"Because they are true words, Baas Allan. Oh, you laugh at the poor Totty; but I had it from my father, and he from his father from generation to generation, amen, and you will see.

You will see, as I have seen before now, and as the Heer Marais will see, who, if the great God had not made him mad—for mad he is, baas, as we know, if you Whites don't—might have lived in his home till he was old, and have had a good son-in-law to bury him in his blanket."

Now I seemed to have had enough of this eerie conversation. Of course it is easy to laugh at natives and their superstitions, but, after a long life of experience, I am bound to admit that they are not always devoid of truth. The native has some kind of sixth sense which the civilised man has lost, or so it seems to me.

" Talking of blankets," I said in order to change the subject, " from whom did you get these karosses ? "

" From whom ? Why, from the Missie, of course, baas. When I heard that you were to sleep in the cart I went to her and borrowed them to cover you. Also, I had forgotten, she gave me a writing for you," and he felt about, first in his dirty shirt, then under his arm, and finally in his fuzzy hair, from which last hiding place he produced a little bit of paper folded into a pellet. I undid it and read these words, written with a pencil and in French :—

" I shall be in the peach orchard half an hour before sunrise. Be there if you would bid me farewell.—M."

" Is there any answer, baas ? " asked Hans when I had thrust the note into my pocket. " If so I can take it without being found out." Then an inspiration seemed to strike him, and he added : " Why do you not take it yourself ? The Missie's window is easy to open, also I am sure she would be pleased to see you."

" Be silent," I said. " I am going to sleep. Wake me an hour before the cock-crow—and, stay—see that the horses have got out of the kraal so that you cannot find them too easily in case the Reverend wishes to start very early. But do not let them wander far, for here we are no welcome guests."

" Yes, baas. By the way, baas, the Heer Pereira, who tried to cheat you over those geese, is sleeping in an empty house not more than two miles away. He drinks coffee when he wakes up in the morning, and his servant, who makes it, is my good friend. Now would you like me to put a little something into it? Not to kill him, for that is against the law in the Book, but just to make him quite mad, for the Book says nothing about that. If so, I have a very good medicine, one that you white people do not know, which improves the taste of the coffee, and it might save much trouble. You see, if he came dancing about the place without any clothes on, like a common Kaffir, the Heer Marais, although *he* is really mad also, might not wish for him as a son-in-law."

" Oh! go to the devil if you are not there already," I replied, and turned over as though to sleep.

There was no need for me to have instructed that faithful creature, the astute but immoral Hans, to call me early, as the lady did her mother in the poem, for I do not think that I closed an eye that night. I spare my reflections, for they can easily be imagined in the case of an earnest-natured lad who was about to be bereft of his first love.

Long before the dawn I stood in the peach orchard, that orchard where we had first met, and waited. At length Marie came stealing between the tree trunks like a grey ghost, for she was wrapped in some light-coloured garment. Oh! once more we were alone together. Alone in the utter solitude and silence which precede the African dawn, when all creatures that love the night have withdrawn to their lairs and hiding places, and those that love the day still sleep their soundest.

She saw me and stood still, then opened her arms and clasped me to her breast, uttering no word. A while later she spoke almost in a whisper, saying :

" Allan, I must not stay long, for I think that if my father found us together, he would shoot you in his madness."

Now as always it was of me she thought, not of herself.

" And you, my sweet? " I asked.

" Oh! " she answered, " that matters nothing. Except for the sin of it I wish he would shoot me, for then I should have done with all this pain. I told you, Allan, when the Kaffirs were on us yonder, that it might be better to die ; and see, my heart spoke truly."

" Is there no hope? " I gasped. " Will he really separate us and take you away into the wilderness? "

" Certainly, nothing can turn him. Yet, Allan, there is this hope. In two years, if I live, I shall be of full age, and can marry whom I will; and this I swear, that I will marry none but you, no, not even if you were to die to-morrow."

" I bless you for those words," I said.

" Why ? " she asked simply. " What others could I speak ? Would you have me do outrage to my own heart and go through life faithless and ashamed ? "

" And I, I swear also," I broke in.

" Nay, swear nothing. While I live I know that you will love me, and if I should be taken, it is my wish that you should marry some other good woman, since it is not well or right that man should live alone. With us maids it is different. Listen, Allan, for the cocks are beginning to crow, and soon there will be light. You must bide here with your father. If possible I will write to you from time to time, telling you where we are and how we fare. But if I do not write, know that it is because I cannot, or because I can find no messenger, or because the letters have miscarried, for we go into wild countries, amongst savages."

" Whither do you go ? " I asked.

" I believe up towards the great harbour called Delagoa Bay, where the Portuguese rule. My cousin Hernan, who accompanies us "—and she shivered a little in my arms—" is half Portuguese. He tells the Boers that he has relations there who have written him many fine promises, saying they will give us good country to dwell in where we cannot be followed by the English, whom he and my father hate so much."

" I have heard that is all fever veld, and that the country between is full of fierce Kaffirs," I said with a groan.

" Perhaps. I do not know, and I do not care. At least, that is the notion in my father's head, though, of course, circumstances may change it. I will try to let you know, Allan, or if I do not, perhaps you will be able to find out for yourself. Then, then, if we both live and you still care for me, who will always care for you, when I am of age, you will join us and, say and do what they may, I will marry you and no other man. And if I die, as may well happen, oh ! then my spirit shall watch over you and wait for you till you join me beneath the wings of God.

Look, it grows light. I must go. Farewell, my love, my first and only love, till in life or death we meet again, as meet we shall."

Once more we clung together and kissed, muttering broken words, and then she tore herself from my embrace and was gone. But oh! as I heard her feet steal through the dew-laden grass, I felt as though my heart were being rent from my breast. I have suffered much in life, but I do not think that ever I underwent a bitterer anguish than in this hour of my parting from Marie. For when all is said and done, what joy is there like the joy of pure, first love, and what bitterness like the bitterness of its loss?

Half an hour later the flowering trees of Maraisfontein were behind us, while in front rolled the fire-swept veld, black as life had become for me.

VII

ALLAN'S CALL

A FORTNIGHT later Marais, Pereira and their companions, a little band in all of about twenty men, thirty women and children, and say fifty half-breeds and Hottentot after-riders, trekked from their homes into the wilderness. I rode to the crest of a table-topped hill and watched the long line of wagons, one of them containing Marie, crawl away northwards across the veld a mile or more beneath.

Sorely was I tempted to gallop after them and seek a last interview with her and her father. But my pride forbade me. Henri Marais had given out that if I came near his daughter he would have me beaten black with *sjambocks* or hide whips. Perhaps he had gained some inkling of our last farewell in the peach orchard. I do not know. But I do know that if anyone had lifted a *sjambock* on me I should have answered with a bullet. Then there would have been blood between us, which is worse to cross than whole rivers of wrath and jealousy. So I just watched the wagons until they vanished, and galloped home down the rock-strewn slope, wishing that the horse would stumble and break my neck.

When I reached the station, however, I was glad that it had not done so, as I found my father sitting on the stoep reading a letter that had been brought by a mounted Hottentot.

It was from Henri Marais, and ran thus :—

" ' REVEREND HEER AND FRIEND QUATERMAIN,—I send this to bid you farewell, for although you are English and we have quarrelled at times, I honour you in my heart. Friend, now that we are starting, your warning words lie on me like lead, I know not why. But what is done cannot be undone, and I trust that all will come right. If not, it is because the Good Lord wills it otherwise.' "

Here my father looked up and said : " When men suffer from their own passion and folly, they always lay the blame on the back of Providence."

Then he went on, spelling out the letter :

" ' I fear your boy Allan, who is a brave lad, as I have reason to know, and honest, must think that I have treated him harshly and without gratitude. But I have only done what I must do. True, Marie, who, like her mother, is very strong and stubborn in mind, swears that she will marry no one else ; but soon Nature will make her forget all that, especially as such a fine husband waits for her hand. So bid Allan forget all about her also, and when he is old enough choose some English girl. I have sworn a great oath before my God that he shall never marry my daughter with my consent.

" ' Friend, I write to ask you something because I trust you more than these slim agents. Half the price, a very poor one, that I have for my farm is still unpaid to me by Jacobus van der Merve, who remains behind and buys up all our lands. It is £100 English, due this day year, and I enclose you power of attorney to receive and give receipt for the same. Also there is due to me from your British Government £253 on account of slaves liberated which were worth quite £1,000. This also the paper gives you authority to receive. As regards my claims against the said cursed Government because of the loss brought on me by the Quabie Kaffirs, it will not acknowledge them, saying that the attack was caused by the Frenchman Leblanc, one of my household.' "

" And with good reason," commented my father.

" ' When you have received these monies, if ever, I pray you take some safe opportunity of sending them to me, where-ever I may be, which doubtless you will hear in due course, although by that time I hope to be rich again and not to need money. Farewell, and God be with you, as I hope He will be with me and Marie and the rest of us trek-Boers. The bearer will overtake us with your answer at our first outspan.

" ' HENRI MARAIS.' "

" Well," said my father with a sigh, " I suppose I must accept his trust, though why he should choose an ' accursed Englishman ' with whom he has quarrelled violently to collect his debts instead of one of his own beloved Boers, I am sure I do not know. I will go and write to him. Allan, see that the messenger and his horse get something to eat."

I nodded and went to the man, who was one of those that had defended Maraisfontein with me, a good fellow unless he got near liquor.

" Heer Allan," he said, looking round to see that we were not overheard, " I have a little writing for you also," and he produced from his pouch a note that was unaddressed.

I tore it open eagerly. Within was written in French, which no Boer would understand if the letter fell into his hands :

" Be brave and faithful, and remember, as I shall. Oh ! love of my heart, adieu, adieu ! "

This message was unsigned ; but what need was there of signature ?

I wrote an answer of a sort that may be imagined, though what the exact words were I cannot remember after the lapse of nearly half a century. Oddly enough, it is the things I said which I recall at such a distance of time rather than the things which I wrote, perhaps because, when once written, my mind being delivered, troubled itself with them no more. So in due course the Hottentot departed with my father's letter and my own, and that was the last direct communication which we had with Henri or Marie Marais for more than a year.

I think that those long months were on the whole the most wretched I have ever spent. The time of life which I was passing through is always trying; that period of emergence from youth into full and responsible manhood which in Africa generally takes place earlier than it does here in England, where young men often seem to me to remain boys up to five-and-twenty. The circumstances which I have detailed made it particularly so in my own case, for here was I who should have been but a cheerful lad, oppressed with the sorrows and anxieties, and fettered by the affections of maturity.

I could not get Marie out of my mind; her image was with me by day and by night, especially by night, which caused me to sleep badly. I became morose, supersensative, and excitable. I developed a cough, and thought, as did others, that I was going into a decline. I remember that Hans even asked me once if I would not come and peg out the exact place where I should like to be buried, so that I might be sure that there would be no mistake made when I could no longer speak for myself. On that occasion I kicked Hans, one of the few upon which I have ever touched a native. The truth was that I had not the slightest intention of being buried. I wanted to live and marry Marie, not to die and be put in a hole by Hans. Only I saw no prospect of marrying Marie, or even of seeing her again, and that was why I felt low-spirited.

Of course, from time to time news of the trek-Boers reached us, but it was extremely confused. There were so many parties of them; their adventures were so difficult to follow, and, I may add, often so terrible; so few of them could write; trustworthy messengers were so scanty; distances were so great. At any rate, we heard nothing of Marais's band except a rumour that they had trekked to a district in what is now the Transvaal, which is called Rustenberg, and thence on towards Delagoa Bay into an unknown veld where they had vanished. From Marie herself no letter came, which showed me clearly enough that she had not found an opportunity of sending one.

Observing my depressed condition, my father suggested as a remedy that I should go to the theological college at Cape Town and prepare myself for ordination. But the Church as a career did not appeal to me, perhaps because I felt that I could never be sufficiently good ; perhaps because I knew that as a clergyman I should find no opportunity of travelling north when my call came. For I always believed that this call would come.

My father, who wished that I should hear another kind of call, was vexed with me over this matter. He desired earnestly that I should follow the profession which he adorned, and indeed saw no other open for me any more than I did myself. Of course he was right in a way, seeing that in the end I found none, unless big game hunting and Kaffir trading can be called a profession. I don't know, I am sure. Still, poor business as it may be, I say now when I am getting towards the end of life that I am glad I did not follow any other. It has suited me ; that was the insignificant hole in the world's affairs which I was destined to fit, whose only gifts were a remarkable art of straight shooting and the more common one of observation mixed with a little untrained philosophy.

So hot did our arguments become about this subject of the Church, for, as may be imagined, in the course of them I revealed some unorthodoxy, especially as regards the matter of our methods of Christianising Kaffirs, that I was extremely thankful when a diversion occurred which took me away from home. The story of my defence of Maraisfontein had spread far, and that of my feats of shooting, especially in the Goose Kloof, still farther. So the end of it was that those in authority commandeered me to serve in one of the continual Kaffir frontier wars which was in progress, and instantly gave me a commission as a kind of lieutenant in a border corps.

Now the events of that particular war have nothing to do with the history that I am telling, so I do not propose even to touch on them. I served in it for a year, meeting with many adventures, one or two successes, and several failures. Once I was wounded slightly, twice I but just escaped with my life. Once I was reprimanded for taking a foolish risk and losing some

men. Twice I was commended for what were called gallant
actions, such as bringing a wounded comrade out of danger
under a warm fire, mostly of assegais, and penetrating by night,
almost alone, into the stronghold of a chieftain, and shooting
him.

At length that war was patched up with an inconclusive peace
and my corpse was disbanded. I returned home, no longer a
lad, but a man with experience of various kinds and a rather
unique knowledge of Kaffirs, their languages, history, and modes
of thought and action. Also I had associated a good deal with
British officers, and from them acquired much that I had found
no opportunity of studying before, especially, I hope, the ideas
and standards of English gentlemen.

I had not been back at the Mission Station more than three
weeks, quite long enough for me to begin to be bored with idle-
ness and inactivity, when that call for which I had been waiting
came at last.

One day a *smous*, that is a low kind of white man, often a Jew,
who travels about trading with unsophisticated Boers and
Kaffirs, and cheating them if he can, called at the station with
his cartful of goods. I was about to send him away, having no
liking for such gentry, when he asked me if I were named
Allan Quatermain. I said " Yes," whereon he replied that he
had a letter for me, and produced a packet wrapped up in sail-
cloth. I asked him whence he had it, and he answered from a
man whom he had met at Port Elizabeth, an east coast trader,
who, hearing that he was coming into the Cradock district,
entrusted him with the letter. The man told him that it was
very important, and that I should reward the bearer well if it
were delivered safely.

While the Jew talked (I think he was a Jew) I was opening
the sail-cloth. Within was a piece of linen which had been
oiled to keep out water, addressed in some red pigment to
myself or my father. This, too, I opened, not without difficulty,
for it was carefully sewn up, and found within it a letter-packet
also addressed to myself or my father, in the handwriting of
Marie.

Great Heaven! How my heart jumped at that sight! Calling
to Hans to make the *smous* comfortable and give him food, I

went into my own room, and there read the letter, which ran
thus :

"MY DEAR ALLAN,—I do not know whether the other
letters I have written to you have ever come to your hands, or
indeed if this one will. Still, I send it on chance by a wandering
Portuguese half-breed who is going to Delagoa Bay, about fifty
miles, I believe, from the place where I now write, near the
Crocodile River. My father has named it Maraisfontein, after
our old home. If those letters reached you, you will have
learned of the terrible things we went through on our journey ;
the attacks by the Kaffirs in the Zoutpansberg region, who
destroyed one of our parties altogether, and so forth. If not,
all that story must wait, for it is too long to tell now, and,
indeed, I have but little paper, and not much pencil. It will be
enough to say, therefore, that to the number of thirty-five white
people, men, women and children, we trekked at the beginning
of the summer season, when the grass was commencing to grow,
from the Lydenburg district—an awful journey over mountains
and through flooded rivers. After many delays, some of them
months long, we reached this place, about eight weeks ago, for I
write to you at the beginning of June, if we have kept correct
account of the time, of which I am not certain.

"It is a beautiful place to look at, a flat country of rich veld,
with big trees growing on it, and about two miles from the
great river that is called the Crocodile. Here, finding good water,
my father and Hernan Pereira, who now rules him in all things,
determined to settle, although some of the others wished to
push on nearer to Delagoa Bay. There was a great quarrel
about it, but in the end my father, or rather Hernan, had his will,
as the oxen were worn out and many had already died from the
bites of a poisonous fly which is called the tsetse. So we lotted
out the land, of which there is enough for hundreds, and began
to build rude houses.

"Then trouble came upon us. The Kaffirs stole most of our
horses, although they have not dared to attack us, and except
two belonging to Hernan, the rest died of the sickness, the last
of them but yesterday. The oxen, too, have all died of the
tsetse bites or other illnesses. But the worst is that although this

country looks so healthy, it is poisoned with fever, which comes up, I think, in the mists from the river. Already out of the thirty-five of us, ten are dead, two men, three women, and five children, while more are sick. As yet my father and I and my cousin Pereira have, by God's mercy, kept quite well; but although we are all very strong, how long this will continue I cannot tell. Fortunately we have plenty of ammunition and the place is thick with game, so that those of the men who remain strong can kill all the food we want, even shooting on foot, and we women have made a great quantity of biltong by salting flesh and drying it in the sun. So we shall not actually starve for a long while, even if the game goes away.

"But, dear Allan, unless help comes to us I think that we shall die every one, for God alone knows the miseries that we suffer and the horrible sights of sickness and death that are around us. At this moment there lies by me a little girl who is dying of fever.

"Oh, Allan, if you can help us, do so! Because of our sick it is impossible for us to get to Delagoa Bay, and if we did we have no money to buy anything there, for all that we had with us was lost in a wagon in a flooded river. It was a great sum, for it included Hernan's rich fortune which he brought from the Cape with him in gold. Nor can we move anywhere else, for we have no cattle or horses. We have sent to Delagoa Bay, where we hear these are to be had, to try to buy them on credit; but my cousin Hernan's relations, of whom he used to talk so much, are dead or gone away, and no one will trust us. With the neighbouring Kaffirs, too, who have plenty of cattle, we have quarrelled since, unfortunately, my cousin and some of the other Boers tried to take certain beasts of theirs without payment. So we are quite helpless, and can only wait for death.

"Allan, my father says that he asked your father to collect some monies that were owing to him. If it were possible for you or other friends to come to Delagoa in a ship with that money, I think that it might serve to buy some oxen, enough for a few wagons. Then perhaps we might trek back and fall in with a party of Boers who, we believe, have crossed the Quathlamba Mountains into Natal. Or perhaps we might get to the Bay and find a ship to take us anywhere from this horrible place. If you could come, the natives would guide you to where we are.

"But it is too much to hope that you will come, or that if you do come you will find us still alive.

"Allan, my dearest, I have one more thing to say, though I must say it shortly, for the paper is nearly finished. I do not know, supposing that you are alive and well, whether you still care for me, who left you so long ago—it seems years and years —but *my* heart is where it was, and where I promised it should remain, in your keeping. Of course, Hernan has pressed me to marry him, and my father has wished it. But I have always said no, and now, in our wretchedness, there is no more talk of marriage at present, which is the one good thing that has happened to me. And, Allan, before so very long I shall be of age, if I live. Still, I dare say you no longer think of marriage with me, who, perhaps, are already married to someone else, especially as now I and all of us are no better than wandering beggars. Yet I have thought it right to tell you these things, which you may like to know.

"Oh, why did God ever put it into my father's heart to leave the Cape Colony just because he hated the British Government and Hernan Pereira and others persuaded him? I know not, but, poor man, he is sorry enough now. It is pitiful to see him; at times I think that he is going mad.

"The paper is done, and the messenger is going; also the sick child is dying and I must attend to her. Will this letter ever come to your hands, I wonder? I am sending with it the little money I have to pay for its delivery—about four pounds English. If not, there is an end. If it does, and you cannot come or send others, at least pray for us. I dream of you by night and think of you by day, for how much I love you I cannot tell.

"In life or death I am

"Your MARIE."

Such was this awful letter. I still have it; it lies before me, those ragged sheets of paper covered with faint pencil-writing that is blotted here and there with tear marks, some of them the tears of Marie who wrote, some of them the tears of me who read. I wonder if there exists a more piteous memorial of the terrible sufferings of the trek-Boers, and especially of such of them as forced their way into the poisonous veld around Delagoa, as did this Marais expedition and those under the command of Triechard. Better, like many of their people, to have perished at once by the spears of Umzilikazi and other savages than to endure these lingering tortures of fever and starvation.

As I finished reading this letter my father, who had been out visiting some of his Mission Kaffirs, entered the house, and I went into the sitting-room to meet him.

" Why, Allan, what is the matter with you ? " he asked, noting my tear-stained face.

I gave him the letter, for I could not speak, and with difficulty he deciphered it.

" Merciful God, what dreadful news ! " he said when he had finished. " Those poor people ! those poor, misguided people ! What can be done for them ? "

" I know one thing that can be done, father, or at any rate can be attempted. I can try to reach them."

" Are you mad ? " he asked. " How is it possible for you, one man, to get to Delagoa Bay, buy cattle, and rescue these folk, who probably are now all dead ? "

" The first two things are possible enough, father. Some ship will take me to the Bay. You have Marais's money, and I have that five hundred pounds which my old aunt in England left me last year. Thank Heaven ! owing to my absence on com-mando, it still lies untouched in the bank at Port Elizabeth. That is about eight hundred pounds in all, which would buy a great many cattle and other things. As for the third, it is not in our hands, is it ? It may be that they cannot be rescued, it may be that they are dead. I can only go to see."

" But, Allan, Allan, you are my only son, and if you go it is probable that I shall never see you more."

" I have been through some dangers lately, father, and am still alive and well. Moreover, if Marie is dead "—I paused, then went on passionately—" Do not try to stop me, for I tell you, father, I will not be stopped. Think of the words in that letter and what a shameless hound I should be if I sat here quiet while Marie is dying yonder. Would you have done so if Marie had been my mother ? "

" No," answered the old gentleman, " I should not. Go, and God be with you, Allan, and me also, for I never expect to see you again." And he turned his head aside for a while.

Then we went into matters. The *smous* was summoned and asked about the ship which brought the letter from Delagoa. It seemed that she was an English-owned brig known as the *Seven Stars*, and that her captain, one Richardson, proposed to sail back to the Bay on the morrow, that was the third of July, or in other words, within twenty-four hours.

Twenty-four hours ! And Port Elizabeth was one hundred and eighteen miles away, and the *Seven Stars* might leave earlier if she had completed her cargo and wind and weather served. Moreover, if she did leave, it might be weeks or months before any other ship sailed for Delagoa Bay, for in those days, of course, there were no mail boats.

I looked at my watch. It was four o'clock in the afternoon, and from a calendar we had, which gave the tides at Port Elizabeth and other South African harbours, it did not seem probable that the *Seven Stars* would sail, if she kept to her date, before about eight on the morrow. One hundred and twenty miles to be covered in, say, fourteen hours over rough country with some hills! Well, on the other hand, the roads were fairly good and dry, with no flooded rivers to cross, although there might be one to swim and there was a full moon. It could be done—barely, and now I was glad indeed that Hernan Pereira had not won my swift mare in that shooting match.

I called to Hans, who was loafing about outside and said quietly :

" I ride to Port Elizabeth, and must be there by eight o'clock to-morrow morning."

" Allemachte ! " exclaimed Hans, who had been that road several times.

" You will go with me, and from Port Elizabeth on to Delagoa Bay. Saddle the mare and the roan horse, and put a headstall on the chestnut to lead with you as a spare. Give them all a feed, but no water. We start in half an hour." Then I added certain directions as to the guns we would take, saddle-bags, clothes, blankets and other details, and bade him start about the business.

Hans never hesitated. He had been with me through my recent campaign, and was accustomed to sudden orders. Moreover, I think that if I had told him I was riding to the moon, beyond his customary exclamation of " Allemachte ! " he would have made no objection to accompanying me thither.

The next half-hour was a busy time for me. Henri Marais' money had to be got out of the strong box and arranged in a belt of buck's hide that I had strapped about me. A letter had to be written by my father to the manager of the Port Elizabeth bank, identifying me as the owner of the sum lodged there in my name. A meal must be eaten and some food prepared for us to carry. The horses' shoes had to be seen to, and a few clothes packed in the saddlebags. Also there were other things which I have forgotten. Yet within five-and-thirty minutes the long, lean mare stood before the door. Behind her, with a tall crane's feather in his hat, was Hans, mounted on the roan stallion, and leading the chestnut, a four-year-old which I had bought as a foal on the mare as part of the bargain. Having been corn fed from a colt it was a very sound and well-grown horse, though not the equal of its mother in speed.

In the passage my poor old father, who was quite be-wildered by the rapidity and urgent nature of this business, embraced me.

" God bless you, my dear boy," he said. " I have had little time to think, but I pray that this may be all for the best, and that we may meet again in the world. But if not, remember what I have taught you, and if I survive you, for my part I shall remember that you died trying to do your duty. Oh, what trouble has the blind madness of Henri Marais brought upon us all ! Well, I warned him that it would be so. Good-bye, my dear boy, good-bye; my prayers will follow you, and for the rest—— Well, I am old, and what does it matter if my grey hairs come with sorrow to the grave ? "

I kissed him back, and with an aching heart sprang to the saddle. In five more minutes the station was out of sight.

Thirteen and a half hours later I pulled rein upon the quay of Port Elizabeth just, only just, in time to catch Captain Richardson, as he was entering his boat to row out to the *Seven Stars*, on which the canvas was already being hoisted. As well as I could in my exhausted state, I explained matters and persuaded him to wait till the next tide. Then, thanking God for the mare's speed—the roan had been left foundered thirty miles away, and Hans was following on the chestnut, but not yet up—I dragged the poor beast to an inn at hand. There she lay down and died. Well, she had done her work, and there was no other horse in the country that could have caught that boat.

An hour or so later Hans came in flogging the chestnut, and here I may add that both it and the roan recovered. Indeed I rode them for many years, until they were quite old. When I had eaten, or tried to eat something and rested awhile, I went to the bank, succeeded in explaining the state of the case to the manager, and after some difficulty, for gold was not very plentiful in Port Elizabeth, procured three hundred pounds in sovereigns. For the other two he gave me a bill upon some agent in Delagoa Bay, together with a letter of recommendation to him and the Portuguese governor, who, it appeared, was in debt to their establishment. By an afterthought, however, although I kept the letters, I returned him the bill and spent the £200 in purchasing a great variety of goods, which I will not enumerate, that I knew would be useful for trading purposes among the east coast Kaffirs. Indeed, I practically cleared out the Port Ellzabeth stores, and barely had time, with the help of Hans and the storekeepers, to pack and ship the goods before the *Seven Stars* put out to sea.

Within twenty-four hours from the time I had left the Mission station, Hans and I saw behind us Port Elizabeth fading into the distance, and in front a waste of stormy waters.

VIII

THE CAMP OF DEATH

EVERYTHING went well upon that voyage, except with me personally. Not having been on the ocean since I was a child, I, who am naturally no good sailor, was extremely ill as day by day we ploughed through seas that grew ever more rough. Also, strong as I was, that fearful ride had overdone me. Added to these physical discomforts was my agonising anxiety of mind, which I leave anyone with imagination to picture for himself. Really there were times when I wished that the *Seven Stars* would plunge headlong to the bottom of the deep and put an end to me and my miseries.

These, however, so far as the bodily side of them was concerned, were, I think, surpassed by those of my henchman Hans, who, as a matter of fact, had never before set foot in any kind of boat. Perhaps this was fortunate, since had he known the horrors of the ocean, much as he loved me, he would, I am sure, by one means or another, have left me to voyage in the *Seven Stars* alone. There he lay upon the floor of my little cabin, rolling to and fro with the violent motion of the brig, overcome with terror. He was convinced that we were going to be drowned, and in the intervals of furious sea-sickness uttered piteous lamentations in Dutch, English, and various native tongues, mingled with curses and prayers of the most primitive and realistic order.

After the first twenty-four hours or so he informed me with many moans that the last bit of his inside had just come out of him, and that he was now quite hollow " like a gourd." Also he declared that all these evils had fallen upon him because he had been fool enough to forsake the religion of his people (what was that, I wonder), and allow himself to be " washed white," that is, be baptised, by my father.

I answered that as he had become white instead of staying yellow, I advised him to remain so, since it was evident that the Hottentot gods would have nothing more to do with one who had deserted them. Thereon he made a dreadful face, which even in the midst of my own woes caused me to laugh at him, uttered a prolonged groan, and became so silent that I thought he must be dead. However, the sailor who brought me my food —such food!—assured me that this was not so, and lashed him tight to the legs of the bunk by his arm and ankle so as to prevent him from being rolled to bits.

Next morning Hans was dosed with brandy, which, in his empty condition, made him extremely drunk, and from that time forward began to take a more cheerful view of things. Especially was this so when the hours for the " brandy medicine " came round. Hans, like most other Hottentots, loved spirits, and would put up with much to get them, even with my father's fiery indignation.

I think it was on the fourth day that at length we pitched and rolled ourselves over the shallow bar of Port Natal and found ourselves at peace for a while under shelter of the Point in the beautiful bay upon the shores of which the town of Durban now stands. Then it was but a miserable place, consisting of a few shanties which were afterwards burnt by the Zulus, and a number of Kaffir huts. For such white men as dwelt there had for the most part native followings, and, I may add, native wives.

We spent two days at this settlement of Durban, where Captain Richardson had some cargo to land for the English settlers, one or two of whom had started a trade with the natives and with parties of the emigrant Boers, who were beginning to enter the territory by the overland route. Those days I passed on shore, though I would not allow Hans to accompany me lest he should desert, employing my time in picking up all the information I could about the state of affairs, especially with reference to the Zulus, a people with whom I was destined ere long to make an intimate acquaintance. Needless to say, I inquired both from natives and from white men whether anything was known of the fate of Marais's party, but no one seemed even to have heard of them. One thing I did learn, however, that my old friend, Pieter Retief, with a large following, had crossed the Quathlamba Mountains, which we now know as the Drakensberg, and entered the territory of Natal. Here they proposed to settle if they could get the leave of the Zulu king,

Dingaan, a savage potentate of whom and of whose armies everyone seemed to live in terror.

On the third morning, to my great relief, for I was terrified lest we should be delayed, the *Seven Stars* sailed with a favouring wind. Three days later we entered the harbour of Delagoa, a sheet of water many miles long and broad. Notwithstanding its shallow entrance, it is the best natural port in south-eastern Africa, but now, alas ! lost to the English.

Six hours later we anchored opposite a sandbank on which stood a dilapidated fort and a dirty settlement known as Lorenzo Marquez, where the Portuguese kept a few soldiers, most of them coloured. I pass over my troubles with the Customs; if such they could be called. Suffice it to say that ultimately I succeeded in landing my goods, on which the duty chargeable was apparently enormous. This I did by distributing twenty-five English sovereigns among various officials, beginning with the acting-governor and ending with a drunken black sweep who sat in a kind of sentry box on the quay.

Early next morning the *Seven Stars* sailed again, because of some quarrel with the officials, who threatened to seize her—I forget why. Her destination was the East African ports and, I think, Madagascar, where a profitable trade was to be done in carrying cattle and slaves. Captain Richardson said he might be back at Lorenzo Marquez in two or three months' time, or he might not. As a matter of fact the latter supposition proved correct, for the *Seven Stars* was lost on a sandbank somewhere up the coast, her crew only escaping to Mombasa after enduring great hardships.

Well, she had served my turn, for I heard afterwards that no other ship put into the Bay for a whole year from the date she left it. So if I had not caught her at Port Elizabeth I could not have come at all, except, of course, overland. This at best must have taken many months, and was moreover a journey that no man could enter on alone.

Now I get back to my story again.

There was no inn at Lorenzo Marquez. Through the kindness of one of his native or half-breed wives, who could talk a little Dutch, I managed, however, to get a lodging in a tumble-down house belonging to a dissolute person who called himself Don

José Ximenes, but who was really himself a half-breed. Here
good fortune befriended me. Don José, when sober, was a
trader with the natives, and a year before had acquired from them
two good buck wagons. Probably they were stolen from some
wandering Boers or found derelict after their murder or death
by fever. These wagons he was only too glad to sell for a song.
I think I gave him twenty pounds English for the two, and thirty
more for twelve oxen that he had bought at the same time as
the wagons. They were fine beasts of the Afrikander breed, that
after a long rest had grown quite fat and strong.

Of course twelve oxen were not enough to draw two wagons,
or even one. Therefore, hearing that there were natives on the
mainland who possessed plenty of cattle, I at once gave out that
I was ready to buy, and pay well in blankets, cloth, beads and
so forth. The result was that within two days I had forty or
fifty to choose from, small animals of the Zulu character and,
I should add, unbroken. Still they were sturdy and used to that
veld and its diseases. Here it was that my twelve trained beasts
came in. By putting six of them to each wagon, two as fore-
and two as after-oxen, and two in the middle, Hans and I were
able to get the other ten necessary to make up a team of sixteen
under some sort of control.

Heavens! how we worked during the week or so which went
by before it was possible for me to leave Lorenzo Marquez.
What with mending up and loading the wagons, buying and
breaking in the wild oxen, purchasing provisions, hiring native
servants—of whom I was lucky enough to secure eight who
belonged to one of the Zulu tribes and desired to get back to
their own country, whence they had wandered with some Boers,
I do not think that we slept more than two or three hours out of
the twenty-four.

But, it may be asked, what was my aim, whither went I, what
inquiries had I made? To answer the last question first, I had
made every possible inquiry, but with little or no result. Marie's
letter had said that they were encamped on the bank of the
Crocodile River, about fifty miles from Delagoa Bay. I asked
everyone I met among the Portuguese—who, after all, were not
many—if they had heard of such an encampment of emigrant
Boers. But these Portuguese appeared to have heard nothing,

except my host, Don José, who had a vague recollection of something—he could not remember what.

The fact was that at this time the few people who lived at Lorenzo Marquez were too sodden with liquor and other vices to take any interest in outside news that did not immediately concern them. Moreover, the natives whom they flogged and oppressed if they were their servants, or fought with, if they were not, told them little, and almost nothing that was true, for between the two races there was an hereditary hate stretching back for generations. So from the Portuguese I gained no information.

Then I turned to the Kaffirs, especially to those from whom I had bought the cattle. *They* had heard that some Boers reached the banks of the Crocodile moons ago—how many they could not tell. But that country, they said, was under the rule of a chief who was hostile to them, and killed any of their people who ventured thither. Therefore they knew nothing for certain. Still, one of them stated that a woman whom he had bought as a slave, and who had passed through the district in question a few weeks before, told him that someone had told her that these Boers were all dead of sickness. She added that she had seen their wagon caps from a distance, so if they were dead, " their wagons were still alive."

I asked to see this woman, but the native refused to produce her. After a great deal of talk, however, he offered to sell her to me, saying that he was tired of her. So I bargained with the man and finally agreed for her purchase for three pounds of copper wire and eight yards of blue cloth. Next morning she was produced, an extremely ugly person with a large, flat nose, who came from somewhere in the interior of Africa, having, I gathered, been taken captive by Arabs and sold from hand to hand. Her name, as near as I can pronounce it, was Jeel.

I had great difficulty in establishing communication with her, but ultimately found that one of my newly hired Kaffirs could understand something of her language. Even then it was hard to make her talk, for she had never seen a white man, and thought I had bought her for some dreadful purpose or other. However, when she found that she was kindly treated, she opened her lips and told me the same story that her late master had repeated, neither more nor less. Finally I asked her whether she could guide me to the place where she had seen the "live wagons."

She answered: "Oh, yes," as she had travelled many roads and never forgot any of them.

This, of course, was all I wanted from the woman, who, I may add, ultimately gave me a good deal of trouble. The poor creature seemed never to have experienced kindness, and her gratitude for the little I showed her was so intense that it became a nuisance. She followed me about everywhere, trying to do me service in her savage way, and even attempted to seize my food and chew it before I put it into my own mouth—to save me the trouble, I suppose. Ultimately I married her, somewhat against her will, I fear, to one of the hired Kaffirs, who made her a very good husband, although when he was dismissed from my service she wanted to leave him and follow me.

At length, under the guidance of this woman, Jeel, we made a start. There were but fifty miles to go, a distance that on a fair road any good horse would cover in eight hours, or less. But we had no horses, and there was no road—nothing but swamps and bush and rocky hills. With our untrained cattle it took us three days to travel the first twelve miles, though after that things went somewhat better.

It may be asked, why did I not send on ? But whom could I send when no one knew the way, except the woman, Jeel, whom I feared to part with lest I should see her no more ? Moreover, what was the use of sending, since the messengers could take no help ? If everyone at the camp was dead, as rumour told us— well, they were dead. And if they lived, the hope was that they might live a little longer. Meanwhile, I dared not part with my guide, nor dared I leave the relief wagons to go on with her alone. If I did so, I knew that I should never see them again, since only the prestige of their being owned by a white man who was not a Portuguese prevented the natives from looting them.

It was a truly awful journey. My first idea had been to follow the banks of the Crocodile River, which is what I should have attempted had I not chanced on the woman, Jeel. Lucky was it that I did not do so, since I found afterwards that this river wound about a great deal, and was joined by impassable tributaries. Also it was bordered by forests. Jeel's track, on the contrary, followed an old slave road, that, bad as it was, avoided the swampy places of the surrounding country, and those native tribes which the experience of generations of the traders in this iniquitous traffic showed to be most dangerous.

Nine days of fearful struggle had gone by. We had camped one night below the crest of a long slope strewn with great rocks, many of which we were obliged to roll out of the path by main force in order to make a way for the wagons. The oxen had to lie in their yokes all night, since we dared not let them loose fearing lest they should stray; also lions were roaring in the distance, although, game being plentiful, these did not come near to us. As soon as there was any light we let out the teams to fill themselves on the tussocky grass that grew about, and meanwhile cooked and ate some food.

Presently the sun rose, and I saw that beneath us was a great stretch of plain covered with mist, and to the north, on our right, several denser billows of mist that marked the course of the Crocodile River.

By degrees this mist lifted, tall tops of trees appearing above it, till at length it thinned into vapour that vanished away as the sun rose. As I watched it idly, the woman, Jeel, crept up to me in her furtive fashion, touched me on the shoulder and pointed to a distant group of trees.

Looking closely at these trees, I saw between them what at first I took for some white rocks. Further examination, as the mist cleared, suggested to my mind, however, that they might be wagon tilts. Just then the Zulu who understood Jeel's talk came up. I asked him as well as I could, for at that time my knowledge of his tongue was very imperfect, what she wished to say. He questioned her, and answered that she desired to tell me that those were the moving houses of the Amaboona (the Boer people), just where she had seen them nearly two moons ago.

At this tidings my heart seemed to stand still, so that for more than a minute I could not speak. There were the wagons at last, but—oh! who and what should I find in them? I called Hans and bade him inspan as quickly as possible, explaining to him that yonder was Marais's camp.

"Why not let the oxen fill themselves first, baas?" he answered. "There is no hurry, for though the wagons are there, no doubt all the people are dead long ago."

"Do what I bid you, you ill-omened beast," I said, "instead of croaking of death like a crow. And listen : I am going to walk forward to that camp; you must follow with the wagons as fast as they can travel."

"No, baas, it is not safe that you should go alone. Kaffirs or wild beasts might take you."

"Safe or not, I am going ; but if you think it wise, tell two of those Zulus to come with me."

A few minutes later I was on the road, followed by the two Kaffirs armed with spears. In my youth I was a good runner, being strong of leg and light in body, but I do not think that I ever covered seven miles, for that was about the distance to the camp, in quicker time than I did that morning. Indeed, I left those active Kaffirs so far behind that when I approached the trees they were not in sight. Here I dropped to a walk, as I said to myself—to get my breath. Really it was because I felt so terrified at what I might find that I delayed the discovery just for one minute more. While I approached, hope, however faint, still remained; when I arrived, hope might be replaced by everlasting despair.

Now I could see that there were some shanties built behind the wagons, doubtless those "rude houses" of which Marie had written. But I could not see anyone moving about them, or any cattle or any smoke, or other sign of life. Nor could I hear a single sound.

Doubtless, thought I to myself, Hans is right. They are all long dead.

My agony of suspense was replaced by an icy calm. At length I knew the worst. It was finished—I had striven in vain. I walked through the outlying trees and between two of the wagons. One of these I noticed, as we do notice things at such times, was the same in which Marais had trekked with his daughter, his favourite wagon that once I had helped to fit with a new dissel-boom.

Before me were the rough houses built of the branches of trees, daubed over with mud, or rather the backs of them, for

" I looked up. There advancing . . . very slowly . . . I saw
Marie Marais ! " (*See page* 107)

they faced west. I stood still for a moment, and as I stood thought that I heard a faint sound as of someone reciting slowly. I crept along the end of the outermost house and, rubbing the cold sweat from my eyes, peeped round the corner, for it occurred to me that savages might be in possession. Then I saw what caused the sound. A tattered, blackened, bearded man stood at the head of a long and shallow hole, saying a prayer.

It was Henri Marais, although at the time I did not recognise him, so changed was he. A number of little mounds to the right and left of him told me, however, that the hole was a grave. As I watched two more men appeared, dragging between them the body of a woman, which evidently they had not strength to carry, as its legs trailed upon the ground. From the shape of the corpse it seemed to be that of a tall young woman, but the features I could not see, because it was being dragged face downwards. Also the long hair hanging from the head hid them. It was dark hair, like Marie's. They reached the grave, and tumbled their sad burden into it; but I—I could not stir!

At length my limbs obeyed my will. I went forward to the men and said in a hollow voice in Dutch:

" Whom do you bury ? "

" Johanna Meyer," answered someone mechanically, for they did not seem to have taken the trouble to look at me. As I listened to those words my heart, which had stood still waiting for the answer, beat again with a sudden bound that I could hear in the silence.

I looked up. There, advancing from the doorway of one of the houses, very slowly, as though overpowered by weakness, and leading by the hand a mere skeleton of a child, who was chewing some leaves, I saw—I saw *Marie Marais!* She was wasted to nothing, but I could not mistake her eyes, those great soft eyes that had grown so unnaturally large in the white, thin face.

She too saw me and stared for one moment. Then, loosing the child, she cast up her hands, through which the sunlight shone as through parchment, and slowly sank to the ground.

" She has gone, too," said one of the men in an indifferent voice. " I thought she would not last another day."

Now for the first time the man at the head of the grave turned.

Lifting his hand, he pointed to me, whereon the other two men turned also.

"God above us!" he said in a choked voice, "at last I am quite mad. Look! there stands the *spook* of young Allan, the son of the English predicant who lived near Cradock."

As soon as I heard the voice I knew the speaker.

"Oh, Mynheer Marais!" I cried, "I am no ghost; I am Allan himself come to save you."

Marais made no answer; he seemed bewildered. But one of the men cried out crazily:

"How can you save us, youngster, unless you are ready to be eaten? Don't you see, we starve, we starve!"

"I have wagons and food," I answered.

"Allemachte! Henri," exclaimed the man, with a wild laugh, "do you hear what your English *spook* says? He says that he has wagons and *food, food, food!*"

Then Marais burst into tears and flung himself upon my breast, nearly knocking me down. I wrenched myself free of him and ran to Marie, who was lying face upwards on the ground. She seemed to hear my step, for her eyes opened and she struggled to a sitting posture.

"Is it really you, Allan, or do I dream?" she murmured.

"It is I, it is I," I answered, lifting her to her feet, for she seemed to weigh no more than a child. Her head fell upon my shoulder, and she too began to weep.

Still holding her, I turned to the men and said:

"Why do you starve when there is game all about?" and I pointed to two fat elands strolling among the trees not more than a hundred and fifty yards away.

"Can we kill game with stones?" asked one of them, "we whose powder was all burnt a month ago. Those buck," he added, with a wild laugh, "come here to mock us every morning; but they will not walk into our pitfalls. They know them too well, and we have no strength to dig others."

Now when I left my wagons I had brought with me that same Purdey rifle with which I had shot the geese in the match against Pereira, choosing it because it was so light to carry. I held up my hand for silence, set Marie gently on the ground, and began to steal towards the elands. Taking what shelter I could I got within a hundred yards of them, when suddenly they took alarm, being frightened, in fact, by my two Zulu servants, who were now arriving.

Off they galloped, the big bull leading, and vanished behind some trees. I saw their line, and that they would appear again between two clumps of bush about two hundred and fifty yards away. Hastily I raised the full sight on the rifle, which was marked for two hundred yards, lifted it, and waited, praying to God as I did so that my skill might not fail me.

The bull appeared, its head held forward, its long horns lying flat upon the back. The shot was very long, and the beast very large to bring down with so small a bullet. I aimed right forward —clear of it, indeed—high too, in a line with its backbone, and pressed the trigger.

The rifle exploded, the bullet clapped, and the buck sprang forward faster than ever. I had failed! But what was this? Suddenly the great bull swung round and began to gallop towards us. When it was not more than fifty yards away, it fell in a heap, rolled twice over like a shot rabbit, and lay still. That bullet was in its heart.

The two Kaffirs appeared breathless and streaming with perspiration.

" Cut meat from the eland's flank; don't stop to skin it," I said in my broken Zulu, helping the words out with signs.

They understood, and a minute later were at work with their assegais. Then I looked about me. Near by lay a store of dead branches placed there for fuel.

" Have you fire? " I asked of the skeleton Boers, for they were nothing more.

" *Nein, nein,*" they answered; " our fire is dead."

I produced the tinder-box which I carried with me, and struck the flint. Ten minutes later we had a cheerful blaze, and within three-quarters of an hour good soup, for iron pots were not wanting—only food to put into them. I think that for the rest of that day those poor creatures did little else but eat, sleeping between their meals. Oh! the joy I had in feeding them, especially after the wagons arrived, bringing with them salt—how they longed for that salt!—sugar and coffee.

IX

THE PROMISE

OF the original thirty-five souls, not reckoning natives, who
had accompanied Henri Marais upon his ill-fated expedition,
there now remained but nine alive at the new Maraisfontein.
These were himself, his daughter, four Prinsloos—a family of
extraordinary constitution—and three Meyers, being the husband of the poor woman I had seen committed to the grave and
two of her six children. The rest, Hernan Pereira excepted, had
died of fever and actual starvation, for when the fever lessened
with the change of the seasons, the starvation set in. It appeared
that, with the exception of a very little, they had stored their
powder in a kind of outbuilding which they constructed,
placing it at a distance for safety's sake. When most of the
surviving men were away, however, a grass fire set light to this
outbuilding and all the powder blew up.

After this, for a while they supplied the camp with food by
the help of such ammunition as remained to them. When that
failed they dug pits in which to catch game. In time the buck
came to know of those pits, so that they snared no more.

Then, as the " biltong " or sun-dried meat they had made was
all consumed, they were driven to every desperate expedient
that is known to the starving, such as the digging up of bulbs,
the boiling of grass, twigs and leaves, the catching of lizards,
and so forth. I believe that they actually ate caterpillars and
earth-worms. But after their last fire went out through the
neglect of the wretched Kaffir who was left to watch it, and
having no tinder, they failed to relight it by friction, of course
even this food failed them. When I arrived they had practically
been three days without anything to eat except green leaves and
grass, such as I saw the child chewing. In another seventy
hours doubtless every one of them would have been dead.

Well, they recovered rapidly enough, for those who had
survived its ravages were evidently now impervious to fever.
Who can tell the joy that I experienced as I watched Marie

returning from the very brink of the grave to a state of full and lovely womanhood? After all, we are not so far away from the primitive conditions of humanity, when the first duty of man was to feed his women and his children, and I think that something of that instinct remains with us. At least, I know I never experienced a greater pleasure than I did when the woman I loved, the poor, starving woman, ate and ate of the food which I was able to give her—she who for weeks had existed upon locusts and herbs.

For the first few days we did not talk much, except of the immediate necessities of the hour, which occupied all our thoughts. Afterwards, when Marais and his daughter were strong enough to bear it, we had some conversation. He began by asking how I came to find them.

I replied, through Marie's letter, which, it appeared, he knew nothing of, for he had forbidden her to write to me.

" It seems fortunate that you were disobeyed, mynheer," I said, to which he answered nothing.

Then I told the tale of the arrival of that letter at the Mission Station in the Cape Colony by the hand of a wandering *smous*, and of my desperate ride upon the swift mare to Port Elizabeth, where I just succeeded in catching the brig *Seven Stars* before she sailed. Also I told them of the lucky chances that enabled me to buy the wagons and find a guide to their camp, reaching it but a few hours before it was too late.

" It was a great deed," said Henry Marais, taking the pipe from his mouth, for I had brought tobacco among my stores. " But tell me, Allan, why did you do it for the sake of one who has not treated you kindly ? "

" I did it," I answered, " for the sake of one who has always treated me kindly," and I nodded towards Marie, who was engaged in washing up the cooking pots at a distance.

" I suppose so, Allan; but you know she is affianced to another."

" I know that she is affianced to me, and to no other," I answered warmly, adding, " And pray where is this other ? If he lives I do not see him here."

" No," replied Marais in a curious voice. " The truth is, Allan, that Hernan Pereira left us about a fortnight before you

came. One horse remained, which was his, and with two Hottentots, who were also his servants, he rode back upon the track
by which we came, to try to find help. Since then we have heard
nothing of him."

"Indeed ; and how did he propose to get food on the way ? "

"He had a rifle, or rather they all three had rifles, and about
a hundred charges between them, which escaped the fire."

"With a hundred charges of powder carefully used your
camp would have been fed for a month, or perhaps two months,"
I remarked. "Yet he went away with all of them—to find
help ? "

"That is so, Allan. We begged him to stay, but he would
not ; and, after all, the charges were his own property. No
doubt he thought he acted for the best, especially as Marie would
have none of him," Marais added with emphasis.

"Well," I replied, "it seems that it is I who have brought
you the help, and not Pereira. Also, by the way, mynheer, I
have brought you the money my father collected on your account,
and some £500 of my own, or what is left of it, in goods and
gold. Moreover, Marie does not refuse me. Say, therefore, to
which of us does she belong ? "

"It would seem that it should be to you," he answered
slowly, "since you have shown yourself so faithful, and were
it not for you she would now be lying yonder," and he pointed
to the little heaps that covered the bones of most of the expedition. "Yes, yes, it would seem that it should be to you, who
twice have saved her life and once have saved mine also."

Now I suppose that he saw on my face the joy which I could
not conceal, for he added hastily : "Yet, Allan, years ago I
swore on the Book before God that never with my will should
my daughter marry an Englishman, even if he were a good
Englishman. Also, just before we left the Colony, I swore
again, in her presence and that of Hernan Pereira, that I would
not give her to you, so I cannot break my oath, can I ? If I did,
the good God would be avenged upon me."   •

"Some might think that when I came here the good God
was in the way of being avenged upon you for the keeping of
that evil oath," I answered bitterly, glancing, in my turn, at the
graves.

" Yes, they might, Allan," he replied without anger, for all his troubles had induced a reasonable frame of mind in him—for a while. " Yet, His ways are past finding out, are they not ? "

Now my anger broke out, and, rising, I said :

" Do you mean, Mynheer Marais, that notwithstanding the love between us, which you know is true and deep, and notwithstanding that I alone have been able to drag both of you and the others out of the claws of death, I am never to marry Marie ? Do you mean that she is to be given to a braggart who deserted her in her need ? "

" And what if I do mean that, Allan ? "

" This : although I am still young, as you know well, I am a master who can think and act for himself. Also, I am your master here—I have cattle and guns and servants. Well, I will take Marie, and if any should try to stop me, I know how to protect myself and her."

This bold speech did not seem to surprise him in the least or to make him think the worse of me. He looked at me for a while, pulling his long beard in a meditative fashion, then answered :

" I dare say that at your age I should have played the same game, and it is true that you have things in your fist. But, much as she may love you, Marie would not go away with you and leave her father to starve."

" Then you can come with us as my father-in-law, Mynheer Marais. At any rate, it is certain that I will not go away and leave her here to starve."

Now I think that something which he saw in my eye showed him that I was in earnest. At least, he changed his tone and began to argue, almost to plead.

" Be reasonable, Allan," he said. " How can you marry Marie when there is no predicant to marry you ? Surely, if you love her so much, you would not pour mud upon her name, even in this wilderness ? "

" She might not think it mud," I replied. " Men and women have been married without the help of priests before now, by open declaration and public report, for instance, and their children held to be born in wedlock. I know that, for I have read of the law of marriage."

"It may be, Allan, though I hold no marriage good unless the holy words are said. But why do you not let me come to the end of my story?"

"Because I thought it was ended, Mynheer Marais."

"Not so, Allan. I told you that I had sworn that she should never marry you with my will. But when she is of age, which will be in some six months' time, my will counts no longer, seeing that then she is a free woman who can dispose of herself. Also I shall be clear of my oath, for no harm will come to my soul if that happens which I cannot help. Now are you satisfied?"

"I don't know," I answered doubtfully, for somehow all Marais's casuistry, which I thought contemptible, did not convince me that he was sincere. "I don't know," I repeated. "Much may chance in six months."

"Of course, Allan. For instance, Marie might change her mind and marry someone else."

"Or I might not be there to marry, mynheer. Accidents sometimes happen to men who are not wanted, especially in wild countries, or, for the matter of that, to those who are."

"Allemachte! Allan, you do not mean that I——"

"No, mynheer," I interrupted; "but there are other people in the world besides yourself—Hernan Pereira, for example, if he lives. Still, I am not the only one concerned in this matter. There is Marie yonder. Shall I call her?"

He nodded, preferring probably that I should speak to her in his presence rather than alone.

So I called to Marie, who was watching our talk somewhat anxiously while she went about her tasks. She came at once, a very different Marie to the starving girl of a while before, for although she was still thin and drawn, her youth and beauty were returning to her fast under the influences of good food and happiness.

"What is it, Allan?" she asked gently. I told her all, repeating our conversation and the arguments which had been used on either side word for word, as nearly as I could remember them.

"Is that right?" I asked of Marais when I had finished.

"It is right; you have a good memory," he answered.

" Very well. And now what have you to say, Marie ? "

" I, dear Allan ? Why, this : My life belongs to you, who have twice saved this body of mine from death, as my love and spirit belong to you. Therefore, I should have thought it no shame if I had been given to you here and now before the people, and afterwards married by a clergyman when we found one. But my father has sworn an oath which weighs upon his mind, and he has shown you that within six months—a short six months—that oath dies of itself, since, by the law, he can no longer control me. So, Allan, as I would not grieve him, or perhaps lead him to say and do what is foolish, I think it would be well that we should wait for those six months, if, on his part, he promises that he will then do nothing to prevent our marriage."

" *Ja, ja,* I promise that then I will do nothing to prevent your marriage," answered Marais eagerly, like one who has suddenly seen some loophole of escape from an impossible position, adding, as though to himself, " But God may do something to prevent it, for all that."

" We are everyone of us in the hand of God," she replied in her sweet voice. " Allan, you hear, my father has promised ? "

" Yes, Marie, he has promised—after a fashion," I replied gloomily, for somehow his words struck a chill through me.

" I have promised, Allan, and I will keep my promise to you, as I have kept my oath to God, attempting to work you no harm, and leaving all in His hands. But you, on your part, must promise also that, till she is of age, you will not take Marie as a wife—no, not if you were left alone together in the veld. You must be as people who are affianced to each other, no more."

So, having no choice, I promised, though with a heavy heart. Then, I suppose in order to make this solemn contract public, Marais called the surviving Boers, who were loitering near, and repeated to them the terms of the contract that we had made.

The men laughed and shrugged their shoulders. But Vrouw Prinsloo, I remember, said outright that she thought the business foolish, since if anyone had a right to Marie, I had, where-ever I chose to take her. She added that, as for Hernan Pereira, he was a " sneak and a stinkcat," who had gone on to save his own life, and left them all to die. If *she* were Marie, should they meet again, she would greet him with a pailful of dirty water in the face, as she herself meant to do if she got the chance.

Vrouw Prinsloo, it will be observed, was a very outspoken woman and, I may add, an honest one.

So this contract was settled. I have set it out at length because of its importance in our story. But now I wish—ah ! how I wish that I had insisted upon being married to Marie then and there. If I had done so, I think I should have carried my point, for I was the " master of many legions " in the shape of cattle, food and ammunition, and rather than risk a quarrel with me, the other Boers would have forced Marais to give way. But we were young and inexperienced ; also it was fated otherwise. Who can question the decrees of Fate written immutably, perhaps long before we were born, in the everlasting book of human destinies ?

Yet, when I had shaken off my first fears and doubts, my lot and Marie's were very happy, a perfect paradise, indeed, compared with what we had gone through during that bitter time of silence and separation. At any rate, we were acknowledged to be affianced by the little society in which we lived, including her father, and allowed to be as much alone together as we liked. This meant that we met at dawn only to separate at nightfall, for, having little or no artificial light, we went to rest with the sun, or shortly after it. Sweet, indeed, was that companionship of perfect trust and love ; so sweet, that even after all these years I do not care to dwell upon the holy memory of those blessed months.

So soon as the surviving Boers began to recover by the help of my stores and medicines and the meat which I shot in plenty, of course great discussions arose as to our future plans. First it was suggested that we should trek to Lorenzo Marquez, and wait for a ship there to take us down to Natal, for none of them would hear of returning beggared to the Cape to tell the story of their failure and dreadful bereavements. I pointed out, however, that no ship might come for a long while, perhaps for one or two years, and that Lorenzo Marquez and its neighbourhood seemed to be a poisonous place to live in !

The next idea was that we should stop where we were, one which I rather welcomed, as I should have been glad to abide in peace with Marie until the six months of probation had gone by.

However, in the end this was rejected for many good reasons. Thus half a score of white people, of whom four were members of a single family, were certainly not strong enough to form a settlement, especially as the surrounding natives might become actively hostile at any moment. Again, the worst fever season was approaching, in which we should very possibly all be carried off. Further, we had no breeding cattle or horses, which would not live in this veld, and only the ammunition and goods that I had brought with me.

So it was clear that but one thing remained to be done, namely, to trek back to what is now the Transvaal territory, or, better still, to Natal, for this route would enable us to avoid the worst of the mountains. There we might join some other party of the emigrant Boers, for choice, that of Retief, of whose arrival over the Drakensberg I was able to tell them.

That point settled, we made our preparations. To begin with, I had only enough oxen for two wagons, whereas, even if we abandoned the rest of them, we must take at least four. Therefore, through my Kaffirs, I opened negotiations with the surrounding natives, who, when they heard that I was not a Boer and was prepared to pay for what I bought, soon expressed a willingness to trade. Indeed, very shortly we had quite a market established, to which cattle were brought that I bargained for and purchased, giving cloth, knives, hoes, and the usual Kaffir goods in payment for the same.

Also, they brought mealies and other corn ; and oh ! the delight with which those poor people, who for months and months had existed upon nothing but flesh-meat, ate of this farinaceous food. Never shall I forget seeing Marie and the surviving children partake of their first meal of porridge, and washing the sticky stuff down with draughts of fresh, sugared milk, for with the oxen I had succeeded in obtaining two good cows. It is enough to say that this change of diet soon completely re-established their health, and made Marie more beautiful than she had ever been before.

Having got the oxen, the next thing was to break them to the yoke; for, although docile creatures enough, they had never even seen a wagon. This proved a long and difficult process, involving many trial trips; moreover, the selected wagons, one of which had belonged to Pereira, must be mended with very insufficient tools and without the help of a forge. Indeed, had it not chanced that Hans, the Hottentot, had worked for a wagon-maker at some indefinite period of his career, I do not think that we could have managed the job at all.

It was while we were busy with these tasks that some news arrived which was unpleasing enough to everyone, except perhaps to Henri Marais. I was engaged on a certain evening in trying to make sixteen of the Kaffir cattle pull together in the yoke, instead of tying themselves into a double knot and over-setting the wagon, when Hans, who was helping me, suddenly called out:

" Look ! baas, here comes one of my brothers," or, in other words, a Hottentot.

Following the line of his hand, I saw a thin and wretched creature, clad only in some rags and the remains of a big hat with the crown out, staggering towards us between the trees.

" Why ! " exclaimed Marie in a startled voice, for, as usual, she was at my side, " it is Klaus, one of my cousin Hernan's after-riders."

" So long as it is not your cousin Hernan himself, I do not care," I said.

Presently the poor, starved " Totty " arrived, and, throwing himself down, begged for food. A cold shoulder of buck was given to him, which he devoured, holding it in both hands and tearing off great lumps of flesh with his teeth like a wild beast.

When at last he was satisfied, Marais, who had come up with the other Boers, asked him whence he came and what was his news of his master.

" Out of the bush," he answered, "and my news of the baas is that he is dead. At least, I left him so ill that I suppose he must be dead by now."

" Why did you leave him if he was ill ? " asked Marais.

" Because he told me to, baas, that I might find help, for we were starving, having fired our last bullet."

" Is he alone, then ? "

" Yes, yes, except for the wild beasts and the vultures. A lion ate the other man, his servant, a long while ago."

" How far is he off ? " asked Marais again.

" Oh ! baas, about five hours' journey on horseback on a good road." (This would be some thirty-five miles.)

Then he told this story : Pereira with his two Hottentot servants, he mounted and they on foot, had traversed about a hundred miles of rough country in safety, when at night a lion killed and carried off one of the Hottentots, and frightened away the horse, which was never seen again. Pereira and Klaus proceeded on foot till they came to a great river, on the banks of which they met some Kaffirs, who appear to have been Zulus on outpost duty. These men demanded their guns and ammunition to take to their king, and, on Pereira refusing to give them up, said that they would kill them both in the morning after they had made him instruct them in the use of the guns by beating him with sticks.

In the night a storm came on, under cover of which Pereira and Klaus escaped. As they dared not go forward for fear lest they should fall into the hands of the Zulus, they fled back northwards, running all night, only to find in the morning that they had lost their way in the bush. This had happened nearly a month before—or, at any rate, Klaus thought so, for no doubt the days went very slowly—during which time they had wandered about, trying to shape some sort of course by the sun with the object of returning to the camp. They met no man, black or white, and supported themselves upon game, which they shot and ate raw or sun-dried, till at length all their powder was done and they threw away their heavy *roers*, which they could no longer carry.

It was at this juncture that from the top of a tall tree Klaus saw a certain *koppie* a long way off, which he recognised as being within fifteen miles or so of Marais's camp. By now they were starving, only Klaus was the stronger of the two, for he found and devoured some carrion, a dead hyena I think it was. Pereira also tried to eat this horrible food, but, not having the stomach of a Hottentot, the first mouthful of it made him dreadfully ill. They sought shelter in a cave on the bank of a stream, where grew water-cresses and other herbs, such as wild asparagus. Here it was that Pereira told Klaus to try to make his way back to the camp, and, should he find anyone alive there, to bring him succour.

So Klaus went, taking the remaining leg of the hyena with him, and on the afternoon of the second day arrived as has been told.

X

VROUW PRINSLOO SPEAKS HER MIND

Now, when the Hottentot's story was finished a discussion arose. Marais said that someone must go to see whether his nephew still lived, to which the other Boers replied " *Ja* " in an indifferent voice. Then the Vrouw Prinsloo took up her parable.

She remarked, as she had done before, that in her judgment Hernan Pereira was " a stinkcat and a sneak," who had tried to desert them in their trouble, and by the judgment of a just God had got into trouble himself. Personally, she wished that the lion had taken him instead of the worthy Hottentot, although it gave her a higher opinion of lions to conclude that it had not done so, because if it did it thought it would have been poisoned. Well, her view was that it would be just as well to let that traitor lie upon the bed which he had made. Moreover, doubtless by now he was dead, so what was the good of bothering about him?

These sentiments appeared to appeal to the Boers, for they remarked : " *Ja*, what is the good ? "

" Is it right," asked Marais, " to abandon a comrade in misfortune, one of our own blood ? "

" *Mein Gott !* " replied Vrouw Prinsloo ; " he is no blood of mine, the evil-odoured Portugee. But I admit he is of yours, Heer Marais, being your sister's son, so it is evident that you should be the one to go to seek after him."

" That seems to be so, Vrouw Prinsloo," said Marais in his meditative manner ; " yet I must remember that I have Marie to look after."

" Ach ! and so had he, too, until he remembered his own skin, and went off with the only horse and all the powder, leaving her and the rest of us to starve. Well, you won't go, and Prinsloo won't go, or my boy either, for I'll see to that ; so Meyer must go."

" *Nein, nein*, good Vrouw," answered Meyer, " I have those children that are left to me to consider."

. " Then," exclaimed Vrouw Prinsloo triumphantly, " nobody will go, so let us forget this stinkcat, as he forgot us."

" Does it seem right," asked Marais again, " that a Christian man should be left to starve in the wilderness ? " and he looked at me.

" Tell me, Heer Marais," I remarked, answering the look, " why should I of all people go to look for the Heer Pereira, one who has not dealt too well with me ? "

" I do not know, Allan. Yet the Book tells us to turn the other cheek and to forget injuries. Still, it is for you to judge, remembering that we must answer for all things at the last day, and not for me. I only know that were I your age, and not burdened with a daughter to watch over, *I* should go."

" Why should you talk to me thus ? " I asked with indignation. " Why do you not go yourself, seeing that I am quite ready to look after Marie ? " (Here the Vrouw Prinsloo and the other Boers tittered.) " And why do you not address your remarks to these other *heeren* instead of to me, seeing that they are the friends and trek-companions of your nephew ? "

At this point the male Prinsloos and Meyer found that they had business elsewhere.

" It is for you to judge, yet remember, Allan, that it is an awful thing to appear before our Maker with the blood of a fellow creature upon our hands. But if you and these other hard-hearted men will not go, I at my age, and weak as I am with all that I have suffered, will go myself."

" Good," said Vrouw Prinsloo, " that is the best way out of it. You will soon get sick of the journey, Heer Marais, and we shall see no more of the stinkcat."

Marais rose in a resigned fashion, for he never deigned to argue with Vrouw Prinsloo, who was too many for him, and said :

"Farewell, Marie. If I do not return, you will remember my wishes, and my will may be found between the first leaves of our Holy Book. Get up, Klaus, and guide me to your master," and he administered a somewhat vicious kick to the gorged and prostrate Hottentot.

Now Marie, who all this while had stood silent, touched me on the shoulder and said :

"Allan, is it well that my father should go alone ? Will you not accompany him ? "

"Of course," I answered cheerfully ; "on such a business there should be two, and some Kaffirs also to carry the man, if he still lives."

Now for the end of the story. As the Hottentot Klaus was too exhausted to move that night, it was arranged that we should start at dawn. Accordingly, I rose before the light, and was just finishing my breakfast when Marie appeared at the wagon in which I slept. I got up to greet her, and, there being no one in sight, we kissed each other several times.

"Have done, my heart," she said, pushing me away. "I come to you from my father, who is sick in his stomach and would see you."

"Which means that I shall have to go after your cousin alone," I replied with indignant emphasis.

She shook her head, and led me to the little shanty in which she slept. Here by the growing light, that entered through the doorway for it had no window, I perceived Marais seated upon a wooden stool, with his hands pressed on his middle and groaning.

"Good morning, Allan," he said in a melancholy voice ; "I am ill, very ill, something that I have eaten perhaps, or a chill in the stomach, such as often precedes fever or dysentery."

"Perhaps you will get better as you walk, mynheer," I suggested, for, to tell the truth, I misdoubted me of this chill, and knew that he had eaten nothing but what was quite wholesome.

"Walk ! God alone knows how I can walk with something gripping my inside like a wagon-maker's vice. Yet I will try, for it is impossible to leave that poor Hernan to die alone ; and if I do not go to seek him, it seems that no one else will."

" Why should not some of my Kaffirs go with Klaus ? " I asked.

" Allan," he replied solemnly, " if you were dying in a cave far from help, would you think well of those who sent raw Kaffirs to succour you when they might have come themselves, Kaffirs who certainly would let you die and return with some false story ? "

" I don't know what I should think, Herr Marais. But I do know that if *I* were in that cave and Pereira were in this camp, neither would he come himself, nor so much as send a savage to save *me*."

" It may be so, Allan. But even if another's heart is black, should yours be black also ? Oh ! I will come, though it be to my death," and, rising from the stool with the most dreadful groan, he began to divest himself of the tattered blanket in which he was wrapped up.

" Oh ! Allan, my father must not go ; it will kill him," exclaimed Marie, who took a more serious view of his case than I did.

" Very well, if you think so," I answered. " And now as it is time for me to be starting, good-bye."

" You have a good heart, Allan," said Marais, sinking back upon his stool and resuming his blanket, while Marie looked despairingly first at one and then at the other of us.

Half an hour later I was on the road in the very worst of tempers.

" Mind what you are about," called Vrouw Prinsloo after me. " It is not lucky to save an enemy, and if I know anything of that stinkcat, he will bite your finger badly by way of gratitude. Bah ! lad, if I were you I should just camp for a few days in the bush, and then come back and say that I could find nothing of Pereira except the dead hyenas that had been poisoned by eating him. Good luck to you all the same, Allan ; may I find such a friend in need. It seems to me that you were born to help others."

Beside the Hottentot Klaus, my companions on this unwelcome journey were three of the Zulu Kaffirs, for Hans I was obliged to leave in charge of my cattle and goods with the other men. Also, I took a pack ox, an active beast that I had been training to carry loads and, if necessary, a man, although as yet it was not very well broken.

All that day we marched over extremely rough country, till at last darkness found us in a mountainous kloof, where we slept, surrounded by watch-fires because of the lions. Next morning at the first light we moved on again, and about ten o'clock waded through a stream to a little natural cave, where Klaus said he had left his master. This cave seemed extremely silent, and, as I hesitated for a moment at its mouth, the thought crossed my mind that if Pereira were still there, he must be dead. Indeed, do what I would to suppress it, with that reflection came a certain feeling of relief and even of pleasure. For well I knew that Pereira alive was more dangerous to me than all the wild men and beasts in Africa put together. Thrusting back this unworthy sentiment as best I could, I entered the cave alone, for the natives, who dread the defilement of the touch of a corpse, lingered outside.

It was but a shallow cavity, washed out of the overhanging rock by the action of water; and as soon as my eyes grew accustomed to its gloom, I saw that at the end of it lay a man. So still did he lie, that now I was almost certain that his troubles were over. I went up to him and touched his face, which was cold and clammy, and then, quite convinced, turned to leave the place, which, I thought, if a few rocks were piled in the mouth of it, would make an excellent sepulchre.

Just as I stepped out into the sunlight, and was about to call to the men to collect the rocks, however, I thought that I heard a very faint groan behind me, which at the moment I set down to imagination. Still, I returned, though I did not much like the job, knelt down by the figure and waited with my hand over its heart. For five minutes or more I stayed here, and then, quite convinced, was about to leave again when, for the second time, I heard that faint groan. Pereira was not dead, but only on the extreme brink of death!

I ran to the entrance of the cave, calling the Kaffirs, and together we carried him out into the sunlight. He was an awful spectacle, mere bone with yellow skin stretched over it, and covered with filth and clotted blood from some hurt. I had brandy with me, of which I poured a little down his throat, whereon his heart began to beat feebly. Then we made some soup, and poured that down his throat with more brandy, and the end of it was he came to life again.

For three days did I doctor that man, and really I believe that if at any time during those days I had relaxed my attentions even for a couple of hours, he would have slipped through my fingers, for at this business Klaus and the Kaffirs were no good at all. But I pulled him round, and on the third morning he came to his senses. For a long while he stared at me, for I had laid him in the mouth of the cave, where the light was good, although the overhanging rocks protected him from the sun. Then he said :

" Allemachte ! you remind me of someone, young man. I know. It is of that damned English boy who beat me at the goose shooting, and made me quarrel with *Oom* [uncle] Retief, the jackanapes that Marie was so fond of. Well, whoever you are, you can't be he, thank God."

" You are mistaken, Heer Pereira," I answered. " I am that same damned young English jackanapes, Allan Quatermain by name, who beat you at shooting. But if you take my advice, you will thank God for something else, namely, that your life has been saved."

" Who saved it ? " he asked.

" If you want to know, I did ; I have been nursing you these three days."

" You, Allan Quatermain ! Now, that is strange, for certainly I would not have saved yours," and he laughed a little, then turned over and went to sleep.

From that time forward his recovery was rapid, and two days later we began our journey back to Marais's camp, the convalescent Pereira being carried in a litter by the four natives. It was a task at which they grumbled a good deal, for the load was heavy over rough ground, and whenever they stumbled or shook him he cursed at them. So much did he curse, indeed, that at length one of the Zulus, a man with a rough temper, said that if it were not for the Inkoos, meaning myself, he would put his assegai through him, and let the vultures carry him. After this Pereira grew much more polite. When the bearers became exhausted we set him on the pack-ox, which two of us led, while the other two supported him on either side. It was in this fashion that at last we arrived at the camp one evening.

Here the Vrouw Prinsloo was the first to greet us. We found her standing in the game path which we were following, quite a quarter of a mile from the wagons, with her hands set upon her broad hips and her feet apart. Her attitude was so defiant, and had about it such an air of premeditation, that I cannot help thinking she had got wind of our return, perhaps from having seen the smoke of our last fires, and was watching for us. Also, her greeting was warm.

"Ah! here you come, Hernan Pereira," she cried, "riding on an ox, while better men walk. Well, now, I want a chat with you. How came it that you went off in the night, taking the only horse and all the powder?"

"I went to get help for you," he replied sulkily.

"Did you, did you, indeed! Well, it seems that it was you who wanted the help, after all. What do you mean to pay the Heer Allan Quatermain for saving your life, for I am sure he has done so? You have got no goods left, although you were always boasting about your riches; they are now at the bottom of a river, so it will have to be in love and service."

He muttered something about my wanting no payment for a Christian act.

"No, he wants no payment, Hernan Pereira, he is one of the true sort, but you'll pay him all the same and in bad coin if you get the chance. Oh! I have come out to tell you what I think of you. You are a stinkcat; do you hear that? A thing that no dog would bite if he could help it! You are a traitor also. You brought us to this cursed country, where you said your relatives would give us wealth and land, and then, after famine and fever attacked us, you rode away, and left us to die to save your own dirty skin. And now you come back here for help, saved by him whom you cheated in the Goose Kloof, by him whose true love you have tried to steal. Oh, *mein Gott!* why does the Almighty leave such fellows alive, while so many that are good and honest and innocent lie beneath the soil because of stink-cats like you?"

So she went on, striding at the side of the pack-ox, and reviling Pereira in a ceaseless stream of language, until at length he thrust his thumbs into his ears and glared at her in speechless wrath.

Thus it was that at last we arrived in the camp, where, having seen us coming, all the Boers were gathered. They are not a particularly humorous people, but this spectacle of the advance of Pereira seated on the pack-ox, a steed that is becoming to few riders, with the furious and portly Vrouw Prinsloo striding at his side and shrieking abuse at him, caused them to burst into laughter. Then Pereira's temper gave out, and he became even more abusive than Vrouw Prinsloo.

" Is this the way you receive me, you veld-hogs, you common Boers, who are not fit to mix with a man of position and learning like myself ? " he began.

" Then in God's name why do you mix with us, Hernan Pereira ? " asked the saturnine Meyer, thrusting his face forward till the Newgate fringe he wore by way of a beard literally seemed to curl with wrath. " When we were hungry you did not wish it, for you slunk away and left us, taking all the powder. But now that we are full again, thanks to the little Englishman, and you are hungry, you come back. Well, if I had my way I would give you a gun and six days' rations, and turn you out to shift for yourself."

" Don't be afraid, Jan Meyer," shouted Pereira from the back of the pack-ox. " As soon as I am strong enough I will leave you in charge of your English captain here "—and he pointed to me—" and go to tell our people what sort of folk you are."

" That is good news," interrupted Prinsloo, a stolid old Boer, who stood by puffing at his pipe. " Get well, get well as soon as you can, Hernan Pereira."

It was at this juncture that Marais arrived accompanied by Marie. Where he came from I do not know, but I think he must have been keeping in the background on purpose to see what kind of a reception Pereira would meet with.

" Silence, brothers," he said. " Is this the way you greet my nephew, who has returned from the gate of death, when you should be on your knees thanking God for his deliverance ? "

" Then go on your knees and thank Him yourself, Henri Marais," screamed the irrepressible Vrouw Prinsloo. " I give thanks for the safe return of Allan here, though it is true they would be warmer if he had left this stinkcat behind him. Alle-machte! Henri Marais, why do you make so much of this Portuguese fellow? Has he bewitched you? Or is it because he is your sister's son, or because you want to force Marie there to marry him? Or is it, perhaps, that he knows of something bad in your past life, and you have to bribe him to keep his mouth shut?"

Now, whether this last unpleasant suggestion was a mere random arrow drawn from Vrouw Prinsloo's well-stored quiver, or whether the vrouw had got hold of the tail-end of some long-buried truth, I do not know. Of course, however, the latter explanation is possible. Many men have done things in their youth which they do not wish to see dug up in their age; and Pereira may have learned a family secret of the kind from his mother.

At any rate, the effect of the old lady's words upon Marais was quite remarkable. Suddenly he went into one of his violent and constitutional rages. He cursed Vrouw Prinsloo. He cursed everybody else, assuring them severally and collectively that Heaven would come even with them. He said there was a plot against him and his nephew, and that I was at the bottom of it, I who had made his daughter fond of my ugly little face. So furious were his words, whereof there were many more which I have forgotten, that at length Marie began to cry and ran away. Presently, too, the Boers strolled off, shrugging their shoulders, one of them saying audibly that Marais had gone quite mad at last, as he always thought he would.

Then Marais followed them, throwing up his arms and still cursing as he went, and, slipping over the tail of the pack-ox, Pereira followed him. So the Vrouw Prinsloo and I were left alone, for the coloured men had departed, as they always do when white people begin to quarrel.

"There, Allan, my boy," said the vrouw in triumph. "I have found the sore place on the mule's back, and didn't I make him squeal and kick, although on most days of the week he seems to be such a good and quiet mule—at any rate, of late."

"I dare say you did, vrouw," I said wrathfully, "but I wish you would leave Mynheer Marais's sore places alone, seeing that if the squeals are for you, the kicks are for me."

" What does that matter, Allan ? " she asked. " He always
was your enemy, so that it is just as well you should see his heels
when you are out of reach of them. My poor boy, I think you
will have a bad time of it between the stinkcat and the mule,
although you have done so much for both of them. Well, there
is one thing—Marie has a true heart. She will never marry any
man except yourself, Allan—even if you are not here to marry,"
she added by an afterthought.

The old lady paused a little, staring at the ground. Then she
looked up and said :

" Allan, my dear " (for she was really fond of me, and called
me thus at times), " you didn't take the advice I gave you,
namely, to look for Pereira and not to find him. Well, I will give
you some more, which you *will* take if you are wise."

" What is it ? " I asked doubtfully ; for, although she was
upright enough in her own way, the Vrouw Prinsloo could
bring herself to look at things in strange lights. Like many
other women, she judged of moral codes by the impulses of her
heart, and was quite prepared to stretch them to suit circumstances or to gain an end which she considered good in itself.

" Just this, lad. Do you make a two days' march with Marie
into the bush. I want a little change, so I will come, too, and marry
you there; for I have got a prayer-book, and can spell out the
service if we go through it once or twice first."

Now, the vision of Marie and myself being married by the
Vrouw Prinsloo in the vast and untrodden veld, although
attractive, was so absurd that I laughed.

" Why do you laugh, Allan ? Anyone can marry people if
there is no one else there ; indeed, I believe that they can marry
themselves."

" I dare say," I answered, not wishing to enter into a legal
argument with the vrouw. " But you see, Tante, I solemnly
promised her father that I would not marry her until she was
of age, and if I broke my word I should not be an honest
man."

" An honest man ! " she exclaimed with the utmost contempt ;
" an honest man ! Well, are Marais and Hernan Pereira honest
men ? Why do you not cut your stick the same length as theirs,
Allan Quatermain ? I tell you that your *verdomde* honesty will

be your ruin. You remember my words later on," and she marched off in high dudgeon.

When she had gone I went to my wagons, where Hans was waiting for me with a detailed and interminable report of everything that had happened in my absence. Glad was I to find that, except for the death of one sickly ox, nothing had gone wrong. When at length he had ended his long story, I ate some food, which Marie sent over for me ready cooked, for I was too tired to join any of the Boers that night. Just as I had finished my meal and was thinking of turning in, Marie herself appeared within the circle of the camp-fire's light. I sprang up and ran to her, saying that I had not expected to see her that evening, and did not like to come to the house.

"No," she answered, drawing me back into the shadows, "I understand. My father seems very much upset, almost mad, indeed. If the Vrouw Prinsloo's tongue had been a snake's fang, it could not have stung him worse."

"And where is Pereira?" I asked.

"Oh! my cousin sleeps in the other room. He is weak and worn out. All the same, Allan, he wanted to kiss me. So I told him at once how matters stood between you and me, and that we were to be married in six months."

"What did he say to that?" I asked.

"He turned to my father and said: 'Is this true, my uncle?' And my father answered: 'Yes, that is the best bargain I could make with the Englishman, seeing that you were not here to make a better.'"

"And what happened then, Marie?"

"Oh, then Hernan thought a while. At last he looked up and said: 'I understand. Things have gone badly. I acted for the best, who went away to try to find help for all of you. I failed. Meanwhile the Englishman came and saved you. Afterwards he saved me also. Uncle, in all this I see God's hand; had it not been for this Allan none of us would be alive. Yes, God used him that we might be kept alive. Well, he has promised that he will not marry Marie for six months. And you know, my uncle, that some of these English are great fools; they keep their promises even to their own loss. Now, in six months much may happen; who knows what will happen?'"

"Were you present when you heard all this, Marie?" I asked.

"No, Allan; I was on the other side of the reed partition. But at those words I entered and said: 'My father and Cousin Hernan, please understand that there is one thing which will never happen.'

"'What is that?' asked my cousin.

"'It will never happen that I shall marry you, Hernan,' I replied.

"'Who knows, Marie, who knows?' he said.

"'I do. Hernan,' I answered. 'Even if Allan were to die to-morrow, I would not marry you, either then or twenty years hence. I am glad that he has saved your life, but henceforth we are cousins, nothing more.'

"'You hear what the girl tells us,' said my father; 'why do you not give up the business? What is the use of kicking against the pricks?'

"'If one wears stout boots and kicks hard enough, the pricks give way,' said Hernan. 'Six months is a long time, my uncle.'

"'It may be so, cousin,' I said; 'but remember that neither six months nor six years, nor six thousand years, are long enough to make me marry any man except Allan Quatermain, who has just rescued you from death. Do you understand?'

"'Yes,' he replied, 'I understand that you will not marry me. Only then I promise that you shall not marry either Allan Quatermain or any other man.'

"'God will decide that,' I answered, and came away, leaving him and my father together. And now, Allan, tell me all that has happened since we parted."

So I told her everything, including the Vrouw Prinsloo's advice.

"Of course, Allan, you were quite right," she remarked when I had finished; "but I am not sure that the Vrouw Prinsloo was not also right in her own fashion. I am afraid of my cousin Hernan, who holds my father in his hand—fast, fast. Still, we have promised, and must keep our word."

XI

THE SHOT IN THE KLOOF

I THINK it was about three weeks after these events that we began our southward trek. On the morning subsequent to our arrival at Marais's camp, Pereira came up to me when several people were present, and taking my hand, thanked me in a loud voice for having saved his life. Thenceforward, he declared, I should be dearer to him than a brother, for was there not a blood bond between us ?

I answered I did not think any such bond existed ; indeed, I was not sure what it meant. I had done my duty by him, neither less nor more, and there was nothing further to be said.

It turned out, however, that there was a great deal further to be said, since Pereira desired to borrow money, or, rather, goods, from me. He explained that owing to the prejudices of the vulgar Boers who remained alive in that camp, and especially of the scandalous-tongued Vrouw Prinsloo, both he and his uncle had come to the conclusion that it would be wise for him to remove himself as soon as possible. Therefore he proposed to trek away alone.

I answered that I should have thought he had done enough solitary travelling in this veld, seeing how his last expedition had ended. He replied that he had, indeed, but everyone here was so bitter against him that no choice was left. Then he added with an outburst of truth :

" Allemachte ! Mynheer Quatermain, do you suppose that it is pleasant for me to see you making love all day to the maid who was my betrothed, and to see her paying back the love with her eyes ? Yes, and doubtless with her lips, too, from all I hear."

" You could leave her whom you called your betrothed, but who never was betrothed to anyone but me with her own will, to starve in the veld, mynheer. Why, then, should you be angry because I picked up that which you threw away, that, too, which was always my own and not yours ? Had it not been for me,

here would now be no maid left for us to quarrel over, as, had
it not been for me, there would be no man left for me to quarrel
with about the maid."

" Are you God, then, Englishman, that you dispose of the
lives of men and women at your will ? It was He Who saved us,
not you."

" He may have saved you, but it was through me. I carried
out the rescue of these poor people whom you deserted, and I
nursed you back to life."

" I did not desert them ; I went to get help for them."

" Taking all the powder and the only horse with you ! Well,
that is done with, and now you want to borrow goods to pay
for cattle—from me, whom you hate. You are not proud,
Mynheer Pereira, when you have an end to serve, whatever that
end may be," and I looked at him. My instinct warned me against
this false and treacherous man, who, I felt, was even then plotting in his heart to bring some evil upon me.

" No, I am not proud. Why should I be, seeing that I mean to
repay you twice over for anything which you may lend me now ?"

I reflected a while. Certainly our journey to Natal would be
pleasanter if Pereira were not of the company. Also, if he went
with us, I was sure that before we came to the end of that trek,
one or other of us would leave his bones on the road. In short,
not to put too fine a point on it, I feared lest in this way or in
that he would bring me to my death in order that he might
possess himself of Marie. We were in a wild country, with few
witnesses and no law courts, where such deeds might be done
again and again and the doer never called to account for lack
of evidence and judges.

So I made up my mind to fall in with his wishes, and we
began to bargain. The end of it was that I advanced him enough
of my remaining goods to buy the cattle he required from the
surrounding natives. It was no great quantity, after all, seeing
that in this uncivilised place an ox could be purchased for a few
strings of beads or a cheap knife. Further, I sold him a few of the
beasts that I had broken, a gun, some ammunition and certain
other necessaries, for all of which things he gave me a note of
hand written in my pocket-book. Indeed, I did more ; for as
none of the Boers would help him I assisted Pereira to break

in the cattle he bought, and even consented when he asked me to give him the services of two of the Zulus whom I had hired.

All these preparations took a long while. If I remember right, twelve more days had gone by before Pereira finally trekked off from Marais's camp, by which time he was quite well and strong again.

We all assembled to see the start, and Marais offered up a prayer for his nephew's safe journey and our happy meeting again in Natal at the laager of Retief, which was to be our rendezvous, if that leader were still in Natal. No one else joined in the prayer. Only Vrouw Prinsloo audibly added another of her own. It was to the effect that he might not come back a second time, and that she might never see his face again, either at Retief's laager or anywhere else, if it would please the good Lord so to arrange matters.

The Boers tittered; even the Meyer children tittered, for by this time the hatred of the Vrouw Prinsloo for Hernan Pereira was the joke of the place. But Pereira himself pretended not to hear, said good-bye to us all affectionately, adding a special petition for the Vrouw Prinsloo, and off we went.

I say " we went " because with my usual luck, to help him with the half-broken oxen, I was commandeered to accompany this man to his first outspan, a place with good water about twelve miles from the camp, where he proposed to remain for the night.

Now, as we started about ten o'clock in the morning and the veld was fairly level, I expected that we should reach this outspan by three or four in the afternoon, which would give me time to walk back before sunset. In fact, however, so many accidents happened of one sort or another, both to the wagon itself, of which the woodwork had shrunk with long standing in the sun, and to the cattle, which, being unused to the yoke, tied themselves in a double knot upon every opportunity, that we only arrived there at the approach of night.

The last mile of that trek was through a narrow gorge cut out by water in the native rock. Here trees grew sparsely, also great ferns, but the bottom of the gorge, along which game were accustomed to travel, was smooth enough for wagons, save for a few fallen boulders, which it was necessary to avoid.

When at length we reached the outspan I asked the Hottentot, Klaus, who was assisting me to drive the team, where his master was, for I could not see him anywhere. He answered that he had gone back down the kloof to look for something that had fallen from the wagon, a bolt I think, he said.

" Very good," I replied. " Then tell him, if we do not meet, that I have returned to the camp."

As I set out the sun was sinking below the horizon, but this did not trouble me overmuch, as I had a rifle with me, that same light rifle with which I had shot the geese in the great match. Also I knew that the moon, being full, would be up presently.

The sun sank, and the kloof was plunged in gloom. The place seemed eerie and lonesome, and suddenly I grew afraid. I began to wonder where Pereira was, and what he might be doing. I even thought of turning back and finding some way round, only having explored all this district pretty thoroughly in my various shooting expeditions from the camp, I knew there was no practicable path across those hills. So I went on with my rifle at full cock, whistling to keep up my courage, which, of course, in the circumstances was a foolish thing to do. It occurred to me at the time that it was foolish, but, in truth, I would not give way to the dark suspicions which crossed my mind. Doubtless by now Pereira had passed me and reached the outspan.

The moon began to shine—that wonderful African moon, which turns night to day—throwing a network of long, black shadows of trees and rocks across the game track I was following. Right ahead of me was a particularly dark patch of this shadow, caused by a projecting wall of cliff, and beyond it an equally bright patch of moonlight. Somehow I misdoubted me of that stretch of gloom, for although, of course, I could see nothing there, my quick ear caught the sound of movements.

I halted for a moment. Then, reflecting that these were doubtless caused by some night-walking creature, which, even should it chance to be dangerous, would flee at the approach of man, I plunged into it boldly. As I emerged at the other end— the shadow was eighteen or twenty paces long—it occurred to me that if any enemy were lurking there, I should be an easy target as I entered the line of clear light. So, almost instinctively, for I do not remember that I reasoned the thing out, after my first two steps forward in the light I gave a little spring to the left, where there was still shadow, although it was not deep. Well was it for me that I did so, for at that moment I felt something touch my cheek and heard the loud report of a gun immediately behind me.

Now, the wisest course would have been for me to run before whoever had fired found time to reload. But a kind of fury seized me, and run I would not. On the contrary, I turned with a shout, and charged back into the shadow. Something heard me coming, something fled in front of me. In a few seconds we were out into the moonlight beyond, and, as I expected, I saw that this something was a man—Pereira!

He halted and wheeled round, lifting the stock of his gun, club fashion.

" Thank God! it is you, Heer Allan," he said; " I thought you were a tiger."

" Then it was your last thought, murderer," I answered, raising my rifle.

" Don't shoot," he said. " Would you have my blood upon you? Why do you want to kill me?"

" Why did you try to kill me?" I answered covering him.

" I try to kill you! Are you mad? Listen, for your own sake. I sat down on the bank yonder waiting for the moon, and, being tired, fell asleep. Then I woke up with a start and, thinking from the sounds that a tiger was after me, fired to scare it. Allemachte! man, if I had aimed at you, could I have missed at that distance?"

" You did not quite miss, and had I not stepped to the left, you would have blown my head off. Say your prayers, you dog!"

" Allan Quatermain," he exclaimed with desperate energy, " you think I lie, who speak the truth. Kill me if you will, only then remember that you will hang for it. We court one woman, that is known, and who will believe this story of yours that I tried to shoot you? Soon the Kaffirs will come to look for me, probably they are starting already, and will find my body with your bullet in my heart. Then they will take it back to Marais's camp, and I say—who will believe your story?"

" He halted and wheeled round, lifting the stock of his gun,
club fashion." (*See page* 136)

" Some, I think, murderer," but as I spoke the words a chill of fear struck me. It was true, I could prove nothing, having no witnesses, and henceforward I should be a Cain among the Boers, one who had slain a man for jealousy. His gun was empty ; yes, but it might be said that I had fired it after his death. And as for the graze upon my cheek—why, a twig might have caused it. What should I do, then ? Drive him before me to the camp, and tell this tale ? Even then it would be but my word against his. No, he had me in a forked stick. I must let him go, and trust that Heaven would avenge his crime, since I could not. Moreover, by now my first rage was cooling, and to execute a man thus——

" Hernan Pereira," I said, " you are a liar and a coward. You tried to butcher me because Marie loves me and hates you, and you want to force her to marry you. Yet I cannot shoot you down in cold blood as you deserve. I leave it to God to punish you, as, soon or late, He will, here or hereafter ; you who thought to slaughter me and trust to the hyenas to hide your crime, as they would have done before morning. Get you gone before I change my mind and be swift."

Without another word he turned and ran swiftly as a buck, leaping from side to side as he ran, to disturb my aim in case I should shoot.

When he was a hundred yards away or more I, too, turned and ran, never feeling safe till I knew there was a mile of ground between us.

It was past ten o'clock that night when I got back to the camp, where I found Hans the Hottentot about to start to look for me, with two of the Zulus, and told him that I had been detained by accidents to the wagon. The Vrouw Prinsloo was still up also, waiting to hear of my arrival.

" What was the accident, Allan ? " she asked. " It looks as though there had been a bullet in it," and she pointed to the bloody smear upon my cheek.

I nodded.

" Pereira's ? " she asked again.

I nodded a second time.

" Did you kill him ? "

"No; I let him go. It would have been said that I murdered him," and I told her what had happened.

"*Ja*, Allan," she remarked when I had finished. "I think you were wise, for you could have proved nothing. But oh! for what fate, I wonder, is God Almighty saving up that stink-cat. Well, I will go and tell Marie that you are back safe, for her father won't let her out of the hut so late; but nothing more unless you wish it."

"No, Tante; I think nothing more, at any rate at present."

Here I may state, however, that within a few days Marie and everyone else in the camp knew the story in detail, except perhaps Marais, to whom no one spoke of his nephew. Evidently Vrouw Prinsloo had found herself unable to keep secret such an example of the villainy of her aversion, Pereira. So she told her daughter, who told the others quickly enough, though I gathered that some of them set down what had happened to accident. Bad as they knew Pereira to be, they could not believe that he was guilty of so black a crime.

About a week later the rest of us started from Marais's camp, a place that, notwithstanding the sadness of many of its associations, I confess I left with some regret. The trek before us, although not so very long, was of an extremely perilous nature. We had to pass through about two hundred miles of country of which all we knew was that its inhabitants were the Ama-tonga and other savage tribes. Here I should explain that after much discussion we had abandoned the idea of retracing the route followed by Marais on his ill-fated journey towards Delagoa.

Had we taken this it would have involved our crossing the terrible Lobombo Mountains, over which it was doubtful whether our light cattle could drag the wagons. Moreover, the country beyond the mountains was said to be very bare of game and also of Kaffirs, so that food might be lacking. On the other hand, if we kept to the east of the mountains the veld through which we must pass was thickly populated, which meant that in all probability we could buy grain.

What finally decided us to adopt this route, however, was that here in these warm, low-lying lands there would be grass for the oxen. Indeed, now, at the beginning of spring, in this part of Africa it was already pushing. Even if it were not, the beasts could live upon what herbage remained over from last summer and on the leaves of trees, neither of which in this winter veld ever become quite lifeless, whereas on the sere and fire-swept plains beyond the mountains they might find nothing at all. So we determined to risk the savages and the lions which followed the game into these hot districts, especially as it was not yet the fever season or that of the heavy rains, so that the rivers would be fordable.

I do not propose to set out our adventures in detail, for these would be too long. Until the great one of which I shall have to tell presently, they were of an annoying rather than of a serious nature. Travelling as we did, between the mountains and the sea, we could not well lose our way, especially as my Zulus had passed through that country ; and when their knowledge failed us, we generally managed to secure the services of local guides. The roads, however, or rather the game tracks and Kaffir paths which we followed, were terrible, for with the single exception of that of Pereira for part of the distance, no wagon had ever gone over them before. Indeed, a little later in the year they could not have been travelled at all. Sometimes we stuck in bogs out of which we had to dig the wheels, and sometimes in the rocky bottoms of streams, while once we were obliged literally to cut our way through a belt of dense bush from which it took us eight days to escape.

Our other chief trouble came from the lions, whereof there were great numbers in this veld. The prevalence of these hungry beasts forced us to watch our cattle very closely while they grazed, and at night, wherever it was possible, to protect them and ourselves in *bomas*, or fences of thorns, within which we lit fires to scare away wild beasts. Notwithstanding these pre-cautions, we lost several of the oxen, and ourselves had some narrow escapes.

Then, one night, just as Marie was about to enter the wagon where the women slept, a great lion, desperate with hunger, sprang over the fence. She leapt away from the beast, and in so doing caught her foot and fell down, whereon the lion came for her. In another few seconds she would have been dead, or carried off living.

But as it chanced, Vrouw Prinsloo was close at hand. Seizing a flaming bough from the fire, that intrepid woman ran at the lion and, as it opened its huge mouth to roar or bite, thrust the burning end of the bough into its throat. The lion closed its jaws upon it, then finding the mouthful not to its taste, departed even more quickly than it had come, uttering the most dreadful noises and leaving Marie quite unhurt. Needless to say, after this I really worshipped the Vrouw Prinsloo, though she, good soul, thought nothing of the business, which in those days was but a common incident of travel.

I think it was on the day after this lion episode that we came upon Pereira's wagon, or rather its remains. Evidently he had tried to trek along a steep rocky back which overhung a stream, with the result that the wagon had fallen into the stream-bed, then almost dry, and been smashed beyond repair.

The Tonga natives of the neighbourhood, who had burned most of the woodwork in order to secure the precious iron bolts and fittings, informed us that the white man and his servants who were with the wagon had gone forward on foot some ten days before, driving their cattle with them. Whether this story were true or not we had no means of finding out. It was quite possible that Pereira and his companions had been murdered, though as we found the Tongas very quiet folk if well treated and given the usual complimentary presents for wayleaves, this did not seem probable. Indeed, a week later our doubts upon this point were cleared up thus.

We had reached a big kraal called Fokoti, on the Umkusi River, which appeared to be almost deserted. We asked an old woman whom we met where its people had gone. She answered that they had fled towards the borders of Swaziland, fearing an attack from the Zulus whose territories began beyond this Umkusi River. It seemed that a few days before a Zulu impi or regiment had appeared upon the banks of the river, and although there was no war at the time between the Zulus and the Tongas, the latter had thought it wise to put themselves out of reach of those terrible spears.

On hearing this news we debated whether it would not be well for us to follow their example and, trekking westwards, try to find a pass in the mountains. Upon this point there was a division of opinion among us. Marais, who was a fatalist, wished to go on, saying that the good Lord would protect us, as He had done in the past.

"Allemachte!" answered the Vrouw Prinsloo. "Did he protect all those who lie dead at Marais's camp, whither your folly led us, mynheer? The good Lord expects us to look after our own skins, and I know that these Zulus are of the same blood as Umsilikazi's Kaffirs, who have killed so many of our people. Let us try the mountains, say I."

Of course her husband and son agreed with her, for to them the vrouw's word was law; but Marais, being as usual, obstinate, would not give way. All that afternoon they wrangled, while I held my tongue, declaring that I was willing to abide by the decision of the majority. In the end, as I foresaw they would, they appealed to me to act as umpire between them.

"Friends," I answered, "if you had asked me my opinion before, I should have voted for trying the mountains, beyond which, perhaps, we might find some Boers. I do not like this story of the Zulu impi. I think that someone has told them of our coming, and that it is us they mean to attack and not the Tongas, with whom they are at peace. My men say that it is not usual for impis to visit this part of the country."

"Who could have told them?" asked Marais.

"I don't know, mynheer. Perhaps the natives have sent on word, or perhaps—Hernan Pereira."

"I knew that you would suspect my nephew, Allan," he exclaimed angrily.

"I suspect no one: I only weigh what is probable. However, it is too late for us to move to-night either south or westwards, so I think I will sleep over the business and see what I can find out from my Zulus."

That night, or rather the following morning, the question was settled for us, for when I woke up at dawn, it was to see the faint light glimmering on what I knew must be spears. We were surrounded by a great company of Zulus, as I discovered afterwards, over two hundred strong. Thinking that after their fashion they were preparing to attack us at dawn, I called the news to the others, whereon Marais rushed forward, just as he had left his bed, cocking his *roer* as he came.

" For the love of God, do not shoot ! " I said. " How can we resist so many ? Soft words are our only chance."

Still he attempted to fire, and would have done so had I not thrown myself upon him and literally torn the gun from his hand. By this time the Vrouw Prinsloo had come up, a very weird spectacle, I recollect, in what she called her " sleep-garments," that included a night-cap made of a worn jackal skin and a kind of otter-pelt stomacher.

" Accursed fool ! " she said to Marais, " would you cause all our throats to be cut ? Go forward, you, Allan, and talk to those *swartzels* " (that is, black creatures), " gently as you would to a savage dog. You have a tongue steeped in oil, and they may listen to you."

" Yes," I answered ; " that seems the best thing to do. If I should not return, give my love to Marie."

So I beckoned to the headman of my Zulus whom I had hired at Delagoa, to accompany me, and marched forward boldly quite unarmed. We were encamped upon a rise of ground a quarter of a mile from the river, and the impi, or those of them whom we could see, were at the foot of this rise about a hundred and sixty yards away. The light was growing now, and when I was within fifty paces of them they saw me. At some word of command a number of men rushed toward me, their fighting shields held over their bodies and their spears up.

" We are dead ! " exclaimed my Kaffir in a resigned voice. I shared his opinion, but thought I might as well die standing as running away.

Now I should explain that though as yet I had never mixed with these Zulus, I could talk several native dialects kindred to that which they used very well indeed. Moreover, ever since I had hired men of their race at Delagoa, I had spent all my spare time in conversing with them and acquiring a knowledge of their language, history and customs. So by this time I knew their tongue fairly, although occasionally I may have used terms which were unfamiliar to them.

Thus it came about that I was able to shout to them, asking what was their business with us. Hearing themselves addressed in words which they understood, the men halted, and seeing that I was unarmed, three of them approached me.

"We come to take you prisoners, white people, or to kill you if you resist," said their captain.

"By whose order?" I asked.

"By the order of Dingaan our king."

"Is it so? And who told Dingaan that we were here?"

"The Boer who came in front of you."

"Is it so?" I said again. "And now what do you need of us?"

"That you should accompany us to the kraal of Dingaan."

"I understand. We are quite willing, since it lies upon our road. But then why do you come against us, who are peaceful travellers, with your spears lifted?"

"For this reason. The Boer told us that there is among you a 'child of George'" (an Englishman), "a terrible man who would kill us unless we killed or bound him first. Show us this child of George that we may make him fast, or slay him, and we will not hurt the rest of you."

"I am the child of George," I answered, "and if you think it necessary to make me fast, do so."

Now the Zulus burst out laughing.

"You! Why, you are but a boy who weighs no more than a fat girl," exclaimed their captain, a great, bony fellow who was named Kambula.

"That may be so," I answered; "but sometimes the wisdom of their fathers dwells in the young. I am the son of George who saved these Boers from death far away, and I am taking them back to their own people. We desire to see Dingaan, your king. Be pleased therefore to lead us to him as he has commanded you to do. If you do not believe what I tell you, ask this man who is with me, and his companions who are of your own race. They will tell you everything."

Then the captain Kambula called my servant apart and talked with him for a long while.

When the interview was finished he advanced to me and said:

"Now I have heard all about you. I have heard that although young you are very clever, so clever that you do not sleep, but watch by night as well as by day. Therefore, that I, Kambula, name you Macumazahn, Watcher-by-night, and by that name you shall henceforth be known among us. Now, Macumazahn, Son of George, bring out these Boers whom you are guiding that I may lead them in their moving huts to the Great Place, Umgungundhlovu, where dwells Dingaan the king. See, we lay down our spears and will come to meet them unarmed, trusting to you to protect us, O Macumazahn, Son of George," and he cast his assegai to the ground.

"Come," I said, and led them to the wagons.

XII

DINGAAN'S BET

As I advanced to the wagons accompanied by Kambula and his two companions, I saw that Marais, in a state of great excitement, was engaged in haranguing the two Prinsloo men and Meyer, while the Vrouw Prinsloo and Marie appeared to be attempting to calm him.

"They are unarmed," I heard him shout. "Let us seize the black devils and hold them as hostages."

Thereon, led by Marais, the three Boer men came towards us doubtfully, their guns in their hands.

"Be careful what you are doing," I called to them. "These are envoys," and they hung back a little while Marais went on with his haranguing.

The Zulus looked at them and at me, then Kambula said :

"Are you leading us into a trap, Son of George ? "

"Not so," I answered ; "but the Boers are afraid of you and think to take you prisoners."

"Tell them," said Kambula quietly, "that if they kill us or lay a hand on us, as no doubt they can do, very soon every one of them will be dead and their women with them."

I repeated this ultimatum energetically enough, but Marais shouted :

"The Englishman is betraying us to the Zulus ! Do not trust him ; seize them as I tell you."

What would have happened I am sure I do not know ; but just then the Vrouw Prinsloo came up and caught her husband by the arm, exclaiming :

"You shall have no part in this fool's business. If Marais wishes to seize the Zulus, let him do so himself. Are you mad or drunk that you should think that Allan would wish to betray Marie to the Kaffirs, to say nothing of the rest of us?" and she began to wave an extremely dirty *vatdoek*, or dishcloth, which she always carried about with her and used for every purpose, towards Kambula as a sign of peace.

Now the Boers gave way, and Marais, seeing himself in a minority, glowered at me in silence.

"Ask these white people, O Macumazahn," said Kambula, "who is their captain, for to the captain I would speak."

I translated the question, and Marais answered:

"I am."

"No," broke in Vrouw Prinsloo, "*I* am. Tell them, Allan, that these men are all fools and have given the rule to me, a woman."

So I told them. Evidently this information surprised them a little, for they discussed together. Then Kambula said:

"So be it. We have heard that the people of George are now ruled by a woman, and as you, Macumazahn, are one of that people, doubtless it is the same among your party."

Here I may add that thenceforward the Zulus always accepted the Vrouw Prinsloo as the *Inkosikaas* or chieftainness of our little band, and with the single exception of myself, whom they looked upon as her "mouth," or *induna*, would only transact business with, or give directions to her. The other Boers they ignored completely.

This point of etiquette settled, Kambula bade me repeat what he had already told me, that we were prisoners whom he was instructed by Dingaan to convey to his Great Place, and that if we made no attempt to escape we should not be hurt upon the journey.

I did so, whereon the vrouw asked as I had done, who had informed Dingaan that we were coming.

I repeated to her word for word what the Zulus had told me, that it was Pereira, whose object seems to have been to bring about my death or capture.

Then the vrouw exploded.

"Do you hear that, Henri Marais?" she screamed. "It is your stinkcat of a nephew again. Oh! I thought I smelt him!

Your nephew has betrayed us to these Zulus that he may bring Allan to his death. Ask them, Allan, what this Dingaan has done with the stinkcat."

So I asked, and was informed they believed that the king had let Pereira go on to his own people in payment of the information that he had given him.

" My God ! " said the vrouw, " I hoped that he had knocked him on the head. Well, what is to be done now ? "

" I don't know," I answered. Then an idea occurred to me, and I said to Kambula :

" It seems to be me, the son of George, that your king wants. Take me, and let these people go on their road."

The three Zulus began to discuss this point, withdrawing themselves a little way so that I could not overhear them. But when the Boers understood the offer that I had made, Marie, who until now had been silent, grew more angry than ever I had seen her before.

" It shall not be ! " she said, stamping her foot. " Father, I have been obedient to you for long, but if you consent to this I will be obedient no more. Allan saved my cousin Hernan's life, as he saved all our lives. In payment for that good deed Hernan tried to murder him in the kloof—oh ! be quiet, Allan ; I know all the story. How he has betrayed him to the Zulus, telling them that he is a terrible and dangerous man who must be killed. Well, if he is to be killed, I will be killed with him, and if the Zulus take him and let us free, I go with him. Now make up your mind."

Marais tugged at his beard, staring first at his daughter and then at me. What he would have answered I do not know, for at that moment Kambula stepped forward and gave his decision.

It was to the effect that although it was the Son of George whom Dingaan wanted, his orders were that all with him were to be taken also. Those orders could not be disobeyed. The king would settle the matter as to whether some of us were to be killed or let free, when we reached his House. Therefore he commanded that " we should tie the oxen to the moving huts and cross the river at once."

This was the end of that scene. Having no choice we inspanned and continued our journey, escorted by the company of two hundred savages. I am bound to say that during the four or five days that it took us to reach Dingaan's kraal they behaved very well to us. With Kambula and his officers, all of them good fellows in their way, I had many conversations, and from them learned much as to the state and customs of the Zulus. Also the peoples of the districts through which we passed flocked round us at every outspan, for most of them had never seen a white man before, and in return for a few beads brought us all the food that we required. Indeed, the beads, or their equivalents, were nothing but a present, since, by the king's command, they must satisfy our wants. This they did very thoroughly. For instance, when on the last day's trek, some of our oxen gave out, numbers of Zulus were inspanned in place of them, and by their help the wagons were dragged to the great kraal, Umgungundh-lovu.

Here an outspan place was assigned to us near to the house, or rather the huts, of a certain missionary of the name of Owen, who with great courage had ventured into this country. We were received with the utmost kindness by him and his wife and household, and it is impossible for me to say what pleasure I found, after all my journeyings, in meeting an educated man of my own race.

Near to our camp was a stone-covered koppie, where, on the morning after our arrival, I saw six or eight men executed in a way that I will not describe. Their crime, according to Mr. Owen, was that they had bewitched some of the king's oxen.

While I was recovering from this dreadful spectacle, which, fortunately, Marie did not witness, the captain Kambula arrived, saying that Dingaan wished to see me. So taking with me the Hottentot Hans and two of the Zulus whom I had hired at Delagoa Bay—for the royal orders were that none of the other white people were to come, I was led through the fence of the vast town in which stood two thousand huts—the " multitude of houses " as the Zulus called it—and across a vast open space in the middle.

On the farther side of this space, where, before long, I was fated to witness a very tragic scene, I entered a kind of labyrinth. This was called *siklohlo*, and had high fences with numerous turns, so that it was impossible to see where one was going or to find the way in or out. Ultimately, however, I reached a great hut named *intunkulu*, a word that means the " house of houses," or the abode of the king, in front of which I saw a fat man seated on a stool, naked except for the *moocha* about his middle and necklaces and armlets of blue beads. Two warriors held their broad shields over his head to protect him from the sun. Otherwise he was alone, although I felt sure that the numerous passages around him were filled with guards, for I could hear them moving.

On entering this place Kambula and his companions flung themselves upon their faces and began to sing praises of which the king took no notice. Presently he looked up, and appearing to observe me for the first time asked :

" Who is that white boy ? "

Then Kambula rose and said :

" O king, this is the Son of George, whom you commanded me to capture. I have taken him and the *Amaboona* " (that is, the Boers), " his companions, and brought them all to you, O king."

" I remember," said Dingaan. " The big Boer who was here, and whom Tambusa "—he was one of Dingaan's captains— " let go against my will, said that he was a terrible man who should be killed before he worked great harm to my people. Why did you not kill him, Kambula, although it is true he does not look very terrible ? "

" Because the king's word was that I should bring him to the king living," answered Kambula. Then he added cheerfully: " Still, if the king wishes it, I can kill him at once."

" I don't know," said Dingaan doubtfully ; " perhaps he can mend guns." Next, after reflecting a while, he bade a shield-holder to fetch someone, I could not hear whom.

" Doubtless," thought I to myself, " it is the executioner," and at that thought a kind of mad rage seized me. " Why should my life be ended thus in youth to satisfy the whim of a savage ? And if it must be so, why should I go alone ? "

In the inside pocket of my ragged coat I had a small loaded pistol with two barrels. One of those barrels would kill Dingaan —at five paces I could not miss that bulk—and the other would blow out my brains, for I was not minded to have my neck twisted or to be beaten to death with sticks. Well, if it was to be done, I had better do it at once. Already my hand was creeping towards the pocket when a new idea, or rather two ideas, struck me.

The first was that if I shot Dingaan the Zulus would probably massacre Marie and the others—Marie, whose sweet face I should never see again. The second was that while there is life there is hope. Perhaps, after all, he had not sent for an executioner, but for someone else. I would wait. A few minutes more of existence were worth the having.

The shield-bearer returned, emerging from one of the narrow, reed-hedged passages, and after him came no executioner, but a young white man, who, as I knew from the look of him, was English. He saluted the king by taking off his hat, which I remember was stuck round with black ostrich feathers, then stared at me.

" O Tho-maas " (that is how he pronounced " Thomas "), said Dingaan, " tell me if this boy is one of your brothers, or is he a Boer ? "

" The king wants to know if you are Dutch or British," said the white lad, speaking in English.

" As British as you are," I answered. " I was born in England, and come from the Cape."

" That may be lucky for you," he said, " because the old witch-doctor, Zikali, has told him that he must not kill any English. What is your name ? Mine is Thomas Halstead. I am interpreter here."

" Allan Quatermain. Tell Zikali, whoever he may be, that if he sticks to his advice I will give him a good present."

" What are you talking about ? " asked Dingaan suspiciously.

" He says he is English, no Boer, O king ; that he was born across the Black Water, and that he comes from the country out of which all the Boers have trekked."

At this intelligence Dingaan pricked up his ears.

" Then he can tell me about these Boers," he said, " and what they are after, or could if he were able to speak my tongue. I do not trust you to interpret, you Tho-maas, whom I know to be a liar," and he glowered at Halstead.

" I can speak your tongue, though not very well, O king," I

interrupted, " and I can tell you all about the Boers, for I have
lived among them."

" *Ow !* " said Dingaan, intensely interested. " But perhaps
you are also a liar. Or are you a praying man, like that fool
yonder, who is named Oweena ? "—he meant the missionary,
Mr. Owen—" whom I spare because it is not lucky to kill one
who is mad, although he tries to frighten my soldiers with tales
of a fire into which they will go after they are dead. As though
it matters what happens to them after they are dead ! " he added
reflectively, taking a pinch of snuff.

" I am no liar," I answered. " What have I to lie about ? "

" You would lie to save your own life, for all white men are
cowards ; not like the Zulus, who love to die for their king. But
how are you named ? "

" Your people call me Macumazahn."

" Well, Macumazahn, if you are no liar, tell me is it true
that these Boers rebelled against their king who was named
George, and fled from him as the traitor Umsilikazi did from
me ? "

" Yes," I answered, " that is true."

" Now I am sure that you are a liar," said Dingaan triumphantly. " You say that you are English and therefore serve your
king, or the *Inkosikaas* " (that is the Great Lady), " who they
tell me now sits in his place. How does it come about then that
you are travelling with a party of these very *Amaboona* who must
be your enemies, since they are the enemies of your king, or of
her who follows after him ? "

Now I knew that I was in a tight place, for on this matter of
loyalty, Zulu, and indeed all native ideas, are very primitive.
If I said that I had sympathy with the Boers, Dingaan would
set me down as a traitor. If I said that I hated the Boers, then
still I should be a traitor because I associated with them, and a
traitor in his eyes would be one to be killed. I do not like to
talk religion, and anyone who has read what I have written in
various works will admit that I have done so rarely, if ever. Yet
at that moment I put up a prayer for guidance, feeling that my
young life hung upon the answer, and it came to me—whence I
do not know. The essence of that guidance was that I should
tell the simple truth to this fat savage. So I said to him :

" The answer is this, O king. Among those Boers is a maiden whom I love and who betrothed herself to me since we were ' so high.' Her father took her north. But she sent a message to me saying that her people died of fever and she starved. So I went up in a ship to save her, and have saved her, and those who remained alive of her people with her."

" *Ow!* " said Dingaan ; " I understand that reason. It is a good reason. However many wives he may have, there is no folly that a man will not commit for the sake of some particular girl who is not yet his wife. I have done as much myself, especially for one who was called Nada the Lily, of whom a certain Umslopogaas robbed me, one of my own blood of whom I am much afraid."[1]

For a while he brooded heavily, then went on :

" Your reason is good, Macumazahn, and I accept it. More, I promise you this. Perhaps I shall kill these Boers, or perhaps I shall not kill them. But if I make up my mind to kill them, this girl of yours shall be spared. Point her out to Kambula here— not to Tho-maas, for he is a liar and would tell me the wrong one—and she shall be spared."

" I thank you, O king," I said ; " but what is the use of that if I am to be killed ? "

" I did not say that you were to be killed, Macumazahn, though perhaps I shall kill you, or perhaps I shall not kill you. It depends upon whether I find you to be a liar, or not a liar. Now the Boer whom Tambusa let go against my wish said that you are a mighty magician as well as a very dangerous man, one who can shoot birds flying on the wing with a bullet, which is impossible. Can you do so ? "

" Sometimes," I answered.

" Very good, Macumazahn. Now we will see if you are a wizard or a liar. I will make a bet with you. Yonder by your camp is a hill called ' Hloma Amabutu,' a hill of stones where evildoers are slain. This afternoon some wicked ones die there, and when they are dead the vultures will come to devour them. Now this is my bet with you. When those vultures come you shall shoot at them, and if you kill three out of the first five on the wing—not on the ground, Macumazahn—then I will spare

[1] *See* the Author's book named " Nada the Lily."

these Boers. But if you miss them, then I shall know that you
are a liar and no wizard, and I will kill them every one on the
hill Hloma Amabutu. I will spare none of them except the girl,
whom perhaps I will take as a wife. As to you, I will not yet
say what I will do with you."

Now my first impulse was to refuse this monstrous wager,
which meant that the lives of a number of people were to be
set against my skill in shooting. But young Thomas Halstead,
guessing the words that were about to break from me, said in
English :

" Accept unless you are a fool. If you don't he will cut the
throats of every one of them and stick your girl into the *emposeni* "
(that is harem), " while you will become a prisoner as I am."

These were words that I could not resent or neglect, so
although despair was in my heart, I said coolly :

" Be it so, O king. I take your wager. If I kill three vultures
out of five as they hover over the hill, then I have your promise
that all those who travel with me shall be allowed to go hence
in safety."

" Yes, yes, Macumazahn ; but if you fail to kill them, remember that the next vultures you shoot at shall be those that come
to feed upon their flesh, for then I shall know that you are no
magician, but a common liar. And now begone, Tho-maas.
I will not have you spying on me ; and you Macumazahn,
come hither. Although you talk my tongue so badly, I would
speak with you about the Boers."

So Halstead went, shrugging his shoulders and muttering as
he passed me :

" I hope you really *can* shoot."

After he had left I sat alone for a full hour with Dingaan while
he cross-examined me about the Dutch, their movements and
their aims in travelling to the confines of his country.

I answered his questions as best I could, trying to make out
a good case for them.

At length, when he grew weary of talking, he clapped his
hands, whereon a number of fine girls appeared, two of whom
carried pots of beer, from which he offered me drink.

I replied that I would have none, since beer made the hand
shake and that on the steadiness of my hand that afternoon

depended the lives of many. To do him justice he quite understood the point. Indeed, he ordered me to be conducted back
to the camp at once that I might rest, and even sent one of his
own attendants with me to hold a shield over my head as I
walked so that I should be protected from the sun.

"*Hamba-gachle*" (that is "Go softly"), said the wicked old
tyrant to me as I departed under the guidance of Kambula.
"This afternoon, one hour before sundown, I will meet you
at Hloma Amabutu, and there shall be settled the fate of these
Amaboona, your companions."

When I reached the camp it was to find all the Boers clustered
together waiting for me, and with them the Reverend Mr. Owen
and his people, including a Welsh servant of his, a woman of
middle age who, I remember, was called Jane.

"Well," said the Vrouw Prinsloo, "and what is your news,
young man?"

"My news, aunt," I answered, "is that one hour before
sundown to-day I have to shoot vultures on the wing against
the lives of all of you. This you owe to that false-hearted hound
Hernan Pereira, who told Dingaan that I am a magician. Now
Dingaan would prove it. He thinks that only by magic can a
man shoot soaring vultures with a bullet, and as he is determined
to kill you all, except perhaps Marie, in the form of a bet he has
set me a task which he believes to be impossible. If I fail, the
bet is lost, and so are your lives. If I succeed I think your lives
will be spared, since Kambula there tells me that the king always
makes it a point of honour to pay his bets. Now you have the
truth, and I hope you like it," and I laughed bitterly.

When I had finished a perfect storm of execration broke from
the Boers. If curses could have killed Pereira, surely he would
have died upon the spot, wherever he might be. Only two of
them were silent. Marie, who turned very pale, poor girl, and
her father. Presently one of them, I think it was Meyer, rounded
on him viciously and asked him what he thought now of that
devil, his nephew.

"I think there must be some mistake," answered Marais
quietly, "since Hernan cannot have wished that we should all
be put to death."

"No," shouted Meyer; "but he wished that Allan Quatermain should, which is just as bad; and now it has come about that once more our lives depend upon this English boy."

"At any rate," replied Marais, looking at me oddly, "it seems that he is not to be killed, whether he shoots the vultures or misses them."

"That remains to be proved, mynheer," I answered hotly, for the insinuation stung me. "But please understand that if all of you, my companions, are to be slaughtered, and Marie is to be put among this black brute's women as he threatens, I have no wish to live on."

"My God! does he threaten that?" said Marais. "Surely you must have misunderstood him, Allan."

"Do you think that I should lie to you on such a matter——" I began.

But before I could proceed, the Vrouw Prinsloo thrust herself between us, crying:

"Be silent, you, Marais, and you too, Allan. Is this a time that you should quarrel and upset yourself, Allan, so that when the trial comes you will shoot your worst and not your best? And is this a time, Henri Marais, that you should throw insults at one on whom all our lives hang, instead of praying for God's vengeance upon your accursed nephew? Come, Allan, and take food. I have fried the liver of that heifer which the king sent us; it is ready and very good. After you have eaten it you must lie down and sleep a while."

Now among the household of the Reverend Mr. Owen was an English boy called William Wood, who was not more than twelve or fourteen years of age. This lad knew both Dutch and Zulu, and acted as interpreter to the Owen family during the absence on a journey of a certain Mr. Hulley, who really filled that office. While this conversation was taking place in Dutch he was engaged in rendering every word of it into English for the benefit of the clergyman and his family. When Mr. Owen understood the full terror of the situation, he broke in saying:

"This is not a time to eat or to sleep, but a time to pray that the heart of the savage Dingaan may be turned. Come, let us pray!"

"Yes," rejoined Vrouw Prinsloo, when William Wood had

translated. " Do you pray, *Predicant*, and all the rest of you who have nothing else to do, and while you are about it pray also that the bullets of Allan Quatermain may not be turned. As for me and Allan, we have other things to see to, so you must pray a little harder to cover us as well as yourselves. Now you come along, nephew Allan, or that liver may be overdone and give you indigestion, which is worse for shooting than even bad temper. No, not another word. If you try to speak any more, Henri Marais, I will box your ears," and she lifted a hand like a leg of mutton, then, as Marais retreated before her, seized me by the collar as though I were a naughty boy and led me away to the wagons.

XIII

THE REHEARSAL

By the women's wagon we found the liver cooked in its frying-pan, as the vrouw had said. Indeed, it was just done to a turn. Selecting a particularly massive slice, she proceeded to take it from the pan with her fingers in order to set it upon a piece of tin, from which she had first removed the more evident traces of the morning meal with her constant companion, the ancient and unwashed *vatdoek*. As it chanced the effort was not very successful, since the boiling liver fat burnt the vrouw's fingers, causing her to drop it on the grass, and, I am sorry to add, to swear as well. Not to be defeated, however, having first sucked her fingers to ease their smart, she seized the sizzling liver with the *vatdoek* and deposited it upon the dirty tin.

" There, nephew," she said triumphantly, " there are more ways of killing a cat than by drowning. What a fool I was not to think of the *vatdoek* at first. Allemachte ! how the flesh has burnt me ; I don't suppose that being killed would hurt much more. Also, if the worst comes to the worst, it will soon be over. Think of it, Allan, by to-night I may be an angel, dressed in a long white nightgown like those my mother gave me when I was married, which I cut up for baby-clothes because I found them chilly wear, having always been accustomed to sleep in my vest and petticoat. Yes, and I shall have wings, too, like those on a white gander, only bigger if they are to carry my weight."

"And a crown of Glory," I suggested.

"Yes, of course, a crown of Glory—very large, since I shall be a martyr; but I hope one will only have to wear it on Sundays, as I never could bear anything heavy on my hair; moreover, it would remind me of a Kaffir's head-ring done in gold, and I shall have had enough of Kaffirs. Then there will be the harp," she went on as her imagination took fire at the prospect of these celestial delights. "Have you ever seen a harp, Allan? I haven't except that which King David carries in the picture in the Book, which looks like a broken *rimpi* chair frame set up edgeways. As for playing the thing, they will have to teach me, that's all, which will be a difficult business, seeing that I would sooner listen to cats on the roof than to music, and as for making it——"

So she chattered on, as I believe with the object of diverting and amusing me, for she was a shrewd old soul who knew how important it was that I should be kept in an equable frame of mind at this crisis in our fates.

Meanwhile I was doing my best with the lump of liver, that tasted painfully of *vatdoek* and was gritty with sand. Indeed, when the vrouw's back was turned I managed to throw most of it to Hans behind me, who swallowed it at a gulp as a dog does, since he did not wish to be caught chewing it.

"God in heaven! how fast you eat, nephew," said the vrouw, catching sight of my empty tin. Then, eyeing the voracious Hottentot suspiciously, she added: "That yellow dog of yours hasn't stolen it, has he? If so, I'll teach him."

"No, no, vrouw," answered Hans in alarm. "No meat has passed my lips this day, except what I licked out of the pan after breakfast."

"Then, Allan, you will certainly have indigestion, which is just what I wanted to avoid. Have I not often told you that you should chew your bit twenty times before you swallow, which I would do myself if I had any back teeth left? Here, drink this milk; it is only a little sour and will settle your stomach," and she produced a black bottle and subjected it to the attentions of the *vatdoek*, growing quite angry when I declined it and sent for water.

Next she insisted upon my getting into her own bed in the wagon to sleep, forbidding me to smoke, which she said made the hand shake. Thither, then, I went, after a brief conversation with Hans, whom I directed to clean my rifle thoroughly. For I wished to be alone and knew that I had little chance of solitude outside of that somewhat fusty couch.

To tell the truth, although I shut my eyes to deceive the vrouw, who looked in occasionally to see how I was getting on, no sleep came to me that afternoon—at least, not for a long while. How could I sleep in that hot place when my heart was torn with doubt and terror? Think of it, reader, think of it! An hour or two, and on my skill would hang the lives of eight white people—men, women, and children, and the safety or the utter shame of the woman whom I loved and who loved me. No, she should be spared the worst. I would give her my pistol, and if there were need she would know what to do.

The fearful responsibility was more than I could bear. I fell into a veritable agony; I trembled and even wept a little. Then I thought of my father and what he would do in such circumstances, and began to pray as I had never prayed before.

I implored the Power above me to give me strength and wisdom; not to let me fail in this hour of trouble, and thereby bring these poor people to a bloody death. I prayed till the perspiration streamed down my face; then suddenly I fell into sleep or swoon. I don't know how long I lay thus, but I think it must have been the best part of an hour. At last I woke up, all in an instant, and as I woke I distinctly heard a tiny voice, unlike any other voice in the whole world, speak inside my head, or so it seemed to me, saying:

" *Go to the hill Hloma Amabutu, and watch how the vultures fly. Do what comes into your mind, and even if you seem to fail, fear nothing.*"

I sat up on the old vrouw's bed, and felt that some mysterious change had come over me. I was no longer the same man. My doubts and terrors had gone; my hand was like a rock; my heart was light. I knew that I should kill those three vultures. Of course the story seems absurd, and easy to be explained by the state of my nerves under the strain which was being put upon them, and for aught I know that may be its true meaning. Yet I am not ashamed to confess that I have always held, and still hold, otherwise. I believe that in my extremity some kindly Power did speak to me in answer to my earnest prayers and to those of others, giving me guidance and, what I needed still more, judgment and calmness. At any rate, that this was my conviction at the moment may be seen from the fact that I hastened to obey the teachings of that tiny, unnatural voice.

Climbing out of the wagon, I went to Hans, who was seated near by in the full glare of the hot sun, at which he seemed to stare with unblinking eyes.

"Where's the rifle, Hans?" I said.

"*Intombi* is here, baas, where I have put her to keep her cool, so that she may not go off before it is wanted," and he pointed to a little grave-like heap of gathered grass at his side.

The natives, I should explain, named this particular gun *Intombi*, which means a young girl, because it was so much slimmer and more graceful than other guns.

"Is it clean?" I asked.

"Never was she cleaner since she was born out of the fire, baas. Also, the powder has been sifted and set to dry in the sun with the caps, and the bullets have been trued to the barrel, so that there may be no accidents when it comes to the shooting. If you miss the *aasvogels*, baas, it will not be the fault of *Intombi* or of the powder and the bullets; it will be your own fault."

"That's comforting," I answered. "Well, come on. I want to go to the Death-hill yonder."

"Why, baas, before the time?" asked the Hottentot, shrinking back a little. "It is no place to visit till one is obliged. These Zulus say that ghosts sit there even in the daylight, haunting the rocks where they were made ghosts."

"Vultures sit or fly there also, Hans; and I would see how they fly, that I may know when and where to shoot at them."

"That is right, baas," said the clever Hottentot. "This is not like firing at geese in the Groote Kloof. The geese go straight, like an assegai to its mark. But the *aasvogels* wheel round and round, always on the turn; it is easy to miss a bird that is turning, baas."

"Very easy. Come on."

Just as we were starting Vrouw Prinsloo appeared from behind the other wagon, and with her Marie, who, I noticed, was very pale and whose beautiful eyes were red, as though with weeping.

The vrouw asked me where we were going. I told her. After considering a little, she said that was a good thought of mine, as it was always well to study the ground before a battle.

I nodded, and led Marie aside behind some thorn trees that grew near.

" Oh ! Allan, what will be the end of this ? " she asked piteously. High as was her courage it seemed to fail her now.

" A good end, dearest," I answered. " We shall come out of this hole safely, as we have of many others."

" How do you know that, Allan, which is known to God alone ? "

" Because God told me, Marie," and I repeated to her the story of the voice I had heard in my dream, which seemed to comfort her.

" Yet, yet," she exclaimed doubtfully, " it was but a dream, Allan, and dreams are such uncertain things. You may fail, after all."

" Do I look like one who will fail, Marie ? "

She studied me from head to foot, then answered :

" No, you do not, although you did when you came back from the king's huts. Now you are quite changed. Still, Allan, you may fail, and then—what ? Some of those dreadful Zulus have been here while you were sleeping, bidding us all make ready to go to the Hill of Death. They say that Dingaan is in earnest. If you do not kill the vultures, he will kill us. It seems that they are sacred birds, and if they escape he will think he has nothing to fear from the white men and their magic, and so will make a beginning by butchering us. I mean the rest of us, for I am to be kept alive, and oh ! what shall I do, Allan ? "

I looked at her, and she looked at me. Then I took the double-barrelled pistol out of my pocket and gave it to her.

" It is loaded and on the half-cock," I said.

She nodded and hid it in her dress beneath her apron. Then without more words we kissed and parted, for both of us feared to prolong that scene.

The hill Hloma Amabutu was quite close to our encampment and the huts of the Reverend Mr. Owen, scarcely a quarter of a mile off, I should say, rising from the flat veld on the further side of a little depression that hardly amounted to a valley. As we approached it I noticed its peculiar and blasted appearance, for whereas all around the grass was vivid with the green of spring, on this place none seemed to grow. An eminence strewn with tumbled heaps of blackish rock, and among them a few struggling, dark-leaved bushes ; that was its appearance. Moreover, many of these boulders looked as though they had been splashed and lined with whitewash, showing that they were the resting-place of hundreds of gorged vultures.

I believe it is the Chinese who declare that particular localities have good or evil influences attached to them, some kind of spirit of their own, and really Hloma Amabutu and a few other spots that I am acquainted with in Africa give colour to the fancy. Certainly as I set foot upon that accursed ground, that Golgotha, that Place of Skulls, a shiver went through me. It may have been caused by the atmosphere, moral and actual, of the mount, or it may have been a prescience of a certain dreadful scene which within a few months I was doomed to witness there. Or perhaps the place itself and the knowledge of the trial before me sent a sudden chill through my healthy blood. I cannot say which it was, but the fact remains as I have stated, although a minute or two later, when I saw what kind of sleepers lay upon that mount, it would not have been necessary for me to seek any far-fetched explanations of my fear.

Across this hill, winding in and out between the rough rocks that lay here, there and everywhere like hailstones after a winter storm, ran sundry paths. It seems that the shortest road to various places in the neighbourhood of the Great Kraal ran over it, and although no Zulu ever dared to set foot there between sun-set and rise, in the daytime they used these paths freely enough. But I suppose that they also held that this evil-omened field of death had some spirit of its own, some invisible but imminent fiend, who needed to be propitiated, lest soon he should claim them also.

This was their method of propitiation, a common one enough, I believe, in many lands, though what may be its meaning I cannot tell. As the traveller came to those spots·where the paths cut across each other, he took a stone and threw it on to a heap that had been accumulated there by the hands of other travellers. There were many such heaps upon the hill, over a dozen, I think, and the size of them was great. I should say that the biggest contained quite fifty loads of stones, and the smallest not fewer than twenty or thirty.

Now, Hans, although he had never set foot there before, seemed to have learned all the traditions of the place, and what rites were necessary to avert its curse. At any rate, when we came to the first heap, he cast a stone upon it, and begged me to do the same. I laughed and refused, but when we reached the second heap the same thing happened. Again I refused, whereon, before we came to a third and larger pile, Hans sat down upon the ground and began to groan, swearing that he would not go one step farther unless I promised to make the accustomed offering.

" Why not, you fool ? " I asked.

" Because if you neglect it, baas, I think that we shall stop here for ever. Oh ! you may laugh, but I tell you that already you have brought ill-luck upon yourself. Remember my words, baas, when you miss two of the five *aasvogels*."

" Bosh ! " I exclaimed, or, rather, its Dutch equivalent. Still, as this talk of missing vultures touched me nearly, and it is always as well to conform to native prejudices, at the next and two subsequent heaps I cast my stone as humbly as the most superstitious Zulu in the land.

By this time we had reached the summit, which may have been two hundred yards long. It was hogbacked in shape, with a kind of depression in the middle cleared of stones, either by the hand of man or nature, and not unlike a large circus in its general conformation.

Oh ! the sight that met my eyes. All about lay the picked and scattered bones of men and women, many of them broken up by the jaws of hyenas. Some were quite fresh, for the hair still clung to the skulls, others blanched and old. But new or ancient, there must have been hundreds of them. Moreover, on the sides of the hill it was the same story, though there, for the most part, the bones had been gathered into gleaming heaps.

No wonder that the vultures loved Hloma Amabutu, the Place of Slaughter of the bloody Zulu king.

Of these horrible birds, however, at the moment not one was to be seen. As there had been no execution for a few hours they were seeking their food elsewhere. Now, for my own purposes, I wanted to see them, since otherwise my visit was in vain, and presently bethought myself of a method of securing their arrival.

"Hans," I said, "I am going to pretend to kill you, and then you must lie quite still out there like one dead. Even if the *aasvogels* settle on you, you must lie quite still, so that I may see whence they come and how they settle."

The Hottentot did not take at all kindly to this suggestion. Indeed, he flatly refused to obey me, giving sundry good reasons. He said that this kind of rehearsal was ill-omened ; that coming events have a way of casting their shadow before, and he did not wish to furnish the event. He said that the Zulus declared that the sacred *aasvogels* of Hloma Amabutu were as savage as lions, and that when once they saw a man down they would tear him to pieces, dead or living. In short, Hans and I came to an acute difference of opinion. As for every reason it was necessary that my view should prevail, however, I did not hesitate to put matters to him very plainly.

"Hans," I said, "you have to be a bait for vultures ; choose if you will be a live bait or a dead bait," and I cocked the rifle significantly, although, in truth, the last thing that I wished or intended to do was to shoot my faithful old Hottentot friend. But Hans, knowing all I had at stake, came to a different conclusion.

"Allemachte ! baas," he said, "I understand, and I do not blame you. Well, if I obey alive, perhaps my guardian Snake " (or spirit) " will protect me from the evil omen, and perhaps the *aasvogels* will not pick out my eyes. But if once you send a bullet through my stomach—why, then everything is finished, and for Hans it is ' Good night, sleep well.' I will obey you, baas, and lie where you wish, only, I pray you, do not forget me and go away, leaving me with those devil birds."

I promised him faithfully that I would not. Then we went through a very grim little pantomime. Proceeding to the centre of the arena-like space, I lifted the gun, and appeared to dash out Hans' brains with its butt. He fell upon his back, kicked about a little, and lay still. This finished Act 1.

Act 2 was that, capering like a brute of a Zulu executioner, I retired from my victim, and hid myself in a bush on the edge of the plateau at a distance of forty yards. After this there was a pause. The place was intensely bright with sunshine and intensely silent; as silent as the skeletons of the murdered men about me; as silent as Hans, who lay there looking so very small and dead in that big theatre where no grass grew. It was an eerie wait in such surroundings, but at length the curtain rang up for Act 3.

In the infinite arch of blue above me I perceived a speck no larger than a mote of dust. The *aasvogel* on watch up there far out of the range of man's vision had seen the deed, and, by sinking downwards, signalled it to his companions that were quartering the sky for fifty miles round; for these birds prey by sight, not by smell. Down he came and down, and long before he had reached the neighbourhood of earth specks appeared in the distant blue. Now he was not more than four or five hundred yards above me, and began to wheel, floating round the place upon his wide wings, and sinking as he wheeled. So he sank softly and slowly until he was about a hundred and fifty feet above Hans. Then suddenly he paused, hung quite steady for a few seconds, shut his wings and fell like a bolt, only opening them again just before he reached the earth.

Here he settled, tilting forward in that odd way which vultures have, and scrambling a few awkward paces until he gained his balance. Then he froze into immobility, gazing with an awful, stony glare at the prostrate Hans, who lay within about fifteen feet of him. Scarcely was this *aasvogel* down, when others, summoned from the depths of sky, did as he had done. They appeared, they sank, they wheeled, always from east to west, the way the sun travels. They hovered for a few seconds, then fell like stones, pitched on to their beaks, recovered themselves, waddled forward into line, and sat gazing at Hans. Soon there was a great ring of them about him, all immovable, all gazing, all waiting for something.

Presently that something appeared in the shape of an *aasvogel* which was nearly twice as big as any of the others. This was what the Boers and the natives call the " king vulture," one of which goes with every flock. He it is who rules the roost and also the carcase, which without his presence and permission none dare to attack. Whether this vile fowl is of a different species from the others, or whether he is a bird of more vigorous growth and constitution that has outgrown the rest and thus become their overlord, is more than I can tell. At least it is certain, as I can testify from long and constant observation, that almost every flock of vultures has its king.

When this particular royalty had arrived, the other *aasvogels*, of which perhaps there were now fifty or sixty gathered round Hans, began to show signs of interested animation. They looked at the king bird, they looked at Hans, stretching out their naked red necks and winking their brilliant eyes. I, however, did not pay particular attention to those upon the earth, being amply occupied in watching their fellows in the air.

With delight I observed that the vulture is a very conservative creature. They all did what doubtless they have done since the days of Adam or earlier—wheeled and then hung that little space of time before they dropped to the ground like lead. This, then, would be the moment at which to shoot them, when for four or five seconds they offered practically a sitting target. Now, at that distance, always under a hundred yards, I knew well that I could hit a tea plate every shot, and a vulture is much larger than a tea plate. So it seemed to me that, barring accidents, I had little to fear from the terrible trial of skill which lay before me. Again and again I covered the hovering birds with my rifle, feeling that if I had pressed the trigger I should have pierced them through.

Thinking it well to practise, I continued this game for a long while, till at last it came to an unexpected end. Suddenly I heard a scuffling sound. Dropping my glance, I saw that the whole mob of *aasvogels* were rushing in upon Hans, helping themselves forward by flapping their great wings, and that about three feet in front of them was their king. Next instant Hans vanished, and from the centre of that fluffy, stinking mass there arose a frightful yell.

As a matter of fact, as I found afterwards, the king vulture had fastened on to his snub nose, whilst its dreadful companions, having seized other portions of his frame, were beginning to hang back after their fashion in order to secure some chosen morsel. Hans kicked and screamed, and I rushed in shouting, causing them to rise in a great, flapping cloud that presently vanished this way and that. Within a minute they had all gone, and the Hottentot and I were left alone.

" That is good," I said. " You played well."

" Good ! baas," he answered, " and I with two cuts in my nose in which I can lay my finger, and bites all over me. Look how my trousers are torn. Look at my head—where is the hair? Look at my nose. Good ! Played well ! It is those *verdomde aasvogels* that played. Oh ! baas, if you had seen and smelt them, you would not say that it was good. See, one more second and I, who have two nostrils should have had four."

" Never mind, Hans," I said, " it is only a scratch, and I will make you a present of some new trousers. Also, here is tobacco for you. Come to the bush ; let us talk."

So we went, and when Hans was a little composed I told him all that I had observed about the habits of the *aasvogel* in the air, and he told me all that he had observed about their habits on the ground, which, as I might not shoot them sitting, did not interest me. Still, he agreed with me that the right moment to fire would be just before they pounced.

Whilst we were still talking we heard a sound of shouts, and, looking over the brow of the hill that faced towards Umgungund-hluvu, we saw a melancholy sight. Being driven up the slope towards us by three executioners and a guard of seven or eight soldiers, their hands tied behind their backs, were three men, one very old, one of about fifty years of age, and one a lad, who did not look more than eighteen. As I soon heard, they were of a single family, the grandfather, the father, and the eldest son, who had been seized upon some ridiculous charge of witchcraft, but really in order that the king might take their cattle.

Having been tried and condemned by the *Nyangas*, or witch-doctors, these poor wretches were now doomed to die. Indeed, not content with thus destroying the heads of the tribe, present and to come, for three generations, all their descendants and collaterals had already been wiped out by Dingaan, so that he might pose as sole heir to the family cattle.

Such were the dreadful cruelties that happened in Zululand in those days.

XIV

THE PLAY

THE doomed three were driven by their murderers into the centre of the depression, within a few yards of which Hans and I were standing.

After them came the head executioner, a great brute who wore a curiously shaped leopard-skin cap—I suppose as a badge of office—and held in his hand a heavy kerry, the shaft of which was scored with many notches, each of them representing a human life.

" See, White Man," he shouted, " here is the bait which the king sends to draw the holy birds to you. Had it not been that you needed such bait, perhaps these wizards would have escaped. But the Black One said the little Son of George, who is named Macumazahn, needs them that he may show his magic, and therefore they must die to-day."

Now, at this information I turned positively sick. Nor did it make me feel better when the youngest of the victims, hearing the executioner's words, flung himself upon his knees, and began to implore me to spare him. His grandfather also addressed me, saying :

" Chief, will it not be enough if I die ? I am old, and my life does not matter. Or if one is not sufficient, take me and my son, and let the lad, my grandson, go free. We are all of us innocent of any witchcraft, and he is not even old enough to practise such things, being but an unmarried boy. Chief, you, also, are young. Would not your heart be heavy if you had to be slain when the sun of your life was still new in the sky ? Think, White Chief, what your father would feel, if you have one, should he be forced to see you killed before his eyes, that some stranger might use your body to show his skill with a magic weapon by slaying the wild things that would eat it."

Now, almost with tears, I broke in, explaining to the venerable man as well as I could that their horrible fate had nothing to do with me. I told him that I was innocent of their blood, who was forced to be there to try to shoot vultures on the wing in order to save my white companions from a doom similar to their own. He listened attentively, asking a question now and again, and when he had mastered my meaning, said with a most dignified calmness :

" Now I understand, White Man, and am glad to learn that you are not cruel, as I thought. My children," he added, turning to the others, " let us trouble this *Inkoos* no more. He only does what he must do to save the lives of his brethren by his skill, if he can. If we continue to plead with him and stir his heart to pity, the sorrow swelling in it may cause his hand to shake, and then they will die also, and their blood be on his head and ours. My children, it is the king's will that we should be slain. Let us make ready to obey the king, as men of our House have always done. White lord, we thank you for your good words. May you live long, and may good fortune sleep in your hut to the end. May you shoot straight, also, with your magic tool, and thereby win the lives of your company out of the hand of the king. Farewell, *Inkoos*," and since he could not lift his bound hands in salutation, he bowed to me, as did the others.

Then they walked to a little distance, and, seating themselves on the ground, began to talk together, and after a while to drone some strange chant in unison. The executioners and the guards also sat down not far away, laughing, chatting, and passing a horn of snuff from hand to hand. Indeed, I observed that the captain of them even took some snuff to the victims, and held it in his palm beneath their noses, while they drew it up their nostrils and politely thanked him between the sneezes.

As for myself, I lit a pipe and smoked it, for I seemed to require a stimulant, or, rather, a sedative. Before it was finished Hans, who was engaged in doctoring his scratches made by the vultures' beaks with a concoction of leaves which he had been chewing, exclaimed suddenly in his matter-of-fact voice :

" See, baas, here they come, the white people on one side

and the black on the other, just like the goats and the sheep at Judgment Day in the Book."

I looked, and there to my right appeared the party of Boers, headed by the Vrouw Prinsloo, who held the remnants of an old umbrella over her head. To the left advanced a number of Zulu nobles and councillors, in front of whom waddled Dingaan arrayed in his bead dancing dress. He was supported by two stalwart body-servants, whilst a third held a shield over his head to protect him from the sun, and a fourth carried a large stool, upon which he was to sit. Behind each party, also, I perceived a number of Zulus in their war-dress, all of them armed with broad stabbing spears.

The two parties arrived at the stone upon which I was sitting almost simultaneously, as probably it had been arranged that they should do, and halted staring at each other. As for me, I sat still upon my stone and smoked on.

" Allemachte ! Allan," puffed the Vrouw Prinsloo, who was breathless with her walk up the hill, " so here you are ! As you did not come back, I thought you had run away and left us, like that stinkcat Pereira."

" Yes, *Tante* (aunt), here I am," I answered gloomily, " and I wish to heaven that I was somewhere else."

Just then Dingaan, having settled his great bulk upon the stool and recovered his breath, called to the lad Halstead, who was with him, and said :

" O Tho-maas, ask your brother, Macumazahn, if he is ready to try to shoot the vultures. If not, as I wish to be fair, I will give him a little more time to make his magic medicine."

I replied sulkily that I was as ready as I was ever likely to be.

Then the Vrouw Prinsloo, understanding that the king of the Zulus was before her, advanced upon him, waving her umbrella. Catching hold of Halstead, who understood Dutch, she forced him to translate an harangue, which she addressed to Dingaan.

Had he rendered it exactly as it came from her lips, we should all have been dead in five minutes, but, luckily, that unfortunate young man had learnt some of the guile of the serpent during his sojourn among the Zulus, and varied her vigorous phrases. The gist of her discourse was that he, Dingaan, was a black-

hearted and bloody-minded villain, with whom the Almighty
would come even sooner or later (as, indeed, He did), and that
if he dared to touch one hair of her or of her companions' heads,
the Boers, her countrymen, would prove themselves to be the
ministers of the Almighty in that matter (as, indeed, they did).
As translated by Halstead into Zulu, what she said was that
Dingaan was the greatest king in the whole world; in fact, that
there was not, and never had been, any such a king either in
power, wisdom, or personal beauty, and that if she and her
companions had to die, the sight of his glory, consoled them for
their deaths.

"Indeed," said Dingaan suspiciously, "if that is what this
man-woman says, her eyes tell one story and her lips another.
Oh! Tho-maas, lie no more. Speak the true words of the white
chieftainess, lest I should find them out otherwise, and give you
to the slayers."

Thus adjured, Halstead explained that he had not yet told all
the words. The "man-woman," who was, as he, Dingaan
supposed, a great chieftainess among the Dutch, added that if he,
the mighty and glorious king, the earth-shaker, the world-eater,
killed her or any of her subjects, her people would avenge her
by killing him and his people.

"Does she say that?" said Dingaan. "Then, as I thought,
these Boers are dangerous, and not the peaceful folk they make
themselves out to be," and he brooded for a while, staring at
the ground. Presently he lifted his head and went on : "Well,
a bet is a bet, and therefore I will not wipe out this handful, as
otherwise I would have done at once. Tell the old cow of a
chieftainess that, notwithstanding her threats, I stick to my
promise. If the little Son of George, Macumazahn, can shoot
three vultures out of five, by help of his magic, then she and her
servants shall go free. If not, the vultures which he has missed
shall feed on them, and afterwards I will talk with her people
when they come to avenge her. Now, enough of this *indaba*.
Bring those evildoers here that they may thank and praise me,
who give them so merciful an end."

So the grandfather, the father, and the son were hustled
before Dingaan by the soldiers, and greeted him with the royal
salute of *bayète*.

" O king," said the old man, " I and my children are innocent. Yet if it pleases you, O king, I am ready to die, and so is my son. Yet we pray you to spare the little one. He is but a boy, who may grow up to do you good service, as I have done to you and your House for many years."

" Be silent, you white-headed dog ! " answered Dingaan fiercely. " This lad is a wizard, like the rest of you, and would grow up to bewitch me and to plot with my enemies. Know that I have stamped out all your family, and shall I then leave him to breed another that would hate me ? Begone to the World of Spirits, and tell them how Dingaan deals with sorcerers."

The old man tried to speak again, for evidently he loved this grandchild of his, but a soldier struck him in the face, and Dingaan shouted :

" What ! Are you not satisfied ? I tell you that if you say more I will force you to kill the boy with your own hand. Take them away."

Then I turned and hid my face, as did all the white folk. Presently I heard the old man, whom they had saved to the last that he might witness the deaths of his descendants, cry in a loud voice :

" On the night of the thirtieth full moon from this day I, the far-sighted, I, the prophet, summon thee, Dingaan, to meet me and mine in the Land of Ghosts, and there to pay——"

Then with a roar of horror the executioners fell on him and he died. When there was silence I looked up, and saw that the king, who had turned a dirty yellow hue with fright, for he was very superstitious, was trembling and wiping the sweat from his brow.

" You should have kept the wizard alive," he said in a shaky voice to the head slayer, who was engaged in cutting three more nicks on the handle of his dreadful kerry. " Fool, I would have heard the rest of his lying message."

The man answered humbly that he thought it best it should remain unspoken, and got himself out of sight as soon as possible. Here I may remark that by an odd coincidence Dingaan actually was killed about thirty moons from that time. Mopo, his general, who slew his brother Chaka, slew him also with the help of Umslopogaas, the son of Chaka. In after years Umslopogaas told me the story of the dreadful ghost-haunted death of this tyrant, but, of course, he could not tell me exactly upon what day it happened. Therefore I do not know whether the prophecy was strictly accurate.*

The three victims lay dead in the hollow of the Hill of Death. Presently the king, recovering himself, gave orders that the spectators should be moved back to places where they could see what happened without frightening the vultures. So the Boers, attended by their band of soldiers, who were commanded to slay them at once if they attempted to escape, went one way, and Dingaan and his Zulus went the other, leaving Hans and myself alone behind our bush. As the white people passed me, Vrouw Prinsloo wished me good luck in a cheerful voice, although I could see that her poor old hand was shaking, and she was wiping her eyes with the *vatdoek*. Henri Marais, also in broken tones, implored me to shoot straight for his daughter's sake. Then came Marie, pale but resolute, who said nothing, but only looked me in the eyes, and touched the pocket of her dress, in which I knew the pistol lay hid. Of the rest of them I took no notice.

The moment, that dreadful moment of trial, had come at last; and oh! the suspense and the waiting were hard to bear. It seemed an age before the first speck, that I knew to be a vulture, appeared thousands of feet above me and began to descend in wide circles.

"Oh baas," said poor Hans, "this is worse than shooting at the geese in the Groote Kloof. Then you could only lose your horse, but now——"

"Be silent," I hissed, "and give me the rifle."

The vulture wheeled and sank, sank and wheeled. I glanced towards the Boers, and saw that they were all of them on their knees. I glanced towards the Zulus, and saw that they were watching as, I think, they had never watched anything before, for to them this was a new excitement. Then I fixed my eyes upon the bird.

Its last circle was accomplished. Before it pounced it hung on wide, outstretched wings, as the others had done, its head towards me. I drew a deep breath, lifted the rifle, got the fore-sight dead upon its breast, and touched the hair-trigger. As the

[1] For the history of the death of Dingaan, see the author's "Nada the Lily."

charge exploded I saw the *aasvogel* give a kind of backward twist. Next instant I heard a loud clap, and a surge of joy went through me, for I thought that the bullet had found its billet. But alas! it was not so.

The clap was that of the air disturbed by the passing of the ball and the striking of this air against the still feathers of the wings. Anyone who has shot at great birds on the wing with a bullet will be acquainted with the sound. Instead of falling, the vulture recovered itself. Not knowing the meaning of this unaccustomed noise, it dropped quietly to earth and sat down near the bodies, pitching forward in the natural way and running a few paces, as the others had done that afternoon. Evidently it was quite unhurt.

" Missed ! " gasped Hans as he grasped the rifle to load it. " Oh ! why did you not throw a stone on to the first heap ? "

I gave Hans a look that must have frightened him ; at any rate, he spoke no more. From the Boers went up a low groan. Then they began to pray harder than ever, while the Zulus clustered round the king and whispered to him. I learned afterwards that he was giving heavy odds against me, ten to one in cattle, which they were obliged to take, unwillingly enough.

Hans finished loading, capped and cocked the rifle, and handed it to me. By now other vultures were appearing. Being desperately anxious to get the thing over one way or another, at the proper moment I took the first of them. Again I covered it dead and pressed. Again as the gun exploded I saw that backward lurch of the bird, and heard the clap of the air upon its wings. Then—oh horror !—this *aasvogel* turned quietly, and began to mount the ladder of the sky in the same fashion as it had descended. I had missed once more.

" The second heap of stones has done this, baas," said Hans and this time I did not even look at him. I only sat down and buried my face in my hands. One more such miss, and then——

Hans began to whisper to me.

" Baas," he said, " those *aasvogels* see the flash of the gun, and shy at it like a horse. Baas, you are shooting into their faces, for they all hang with their beaks toward you before they drop. You must get behind them, and fire into their tails, for even an *aasvogel* cannot see with its tail."

I let fall my hands and stared at him. Surely the poor fellow had been inspired from on high! I understood it all now. While their beaks were towards me, I might fire at fifty vultures and never hit one, for each time they would swerve from the flash, causing the bullet to miss them, though but by a little.

" Come," I gasped, and began to walk quickly round the edge of the depression to a rock, which I saw opposite about a hundred yards away. My journey took me near the Zulus, who mocked me as I passed, asking where my magic was, and if I wished to see the white people killed presently. Dingaan was now offering odds of fifty cattle to one against me, but no one would take the bet even with the king.

I made no answer; no, not even when they asked me " if I had thrown down my spear and was running away." Grimly, despairingly, I marched on to the rock, and took shelter behind it with Hans. The Boers, I saw, were still upon their knees, but seemed to have ceased praying. The children were weeping; the men stared at each other; Vrouw Prinsloo had her arm about Marie's waist. Waiting there behind the rock, my courage returned to me, as it sometimes does in the last extremity. I remembered my dream and took comfort. Surely God would not be so cruel as to suffer me to fail and thereby bring all those poor people to their deaths.

Snatching the rifle from Hans, I loaded it myself; nothing must be trusted to another. As I put on the cap a vulture made its last circle. It hung in the air just as the others had done, and oh! its tail was towards me. I lifted, I aimed between the gathered-up legs, I pressed and shut my eyes, for I did not dare to look.

I heard the bullet strike, or seem to strike, and a few seconds later I heard something else—the noise of a heavy thud upon the ground. I looked, and there with outstretched wings lay the foul bird dead, stone dead, eight or ten paces from the bodies.

" Allemachte! that's better," said Hans. " You threw stones on to *all* the other heaps, didn't you, baas ? "

The Zulus grew excited, and the odds went down a little. The Boers stretched out their white faces and stared at me; I saw them out of the corner of my eye as I loaded again. Another vulture came; seeing one of its companions on the ground, if in a somewhat unnatural attitude, perhaps it thought that there could be nothing to fear. I leaned against my rock, aimed, and fired, almost carelessly, so sure was I of the result. This time I did not shut my eyes, but watched to see what happened.

The bullet struck the bird between its thighs, raked it from end to end, and down it came like a stone almost upon the top of its fellow.

" Good, good ! " said Hans with a guttural chuckle of delight. " Now, baas, make no mistake with the third, and ' *als sall recht kommen* ' (all shall be well)."

" Yes," I answered; " *if* I make no mistake with the third."

I loaded the rifle again myself, being very careful to ram down the powder well and to select a bullet that fitted perfectly true to the bore. Moreover, I cleaned the nipple with a thorn, and shook a little fine powder into it, so as to obviate any chance of a miss-fire. Then I set on the cap and waited. What was going on among the Boers or the Zulus I do not know. In this last crisis of all our fates I never looked, being too intent upon my own part in the drama.

By now the vultures appeared to have realised that something unusual was in progress, which threatened danger to them. At any rate, although by this time they had collected in hundreds from east, west, north, and south, and were wheeling the heavens above in their vast, majestic circles, none of them seemed to care to descend to prey upon the bodies. I watched, and saw that among their number was that great king bird which had bitten Hans in the face; it was easy to distinguish him, because he was so much larger than the others. Also, he had some white at the tips of his wings. I observed that certain of his company drew near to him in the skies, where they hung together in a knot, as though in consultation.

They separated out again, and the king began to descend, deputed probably to spy out the land. Down he came in ever-narrowing turns, till he reached the appointed spot for the plunge, and, according to the immemorial custom of these birds, hung a while before he pounced with his head to the south and his great, spreading tail towards me.

This was my chance, and, rejoicing in having so large a

mark, I got the sight upon him and pulled. The bullet thudded, some feathers floated from his belly, showing that it had gone home, and I looked to see him fall as the others had done. But alas! he did not fall. For a few seconds he rocked to and fro upon his great wings, then commenced to travel upwards in vast circles, which grew gradually more narrow, till he appeared to be flying almost straight into the empyrean. I stared and stared. Everybody stared, till that enormous bird became, first a mere blot upon the blue, and at length but a speck. Then it vanished altogether into regions far beyond the sight of man.

" Now there is an end," I said to Hans.

" *Ja*, baas," answered the Hottentot between his chattering teeth, " there is an end. You did not put in enough powder. Presently we shall all be dead."

" Not quite," I said with a bitter laugh. " Hans, load the rifle, load it quick. Before they die there shall be another king in Zululand."

" Good, good ! " he exclaimed as he loaded desperately. " Let us take that fat pig of a Dingaan with us. Shoot him in the stomach, baas ; shoot him in the stomach, so that he too may learn what it is to die slowly. Then cut my throat, here is my big knife, and afterwards cut your own, if you have not time to load the gun again and shoot yourself, which is easier."

I nodded, for it was in my mind to do these things. Never could I stand still and see those poor Boers killed, and I knew that Marie would look after herself.

Meanwhile, the Zulus were coming towards me, and the soldiers who had charge of them were driving up Marais's people, making pretence to thrust them through with their assegais, and shouting at them as men do at cattle. Both parties arrived in the depression at about the same time, but remained separated by a little space. In this space lay the corpses of the murdered men and the two dead *aasvogels*, with Hans and myself standing opposite to them.

" Well, little Son of George," puffed Dingaan, " you have lost your bet, for you did but kill two vultures out of five with your magic, which was good as far as it went, but not good enough. Now you must pay, as I would have paid had you won."

Then he stretched out his hand, and issued the dreadful

order of "*Bulala amalongu!*" (Kill the white people). "Kill them one by one, that I may see whether they know how to die, all except Macumazahn and the tall girl, whom I keep."

Some of the soldiers made a dash and seized the Vrouw Prinsloo, who was standing in front of the party.

"Wait a little, King," she called out as the assegais were lifted over her. "How do you know that the bet is lost? He whom you call Macumazahn hit that last vulture. It should be searched for before you kill us."

"What does the old woman say?" asked Dingaan, and Halstead translated slowly.

"True," said Dingaan. "Well, now I will send her to search for the vulture in the sky. Come back thence, Fat One, and tell us if you find it."

The soldiers lifted their assegais, waiting the king's word. I pretended to look at the ground, and cocked my rifle, being determined that if he spoke it, it should be his last. Hans stared upwards—I suppose to avoid the sight of death—then suddenly uttered a wild yell, which caused everyone, even the doomed people, to turn their eyes to him. He was pointing to the heavens, and they looked to see at what he pointed.

This was what they saw. Far, far above in that infinite sea of blue there appeared a tiny speck, which his sharp sight had already discerned, a speck that grew larger and larger as it descended with terrific and ever-growing speed.

It was the king vulture falling from the heavens—dead!

Down it came between the Vrouw Prinsloo and the slayers, smashing the lifted assegai of one of them and hurling him to the earth. Down it came, and lay there a mere mass of pulp and feathers.

"O Dingaan," I said in the midst of the intense silence that followed, "it seems that it is I who have won the bet, not you. I killed this king of birds, but being a king it chose to die high up and alone, that is all."

Dingaan hesitated, for he did not wish to spare the Boers, and I, noting his hesitation, lifted my rifle a little. Perhaps he saw it, or perhaps his sense of honour, as he understood the word, overcame his wish for their blood. At any rate, he said to one of his councillors:

"It was the king vulture falling from the heavens—
DEAD!" (*See page* 176)

" Search the carcase of that vulture and see if there is a bullet hole in it."

The man obeyed, feeling at the mass of broken bones and flesh. By good fortune he found, not the hole, for that was lost in the general destruction of the tissues, but the ball itself, which, having pierced the thick body from below upwards, had remained fast in the tough skin just by the backbone where the long, red neck emerges from between the wings. He picked it out, for it was only hanging in the skin, and held it up for all to see.

" Macumazahn has won his bet," said Dingaan. " His magic has conquered, though by but a very little. Macumazahn, take these Boers, they are yours, and begone with them out of my country."

XV

RETIEF ASKS A FAVOUR

Now and again during our troubled journey through life we reach little oases of almost perfect happiness, set jewel-like here and there in the thorny wilderness of time. Sometimes these are hours of mere animal content. In others they are made beautiful by waters flowing from our spiritual springs of being, as in those rare instances when the material veil of life seems to be rent by a mighty hand, and we feel the presence and the comfort of God within us and about us, guiding our footsteps to the ineffable end, which is Himself. Occasionally, however, all these, physical satisfaction and love divine and human are blended to a whole, like soul and body, and we can say, " Now I know what is joy."

Such an hour came to me on the evening of that day of the winning of my bet with Dingaan, when a dozen lives or so were set against my nerve and skill. These had not failed me, although I knew that had it not been for the inspiration of the Hottentot Hans (who sent it, I wonder ?) they would have been of no service at all. With all my thought and experience, it had never occurred to me that the wonderful eyes of the vultures would see the flash of the powder even through the pervading sunlight, and swerve before the deadly bullet could reach them.

On that night I was indeed a hero in a small way. Even Henri Marais thawed and spoke to me as a father might to his child, he who always disliked me in secret, partly because I was an Englishman, partly because I was everything to his daughter and he was jealous, and partly for the reason that I stood in the path of his nephew, Hernan Pereira, whom he either loved or feared, or both. As for the rest of them, men, women and children, they thanked and blessed me with tears in their eyes, vowing that, young as I was, thenceforth I and no other should be their leader. As may be imagined, although it is true that she set down my success to her meal of bullock's liver and the nap which she had insisted on my taking, the Vrouw Prinsloo was the most enthusiastic of them all.

"Look at him," she said, pointing with her fat finger at my insignificant self and addressing her family. "If only I had such a husband or a son, instead of you lumps that God has tied to me like clogs to the heels of a she-ass, I should be happy."

"God did that in order to prevent you from kicking, old vrouw," said her husband, a quiet man with a vein of sardonic humour. "If only He had tied another clog to your tongue, I should be happy also"; whereon the vrouw smacked his head and her children got out of the way sniggering.

But the most blessed thing of all was my interview with Marie. All that took place between us can best be left to the imagination, since the talk of lovers, even in such circumstances, is not interesting to others. Also, in a sense, it is too sacred to repeat. One sentence I will set down, however, because in the light of after events I feel that it was prophetic, and not spoken merely by chance. It was at the end of our talk, as she was handing me back the pistol that I had given her for a certain dreadful purpose.

"Three times you have saved my life, Allan—once at Marais-fontein, once from starvation, and now from Dingaan, whose touch would have meant my death. I wonder whether it will ever be my turn to save yours?"

She looked down for a little while, then lifted her head and laid her hand upon my shoulder, adding slowly: "Do you

know, Allan, I think that it will at the——" and suddenly she
turned and left me with her sentence unfinished.

So thus it came about that by the help of Providence I was
enabled to rescue all these worthy folk from a miserable and a
bloody death. And yet I have often reflected since that if things
had gone differently; if, for instance, that king *aasvogel* had
found strength to carry itself away to die at a distance instead of
soaring straight upwards like a towering partridge, as birds
injured in the lungs will often do—I suppose in search of air—
it might have been better in the end. Then I should certainly have
shot Dingaan dead and every one of us would as certainly have
been killed on the spot. But if Dingaan had died that day, Retief
and his companions would never have been massacred. Also
as the peaceful Panda, his brother, would, I suppose, have
succeeded to the throne, probably the subsequent slaughter at
Weenen, and all the after fighting, would never have taken
place. But so it was fated, and who am I that I should quarrel
with or even question the decrees of fate? Doubtless these
things were doomed to happen, and they happened in due
course. There is nothing more to be said.

Early on the following morning we collected our oxen, which,
although still footsore, were now full fed and somewhat rested.
An hour or two later began our trek, word having come to us
from Dingaan that we must start at once. Also he sent us guides,
under the command of the captain Kambula, to show us the road
to Natal.

I breakfasted that day with the Reverend Mr. Owen and his
people, my object being to persuade him to come away with us,
as I did not consider that Zululand was a safe place for white
women and children. My mission proved fruitless. Mrs. Hulley,
the wife of the absent interpreter, who had three little ones,
Miss Owen and the servant, Jane Williams, were all of them
anxious enough to do as I suggested. But Mr. and Mrs. Owen,
who were filled with the true fervour of missionaries, would
not listen. They said that God would protect them; that they
had only been a few weeks in the country, and that it would be
the act of cowards and of traitors to fly at the very beginning of
their work. Here I may add that after the massacre of Retief

they changed their opinion, small blame to them, and fled as fast as anyone else.

I told Mr. Owen how very close I had gone to shooting Dingaan, in which event they might all have been killed with us. This news shocked him much. Indeed he lectured me severely on the sins of bloodthirstiness and a desire for revenge. So, finding that we looked at things differently, and that it was of no use wasting breath in argument, I wished him and his people good-bye and good fortune and went upon my way, little guessing how we should meet again.

An hour later we trekked. Passing by the accursed hill, Hloma Amabutu, where I saw some gorged vultures sleeping on the rocks, we came to the gate of the Great Kraal. Here, to my surprise, I saw Dingaan with some of his councillors and an armed guard of over a hundred men, seated under the shade of two big milk trees. Fearing treachery, I halted the wagons and advised the Boers to load their rifles and be ready for the worst. A minute or so later young Thomas Halstead arrived and told me that Dingaan wished to speak with us. I asked him if that meant that we were to be killed. He answered, " No, you are quite safe." The king had received some news that had put him in a good humour with the white people, and he desired to bid us farewell, that was all.

So we trekked boldly to where Dingaan was, and, stopping the wagons, went up to him in a body. He greeted us kindly enough, and even gave me his fat hand to shake.

" Macumazahn," he said, " although it has cost me many oxen, I am glad that your magic prevailed yesterday. Had it not done so I should have killed all these your friends, which would have been a cause of war between me and the Amaboona. Now, this morning I have learned that these Amaboona are sending a friendly embassy to me under one of their great chiefs, and I think that you will meet them on the road. I charge you, therefore, to tell them to come on, having no fear, as I will receive them well and listen to all they have to say."

I answered that I would do so.

" Good," he replied. " I am sending twelve head of cattle with you, six of them for your food during your journey, and six as a present to the embassy of the Amaboona. Also Kambula, my captain, has charge to see you safely over the Tugela River."

I thanked him and turned to go, when suddenly his eye fell upon Marie, who, foolishly enough, took this opportunity to advance from among the others and speak to me about something—I forget what.

" Macumazahn, is that the maiden of whom you spoke to me ? " asked Dingaan ; " she whom you are going to marry ? "

I answered " Yes."

" By the head of the Black One," he exclaimed, " she is very fair. Will you not make a present of her to me, Macumazahn ? "

I answered, " No ; she is not mine to give away."

" Well, then, Macumazahn, I will pay you a hundred head of cattle for her, which is the price of a royal wife, and give you ten of the fairest girls in Zululand in exchange."

I answered that it could not be.

Now the king began to grow angry.

" I will keep her, whether you wish it or no," he said.

" Then you will keep her dead, O Dingaan," I replied, " for there is more of that magic which slew the vultures."

Of course, I meant that Marie would be dead. But as my knowledge of the Zulu tongue was imperfect, he understood the words to mean that *he* would be dead, and I think they frightened him. At any rate, he said :

" Well, I promised you all safe-conduct if you won your bet, so *hamba gachlé* (go in peace). I wish to have no quarrel with the white folk, but, Macumazahn, you are the first of them who has refused a gift to Dingaan. Still, I bear you no grudge, and if you choose to come back again, you will be welcome, for I perceive that, although so small, you are very clever and have a will of your own ; also that you mean what you say and speak the truth. Tell the People of George that my heart is soft towards them." Then he turned and walked away through the gates of the kraal.

Glad enough was I to see the last of him, for now I knew that we were safe, except from such accidents as may overtake any travellers through a wild country. For the present, at any rate until after he had seen this embassy, Dingaan wished to stand well with the Boers. Therefore it was obvious that he would never make an irreparable quarrel with them by treacherously putting us to death, as we trekked through his country. Being sure of this, we went on our way with light hearts, thanking Heaven for the mercies which had been shown to us.

It was on the third day of our trek, when we were drawing near to the Tugela, that we met the Boer embassy, off-saddled by a little stream where we proposed to outspan to rest the oxen while we ate our midday meal. They were sleeping in the heat of the day and saw nothing of us till we were right on to them, when, catching sight of our Zulu advance guard, they sprang up and ran for their rifles. Then the wagons emerged from the bush, and they stared astonished, wondering who could be trekking in that country.

We called to them in Dutch not to be afraid and in another minute we were among them. While we were yet some way off my eye fell upon a burly, white-bearded man whose figure seemed to be familiar to me, and towards him I went, taking no heed of the others, of whom there may have been six or seven. Soon I was sure, and advancing with outstretched hand, said :

" Good day, Mynheer Piet Retief. Who would have thought that we who parted so far away and so long ago would live to meet among the Zulus ? "

He stared at me.

" Who is it ? Who is it ? Allemachte ! I know now. The little Englishman, Allan Quatermain, who shot the geese down in the Old Colony. Well, I should not be surprised, for the man you beat in that match told me that you were travelling in these parts. Only I understood him to say that the Zulus had killed you."

" If you mean Hernan Pereira," I answered, " where did you meet him ? "

" Why, down by the Tugela there, in a bad way. However, he can tell you all about that himself, for I have brought him with me to show us the path to Dingaan's kraal. Where is Pereira ? Send Pereira here. I want to speak with him."

" Here I am," answered a sleepy voice, the hated voice of Pereira himself, from the other side of a thick bush, where he had been slumbering. " What is it, commandant ? I come," and he emerged, stretching himself and yawning, just as the remainder of my party came up. He caught sight of Henri Marais first of all, and began to greet him, saying : " Thank God, my uncle, you are safe ! "

Then his eyes fell on me, and I do not think I ever saw a man's face change more completely. His jaw dropped, the colour left his cheeks, leaving them of the yellow which is common to persons of Portuguese descent ; his outstretched hand fell to his side.

" Allan Quatermain ! " he ejaculated. " Why, I thought that you were dead."

" As I should have been, Mynheer Pereira, twice over if you could have had your way," I replied.

" What do you mean, Allan ? " broke in Retief.

" I will tell you what he means," exclaimed the Vrouw Prinsloo, shaking her fat fist at Pereira. " That yellow dog means that twice he has tried to murder Allan—Allan, who saved his life and ours. Once he shot at him in a kloof and grazed his cheek ; look, there is the scar of it. And once he plotted with the Zulus to slaughter him, telling Dingaan that he was an evildoer and a wizard, who would bring a curse upon his land."

Now Retief looked at Pereira.

" What do you say to this ? " he asked.

" What do I say ? " repeated Pereira, recovering himself. " Why, that it is a lie or a misunderstanding. I never shot at Heer Allan in any kloof. Is it likely that I should have done so when he had just nursed me back to life ? I never plotted with the Zulus for his death, which would have meant the deaths of my uncle and my cousin and of all their companions. Am I mad that I should do such a thing ? "

" Not mad, but bad," screamed the vrouw. " I tell you, Heer Retief, it is no lie. Ask those with me," she added, appealing to the others, who, with the exception of Marais, answered as with one voice :

" No ; it is no lie."

" Silence ! " said the commandant. " Now, nephew Allan, tell us your story."

So I told him everything, of course, leaving out all details. Even then the tale was long, though it did not seem to be one that wearied my hearers.

"Allemachte!" said Retief when I had finished, "this is a strange story, the strangest that ever I heard. If it is true, Hernan Pereira, you deserve to have your back set against a tree and to be shot."

"God in heaven!" he answered, "am I to be condemned on such a tale—I, an innocent man? Where is the evidence? This Englishman tells all this against me for a simple reason—that he has robbed me of the love of my cousin, to whom I was affianced. Where are his witnesses?"

"As to the shooting at me in the kloof, I have none except God who saw you," I answered. "As to the plot that you laid against me among the Zulus, as it chances, however, there is one, Kambula, the captain who was sent to take me as you had arranged, and who now commands our escort."

"A savage!" exclaimed Pereira. "Is the tale of a savage to be taken against that of a white man? Also, who will translate his story? You, Mynheer Quatermain, are the only one here who knows his tongue, if you do know it, and you are my accuser."

"That is true," remarked Retief. "Such a witness should not be admitted without a sworn interpreter. Now listen; I pass judgment as commandant in the field. Hernan Pereira, I have known you to be a rogue in the past, for I remember that you cheated this very young man, Allan Quatermain, at a friendly trial of skill at which I was present; but since then till now I have heard nothing more of you, good or bad. To-day this Allan Quatermain and a number of my own countrymen bring grave charges against you, which, however, at present are not capable of proof or disproof. Well, I cannot decide those charges, whatever my own opinion may be. I think that you had better go back with your uncle, Henri Marais, to the trek-Boers, where they can be laid before a court and settled according to law."

"If so, he will go back alone," said the Vrouw Prinsloo. "He will not go back with us, for we will elect a field-cornet and shoot him—the stinkcat, who left us to starve and afterwards tried to kill little Allan Quatermain, who saved our lives"; and the chorus behind her echoed:

"*Ja, ja*, we will shoot him."

"Hernan Pereira," said Retief, rubbing his broad forehead,

"I don't quite know why it is, but no one seems to want you as a companion. Indeed, to speak truth, I don't myself. Still, I think you would be safer with me than with these others whom you seem to have offended. Therefore, I suggest that you come on with us. But listen here, man," he added sternly, " if I find you plotting against us among the Zulus, that hour you are dead. Do you understand ? "

" I understand that I am one slandered," replied Pereira. " Still, it is Christian to submit to injuries, and therefore I will do as you wish. As to these bearers of false witness, I leave them to God."

" And I leave you to the devil," shouted Vrouw Prinsloo, " who will certainly have you soon or late. Get out of my sight, stinkcat, or I will pull your hair off." And she rushed at him, flapping her dreadful *vatdoek*—which she produced from some recess in her raiment—in his face, driving him away as though he were a noxious insect.

Well, he went I know not where, and so strong was public opinion against him that I do not think that even his uncle, Henri Marais, sought him out to console him.

When Pereira was gone, our party and that of Retief fell into talk, and we had much to tell. Especially was the commandant interested in the story of my bet with Dingaan, whereby I saved the lives of all my companions by shooting the vultures.

" It was not for nothing, nephew, that God Almighty gave you the power of holding a gun so straight," said Retief to me when he understood the matter. " I remember that when you killed those wildfowl in the Groote Kloof with bullets, which no other man could have done, I wondered why you should have such a gift above all the rest of us, who have practised for so many more years. Well, now I understand. God Almighty is no fool ; He knows His business. I wish you were coming back with me to Dingaan ; but as that tainted man, Hernan Pereira, is of my company, perhaps it is better that you should stay away. Tell me, now, about this Dingaan ; does he mean to kill us ? "

" Not this time, I think, uncle," I answered ; " because, first he wishes to learn all about the Boers. Still, do not trust him too far just because he speaks you softly. Remember, that if I had missed the third vulture, we should all have been dead by now. And, if you are wise, keep an eye upon Hernan Pereira."

" These things I will do, nephew, especially the last of them ; and now we must be getting on. Stay ; come here, Henri Marais ; I have a word to say to you. I understand that this little Englishman, Allan Quatermain, who is worth ten bigger men, loves your daughter, whose life he has saved again and again, and that she loves him. Why, then, do you not let them marry in a decent fashion ? "

" Because before God I have sworn her to another man— to my nephew, Hernan Pereira, whom every one slanders," answered Marais sulkily. " Until she is of age that oath holds."

" Oho ! " said Retief, " you have sworn your lamb to that hyena, have you ? Well, look out, that he does not crack your bones as well as hers, and perhaps some others also. Why does God give some men a worm in their brains, as He does to the *wildebeeste*, a worm that always makes them run the wrong way ? I don't know, I am sure ; but you who are very religious, Henri Marais, might think the matter over and tell me the answer when next we meet. Well, this girl of yours will soon be of age, and then, as I am commandant down yonder where she is going, I'll see she marries the man she wants, whatever you say, Henri Marais. Heaven above us ! I only wish it were my daughter he was in love with. A fellow who can shoot to such good purpose might have the lot of them " ; and uttering one of his great, hearty laughs, he walked off to his horse.

On the morrow of this meeting we forded the Tugela and entered the territory that is now called Natal. Two days' short trekking through a beautiful country brought us to some hills that I think were called Pakadi, or else a chief named Pakadi lived there, I forget which. Crossing these hills, on the further side of them, as Retief had told us we should do, we found a large party of the trek-Boers, who were already occupying this land on the hither side of the Bushman River, little knowing, poor people, that it was fated to become the grave of many of them. To-day, and for all future time, that district is and will be known by the name of Weenen, or the Place of Weeping, because of those pioneers who here were massacred by Dingaan within a few weeks of the time of which I write.

Nice as the land was, for some reason or other it did not quite suit my fancy, and therefore, in view of my approaching marriage with Marie, having purchased a horse from one of the trek-Boers, I began to explore the country round. My object was to find a stretch of fertile veld where we could settle when we were wedded, and such a spot I discovered after some trouble. It lay about thirty miles away to the east, in the loop of a beautiful stream that is now known as the Mooi River.

Enclosed in this loop were some thirty thousand acres of very rich, low-lying soil, almost treeless and clothed with luxuriant grasses where game was extraordinarily numerous. At the head of it rose a flat-topped hill, from the crest of which, oddly enough, flowed a plentiful stream of water fed by a strong spring. Half-way down this hill, facing to the east, and irrigable by the stream, was a plateau several acres in extent, which furnished about the best site for a house that I know in all South Africa. Here I determined we would build our dwelling-place and become rich by the breeding up of great herds of cattle. I should explain that this ground, which once, as the remains of their old kraals showed, had belonged to a Kaffir tribe killed out by Chaka, the Zulu king, was to be had for the taking.

Indeed, as there was more land than we could possibly occupy, I persuaded Henri Marais, the Prinsloos and the Meyers, with whom I had trekked from Delagoa, to visit it with me. When they had seen it they agreed to make it their home in the future, but meanwhile elected to return to the other Boers for safety's sake. So with the help of some Kaffirs, of whom there were a few in the district, remnants of those tribes which Chaka had destroyed, I pegged out an estate of about twelve thousand acres for myself, and, selecting a site, set the natives to work to build a rough mud house upon it which would serve as a temporary dwelling. I should add that the Prinsloos and the Meyers also made arrangements for the building of similar shelters almost alongside of my own. This done, I returned to Marie and the trek-Boers.

On the morning after my return to the camp Piet Retief

appeared there with his five or six companions. I asked him how he had got on with Dingaan.

"Well enough, nephew," he answered. "At first the king was somewhat angry, saying that we Boers had stolen six hundred head of his cattle. But I showed him that it was the chief, Sikonyela, who lives yonder on the Caledon River, who had dressed up his people in white men's clothes and put them upon horses, and afterwards drove the cattle through one of our camps to make it appear that we were the thieves. Then he asked me what was my object in visiting him. I answered that I sought a grant of the land south of the Tugela to the sea.

"'Bring me back the cattle that you say Sikonyela has stolen,' he said, 'and we will talk about this land.' To this I agreed and soon after left the kraal."

"What did you do with Hernan Pereira, uncle?" I asked.

"This Allan. When I was at Umgungundhlovu I sought out the truth of that story you told me as to his having made a plot to get you killed by the Zulus on the ground that you were a wizard."

"And what did you discover, uncle?"

"I discovered that it was true, for Dingaan told me so himself. Then I sent for Pereira and ordered him out of my camp, telling him that if he came back among the Boers I would have him put on his trial for attempted murder. He said nothing, but went away."

"Whither did he go?"

"To a place that Dingaan gave him just outside his kraal. The king said that he would be useful to him, as he could mend guns and teach his soldiers to shoot with them. So there, I suppose, he remains, unless he has thought it wiser to make off. At any rate, I am sure that he will not come here to trouble you or anyone."

"No, uncle, but he may trouble you *there*," I said doubtfully.

"What do you mean, Allan?"

"I don't quite know, but he is black-hearted, a traitor by nature, and in one way or the other he will stir up sorrow. Do you think that he will love you, for instance, after you have hunted him out like a thief?"

Retief shrugged his shoulders and laughed as he answered:

"I will take my chance of that. What is the use of troubling

one's head about such a snake of a man? And now, Allan, I
have something to ask you. Are you married yet?"

"No, uncle, nor can be for another five weeks, when Marie
comes of age. Her father still holds that his oath binds him, and
I have promised that I will not take her till then."

"Does he indeed, Allan? I think that Henri Marais is
'*kransick*' (that is, cracked), or else his cursed nephew, Hernan,
has fascinated him, as a snake does a bird. Still, I suppose that
he has the law on his side, and, as I am commandant, I cannot
advise anyone to break the law. Now listen. It is no use your
staying here looking at the ripe peach you may not pluck, for
that only makes the stomach sick. Therefore the best thing that
you can do is to come with me to get those cattle from Sikonyela,
for I shall be very glad of your company. Afterwards, too, I
want you to return with me to Zululand when I go for the grant
of all this country."

"But how about my getting married?" I asked in dismay.

"Oh! I dare say you will be able to marry before we start.
Or if not, it must be when we return. Listen now; do not
disappoint me in this matter, Allan. None of us can speak Zulu
except you, who take to these savage languages like a duck to
water, and I want you to be my interpreter with Dingaan.
Also the king specially asked that you should come with me when
I brought the cattle, as he seems to have taken a great fancy to
you. He said that you would render his words honestly, but that
he did not trust the lad whom he has there to translate into
Dutch and English. So you see it will help me very much in
this big business if you come with me."

Still I hesitated, for some fear of the future lay heavy on my
heart, warning me against this expedition.

"Allemachte!" said Retief angrily, "if you will not grant
me a favour, let it be. Or is it that you want reward? If so, all
I can promise you is twenty thousand acres of the best land in
the country when we get it."

"No, Mynheer Retief," I replied; "it is no question of
reward; and as for the land, I have already pegged out my
farm on a river about thirty miles to the east. It is that I do not
like to leave Marie alone, fearing lest her father should play
some trick on me as regards her and Hernan Pereira."   •

" Oh, if that is all you are afraid of, Allan, I can soon settle matters ; for I will give orders to the Predicant Celliers that he is not to marry Marie Marais to anyone except yourself, even if she asks him. Also I will order that if Hernan Pereira should come to the camp, he is to be shut up until I return to try him. Lastly, as commandant, I will name Henri Marais as one of those who are to accompany us, so that he will be able to plot nothing against you. Now are you satisfied ? "

I said " Yes " as cheerfully as I could, though I felt anything but cheerful, and we parted, for, of course, the Commandant Retief had much to occupy him.

Then I went and told Marie what I had promised. Somewhat to my surprise she said that she thought I had acted wisely.

" If you stayed here," she added, " perhaps some new quarrel would arise between you and my father which might make bitterness afterwards. Also, dear, it would be foolish for you to offend the Commandant Retief, who will be the great man in this country, and who is very fond of you. After all, Allan, we shall only be separated for a little while, and when that is done we have the rest of our lives to spend together. As for me, do not be afraid, for you know I will never marry anyone but you—no, not to save myself from death."

So I left her somewhat comforted, knowing how sound was her judgment, and went off to make my preparations for the expedition to Sikonyela's country.

All this conversation with Retief I have set down in full, as nearly as I can remember it, because of its fateful consequences. Ah ! if I could have foreseen ; if only I could have foreseen !

XVI

THE COUNCIL

Two days later we started to recover Dingaan's cattle, sixty or seventy of us, all well armed and mounted. With us went two of Dingaan's captains and a number of Zulus, perhaps a hundred, who were to drive the cattle if we recovered them. As I could speak their language, I was more or less in command of this Zulu contingent, and managed to make myself very useful in that capacity. Also, during the month or so of our absence, by continually conversing with them, I perfected myself considerably in my knowledge of their beautiful but difficult tongue.

Now it is not my intention to write down the details of this expedition, during which there was no fighting and nothing serious happened. We arrived in due course at Sikonyela's and stated our errand. When he saw how numerous and well-armed we were, and that behind us was all the might of the Zulu army, that wily old rascal thought it well to surrender the stolen cattle without further to do, and with these some horses which he had lifted from the Boers. So, having received them, we delivered them over to the Zulu captains, with instructions to drive them carefully to Umgungundhlovu. The commandant sent a message by these men to the effect that, having fulfilled his part of the compact, he would wait upon Dingaan as soon as possible in order to conclude the treaty about the land.

This business finished, Retief took me and a number of the Boers to visit other bodies of the emigrant Dutch who were beyond the Drakensberg, in what is now the Transvaal territory. This occupied a long time, as these Boers were widely scattered, and at each camp we had to stop for several days while Retief explained everything to its leaders. Also he arranged with them to come down into Natal, so as to be ready to people it as soon as he received the formal cession of the country from Dingaan. Indeed, most of them began to trek at once, although jealousies between the various commandants caused some of the bands, luckily for themselves, to remain on the farther side of the mountains.

At length, everything being settled, we rode away, and reached the Bushman's River camp on a certain Saturday afternoon. Here, to my joy, we found all well. Nothing had been heard of Hernan Pereira, while the Zulus, if we might judge from messengers who came to us, seemed to be friendly. Marie, also, had now quite recovered from the fears and hardships which she had undergone. Never had I seen her look so sweet and beautiful as she did when she greeted me, arrayed no longer in rags, but in a simple yet charming dress made of some stuff that she had managed to buy from a trader who came up to the camp from Durban. Moreover, I think that there was another reason for the change, since the light of dawning happiness shone in her deep eyes.

The day, as I have said, was Saturday, and on the Monday she would come of age and be free to dispose of herself in marriage, for on that day lapsed the promise which we had given to her father. But, alas! by a cursed perversity of fate, on this very Monday at noon the Commandant Retief had arranged to ride into Zululand on his second visit to Dingaan, and with Retief I was in honour bound to go.

"Marie," I said, "will not your father soften towards us and let us be married to-morrow, so that we may have a few hours together before we part?"

"I do not know, my dear," she answered, blushing, "since about this matter he is very strange and obstinate. Do you know that all the time you were absent he never mentioned your name, and if anyone else spoke it he would get up and go away!"

"That's bad," I said. "Still, if you are willing, we might try."

"Indeed and indeed, Allan, I am willing, who am sick of being so near to you and yet so far. But how shall we do so?"

"I think that we will ask the Commandant Retief and the Vrouw Prinsloo to plead for us, Marie. Let us go and seek them."

She nodded, and hand in hand we walked through the Boers, who nudged each other and laughed at us as we passed to where the old vrouw was seated on a stool by her wagon drinking coffee. I remember that her *vatdoek* was spread over her knees, for she also had a new dress, which she was afraid of staining.

"Well, my dears," she said in her loud voice, "are you married already that you hang so close together?"

"No, my aunt," I answered; "but we want to be, and have come to you to help us."

"That I will do with all my heart, though to speak truth, young people, at your age, as things are, I should have been inclined to help myself, as I have told you before. Heaven above us! what is it that makes marriage in the sight of God? It is that male and female should declare themselves man and wife before all folk, and live as such. The pastor and his mumblings are very well if you can get them, but it is the giving of the hand, not the setting of the ring upon it; it is the vowing of two true hearts, and not words read out of a book, that make marriage. Still, this is bold talk, for which any reverend predicant would reprove me, for if young folk acted on it, although the tie might hold good in law, what would become of his fee? Come, let us seek the commandant and hear what he has to say. Allan, pull me up off this stool, where, if I had my way, after so much travelling, I should like to sit while a house was built over my head, and for the rest of my life."

I obeyed, not without difficulty, and we went to find Retief.

At the moment he was standing alone, watching two wagons that had just trekked away. These contained his wife with other members of his family, and some friends whom he was sending, under the charge of the Heer Smit, to a place called Doornkop, that lay at a distance of fifteen miles or more. At this Doornkop he had already caused a rough house, or rather shed, to be built for the Vrouw Retief's occupation, thinking that she would be more comfortable and perhaps safer there during his absence than at the crowded camp in a wagon.

"Allemachte! Allan," he said, catching sight of me, "my heart is sore; I do not know why. I tell you that when I kissed my old woman good-bye just now I felt as though I should never see her again, and the tears came into my eyes. I wish we were all safe back from Dingaan. But there, there, I will try to get over to see her to-morrow, as we don't start till Monday. What is it that you want, Allan, with that *mooi mesje* of yours?"— and he pointed to the tall Marie.

"What would any man want with such a one, save to marry her?" broke in the Vrouw Prinsloo. "Now, commandant, listen while I set out the tale."

"All right, aunt, only be brief, for I have no time to spare." She obeyed, but I cannot say that she was brief.

When at last the old lady paused, breathless, Retief said:

"I understand everything; there is no need for you young people to talk. Now we will go and see Henri Marais, and if he is not madder than usual, make him listen to reason."

So we walked to where Marais's wagon stood at the end of the line, and found him sitting on the *disselboom* cutting up tobacco with his pocket-knife.

"Good-day, Allan," he said, for we had not met since my return. "Have you had a nice journey?"

I was about to answer when the commandant broke in impatiently:

"See here, see here, Henri, we have not come to talk about Allan's journey, but about his marriage, which is more important. He rides with me to Zululand on Monday, as you do, and wants to wed your daughter to-morrow, which is Sunday, a good day for the deed."

"It is a day to pray, not to give and be given in marriage," commented Marais sulkily. "Moreover, Marie does not come of age before Monday, and until then the oath that I made to God holds."

"My *vatdoek* for your oath!" exclaimed the vrouw, flapping that awful rag in his face. "How much do you suppose that God cares what you in your folly swore to that stinkcat of a nephew of yours? Do you be careful, Henri Marais, that God does not make of your precious oath a stone to fall upon your head and break it like a peanut shell."

"Hold your chattering tongue, old woman," said Marais furiously. "Am I to be taught my duty to my conscience and my daughter by you?"

"Certainly you are, if you cannot teach them to yourself," began the vrouw, setting her hands upon her hips.

But Retief pushed her aside, saying:

"No quarrelling here. Now, Henri Marais, your conduct about these two young people who love each other is a scandal. Will you let them be married to-morrow or not?"

"No, commandant, I will not. By the law I have power over my daughter till she is of age, and I refuse to allow her to marry a cursed Englishman. Moreover, the Predicant Celliers is away, so there is none to marry them."

"You speak strange words, Mynheer Marais," said Retief quietly, "especially when I remember all that this 'cursed Englishman' has done for you and yours, for I have heard every bit of that story, though not from him. Now hearken. You have appealed to the law, and, as commandant, I must allow your appeal. But after twelve o'clock to-morrow night, according to your own showing, the law ceases to bind your daughter. Therefore, on Monday morning, if there is no clergyman in the camp and these two wish it, I, as commandant, will marry them before all men, as I have the power to do."

Then Marais broke into one of those raving fits of temper which were constitutional in him, and to my mind showed that he was never quite sane. Oddly enough, it was on poor Marie that he concentrated his wrath. He cursed her horribly because she had withstood his will and refused to marry Hernan Pereira. He prayed that evil might fall on her; that she might never bear a child, and that if she did, it might die, and other things too unpleasant to mention.

We stared at him astonished, though I think that had he been any other man than the father of my betrothed, I should have struck him. Retief, I noticed, lifted his hand to do so, then let it fall again, muttering: "Let be; he is possessed with a devil."

At last Marais ceased, not, I think, from lack of words, but because he was exhausted, and stood before us, his tall form quivering, and his thin, nervous face working like that of a person in convulsions. Then Marie, who had drooped her head beneath this storm, lifted it, and I saw that her deep eyes were all ablaze and that she was very white.

"You are my father," she said in a low voice, "and therefore I must submit to whatever you choose to say to me. Moreover, I think it likely that the evil which you call down will fall upon me, since Satan is always at hand to fulfil his own wishes. But if so, my father, I am sure that this evil will recoil upon your own head, not only here, but hereafter. There justice will be done to both of us, perhaps before very long, and also to your nephew, Hernan Pereira."

Marais made no answer; his rage seemed to have spent itself. He only sat himself again upon the *disselboom* of the wagon and went on cutting up the tobacco viciously, as though he were slicing the heart of a foe. Even the Vrouw Prinsloo was silent and stared at him whilst she fanned herself with the *vatdoek*. But Retief spoke.

" I wonder if you are mad, or only wicked, Henri Marais,"
he said. " To curse your own sweet girl like this you must be
one or the other—a single child who has always been good to
you. Well, as you are to ride with me on Monday, I pray that
you will keep your temper under control, lest it should bring
us into trouble, and you also. As for you, Marie, my dear, do
not fret because a wild beast has tried to toss you with his horns,
although he happens to be your father. On Monday morning
you pass out of his power into your own, and on that day I will
marry you to Allan Quatermain here. Meanwhile, I think you
are safest away from this father of yours, who might take to
cutting your throat instead of that tobacco. Vrouw Prinsloo,
be so good as to look after Marie Marais, and on Monday
morning next bring her before me to be wed. Until then, Henri
Marais, I, as commandant, shall set a guard over you, with
orders to seize you if it should be necessary. Now I advise you
to take a walk, and when you are calm again, to pray God to
forgive you your wicked words, lest they should be fulfilled
and drag you down to judgment."

Then we all went, leaving Henri Marais still cutting up his
tobacco on the *disselboom*.

On the Sunday I met Marais walking about the camp, followed
by the guard whom Retief had set over him. To my surprise
he greeted me almost with affection.

" Allan," he said, " you must not misunderstand me. I do
not really wish ill to Marie, whom I love more dearly than I
do my life ; God alone knows how much I love her. But I
made a promise to her cousin, Hernan, my only sister's only
child, and you will understand that I cannot break that promise,
although Hernan has disappointed me in many ways—yes,
in many ways. But if he is bad, as they say, it comes with that
Portuguese blood, which is a misfortune that he cannot help,
does it not ? However bad he may be, as an honest man I am
bound to keep my promise, am I not ? Also, Allan, you must
remember that you are English, and although you may be a
good fellow in yourself, that is a fault which you cannot expect
me to forgive. Still, if it is fated that you should marry my
daughter and breed English children—Heaven above ! to think
of it, English children !—well, there is nothing more to be said.

Don't remember the words I spoke to Marie. Indeed, I can't remember them myself. When I grow angry, a kind of rush of blood comes into my brain, and then I forget what I have said," and he stretched out his hand to me.

I shook it and answered that I understood he was not himself when he spoke those dreadful words, which both Marie and I wished to forget.

" I hope you will come to our wedding tomorrow," I added, " and wipe them out with a father's blessing."

" To-morrow! Are you really going to be married to-morrow?" he exclaimed, his sallow face twitching nervously. " O God, it was another man that I dreamed to see standing by Marie's side. But he is not here; he has disgraced and deserted me. Well, I will come, if my gaolers will suffer it. Good-bye, you happy bridegroom of to-morrow, good-bye."

Then he swung round and departed, followed by the guards, one of whom touched his brow and shook his head significantly as he passed me.

I think that Sunday seemed the longest day I ever spent. The Vrouw Prinsloo would scarcely allow me even a glimpse of Marie, because of some fad she had got into her mind that it was either not proper or not fortunate, I forget which, that a bride and bridegroom should associate on the eve of their marriage. So I occupied myself as best I could. First I wrote a long letter to my father, the third that I had sent, telling him everything that was going to happen, and saying how grieved I was that he could not be present to marry us and give us his blessing.

This letter I gave to a trader who was trekking to the bay on the following morning, begging him to forward it by the first opportunity.

That duty done, I saw about the horses which I was taking into Zululand, three of them, two for myself and one for Hans, who accompanied me as after-rider. Also the saddlery, saddle-bags, guns and ammunition must be overhauled, all of which took some time.

" You are going to spend a strange *wittebroodsweek* [white-bread-week, or, in other words, honeymoon], baas," said Hans, squinting at me with his little eyes, as he brayed away at a buckskin which was to serve as a saddle-cloth. " Now, if *I* was to be married to-morrow, I should stop with my pretty for a few days, and only ride off somewhere else when I was tired of her, especially if that somewhere else chanced to be Zululand, where they are so fond of killing people."

" I dare say you would, Hans ; and so would I, if I could, you be sure. But, you see, the commandant wants me to interpret and therefore it is my duty to go with him."

" Duty ; what is duty, baas ? Love I understand. It is for love of you that I go with you ; also for fear lest you should cause me to be beaten if I refused. Otherwise, I would certainly stop here in the camp, where there is plenty to eat and little work to do, as, were I you, I should do also for love of the white missie. But duty—pah ! that is a fool-word, which makes bones of a man before his time and leaves his girl to others."

" Of course, you do not understand, Hans, any more than you coloured people understand what gratitude is. But what do you mean about this trek of ours ? Are you afraid ? "

He shrugged his shoulders. " A little, perhaps, baas. At least I should be if I thought about the morrow, which I don't, since to-day is enough for me, and thinking about what one can't know makes the head ache. Dingaan is not a nice man, baas ; we saw that, didn't we ? He is a hunter who knows how to set a trap. Also he has the Baas Pereira up there to help him. So perhaps you might be more comfortable here kissing Missie Marie. Why do you not say that you have hurt your leg and cannot run ? It would not be much trouble to walk about on a crutch for a day or two, and when the commandant was well gone, your leg might heal and you could throw the stick away."

" Get thee behind me, Satan," I muttered to myself, and was about to give Hans a piece of my mind when I recollected that the poor fellow had his own way of looking at things and could not be blamed. Also, as he said, he loved me, and only suggested what he thought would tend to my joy and safety. How could I suppose that he would be interested in the success of a diplomatic mission to Dingaan, or think anything about it except that it was a risky business ? So I only said :

" Hans, if you are afraid, you had better stop behind. I can easily find another after-rider."

" Is the baas angry with me that he should speak so ? " asked the Hottentot. " Have I not always been true to him ; and if I should be killed, what does it matter ? Have I not said that I do not think about to-morrow, and we must all go to sleep some-time ? No ; unless the baas beats me back, I shall come with him. But, baas "—this in a wheedling tone—" you might give me some brandy to drink your health in to-night. It is very good to get drunk when one has to be sober, and perhaps dead, for a long time afterwards. It would be nice to remember when one is a spook, or an angel with white wings, such as the old baas, your father, used to tell us about in school on the Sabbath."

At this point, finding Hans hopeless, I got up and walked away, leaving him to finish our preparations.

That evening there was a prayer-meeting in the camp, for although no pastor was present, one of the Boer elders took his place and offered up supplications which, if simple and even absurd in their wording, at least were hearty enough. Amongst other requests, I remember that he petitioned for the safety of those who were to go on the mission to Dingaan and of those who were to remain behind. Alas ! those prayers were not heard, for it pleased the Power to Whom they were addressed to decree otherwise.

After this meeting, in which I took an earnest share, Retief, who just before it began had ridden in from Doornkop, whither he had been to visit his wife, held a kind of council, whereat the names of those who had volunteered or been ordered to accompany him, were finally taken down. At this council there was a good deal of discussion, since many of the Boers did not think the expedition wise—at any rate, if it was to be carried out on so large a scale. One of them, I forget which, an old man, pointed out that it might look like a war party, and that it would be wiser if only five or six went, as they had done before, since then there could be no mistake as to the peaceful nature of their intentions.

Retief himself combated this view, and at last turned suddenly to me, who was listening near by and said :

" Allan Quatermain, you are young, but you have a good judgment ; also, you are one of the very few who know Dingaan and can speak his language. Tell us now, what do you think ? "

Thus adjured, I answered, perhaps moved thereto more than I thought by Hans' talk, that I, too, considered the thing dangerous, and that someone whose life was less valuable than the commandant's should go in command.

"Why do you say so, nephew," he said irritably, "seeing that all white men's lives are of equal value, and I can smell no danger in the business?"

"Because, commandant, I do smell danger, though what danger I cannot say, any more than a dog or a buck can when it sniffs something in the air and barks or runs. Dingaan is a tamed tiger just now, but tigers are not house cats that one can play with them, as I know, who have felt his claws and just, only just, come out from between them."

"What do you mean, nephew?" asked Retief in his direct fashion. "Do you believe that this *swartsel*" (that is, black creature) "means to kill us?"

"I believe that it is quite possible," I answered.

"Then, nephew, being a reasonable man as you are, you must have some ground for your belief. Come now, out with it."

"I have none, commandant, except that one who can set the lives of a dozen folk against a man's skill in shooting at birds on the wing, and who can kill people to be a bait for those birds, is capable of anything. Moreover, he told me that he did not love you Boers, and why should he?"

Now, all those who were standing about seemed to be impressed with this argument. At any rate, they turned towards Retief, anxiously waiting for his reply.

"Doubtless," answered the commandant, who, as I have said, was irritable that night, "doubtless those English missionaries have poisoned the king's mind against us Boers. Also," he added suspiciously, "I think you told me, Allan, that the king said he liked you and meant to spare you, even if he killed your companions, just because you also are English. Are you sure that you do not know more than you choose to tell us? Has Dingaan perhaps confided something to you—just because you are English?"

Then noting that these words moved the assembled Boers, in whom race prejudice and recent events had created a deep distrust of any born of British blood, I grew very angry and answered:

" Commandant, Dingaan confided nothing to me, except that some Kaffir witch-doctor, who is named Zikali, a man I never saw, had told him that he must not kill an Englishman, and therefore he wished to spare me, although one of your people, Hernan Pereira, had whispered to him that I ought to be killed. Yet I say outright that I think you are foolish to visit this king with so large a force. Still, I am ready to do so myself with one or two others. Let me go, then, and try to persuade him to sign this treaty as to the land. If I am killed or fail, you can follow after me and do better."

" Allemachte ! " exclaimed Retief; " that is a fair offer. But how do I know, nephew, that when we came to read the treaty we should not find that it granted all the land to you English, and not to us Boers ? No, no, don't look angry. That was not a right thing to say, for you are honest whatever most of your blood may be. Nephew Allan, you who are a brave man, are afraid of this journey. Now, why is that, I wonder ? Ah ! I have it. I had forgotten. You are to be married to-morrow morning to a very pretty girl, and it is not natural that you should wish to spend the next fortnight in Zululand. Don't you see, brothers, he wants to get out of it because he is going to be married, as it is natural that he should, and therefore he tries to frighten us all ? When we were going to be married, should we have wished to ride away at once to visit some stinking savage? Ach ! I am glad I thought of that just as I was beginning to turn his gloomy colour, like a chameleon on a black hat, for it explains everything," and he struck his thigh with his big hand and burst into a roar of laughter.

All the company of Boers who stood around began to laugh also, uproariously, for this primitive joke appealed to them. Moreover, their nerves were strained ; they also dreaded this expedition, and therefore they were glad to relieve themselves in bucolic merriment. Everything was clear to them now Feeling myself in honour bound to go on the embassy, as I was their only interpreter, I, artful dog, was trying to play upon their fears in order to prevent it from starting, so that I might have a week or two of the company of my new-wed wife. They saw and appreciated the joke.

" He's slim, this little Englishman," shouted one.

"Don't be angry with him. We should have done as much ourselves," replied another.

"Leave him behind," said a third. "Even the Zulus do not send a new-married man on service." Then they smacked me on the back, and hustled me in their rude, kindly manner, till at length I fell into a rage and hit one of them on the nose, at which he only laughed the louder, although I made it bleed.

"See here, friends," I said, as soon as silence was restored; "married or no, whoever does not ride to Dingaan, I ride to him, although it is against my judgment. Let those laugh loudest who laugh last."

"Good!" cried one; "if you set the pace we shall soon be home again, Allan Quatermain. Who would not with Marie Marais at the end of the journey?"

Then, followed by their rough and mocking laughter, I broke away from them, and took refuge in my wagon, little guessing that all this talk would be brought up against me on a day to come.

In a certain class of uneducated mind foresight is often interpreted as guilty knowledge.

XVII

THE MARRIAGE

I WAS awakened on my wedding morning by the crash and bellowing of a great thunderstorm. The lightning flashed fearfully all about us, killing two oxen quite near to my wagon, and the thunder rolled and echoed till the very earth seemed to shake. Then came a wail of cold wind, and after that the swish of torrential rain. Although I was well accustomed to such natural manifestations, especially at this season of the year, I confess that these sights and sounds did not tend to raise my spirits, which were already lower than they should have been on that eventful day. Hans, however, who arrived to help me put on my best clothes for the ceremony, was for once consoling.

"Don't look sick, baas," he said, "for if there is storm in the morning, there is shine at night."

" Yes," I answered, speaking more to myself than to him, " but what will happen between the storm of the morning and the peace of the night ? "

It was arranged that the commission, which, counting the native after-riders, consisted of over a hundred people, among them several boys, who were little more than children, was to ride at one hour before noon. Nobody could get about to make the necessary preparations until the heavy rain had passed away, which it did a little after eight o'clock. Therefore when I left the wagon to eat, or try to eat some breakfast, I found the whole camp in a state of bustle.

Boers were shouting to their servants, horses were being examined, women were packing the saddle-bags of their husbands and fathers with spare clothes, the pack-beasts were being laden with biltong and other provisions, and so forth.

In the midst of all this tumult I began to wonder whether my private business would not be forgotten, since it seemed unlikely that time could be found for marriages. However, about ten o'clock when, having done everything that I had to do, I was sitting disconsolately upon my wagon box, being too shy to mix with that crowd of busy mockers or to go to the Prinsloos' camp to make inquiries, the vrouw herself appeared.

" Come on, Allan," she said, " the commandant is waiting and swearing because you are not there. Also, there is another waiting, and oh ! she looks lovely. When they see her, every man in the camp will want her for himself, whether he has got a wife or not, for in that matter, although you mayn't think so just now, they are all the same as the Kaffirs. Oh ! I know them, a white skin makes no difference."

While she held forth thus in her usual outspoken fashion, the vrouw was dragging me along by the hand, just as though I were a naughty little boy. Nor could I get free from that mighty grip, or, when once her great hulk was in motion, match my weight against it. Of course, some of the younger Boers, who, knowing her errand, had followed her, set up a shout of cheers and laughter, which attracted everybody to the procession.

" It is too late to hang back now, Englishman." " You must make the best of a bad business." " If you wanted to change your mind, you should have done it before," men and women roared and screamed with many other such bantering words, till at length I felt myself turn the colour of a red *vlei* lily.

So we came at last to where Marie stood, the centre of an admiring circle. She was clothed in a soft white gown made of some simple but becoming stuff, and she wore upon her dark hair a wreath woven by the other maidens in the camp, a bevy of whom stood behind her.

Now we were face to face. Our eyes met, and oh ! hers were full of love and trust. They dazzled and bewildered me. Feeling that I ought to speak, and not knowing what to say, I merely stammered " Good morning," whereon everyone broke into a roar of laughter, except Vrouw Prinsloo, who exclaimed :

" Did anyone ever see such a fool ? " and even Marie smiled.

Then Piet Retief appeared from somewhere dressed in tall boots and rough riding clothes. Handing the *roer* he was carrying to one of his sons, after much fumbling he produced a book from his pocket, in which the place was marked with a piece of grass.

" Now then," he said, " be silent all, and show respect, for remember I am not a man just now. I am a parson, which is quite a different thing, and, being a commandant and a veld cornet and other officers all rolled into one, by virtue of the law I am about to marry these young people, so help me God. Don't any of you witnesses ever say afterwards that they are not rightly and soundly married, because I tell you that they are, or will be." He paused for breath, and someone said, " Hear, hear," or its Dutch equivalent, whereon, having glared the offender into silence, Retief proceeded :

" Young man and young woman, what are your names ? "

" Don't ask silly questions, commandant," broke in Vrouw Prinsloo ; " you know their names well enough."

" Of course I do, aunt," he answered ; " but for this purpose I must pretend not to know them. Are you better acquainted with the law than I am? But stay, where is the father, Henri Marais ? "

Someone thrust Marais forward, and there he stood quite silent, staring at us with a queer look upon his face and his gun in his hand, for he, too, was ready to ride.

" Take away that gun," said Retief ; " it might go off and

" So we came at last to where Marie stood, the centre of an
admiring circle."   (*See page* 204)

cause disturbance or perhaps accidents," and somebody obeyed.
" Now, Henri Marais, do you give your daughter to be married
to this man ? "

" No," said Marais softly.

" Very well, that is just like you, but it doesn't matter, for she
is of age and can give herself. Is she not of age, Henri Marais ?
Don't stand there like a horse with the staggers, but tell me ; is
she not of age ? "

" I believe so," he answered in the same soft voice.

" Then take notice, people all, that this woman is of age, and
gives herself to be married to this man, don't you, my dear ? "

" Yes," answered Marie.

" All right, now for it," and, opening the book, he held it
up to the light, and began to read, or, rather, to stumble, through
the marriage service.

Presently he stuck fast, being, like most Boers of his time,
no great scholar, and exclaimed :

" Here, one of you help me with these hard words."

As nobody volunteered, Retief handed the book to me, for
he knew that Marais would not assist him, saying :

" You are a scholar, Allan, being a clergyman's son. Read
on till we come to the important bits, and I will say the words
after you, which will do just as well and be quite according to
law."

So I read, Heaven knows how, for the situation was trying
enough, until I came to the crucial questions, when I gave the
book back.

" Ah ! " said Retief ; " this is quite easy. Now then, Allan,
do you take this woman to be your wife ? Answer, putting in
your name, which is left blank in the book."

I replied that I did, and the question was repeated to Marie,
who did likewise.

" Well then, there you are," said Retief, " for I won't trouble
you with all the prayers, which I don't feel myself parson enough
to say. Oh ! no, I forgot. Have you a ring ? "

I drew one off my finger that had been my mother's—I believe
it had served this same purpose at the wedding of her grandmother—and set the thin little hoop of gold upon the third
finger of Marie's left hand. I still wear that ring to-day.

"It should have been a new one," muttered Vrouw Prinsloo.

"Be silent, aunt," said Retief; "are there any jewellers' shops here in the veld? A ring is a ring, even if it came off a horse's bit. There, I think that is all. No, wait a minute, I am going to say a prayer of my own over you, not one out of this book, which is so badly printed that I cannot read it. Kneel down, both of you; the rest may stand, as the grass is so wet."

Now, bethinking herself of Marie's new dress, the vrouw produced her *vatdoek* from a capacious pocket, and doubled up that dingy article for Marie to kneel on, which she did. Then Pieter Retief, flinging down the book, clasped his hands and uttered this simple, earnest prayer, whereof, strangely enough, every word remains fast in my mind. Coming as it did not from a printed page, but from his honest and believing heart, it was very impressive and solemn.

"O God above us, Who sees all and is with us when we are born, when we are married, when we die, and if we do our duty for all time afterwards in Heaven, hear our prayer. I pray Thee bless this man and this woman who appear here before Thee to be wed. Make them love each other truly all their lives, be these long or short, be they sick or well, be they happy or in sorrow, be they rich or poor. Give them children to be reared up in Thy Word, give them an honest name, and the respect of all who know them, and at last give them Thy Salvation through the Blood of Jesus the Saviour. If they are together, let them rejoice in each other. If they are apart, let them not forget each other. If one of them dies and the other lives, let that one who lives look forward to the day of reunion and bow the head to Thy Will, and keep that one who dies in Thy holy Hand. O Thou Who knowest all things guide the lives of these two according to Thy eternal purpose, and teach them to be sure that whatever Thou doest, is done for the best. For Thou art a faithful Creator, Who wishes good to His children and not evil, and at the last Thou wilt give them that good if they do but trust in Thee through daylight and through darkness. Now let no man dare to put asunder those whom Thou hast joined together, O Lord God Almighty, Father of us all. Amen."

So he prayed, and all the company echoed that Amen from their hearts. That is all except one, for Henri Marais turned his back on us and walked away.

"So," said Retief, wiping his brow with the sleeve of his coat, "you are the last couple that ever I mean to marry. The work is too hard for a layman who has bad sight for print. Now kiss each other; it is the right thing to do."

So we kissed and the congregation cheered.

"Allan," went on the commandant, pulling out a silver watch like a turnip, "you have just half an hour before we ride, and the Vrouw Prinsloo says that she has made you a wedding meal in that tent there, so you had best go eat it."

To the tent we went accordingly, to find a simple but bounteous feast prepared, of which we partook, helping each other to food, as is, or was, the custom with new-wedded folk. Also, many Boers came in and drank our healths, although the Vrouw Prinsloo told them that it would have been more decent to leave us alone. But Henri Marais did not come or drink our healths.

Thus the half hour went all too swiftly, and not a word did we get alone. At last in despair, seeing that Hans was already waiting with the horses, I drew Marie aside, motioning to everyone to stand back.

"Dearest wife," I said in broken words, "this is a strange beginning to our married life, but you see it can't be helped."

"No, Allan," she answered, "it can't be helped; but oh! I wish my heart were happier about your journey. I fear Dingaan, and if anything should chance to you I shall die of grief."

"Why should anything chance, Marie? We are a strong and well-armed party, and Dingaan looks on us peacefully."

"I don't know, husband, but they say Hernan Pereira is with the Zulus, and he hates you."

"Then he had better mind his manners, or he will not be here long to hate anybody," I answered grimly, for my gorge rose at the thought of this man and his treacheries.

"Vrouw Prinsloo," I called to the old lady, who was near, "be pleased to come hither and listen. And, Marie, do you listen also. If by chance I should hear anything affecting your safety, and send you a message by someone you can trust, such as that you should remove yourselves elsewhere or hide, promise me that you will obey it without question."

"Of course I will obey you, husband. Have I not just sworn to do so?" Marie said with a sad smile.

"And so will I, Allan," said the vrouw; "not because I have sworn anything, but because I know you have a good head on your shoulders, and so will my man and the others of our party. Though why you should think you will have any message to send, I can't guess, unless you know something that is hidden from us," she added shrewdly. "You say you don't; well, it is not likely you would tell us if you did. Look! They are calling, you must go. Come on, Marie, let us see them off."

So we went to where the commission was gathered on horseback, just in time to hear Retief addressing the people, or, rather, the last of his words.

"Friends," he said, "we go upon an important business, from which I hope we shall return happily within a very little time. Still, this is a rough country, and we have to deal with rough people. Therefore my advice to all you who stay behind is that you should not scatter, but keep together, so that in case of any trouble the men who are left may be at hand to defend this camp. For if they are here you have nothing to fear from all the savages in Africa. And now God be with you, and goodbye. Come, trek, brothers, trek!"

Then followed a few moments of confusion while men kissed their wives, children and sisters in farewell, or shook each other by the hand. I, too, kissed Marie, and, tumbling on to my horse somehow, rode away, my eyes blind with tears, for this parting was bitter. When I could see clearly again I pulled up and looked back at the camp, which was now at some distance. It seemed a peaceful place indeed, for although the storm of the morning was returning and a pall of dark cloud hung over it, the sun still shone upon the white wagon caps and the people who went to and fro among them.

Who could have thought that within a little time it would be but a field of blood, that those wagons would be riddled with assegais, and that the women and children who were moving there must most of them lie upon the veld mutilated corpses dreadful to behold? Alas! the Boers, always impatient of authority and confident that their own individual judgment was the best, did not obey their commandant's order to keep together. They went off this way and that, to shoot the game which was then so plentiful, leaving their families almost without protection. Thus the Zulus found and slew them.

Presently as I rode forward a little apart from the others someone overtook me, and I saw that it was Henri Marais.

"Well, Allan," he said, "so God has given you to me for a son-in-law. Who would have thought it? You do not look to me like a new-married man, for this marriage is not natural when the bridegroom rides off and leaves the bride of an hour. Perhaps you will never be really married after all, for God, Who gives sons-in-law, can also take them away, especially when He was not asked for them. Ah!" he went on, lapsing into French, as was his wont when moved, "*qui vivra verra! qui vivra verra!*" Then, shouting this excellent but obvious proverb at the top of his voice, he struck his horse with the butt of his gun, and galloped away before I could answer him.

At that moment I hated Henri Marais as I had never hated anyone before, not even his nephew Hernan. Almost did I ride to the commandant to complain of him, but reflecting to myself, first that he was undoubtedly half mad, and therefore not responsible for his actions, and secondly that he was better here with us than in the same camp with my wife, I gave up the idea. Yet alas! it is the half-mad who are the most dangerous of lunatics.

Hans, who had observed this scene and overheard all Marais's talk, and who also knew the state of the case well enough, sidled his horse alongside of me, and whispered in a wheedling voice:

"Baas, I think the old baas is *kransick* and not safe. He looks like one who is going to harm someone. Now, baas, suppose I let my gun off by accident; you know we coloured people are very careless with guns! The Heer Marais would never be troubled with any more fancies, and you and the Missie Marie and all of us would be safer. Also, *you* could not be blamed, nor could I, for who can help an accident? Guns will go off sometimes, baas, when you don't want them to."

"Get out," I answered. Yet if Hans's gun had chanced to "go off," I believe it might have saved a multitude of lives!

XVIII

THE TREATY

Our journey to Umgungundhlovu was prosperous and without incident. When we were within half a day's march from the Great Kraal we overtook the herd of cattle that we had recaptured from Sikonyela, for these beasts had been driven very slowly and well rested that they might arrive in good condition. Also the commandant was anxious that we should present them ourselves to the king.

Driving this multitude of animals before us—there were over five thousand head of them—we reached the Great Place on Saturday the 3rd of February about midday and forced them through its gates into the cattle kraals. Then we off-saddled and ate our dinner under those two milk trees near the gate of the kraal where I had bid good-bye to Dingaan.

After dinner messengers came to ask us to visit the king, and with them the youth, Thomas Halstead, who told the commandant that all weapons must be left behind, since it was the Zulu law that no man might appear before the king armed. To this Retief demurred, whereon the messengers appealed to me, whom they had recognised, asking if that were not the custom of their country.

I answered that I had not been in it long enough to know. Then there was a pause while they sent for someone to bear evidence; at the time I did not know whom, as I was not near enough to Thomas Halstead to make inquiries. Presently this someone appeared and turned out to be none other than Hernan Pereira.

He advanced towards us attended by Zulus, as though he were a chief, looking fat and well and handsomer than ever. Seeing Retief, he lifted his hat with a flourish and held out his hand, which, I noted, the commandant did not take.

"So you are still here, Mynheer Pereira!" he said coldly. "Now be good enough to tell me, what is this matter about the abandoning of our arms?"

" The king charges me to say'——" began Hernan.

" Charges you to say, Mynheer Pereira ! Are you then this black man's servant ? But continue."

" That none must come into his private enclosure armed."

" Well, then, mynheer, be pleased to go tell this king that we do not wish to come to his private enclosure. I have brought the cattle that he desired me to fetch, and I am willing to deliver them to him wherever he wishes, but we will not unarm in order to do so."

Now there was talk, and messengers were despatched, who returned at full speed presently to say that Dingaan would receive the Boers in the great dancing place in the midst of the kraal, and that they might bring their guns, as he wished to see how they fired them.

So we rode in, making as fine a show as we could, to find that the dancing place, which measured a good many acres in extent, was lined round with thousands of plumed but unarmed warriors arranged in regiments.

" You see," I heard Pereira say to Retief, " these have no spears."

" No," answered the commandant, " but they have sticks, which when they are a hundred to one would serve as well."

Meanwhile the vast mob of cattle were being driven in a double stream past a knot of men at the head of the space, and then away through gates behind. When the beasts had all gone we approached these men, among whom I recognised the fat form of Dingaan draped in a bead mantle. We ranged ourselves in a semicircle before him, and stood while he searched us with his sharp eyes. Presently he saw me, and sent a councillor to say that I must come and interpret for him.

So, dismounting, I went with Retief, Thomas Halstead, and a few of the leading Boers.

" *Sakubona* [Good day], Macumazahn," said Dingaan. " I am glad that you have come, as I know that you will speak my words truly, being one of the People of George, whom I love, for Tho-maas here I do not trust, although he is also a Son of George."

I told Retief what he said.

" Oh ! " he exclaimed with a grunt, " it seems that you English are a step in front of us Boers, even here."

Then he went forward and shook hands with the king, whom, it will be remembered, he had visited before.

After that the *indaba* or talk began, which I do not propose to set out at length, for it is a matter of history. It is enough to say that Dingaan, after thanking Retief for recovering the cattle, asked where was Sikonyela, the chief who had stolen them, as he wished to kill him. When he learned that Sikonyela remained in his own country, he became, or affected to become, angry. Then he asked where were the sixty horses which he heard we had captured from Sikonyela, as they must be given up to him.

Retief, by way of reply, touched his grey hairs and inquired whether Dingaan thought that he was a child that he, Dingaan, should demand horses which did not belong to him. He added that these horses had been restored to the Boers, from whom Sikonyela had stolen them.

When Dingaan had expressed himself satisfied with this answer, Retief opened the question of the treaty. The King replied, however, that the white men had but just arrived, and he wished to see them dance after their own fashion. As for the business, it might " sit still " till another day.

So in the end the Boers " danced " for his amusement. That is, they divided into two parties, and charged each other at full gallop, firing their guns into the air, an exhibition which seemed to fill all present with admiration and awe. When they paused, the king wished them to go on firing " a hundred shots apiece," but the commandant declined, saying he had no more powder to waste.

" What do you want powder for in a peaceful country ? " asked Dingaan suspiciously.

Retief answered through me :

" To kill food for ourselves, or to protect ourselves if any evil-minded men should attack us."

" Then it will not be wanted here," said Dingaan, " since I will give you food, and as I, the king, am your friend, no man in Zululand dare be your enemy."

Retief said he was glad to hear it, and asked leave to retire with the Boers to his camp outside the gate, as they were all tired with riding. This Dingaan granted, and we said good-bye

and went away. Before I reached the gate, however, a messenger,
I remember it was my old friend Kambula, overtook me, and
said that the king wished to speak with me alone. I answered
him that I could not speak with the king alone without the
permission of the commandant. Thereon Kambula said:

"Come with me, I pray you, O Macumazahn, since otherwise you will be taken by force."

Now, I told Hans to gallop on to Retief, and tell him of my
predicament, for already I saw that at some sign from Kambula
I was being surrounded by Zulus. He did so, and presently
Retief came back himself accompanied only by one man, and
asked me what was the matter now. I informed him, translating
Kambula's words, which he repeated in his presence.

"Does the fellow mean that you will be seized if you do not
go, or I refuse to allow you to do so?"

To this question Kambula's answer was:

"That is so, *Inkoos*, since the king has private words for the
ear of Macumazahn. Therefore we must obey orders, and take
him before the king, living or dead."

"Allemachte!" exclaimed Retief, "this is serious," and, as
though to summon them to my help, he looked behind him
towards the main body of the Boers, who by this time were
nearly all of them through the gate, which was guarded by a
great number of Zulus. "Allan," he went on, "if you are not
afraid, I think that you must go. Perhaps it is only that Dingaan
has some message about the treaty to send to me through you."

"I am not afraid," I answered. "What is the use of being
afraid in a place like this?"

"Ask that Kaffir if the king gives you safe conduct," said
Retief.

I did so and Kambula answered:

"Yes, for this visit. Who am I that I can speak the king's
unspoken words?" [which meant, guarantee his will in the
future.]

"A dark saying," commented Retief. "But go, Allan, since
you must, and God bring you back safe again. It is clear that
Dingaan did not ask that you should come with me for nothing.
Now I wish I had left you at home with that pretty wife of
yours."

So we parted, I going to the king's private enclosure on foot and without my rifle, since I was not allowed to appear before him armed, and the commandant towards the gate of the kraal accompanied by Hans, who led my horse. Ten minutes later I stood before Dingaan, who greeted me kindly enough, and began to ask a number of questions about the Boers, especially if they were not people who had rebelled against their own king and run away from him.

I answered, Yes, they had run away, as they wanted more room to live ; but I had told him all about that when I saw him before. He said he knew I had, but he wished to hear " whether the same words came out of the same mouth, or different words," so that he might know if I were a true man or not. Then, after pausing a while, he looked at me in his piercing fashion and asked :

" Have you brought me a present of that tall white girl with eyes like two stars, Macumazahn ? I mean the girl whom you refused to me, and whom I could not take because you had won your bet, which gave all the white people to you ; she for whose sake you make brothers of those Boers, who are traitors to their king ? "

" No, O Dingaan," I answered ; " there are no women among us. Moreover, this maid is now my wife."

" Your wife ! " he exclaimed angrily. " By the Head of the Black One, have you dared to make a wife of her whom I desired ? Now say, boy, you clever Watcher by Night, you little white ant, who work in the dark and only peep out at the end of your tunnel when it is finished ; you wizard, who by your magic can snatch his prey out of the hand of the greatest king in all the world—for it was magic that killed those vultures on Hloma Amabutu, not your bullets, Macumazahn—say, why should I not make an end of you at once for this trick ? "

I folded my arms and looked at him. A strange contrast we must have made, this huge, black tyrant with the royal air, for to do him justice he had that, at whose nod hundreds went the way of death, and I, a mere insignificant white boy, for in appearance, at any rate, I was nothing more.

" O Dingaan," I said coolly, knowing that coolness was my only chance, " I answer you in the words of the Commandant

Retief, the great chief. Do you take me for a child that I should give up my own wife to you who already have so many? Moreover, you canot kill me because I have the word of your captain, Kambula, that I am safe with you."

This reply seemed to amuse him. At any rate, with one of those almost infantile changes of mood which are common to savages of every degree, he passed from wrath to laughter.

" You are quick as a lizard," he said. " Why should I, who 'have so many wives, want one more, who would certainly hate me? Just because she is white, and would make the others, who are black, jealous, I suppose. Indeed, they would poison her, or pinch her to death in a month, and then come to tell me she had died of fretting. Also, you are right, you have my safe conduct, and must go hence unharmed this time. But look you, little lizard, although you escape me between the stones, I will pull off your tail. I have said that I want to pluck this tall white flower of yours, and I will pluck her. I know where she dwells. Yes, just where the wagon she sleeps in stands in the line, for my spies have told me, and I will give orders that whoever is killed, she is to be spared and brought to me living. So perhaps you will meet this wife of yours here, Macumazahn."

Now, at these ominous words, that might mean so much or so little, the sweat started to my brow, and a shiver went down my back.

" Perhaps I shall and perhaps I shall not, O king," I answered. " The world is as full of chances to-day as it was not long ago when I shot at the sacred vultures on Hloma Amabutu. Still, I think that my wife will never be yours, O king."

" Ow ! " said Dingaan; "this little white ant is making another tunnel, thinking that he will come up at my back. But what if I put down my heel and crush you, little white ant? Do you know," he added confidentially, " that the Boer who mends my guns and whom here we call ' Two-faces,' because he looks towards you Whites with one eye and towards us Blacks with the other, is still very anxious that I should kill you? Indeed, when I told him that my spies said that you were to ride with the Boers, as I had requested that you should be their Tongue, he answered that unless I promised to give you to the vultures, he would warn them against coming. So, since I wanted them to come as I had arranged with him, I promised."

"Is it so, O king?" I asked. "And pray why does this Two-faces, whom we name Pereira, desire that I should be killed?"

"*Ow!*" chuckled the obese old ruffian; "cannot you with all your cleverness guess that, O Macumazahn? Perhaps it is he who needs the tall white maiden, and not I. Perhaps if he does certain things for me, I have promised her to him in payment. And perhaps," he added, laughing quite loud, "I shall trick him after all, keeping her for myself, and paying him in another way, for can a cheat grumble if he is out-cheated?"

I answered that I was an honest man, and knew nothing about cheats, or at what they could or could not grumble.

"Yes, Macumazahn," replied Dingaan quite genially. "That is where you and I are alike. We are both honest, quite honest, and therefore friends, which I can never be with these Amaboona, who, as you and others have told me are traitors. We play our game in the light, like men, and who wins, wins, and who loses, loses. Now hear me, Macumazahn, and remember what I say. Whatever happens to others, whatever you may see, you are safe while I live. Dingaan has spoken. Whether I get the tall white girl, or do not get her, still *you* are safe; it is on my head," and he touched the gum-ring in his hair.

"And why should I be safe if others are unsafe, O king?" I asked.

"Oh! if you would know that, ask a certain ancient prophet named Zikali, who was in this land in the days of Senzangacona, my father, and before then—that is, if you can find him. Also, I like you, who are not a flat-faced fool like these Amaboona, but have a brain that turns in and out through difficulties, as a snake does through reeds; and it would be a pity to kill one who can shoot birds wheeling high above him in the air, which no one else can do. So whatever you see and whatever you hear, remember that you are safe, and shall go safely from this land, or stay safely in it if you will, to be my voice to speak with the Sons of George.

"Now return to the commandant, and say to him that my heart is his heart, and that I am very pleased to see him here.

Tomorrow, and perhaps the next day, I will show him some of the dances of my people, and after that I will sign the writing, giving him all the lands he asks and everything else he may desire, more than he can wish, indeed. *Hamba gachlé*, Macuma-zahn," and, rising with surprising quickness from his chair, which was cut out of a single block of wood, he turned and vanished through the little opening in the reed fence behind him that led to his private huts.

As I was being conducted back to the Boer camp by Kambula, who was waiting for me outside the gate of the labyrinth which is called *isiklohlo*, I met Thomas Halstead, who was lounging about, I think in order to speak with me. Halting, I asked him straight out what the king's intentions were towards the Boers.

" Don't know," he answered, shrugging his shoulders, " but he seems so sweet on them that I think he must be up to mischief. He is wonderfully fond of you, too, for I heard him give orders that the word was to be passed through all the regiments that if anyone so much as hurt you he should be killed at once. Also, you were pointed out to the soldiers when you rode in with the rest, that they might all of them know you."

" That's good for me as far as it goes," I replied. " But I don't know why I should need special protection above others, unless there is someone who wants to harm me."

" There is that, Allan Quatermain. The *indunas* tell me that the good-looking Portugee, whom they call ' Two-faces,' asks the king to kill you every time he sees him. Indeed, I've heard him myself."

" That's kind of him," I answered, " but, then, Hernan Pereira and I never got on. Tell me what is he talking about to the king when he isn't asking him to kill me ? "

" Don't know," he said again. " Something dirty, I'll be bound. One may be sure of that by the native name they have given him. I think, however," he added in a whisper, " that he has had a lot to do with the Boers being allowed to come here at all in order to get their treaty signed. At least, one day when I was interpreting and Dingaan swore that he would not give them more land than was enough to bury them in, Pereira told him that it didn't matter what he signed, as ' what was written with the pen could be scratched out with the spear.' "

"Indeed! And what did the king say to that?"

"Oh! he laughed and said it was true, and that he would give the Boer commission all their people wanted and something over for themselves. But don't you repeat that, Quatermain, for if you do, and it gets to the ear of Dingaan, I shall certainly be killed. And, I say, you're a good fellow, and I won a big bet on you over that vulture shooting, so I will give you a bit of advice, which you will be wise to take. You get out of this country as soon as you can, and go to look after that pretty Miss Marais, whom you are sweet on. Dingaan wants her, and what Dingaan wants he gets in this part of the world."

Then, without waiting to be thanked, he turned and disappeared among a crowd of Zulus, who were following us from curiosity, leaving me wondering whether or no Dingaan was right when he called this young man a liar. His story seemed to tally so well with that told by the king himself, that on the whole I thought he was not.

Just after I had passed the main gateway of the great town, where, his office done, Kambula saluted and left me, I saw two white men engaged in earnest conversation beneath one of the milk trees which, as I think I have already mentioned, grow, or grew, there. They were Henri Marais and his nephew. Catching sight of me, Marais walked off, but Pereira advanced and spoke to me, although, warned perhaps by what had happened to him in the case of Retief, I am glad to say he did not offer me his hand.

"Good day to you, Allan," he said effusively. "I have just heard from my uncle that I have to congratulate you, about Marie I mean, and, believe me, I do so with all my heart."

Now, as he spoke these words, remembering what I had just heard, my blood boiled in me, but I thought it wise to control myself, and therefore only answered:

"Thank you."

"Of course," he went on, "we have both striven for this prize, but as it has pleased God that you should win it, why, I am not one to bear malice."

"I am glad to hear it," I replied. "I thought that perhaps you might be. Now tell me, to change the subject, how long will Dingaan keep us here?"

" Oh! two or three days at most. You see, Allan, luckily
I have been able to persuade him to sign the treaty about the
land without further trouble. So as soon as that is done, you
can all go home."

" The commandant will be very grateful to you," I said.
" But what are you going to do? "

" I do not know, Allan. You see, I am not a lucky fellow
like yourself with a wife waiting for me. I think that perhaps I
shall stop here a while. I see a way of making a great deal of
money out of these Zulus; and having lost everything upon that
Delagoa Bay trek, I want money."

" We all do," I answered, " specially if we are starting in life.
So when it is convenient to you to settle your debts I shall be
glad."

" Oh! have no fear," he exclaimed with a sudden lighting
up of his dark face, " I will pay you what I owe you, every
farthing, with good interest thrown in."

" The king has just told me that is your intention," I remarked
quietly, looking him full in the eyes. Then I walked on, leaving
him staring after me, apparently without a word to say.

I went straight to the hut that was allotted to Retief in the
little outlying guard-kraal, which had been given to us for a
camp. Here I found the commandant seated on a Kaffir stool
engaged in painfully writing a letter, using a bit of board placed
on his knees as a desk.

He looked up, and asked me how I had got on with Dingaan,
not being sorry, as I think, of an excuse to pause in his clerical
labours.

" Listen, Commandant," I said, and, speaking in a low
voice, so as not to be overheard, I told him every word that had
passed in the interviews I had just had with Dingaan, with
Thomas Halstead, and with Pereira.

He heard me out in silence, then said:

" This is a strange and ugly story, Allan, and if it is true,
Pereira must be an even bigger scoundrel that I thought him.
But I can't believe that it is true. I think that Dingaan has been
lying to you for his own purposes; I mean about the plot to
kill you."

" Perhaps, Commandant. I don't know, and I don't much

care. But I am sure that he was not lying when he said he meant to steal away my wife either for himself or for Pereira."

" What, then, do you intend to do, Allan ? "

" I intend, Commandant, with your permission to send Hans, my after-rider, back to the camp with a letter for Marie, telling her to remove herself quietly to the farm I have chosen down on the river, of which I told you, and there to lie hid till I come back."

" I think it needless, Allan. Still, if it will ease your mind, do so, since I cannot spare you to go yourself. Only you must not send this Hottentot, who would talk and frighten the people. I am dispatching a messenger to the camp to tell them of our safe arrival and good reception by Dingaan. He can take your letter, in which I order you to say to your wife that if she and the Prinloos and the Meyers go to this farm of yours they are to go without talking, just as though they wanted a change, that is all. Have the letter ready by dawn to-morrow morning, as I trust mine may be," he added with a groan.

" It shall be ready, Commandant ; but what about Hernan Pereira and his tricks ? "

" This about the accursed Hernan Pereira," exclaimed Retief, striking the writing-board with his fist. " On the first opportunity I will myself take the evidence of Dingaan and of the English lad, Halstead. If I find they tell me the same story they have told you, I will put Pereira on his trial, as I threatened to do before ; and should he be found guilty, by God ! I will have him shot. But for the present it is best to do nothing, except keep an eye on him, lest we should cause fear and scandal in the camp, and, after all, not prove the case. Now go and write your letter, and leave me to write mine."

So I went and wrote, telling Marie something, but by no means all of that I have set down. I bade her, and the Prinsloos and the Meyers, if they would accompany her, as I was sure they would, move themselves off at once to the farm I had beaconed out thirty miles away from the Bushman's River, under pretence of seeing how the houses that were being built there were getting on. Or if they would not go, I bade her go alone with a few Hottentot servants, or any other companions she could find.

This letter I took to Retief, and read it to him. At my request, also, he scrawled at the foot of it :

" I have seen the above and approve it, knowing all the story, which may be true or false. Do as your husband bids you, but do not talk of it in the camp except to those whom he mentions. —PIETER RETIEF."

So the messenger departed at dawn, and in due course delivered my letter to Marie.

The next day was Sunday. In the morning I went to call upon the Reverend Mr. Owen, the missionary, who was very glad to see me. He informed me that Dingaan was in good mind towards us, and had been asking him if he would write the treaty ceding the land which the Boers wanted. I stopped for service at the huts of Mr. Owen, and then returned to the camp. In the afternoon Dingaan celebrated a great war dance for us to witness, in which about twelve thousand soldiers took part.

It was a wonderful and awe-inspiring spectacle, and I remember that each of the regiments employed had a number of trained oxen which manœuvred with them, apparently at given words of command. We did not see Dingaan that day, except at a distance, and after the dance was over returned to our camp to eat the beef which he had provided for us in plenty.

On the third day—that was Monday, the 5th of February, there were more dancings and sham fights, so many more, indeed, that we began to weary of this savage show. Late in the afternoon, however, Dingaan sent for the commandant and his men to come to see him, saying that he wished to talk with him about the matter of the treaty. So we went : but only three or four, of whom I was one, were admitted to Dingaan's presence, the rest remaining at a little distance, where they could see us but were out of earshot.

Dingaan then produced a paper which had been written by the Reverend Mr. Owen. This document, which I believe still exists, for it was found afterwards, was drawn up in legal or semi-legal form, beginning like a proclamation, " Know all men."

It ceded " the place called Port Natal, together with all the land annexed—that is to say, from Tugela to the Umzimvubu

River westward, and from the sea to the north "—to the Boers, " for their everlasting property." At the king's request, as the deed was written in English by Mr. Owen, I translated it to him, and afterwards the lad Halstead translated it also, being called in to do so when I had finished.

This was done that my rendering might be checked, and the fact impressed all the Boers very favourably. It showed them that the king desired to understand exactly what he was to sign, which would not have been the case had he intended any trick or proposed to cheat them afterwards. From that moment forward Retief and his people had no further doubts as to Dingaan's good faith in this matter, and foolishly relaxed all precautions against treachery.

When the translating was finished, the commandant asked the king if he would sign the paper then and there. He answered, " No ; he would sign it on the following morning, before the commission returned to Natal." It was then that Retief inquired of Dingaan, through Thomas Halstead, whether it was a true story which he had heard, that the Boer called Pereira, who had been staying with him, and whom the Zulus knew by the name of " Two-faces," had again asked him, Dingaan, to have me, Allan Quatermain, whom they called Macumazahn, killed. Dingaan laughed and answered :

" Yes, that is true enough, for he hates this Macumazahn. But let the little white Son of George have no fear, since my heart is soft towards him, and I swear by the head of the Black One that he shall come to no harm in Zululand. Is he not my guest, as you are ? "

He then went on to say that if the commandant wished it, he would have " Two-faces " seized and killed because he had dared to ask for my life. Retief answered that he would look into that matter himself, and after Thomas Halstead had confirmed the king's story, as to Pereira's conduct, he rose and said good-bye to Dingaan.

Of this matter of Hernan Pereira, Retief said little as we went back to the camp outside the kraal, though the little that he did say showed his deep anger. When we arrived at the camp, however, he sent for Pereira and Marais and several of the older Boers. I remember that among these were Gerrit Bothman, Senior,

Hendrik Labuschagne and Matthys Pretorious, Senior, all of them persons of standing and judgment. I also was ordered to be present. When Pereira arrived, Retief charged him openly with having plotted my murder, and asked him what he had to say. Of course, his answer was a flat denial, and an accusation against me of having invented the tale because we had been at enmity over a maiden whom I had since married.

"Then, Mynheer Pereira," said Retief, "as Allan Quatermain here has won the maiden who is now his wife, it would seem that his cause of enmity must have ceased, whereas yours may well have remained. However, I have no time to try cases of the sort now. But I warn you that this one will be looked into later on when we get back to Natal, whither I shall take you with me, and that meanwhile an eye is kept on you and what you do. Also I warn you that I have evidence for all that I say. Now be so good as to go, and to keep out of my sight as much as possible, for I do not like a man whom these Kaffirs name 'Two-faces.' As for you, friend Henri Marais, I tell you that you would do well to associate yourself less with one whose name is under so dark a cloud, although he may be your own nephew, whom all know you love blindly."

So far as I recollect neither of them made any answer to this direct speech. They simply turned and went away. But on the next morning, that of the fatal 6th of February, when I chanced to meet the Commandant Retief as he was riding through the camp, making arrangements for our departure to Natal, he pulled up his horse and said :

"Allan, Hernan Pereira has gone, and Henri Marais with him, and for my part I am not sorry, for doubtless we shall meet again, in this world or the next, and find out all the truth. Here, read this, and give it back to me afterwards" ; and he threw me a paper and rode on.

I opened the folded sheet and read as follows :

"To the Commandant Retief, Governor of the Emigrant Boers,

"Mynheer Commandant,

"I will not stay here, where such foul accusations are laid on me by black Kaffirs and the Englishman, Allan Quatermain,

who, like all his race, is an enemy of us Boers, and, although you
do not know it, a traitor who is plotting great harm against you
with the Zulus. Therefore I leave you, but am ready to meet
every charge at the right time before a proper Court. My uncle,
Henri Marais, comes with me, as he feels that his honour is also
touched. Moreover, he has heard that his daughter, Marie, is
in danger from the Zulus, and returns to protect her, which
he who is called her husband neglects to do. Allan Quatermain,
the Englishman, who is the friend of Dingaan, can explain what
I mean, for he knows more about the Zulu plans than I do, as
you will find out before the end."

Then followed the signatures of Hernan Pereira and Henri
Marais.

I put the letter in my pocket, wondering what might be its
precise meaning, and in particular that of the absurd and un-
defined charge of treachery against myself. It seemed to me that
Pereira had left us because he was afraid of something—either
that he might be placed upon his trial or of some ultimate
catastrophe in which he would be involved. Marais probably
had gone with him for the same reason that a bit of iron follows
a magnet, because he never could resist the attraction of this
evil man, his relative by birth. Or perhaps he had learned from
him the story of his daughter's danger, upon which I had already
acted, and really was anxious about her safety. For it must
always be remembered that Marais loved Marie passionately,
however ill the reader of this history may think that he behaved
to her. She was his darling, the apple of his eye, and her great
offence in his sight was that she cared for me more than she did
for him. That is one of the reasons why he hated me as much as
he loved her.

Almost before I had finished reading this letter, the order
came that we were to go in a body to bid farewell to Dingaan,
leaving our arms piled beneath the two milk trees at the gate of
the town. Most of our after-riders were commanded to accompany us—I think because Retief wished to make as big a show
as possible to impress the Zulus. A few of these Hottentots,
however, were told to stay behind that they might collect the
horses, that were knee-haltered and grazing at a distance, and
saddle them up. Among these was Hans, for, as it chanced, I

saw and sent him with the others, so that I might be sure that my own horses would be found and made ready for the journey.

Just as we were starting, I met the lad William Wood, who had come down from the Mission huts, where he lived with Mr. Owen, and was wandering about with an anxious face.

" How are you, William ? " I asked.

" Not very well, Mr. Quatermain," he answered. " The fact is," he added with a burst of confidence, " I feel queerly about you all. The Kaffirs have told me that something is going to happen to you, and I think you ought to know it. I daren't say any more," and he vanished into the crowd.

At that moment I caught sight of Retief riding to and fro and shouting out orders. Going to him, I caught him by the sleeve, saying :

" Commandant, listen to me."

" Well, what is it now, nephew ? " he asked absently.

I told him what Wood had said, adding that I also was uneasy ; I did not know why.

" Oh ! " he answered with impatience, " this is all hailstones and burnt grass " (meaning that the one would melt and the other blow away, or in our English idiom, stuff and rubbish). " Why are you always trying to scare me with your fancies, Allan ? Dingaan is our friend, not our enemy. So let us take the gifts that fortune gives us and be thankful. Come, march."

This he said about eight o'clock in the morning.

We strolled through the gates of the Great Kraal, most of the Boers, who, as usual, had piled their arms under the two milk trees, lounging along in knots of four or five, laughing and chatting as they went. I have often thought since, that although every one of them there, except myself, was doomed within an hour to have taken the dreadful step from time into eternity, it seems strange that advancing fate should have thrown no shadow on their hearts. On the contrary, they were quite gay, being extremely pleased at the successful issue of their mission and the prospect of an immediate return to their wives and children. Even Retief was gay, for I heard him joking with his companions about myself and my " white-bread-week," or honeymoon, which, he said, was drawing very near.

As we went, I noticed that most of the regiments who had

performed the great military dances before us on the previous day were gone. Two, however, remained—the *Ischlangu Inhlope*, that is, the " White Shields," who were a corps of veterans wearing the ring on their heads, and the *Ischlangu Umnyama*, that is, the " Black Shields," who were all of them young men without rings. The " White Shields " were ranged along the fence of the great open place to our left, and the " Black Shields " were similarly placed to our right, each regiment numbering about fifteen hundred men. Except for their kerries and dancing-sticks they were unarmed.

Presently we reached the head of the dancing ground, and found Dingaan seated in his chair with two of his great *indunas*, Umhlela and Tambusa, squatting on either side of him. Behind him, standing in and about the entrance to the labyrinth through which the king had come, were other *indunas* and captains. On arriving in front of Dingaan we saluted him, and he acknowledged the salutation with pleasant words and smiles. Then Retief, two or three of the other Boers, Thomas Halstead and I went forward, whereon the treaty was produced again and identified as the same document that we had seen on the previous day.

At the foot of it someone—I forget who—wrote in Dutch, " De merk van Koning Dingaan " [that is, The mark of King Dingaan.] In the space left between the words " *merk* " and " *van* " Dingaan made a cross with a pen that was given to him, Thomas Halstead holding his hand and showing him what to do.

After this, three of his *indunas*, or great councillors, who were named Nwara, Yuliwana and Manondo, testified as witnesses for the Zulus, and M. Oosthuyzen, A. C. Greyling and B. J. Liebenberg, who were standing nearest to Retief, as witnesses for the Boers.

This done, Dingaan ordered one of his *isibongos*, or praisers, to run to and fro in front of the regiments and others there assembled, and proclaim that he had granted Natal to the Boers to be their property for ever, information which the Zulus received with shouts. Then Dingaan asked Retief if he would not eat, and large trenchers of boiled beef were brought out and handed round. This, however, the Boers refused, saying they had already breakfasted. Thereon the king said that at least they must drink, and pots of *twala*, or Kaffir beer, were handed round, of which all the Boers partook.

While they were drinking, Dingaan gave Retief a message to the Dutch farmers, to the effect that he hoped they would soon come and occupy Natal, which henceforth was their country. Also, black-hearted villain that he was, that they would have a pleasant journey home. Next he ordered the two regiments to dance and sing war songs, in order to amuse his guests.

This they began to do, drawing nearer as they danced.

It was at this moment that a Zulu appeared, pushing his way through the captains who were gathered at the gate of the labyrinth, and delivered some message to one of the *indunas*, who in turn passed it on to the king.

" *Ow !* is it so ? " said the king with a troubled look. Then his glance fell on me as though by accident, and he added : " Macumazahn, one of my wives is taken very ill suddenly, and says she must have some of the medicine of the white men before they go away. Now, you tell me that you are a new-married man, so I can trust you with my wives. I pray you to go and find out what medicine it is that she needs, for you can speak our tongue."

I hesitated, then translated what he had said to Retief.

" You had best go, nephew," said the commandant ; " but come back quickly, for we ride at once."

Still I hesitated, not liking this business ; whereon the king began to grow angry.

" What ! " he said, " do you white men refuse me this little favour, when I have just given you so much—you who have wonderful medicines that can cure the sick ? "

" Go, Allan, go," said Retief, when he understood the words, " or he will grow cross and everything may be undone."

So, having no choice I went through the gateway into the labyrinth.

Next moment men pounced on me, and before I could utter a word a cloth was thrown over my mouth and tied tight behind my head.

I was a prisoner and gagged.

XIX

DEPART IN PEACE

A TALL Kaffir, one of the king's household guards, who carried
an assegai, came up to me and whispered :

" Hearken, little Son of George. The king would save you,
if he can, because you are not Dutch, but English. Yet, know
that if you try to cry out, if you even struggle, you die," and he
lifted the assegai so as to be ready to plunge it through my
heart.

Now I understood, and a cold sweat broke out all over me.
My companions were to be murdered, every one ! Oh ! gladly
would I have given my life to warn them. But alas ! I could not,
for the cloth upon my mouth was so thick that no sound could
pass it.

One of the Zulus inserted a stick between the reeds of the
fence. Working it to and fro sideways, he made an opening
just in line with my eyes—out of cruelty, I suppose, for now I
must see everything.

For some time—ten minutes, I dare say—the dancing and
beer-drinking went on. Then Dingaan rose from his chair and
shook the hand of Retief warmly, bidding him " *Hamba
gachlé*," that is, Depart gently, or in peace. He retreated towards
the gate of the labyrinth, and as he went the Boers took off
their hats, waving them in the air and cheering him. He was
almost through it, and I began to breathe again.

Doubtless I was mistaken. After all, no treachery was
intended.

In the very opening of the gate Dingaan turned, however, and
said two words in Zulu which mean :

" Seize them ! "

Instantly the warriors, who had now danced quite close and
were waiting for these words, rushed upon the Boers. I heard
Thomas Halstead call out in English :

" We are done for," and then add in Zulu, " Let me speak to
the king ! "

Dingaan heard also, and waved his hand to show that he refused to listen, and as he did so shouted thrice :

" *Bulala abatagati !* " that is, Slay the wizards !

I saw poor Halstead draw his knife and plunge it into a Zulu who was near him. The man fell, and again he struck at another soldier, cutting his throat. The Boers also drew their knives— those of them who had time—and tried to defend themselves against these black devils, who rushed on them in swarms. I heard afterwards that they succeeded in killing six or eight of them and wounding perhaps a score. But it was soon over, for what could men armed only with pocket-knives do against such a multitude ?

Presently, amidst a hideous tumult of shouts, groans, curses, prayers for mercy, and Zulu battle cries, the Boers were all struck down—yes, even the two little lads and the Hottentot servants. Then they were dragged away, still living, by the soldiers, their heels trailing on the ground, just as wounded worms or insects are dragged by the black ants.

Dingaan was standing by me now, laughing, his fat face working nervously.

" Come, Son of George," he said, " and let us see the end of these traitors to your sovereign."

Then I was pulled along to an eminence within the labyrinth, whence there was a view of the surrounding country. Here we waited a little while, listening to the tumult that grew more distant, till presently the dreadful procession of death reappeared, coming round the fence of the Great Kraal and heading straight for the Hill of Slaughter, Hloma Amabutu. Soon its slopes were climbed, and there among the dark leaved bushes and the rocks the black soldiers butchered them, every one.

I saw and swooned away.

I believe that I remained senseless for many hours, though towards the end of that time my swoon grew thin, as it were, and I heard a hollow voice speaking over me in Zulu.

" I am glad that the little Son of George has been saved," said the echoing voice, which I did not know, " for he has a great destiny, and will be useful to the black people in time to come." Then the voice went on :

" O House of Senzangacona ! now you have mixed your milk with blood, with white blood. Of that bowl you shall drink to the dregs, and afterwards must the bowl be shattered " ; and the speaker laughed—a deep, dreadful laugh that I was not to hear again for years.

I heard him go away, shuffling along like some great reptile, and then, with an effort, opened my eyes. I was in a large hut, and the only light in the hut came from a fire that burned in its centre, for it was night-time. A Zulu woman, young and good-looking, was bending over a gourd near the fire, doing something to its contents. I spoke to her light-headedly.

" O woman," I said, " is that a man who laughed over me ? "

" Not altogether, Macumazahn," she answered in a pleasant voice. " That was Zikali, the Mighty Magician, the Counsellor of Kings, the Opener of Roads ; he whose birth our grand-fathers do not remember ; he whose breath causes the trees to be torn out by the roots ; he whom Dingaan fears and obeys."

" Did he cause the Boers to be killed ? " I asked.

" Mayhap," she answered. " Who am I, that I should know of such matters ? "

" Are you the woman who was sick whom I was sent to visit ? " I asked again.

" Yes, Macumazahn, I was sick, but now I am well and you are sick, for so things go round. Drink this," and she handed me a gourd of milk.

" How are you named ? " I inquired as I took it.

" Naya is my name," she replied, " and I am your jailer. Don't think that you can escape me, though, Macumazahn, for there are other jailers without who carry spears. Drink."

So I drank and bethought me that the draught might be poisoned. Yet so thirsty was I that I finished it, every drop.

" Now am I a dead man ? " I asked, as I put down the gourd.

" No, no, Macumazahn," she who called herself Naya replied in a soft voice : " not a dead man, only one who will sleep and forget."

Then I lost count of everything and slept—for how long I know not.

When I awoke again it was broad daylight ; in fact, the sun stood high in the heavens. Perhaps Naya had put some drug into my milk, or perhaps I had simply slept. I do not know. At any rate, I was grateful for that sleep, for without it I think that I should have gone mad. As it was, when I remembered, which it took me some time to do, for a while I went near to insanity.

I recollect lying there in that hut and wondering how the Almighty could have permitted such a deed as I had seen done. How could it be reconciled with any theory of a loving and merciful Father? Those poor Boers, whatever their faults, and they had many, like the rest of us, were in the main good and honest men according to their lights. Yet they had been doomed to be thus brutally butchered at the nod of a savage despot, their wives widowed, their children left fatherless, or, as it proved in the end, in most cases, murdered or orphaned!

The mystery was too great—great enough to throw off its balance the mind of a young man who had witnessed such a fearsome scene as I have described.

For some days really I think that my reason hung just upon the edge of that mental precipice. In the end, however, reflection and education, of which I had a certain amount, thanks to my father, came to my aid. I recalled that such massacres, often on an infinitely larger scale, had happened a thousand times in history, and that still through them, often, indeed, by means of them, civilisation has marched forward, and mercy and peace have kissed each other over the bloody graves of the victims.

Therefore even in my youth and inexperience I concluded that some ineffable purpose was at work through this horror, and that the lives of those poor men which had been thus sacrificed were necessary to that purpose. This may appear a dreadful and fatalistic doctrine, but it is one that is corroborated in Nature every day, and doubtless the sufferers meet with their compensations in some other state. Indeed, if it be not so, faith and all the religions are vain.

Or, of course, it may chance that such monstrous calamities happen, not through the will of the merciful Power of which I have spoken, but in its despite. Perhaps the devil of Scripture, at whom we are inclined to smile, is still very real and active in this world of ours. Perhaps from time to time some evil principle breaks into eruption, like the prisoned forces of a volcano, bearing death and misery on its wings, until in the end it must depart strengthless and overcome. Who can say?

The question is one that should be referred to the Archbishop of Canterbury and the Pope of Rome in conclave, with the Lama of Thibet for umpire in case they disagreed. I only try to put down the thoughts that struck me so long ago as my mind renders them to-day. But very likely they are not quite the same thoughts, for a full generation has gone by me since then, and in that time the intelligence ripens as wine does in a bottle.

Besides these general matters, I had questions of my own to consider during those days of imprisonment—for instance, that of my own safety, though of this, to be honest, I thought little. If I were going to be killed, I was going to be killed, and there was an end. But my knowledge of Dingaan told me that he had not massacred Retief and his companions for nothing. This would be but the prelude to a larger slaughter, for I had not forgotten what he said as to the sparing of Marie and the other hints he gave me.

From all this I concluded quite rightly as it proved, that some general onslaught was being made upon the Boers, who probably would be swept out to the last man. And to think that here I was, a prisoner in a Kaffir kraal, with only a young woman as a jailer, and yet utterly unable to escape to warn them. For round my hut lay a courtyard, and round it again ran a reed fence about five feet six inches high. Whenever I looked over this fence, by night or by day, I saw soldiers stationed at intervals of about fifteen yards. There they stood like statues, their broad spears in their hands, all looking inwards towards the fence. There they stood—only at night their number was doubled. Clearly it was not meant that I should escape.

A week went by thus—believe me, a very terrible week. During that time my sole companion was the pretty young woman, Naya. We became friends in a way and talked on a variety of subjects. Only, at the end of our conversations I always found that I had gained no information whatsoever about any matter of immediate interest. On such points as the history of the Zulu and kindred tribes, or the character of Chaka, the great king, or anything else that was remote she would discourse by the hour. But when we came to current events, she dried up like water on a red-hot brick. Still, Naya grew, or pretended to grow, quite attached to me. She even suggested naïvely that I might do worse than marry her, which she said Dingaan was quite ready to allow, as he was fond of me and thought I should be useful to his country. When I told her that I was already married, she shrugged her shining shoulders and asked with a laugh that revealed her beautiful teeth :

" What does that matter ? Cannot a man have more wives than one ? And, Macumazahn," she added, leaning forward and looking at me, " how do you know that you have even one ? You may be divorced or a widower by now."

" What do you mean ? " I asked.

" I ? I mean nothing ; do not look at me so fiercely, Macumazahn. Surely such things happen in the world, do they not ? "

" Naya," I said, " you are two bad things—a bait and a spy— and you know it."

" Perhaps I do, Macumazahn," she answered. " Am I to blame for that if my life is on it, especially when I really like you for yourself ? "

" I don't know," I said. " Tell me, when am I going to get out of this place ? "

" How can I tell you, Macumazahn ? " Naya replied, patting my hand in her genial way, " but I think before long. When you are gone, Macumazahn, remember me kindly sometimes, as I have really tried to make you as comfortable as I could with a watcher staring through every straw in the hut."

I said whatever seemed to be appropriate, and next morning my deliverance came. While I was eating my breakfast in the courtyard at the back of the hut, Naya thrust her handsome and pleasant face round the corner and said that there was a messenger to see me from the king. Leaving the rest of the meal unswallowed I went to the doorway of the yard and there found my old friend, Kambula.

" Greeting, *Inkoos*," he said to me ; " I am come to take you back to Natal with a guard. But I warn you to ask me no questions, for if you do I must not answer them. Dingaan is ill, and you cannot see him, nor can you see the white praying-man, or anyone : you must come with me at once."

"I do not want to see Dingaan," I replied, looking him in the eyes.

"I understand," answered Kambula: "Dingaan's thoughts are his thoughts and your thoughts are your thoughts, and perhaps that is why he does not want to see *you*. Still, remember, *Inkoos*, that Dingaan has saved your life, snatching you unburned out of a very great fire, perhaps because you are of a different sort of wood, which he thinks it a pity to burn. Now, if you are ready, let us go."

"I am ready," I answered.

At the gate I met Naya, who said:

"You never thought to say good-bye to me, White Man, although I have tended you well. Ah! what else could I expect? Still, I hope that if I should have to fly from this land for *my* life, as may chance, you will do for me what I have done for you."

"That I will," I answered, shaking her by the hand; and, as it happened, in after years I did.

Kambula led me, not through the kraal Umgungundhlovu, but round it. Our road lay immediately past the death mount, Hloma Amabutu, where the vultures were still gathered in great numbers. Indeed, it was actually my lot to walk over the new-picked bones of some of my companions who had been despatched at the foot of the hill. One of these skeletons I recognised by his clothes to be that of Samuel Esterhuizen, a very good fellow, at whose side I had slept during all our march. His empty eye-sockets seemed to stare at me reproach-fully, as though they asked me why I remained alive when he and all his brethren were dead. I echoed the question in my own mind. Why of that great company did I alone remain alive?

An answer seemed to rise within me: That I might be one of the instruments of vengeance upon that devilish murderer, Dingaan. Looking upon those poor shattered and desecrated frames that had been men, I swore in my heart that if I lived I would not fail in that mission. Nor did I fail, although the history of that great repayment cannot be told in these pages.

Turning my eyes from this dreadful sight, I saw that on the opposite slope, where we had camped during our southern trek from Delagoa, still stood the huts and wagons of the Reverend Mr. Owen. I asked Kambula whether he and his people were also dead.

"No, *Inkoos*," he answered; "they are of the Children of George, as you are, and therefore the king has spared them, although he is going to send them out of the country."

This was good news, so far as it went, and I asked again if Thomas Halstead had also been spared, since he, too, was an Englishman.

"No," said Kambula. "The king wished to save him, but he killed two of our people and was dragged off with the rest. When the slayers got to their work it was too late to stay their hands."

Again I asked whether I might not join Mr. Owen and trek with him, to which Kambula answered briefly :

"No, Macumazahn; the king's orders are that you must go by yourself."

So I went; nor did I ever again meet Mr. Owen or any of his people. I believe, however, that they reached Durban safely and sailed away in a ship called the *Comet*.

In a little while we came to the two milk trees by the main gate of the kraal, where much of our saddlery still lay scattered about, though the guns had gone. Here Kambula asked me if I could recognise my own saddle.

"There it is," I answered, pointing to it ; "but what is the use of a saddle without a horse ? "

"The horse you rode has been kept for you, Macumazahn," he replied.

Then he ordered one of the men with us to bring the saddle and bridle, also some other articles which I selected, such as a couple of blankets, a water-bottle, two tins containing coffee and sugar, a little case of medicines, and so forth.

About a mile further on I found one of my horses tethered by an outlying guard hut, and noted that it had been well fed and cared for. By Kambula's leave I saddled it and mounted. As I did so, he warned me that if I tried to ride away from the escort I should certainly be killed, since even if I escaped them, orders had been given throughout the land to put an end to me should I be seen alone.

I replied that, unarmed as I was, I had no idea of making any such attempt. So we went forward, Kambula and his soldiers walking or trotting at my side.

For four full days we journeyed thus, keeping, so far as I could judge, about twenty or thirty miles to the east of that road by which I had left Zululand before and re-entered it with Retief and his commission. Evidently I was an object of great interest to the Zulus of the country through which we passed, perhaps because they knew me to be the sole survivor of all the white men who had gone up to visit the king. They would come down in crowds from the kraals and stare at me almost with awe, as though I were a spirit and not a man. Only, not one of them would say anything to me, probably because they had been forbidden to do so. Indeed, if I spoke to any of them, invariably they turned and walked or ran out of hearing.

It was on the evening of the fourth day that Kambula and his soldiers received some news which seemed to excite them a great deal. A messenger in a state of exhaustion, who had an injury to the fleshy part of his left arm, which looked to me as though it had been caused by a bullet, appeared out of the bush and said something of which, by straining my ears, I caught two words—"Great slaughter." Then Kambula laid his fingers on his lips as a signal for silence and led the man away, nor did I see or hear any more of him. Afterwards I asked Kambula who had suffered this great slaughter, whereon he stared at me innocently and replied that he did not know of what I was speaking.

"What is the use of lying to me, Kambula, seeing that I shall find out the truth before long?"

"Then, Macumazahn, wait till you do find it out, and may it please you," he replied, and went off to speak with his people at a distance.

All that night I heard them talking off and on—I, who lay awake plunged into new miseries. I was sure that some other dreadful thing had happened. Probably Dingaan's armies had destroyed all the Boers, and, if so, oh! what had become of Marie? Was she dead, or had she perhaps been taken prisoner, as Dingaan had told me would be done for his own vile purposes? For aught I knew she might now be travelling under escort to Umgungundhlovu, as I was travelling to Natal.

The morning came at last, and that day, about noon, we reached a ford of the Tugela which luckily was quite passable. Here Kambula bade me farewell, saying that his mission was finished. Also he delivered to me a message that I was to give from Dingaan to the English in Natal. It was to this effect: That he, Dingaan, had killed the Boers who came to visit him because he found out that they were traitors to their chief, and therefore not worthy to live. But that he loved the Sons of George, who were true-hearted people, and therefore had nothing to fear from him. Indeed, he begged them to come and see him at his Great Place, where he would talk matters over with them.

I said that I would deliver the message if I met any English people, but, of course, I could not say whether they would accept Dingaan's invitation to Umgungundhlovu. Indeed, I feared lest that town might have acquired such a bad name that they would prefer not to come there without an army.

Then, before Kambula had time to take any offence, I shook his outstretched hand and urged my horse into the stream. I never met Kambula again living, though after the battle of Blood River I saw him dead.

Once over the Tugela I rode forward for half a mile or so till I was clear of the bush and reeds that grew down to the water, fearing lest the Zulus should follow and take me back to Dingaan to explain my rather imprudent message. Seeing no signs of them, I halted, a desolate creature in a desolate country which I did not know, wondering what I should do and whither I should ride. Then it was that there happened one of the strangest experiences of all my adventurous life.

As I sat dejectedly upon my horse, which was also dejected, amidst some tumbled rocks that at a distant period of the world's history had formed the bank of the great river, I heard a voice which seemed familiar to me say:

" Baas, is that *you*, baas ? "

I looked round and could see no one, so, thinking that I had been deceived by my imagination, I held my peace.

" Baas," said the voice again, " are you dead or are you alive ? Because, if you are dead, I don't want to have anything to do with spooks until I am obliged."

Now I answered, "Who is it that speaks, and whence?" though, really, as I could see no one, I thought that I must be demented.

The next moment my horse snorted and shied violently, and no wonder, for out of a great ant-bear hole not five paces away appeared a yellow face crowned with black wool, in which was set a broken feather. I looked at the face and the face looked at me.

"Hans," I said, "is it you? I thought that *you* were killed with the others."

"And I thought that *you* were killed with the others, baas. Are you sure that you are alive?"

"What are you doing there, you old fool?" I asked.

"Hiding from the Zulus, baas. I heard them on the other bank, and then saw a man on a horse crossing the river, and went to ground like a jackal. I have had enough of Zulus."

"Come out," I said, "and tell me your story."

He emerged, a thin and bedraggled creature, with nothing left on him but the upper part of a pair of old trousers, but still Hans, undoubtedly Hans. He ran to me, and seizing my foot, kissed it again and again, weeping tears of joy and stuttering:

"Oh, baas, to think that I should find you who were dead, alive, and find myself alive, too. Oh! baas, never again will I doubt about the Big Man in the sky of whom your reverend father is so fond. For after I had tried all our own spirits, and even those of my ancestors, and met with nothing but trouble, I said the prayer that the reverend taught us, asking for my daily bread because I am so very hungry. Then I looked out of the hole and there you were. Have you anything to eat about you, baas?"

As it chanced, in my saddle-bags I had some biltong that I had saved against emergencies. I gave it to him, and he devoured it as a famished hyena might do, tearing off the tough meat in lumps and bolting them whole. When it was all gone he licked his fingers and his lips and stood still staring at me.

"Tell me your story," I repeated.

"Baas, I went to fetch the horses with the others, and ours had strayed. I got up a tree to look for them. Then I heard a noise, and saw that the Zulus were killing the Boers; so knowing that

presently they would kill us, too, I stopped in that tree, hiding
myself as well as I could in a stork's nest. Well, they came and
assegaied all the other Totties, and stood under my tree cleaning
their spears and getting their breath, for one of my brothers had
given them a good run. But they never saw me, although I
was nearly sick from fear on the top of them. Indeed, I was sick,
but into the nest.

"Well, I sat in that nest all day, though the sun cooked me
like beef on a stick; and when night came I got down and ran,
for I knew it was no good to stop to look for you, and ' every
man for himself when a black devil is behind you,' as your
reverend father says. All night I ran, and in the morning hid
up in a hole. Then when night came again I went on running.
Oh! they nearly caught me once or twice, but never quite, for
I know how to hide, and I kept where men do not go. Only
I was hungry, hungry; yes, I lived on snails and worms, and
grass like an ox, till my middle ached. Still, at last I got across
the river and near to the camp.

"Then just before the day broke and I was saying, ' Now,
Hans, although your heart is sad, your stomach will rejoice and
sing,' what did I see but those Zulu devils, thousands of them,
rush down on the camp and kill all the poor Boers. Men and
women and the little children, they killed them by the hundred,
till at last other Boers came and drove them away, although
they took all the cattle with them. Well, as I was sure that they
would come back, I did not stop there. I ran down to the side
of the river, and have been crawling about in the reeds for days,
living on the eggs of water-birds and a few small fish that I
caught in the pools, till this morning, when I heard the Zulus
again and slipped up here into this hole. Then you came and
stood over the hole, and for a long while I thought you were
a ghost.

"But now we are together once more and all is right, just as
what your reverend father always said it would be with those who
go to church on Sunday, like me when there was nothing else
to do." And again he fell to kissing my foot.

"Hans," I said, "you saw the camp. Was the Missie Marie
there?"

"Baas, how can I tell, who never went into it? But the wagon

she slept in was not there; no, nor that of the Vrouw Prinsloo
or of the Heer Meyer."

"Thank God!" I gasped, then added: "Where were you
trying to get to, Hans, when you ran away from the camp?"

"Baas, I thought perhaps that the Missie and the Prinsloos
and the Meyers had gone to that fine farm which you pegged
out, and that I would go and see if they were there. Because if
so, I was sure that they would be glad to know that you were
really dead, and give me some food in payment for my news.
But I was afraid to walk across the open veld for fear lest the
Zulus should see me and kill me. Therefore I came round
through the thick bush along the river, where one can only
travel slowly, especially if hollow," and he patted his wasted
stomach.

"But, Hans," I asked, "are we near my farm where I set
the men to build the houses on the hill above the river?"

"Of course, baas. Has your brain gone soft that you cannot
find your way about the veld? Four, or at most five, hours on
horseback, riding slow, and you are there."

"Come on, Hans," I said, "and be quick, for I think that
the Zulus are not far behind."

So we started, Hans hanging to my stirrup and guiding me,
for I knew well enough that although he had never travelled
this road, his instinct for locality would not betray a coloured
man, who can find his way across the pathless veld as surely as a
buck or a bird of the air.

On we went over the rolling plain, and as we travelled I
told him my story, briefly enough, for my mind was too torn
with fears to allow me to talk much. He, too, told me more of
his escape and adventures. Now I understood what was that
news which had so excited Kambula and his soldiers. It was
evident that the Zulu impis had destroyed a great number of
the Boers whom they found unprepared for attack, and then
had been driven off by reinforcements that arrived from other
camps.

That was why I had been kept prisoner for all those days.
Dingaan feared lest I should reach Natal in time to warn his
victims!

XX

THE COURT-MARTIAL

ONE hour, two hours, three hours, and then suddenly from the top of a rise the sight of the beautiful Mooi River winding through the plain like a vast snake of silver, and there, in a loop of it, the flat-crested koppie on which I had hoped to make my home. Had hoped!—why should I not still hope? For aught I knew everything might yet be well. Marie might have escaped the slaughter as I had done, and if so, after all our troubles perchance many years of life and happiness awaited us. Only it seemed too good to be true.

I flogged my horse, but the poor beast was tired out and could only break into short canters, that soon lapsed to a walk again. But whether it cantered or whether it walked, its hoofs seemed to beat out the words—" Too good to be true!" Sometimes they beat them fast, and sometimes they beat them slow, but always their message seemed the same.

Hans, too, was outworn and weak from starvation. Also he had a cut upon his foot which hampered him so much that at last he said I had better go on alone; he would follow more slowly. Then I dismounted and set him on the horse, walking by it myself.

Thus it came about that the gorgeous sunset was finished and the sky had grown grey with night before we reached the foot of the koppie. Yet the last rays of the sinking orb had shown me something as they died. There on the slope of the hill stood some mud and wattle houses, such as I had ordered to be built, and near to them several white-capped wagons. Only I did not see any smoke rising from those houses as there should have been at this hour of the day, when men cooked their evening food. The moon would be up presently, I knew, but meanwhile it was dark and the tired horse stumbled and floundered among the stones which lay about at the foot of the hill.

I could bear it no longer.

"Hans," I said, "do you stay here with the horse. I will creep to the houses and see if any dwell there."

"Be careful, baas," he answered, "lest you should find Zulus, for those black devils are all about."

I nodded, for I could not speak, and then began the ascent. For several hundred yards I crept from stone to stone, feeling my way, for the Kaffir path that led to the little plateau where the spring was, above which the shanties stood, ran at the other end of the hill. I struck the spruit or rivulet that was fed by this spring, being guided to it by the murmur of the water, and followed up its bank till I heard a sound which caused me to crouch and listen.

I could not be sure because of the ceaseless babble of the brook, but the sound seemed like that of sobs. While I waited the great moon appeared suddenly above a bank of inky cloud, flooding the place with light, and oh! by that light, looking more ethereal than woman, I saw—I saw Marie!

She stood not five paces from me, by the side of the stream, whither she had come to draw water, for she held a vessel in her hand. She was clothed in some kind of a black garment such as widows wear, but made of rough stuff, and above it her face showed white in the white rays of the moon. Gazing at her from the shadow, I could even see the tears running down her cheeks, for it was she who wept in this lonely place, wept for one who would return no more.

My voice choked in my throat; I could not utter a single word. Rising from behind a rock I moved towards her. She saw me and started, then said in a thrilling whisper:

"Oh! husband, has God sent you to call me? I am ready, husband, I am ready!" and she stretched out her arms wildly, letting fall the vessel, that clanked upon the ground.

"Marie!" I gasped at length; and at that word the blood rushed to her face and brow, and I saw her draw in her breath as though to scream.

"Hush!" I whispered. "It is I, Allan, who have escaped alive." The next thing I remember was that she lay in my arms.

"What has happened here?" I asked when I had told my tale, or some of it.

"Nothing, Allan," she answered. "I received your letter at the camp, and we trekked away as you bade us, without telling the others why, because you remember the Commandant Retief wrote to us not to do so. So we were out of the great slaughter, for the Zulus did not know where we had gone, and never followed us here, although I have heard that they sought for me. My father and my cousin Hernan only arrived at the camp two days after the attack, and discovering or guessing our hiding-place—I know not which—rode on hither. They say they came to warn the Boers to be careful, for they did not trust Dingaan, but were too late. So they too were out of the slaughter, for, Allan, many, many have been killed—they say five or six hundred, most of them women and children. But thank God! many more escaped, since the men came in from the other camps farther off and from their shooting parties, and drove away the Zulus, killing them by scores."

"Are your father and Pereira here now?" I asked.

"No, Allan. They learned of the massacre and that the Zulus were all gone yesterday morning. Also they got the bad news that Retief and everyone with him had been killed at Dingaan's town, it is said through the treachery of the English, who arranged with Dingaan that he should kill them."

"That is false," I said; "but go on."

"Then, Allan, they came and told me that I was a widow like many other women—I who had never been a wife. Allan, Hernan said that I should not grieve for you, as you deserved your fate, since you had been caught in your own snare, being one of those who had betrayed the Boers. The Vrouw Prinsloo answered to his face that he lied, and, Allan, I said that I would never speak to him again until we met before the Judgment Seat of God; nor will I do so."

"But I will speak to him," I muttered. "Well, where are they now?"

"They rode this morning back to the other Boers. I think they want to bring a party of them here to settle, if they like this place, as it is so easy to defend. They said they would return to-morrow and that meanwhile we were quite safe, as they had sure tidings that all the Zulus were back over the Tugela, taking some of their wounded with them, and also the Boer cattle as an offering to Dingaan. But come to the house, Allan—our home that I had made ready for you as well as I could. Oh! my God! our home on the threshold of which I believed you would never set a foot. Yes, when the moon rose from that cloud I believed it, and look, they are still quite close together. Hark, what is that?"

I listened and caught the sound of a horse's hoofs stumbling among the rocks.

"Don't be frightened," I answered; "it is only Hans with my horse. He escaped also; I will tell you how afterwards." And as I spoke he appeared, a woebegone and exhausted object.

"Good day, missie," he said with an attempt at cheerfulness. "Now you should give me a fine dinner, for you see I have brought the baas back safe to you. Did I not tell you, baas, that everything would come right?"

Then he grew silent from exhaustion. Nor were we sorry, who at that moment did not wish to listen to the poor fellow's talk.

Something over two hours had gone by since the moon broke out from the clouds. I had greeted the Vrouw Prinsloo and all my other friends, and been received by them with rapture as one risen from the dead. If they had loved me before, now a new gratitude was added to their love, since had it not been for my warning they also must have made acquaintance with the Zulu spears and perished. It was on their part of the camp that the worst of the attack fell. Indeed, from those wagons hardly anyone escaped.

I had told them all the story, to which they listened in dead silence. Only when it was finished the Heer Meyer, whose natural gloom had been deepened by all these events, said:

"Allemachte! but you have luck, Allan, to be left when everyone else is taken. Now, did I not know you so well, like Hernan Pereira I should think that you and that devil Dingaan had winked at each other."

The Vrouw Prinsloo turned on him furiously.

"How dare you say such words, Carl Meyer?" she exclaimed. "Must Allan always be insulted just because he is English, which he cannot help? For my part, I think that if anyone winked at Dingaan it was the stinkcat Pereira. Otherwise why did he come away before the killing and bring that madman, Henri Marais, with him ? "

" I don't know, I am sure, aunt," said Meyer humbly, for like everyone else he was afraid of the Vrouw Prinsloo.

" Then why can't you hold your tongue instead of saying silly things which must give pain ? " asked the vrouw. " No, don't answer, for you will only make matters worse ; but take the rest of that meat to the poor Hottentot, Hans "—I should explain that we had been supping—" who, although he has eaten enough to burst any white stomach, I dare say can manage another pound or two."

Meyer obeyed meekly, and the others melted away also as they were wont to do when the vrouw showed signs of war, so that she and we two were left alone.

" Now," said the vrouw, " everyone is tired, and I say that it is time to go to rest. Good night, nephew Allan and niece Marie," and she waddled away leaving us together.

" Husband," said Marie presently, " will you come and see the home that I made ready for you before I thought that you were dead ? It is a poor place, but I pray God that we may be happy there," and she took me by the hand and kissed me once and twice and thrice.

About noon on the following day, when my wife and I were laughing and arguing over some little domestic detail of our meagre establishment—so soon are great griefs forgotten in an overwhelming joy, of a sudden I saw her face change, and asked what was the matter.

" Hist ! " she said, " I hear horses," and she pointed in a certain direction.

I looked, and there, round the corner of the hill, came a body of Boers with their after-riders, thirty-two or -three of them in all, of whom twenty were white men.

" See," said Marie, " my father is among them, and my cousin Hernan rides at his side."

It was true. There was Henri Marais, and just behind him, talking into his ear, rode Hernan Pereira. I remember that the two of them reminded me of a tale I had read about a man who was cursed with an evil genius that drew him to some dreadful doom in spite of the promptings of his better nature. The thin, worn, wild-eyed Marais, and the rich-faced, carnal Pereira whispering slyly into his ear; they were exact types of that man in the story and his evil genius who dragged him down to hell. Prompted by some impulse, I threw my arms round Marie and embraced her, saying:

"At least we have been very happy for a while."

"What do you mean, Allan?" she asked doubtfully.

"Only that I think our good hours are done with for the present."

"Perhaps," she answered slowly; "but at least they have been very good hours, and if I should die to-day I am glad to have lived to win them."

Then the cavalcade of Boers came up.

Hernan Pereira, his senses sharpened perhaps by the instincts of hate and jealousy, was the first to recognise me.

"Why, Mynheer Allan Quatermain," he said, "how is it that you are here? How is that you still live? Commandant," he added, turning to a dark, sad-faced man of about sixty whom at that time I did not know, "here is a strange thing. This Heer Quatermain, an Englishman, was with the Governor Retief at the town of the Zulu king, as the Heer Henri Marais can testify. Now, as we know for sure Pieter Retief and all his people are dead, murdered by Dingaan, how then does it happen that this man has escaped?"

"Why do you put riddles to me, Mynheer Pereira?" asked the dark Boer. "Doubtless the Englishman will explain."

"Certainly I will, mynheer," I said. "Is it your pleasure that I should speak now?"

The commandant hesitated. Then, having called Henri Marais apart and talked to him for a little while, he replied:

"No, not now, I think; the matter is too serious. After we have eaten we will listen to your story, Mynheer Quatermain, and meanwhile I command you not to leave this place."

"Do you mean that I am a prisoner, Commandant?" I asked.

"If you put it so—yes, Mynheer Quatermain—a prisoner who has to explain how some sixty of our brothers, who were your companions, came to be butchered like beasts in Zululand, while you escaped. Now, no more words ; by and by doubtless there will be plenty of them. Here you, Carolus and Johannes, keep watch upon this Englishman, of whom I hear strange stories, with your guns loaded, please, and when we send to you, lead him before us."

" As usual, your cousin Hernan brings evil gifts," I said to Marie bitterly. " Well, let us also eat our dinner, which perhaps the Heeren Carolus and Johannes will do us the honour to share —bringing their loaded guns with them."

Carolus and Johannes accepted the invitation and from them we heard much news, all of it terrible enough to learn, especially the details of the massacre in that district, which because of this fearful event is now and always will be known as Weenen, or The Place of Weeping. Suffice it to say that they were quite enough to take away all our appetite, although Carolus and Johannes, who by this time had recovered somewhat from the shock of that night of blood and terror, ate in a fashion which might have filled Hans himself with envy.

Shortly after we had finished our meal, Hans, who, by the way, seemed to have quite recovered from his fatigues, came to remove the dishes. He informed us that all the Boers were having a great " talk," and that they were about to send for me. Sure enough, a few minutes later two armed men arrived and ordered me to follow them. I turned to say some words of farewell to Marie, but she said :

" I go where you do, husband," and, as no objection was made by the guard, she came.

About two hundred yards away, sitting under the shade of one of the wagons, we found the Boers. Six of them were seated in a semicircle upon stools or whatever they could find, the black-browed commandant being in the centre and having in front of him a rough table on which were writing materials.

To the left of these six were the Prinsloos and Meyers, being those folk whom I had rescued from Delagoa, and to the right the other Boers who had ridden into the camp that morning. I saw at a glance that a court-martial had been arranged and that the six elders were the judges, the commandant being the president of the court.

I do not give their names purposely, since I have no wish that the actual perpetrators of the terrible blunder that I am about to describe should be known to posterity. After all, they acted honestly according to their lights, and were but tools in the hand of that villain Hernan Pereira.

" Allan Quatermain," said the commandant, " you are brought here to be tried by a court-martial duly constituted according to the law published in the camps of the emigrant Boers. Do you acknowledge that law ? "

" I know that there is such a law, Commandant," I answered, " but I do not acknowledge the authority of your court-martial to try a man who is no Boer, but a subject of the Queen of Great Britain."

" We have considered that point, Allan Quatermain," said the commandant, " and we disallow it. You will remember that in the camp at Bushman's River, before you rode with the late Pieter Retief to the chief Sikonyela, when you were given command of the Zulus who went with him, you took an oath to interpret truly and to be faithful in all things to the General Retief, to his companions and to his cause. That oath we hold gives this court jurisdiction over you."

" I deny your jurisdiction," I answered, " although it is true that I took an oath to interpret faithfully and I request that a note of my denial may be made in writing."

" It shall be done," said the commandant, and laboriously he made the note on the paper before him.

When he had finished he looked up and said : " The charge against you, Allan Quatermain, is that, being one of the commission who recently visited the Zulu king Dingaan, under command of the late Governor and General Pieter Retief, you did falsely and wickedly urge the said Dingaan to murder the said Pieter Retief and his companions, and especially Henri Marais, your father-in-law, and Hernando Pereira, his nephew, with both of whom you had a quarrel. Further, that afterwards you brought about the said murder, having first arranged with the king of the Zulus that you should be removed to a place of safety while it was done. Do you plead Guilty or Not Guilty ? "

Now when I heard this false and abominable charge my rage and indignation caused me to laugh aloud.

" Are you mad, Commandant," I exclaimed, " that you should say such things ? On what evidence is this wicked lie advanced against me ? "

" No, Allan Quatermain, I am not mad," he replied, " although it is true that through your evil doings I, who had lost my wife and three children by the Zulu spears, have suffered enough to make me mad. As for the evidence against you, you shall hear it. But first I will write down that you plead Not guilty."

He did so, then said :

" If you will acknowledge certain things it will save us all much time, of which at present we have little to spare. Those things are that knowing what was going to happen to the commission you tried to avoid accompanying it. Is that true ? "

" No," I answered. " I knew nothing of what was going to happen to the commission, though I feared something, having but just saved my friends there "—and I pointed to the Prinsloos —" from death at the hands of Dingaan. I did not wish to accompany it for another reason : that I had been married on the day of its starting to Marie Marais. Still, I went after all because the General Retief, who was my friend, asked me to come, to interpret for him."

Now some of the Boers present said :

" That is true. We remember."

But the commandant continued, taking no heed of my answer or these interruptions.

" Do you acknowledge that you were on bad terms with Henri Marais and with Hernan Pereira ? "

" Yes," I answered ; " because Henri Marais did all in his power to prevent my marriage with his daughter Marie, behaving very ill to me who had saved his life and that of his people who remained to him up by Delagoa, and afterwards at Umgungundhlovu. Because, too, Hernan Pereira strove to rob me of Marie, who loved me. Moreover, although I had saved him when he lay sick to death, he afterwards tried to murder me by shooting me down in a lonely place. Here is the mark of it," and I touched the little scar upon the side of my forehead.

" That is true; he did so, the stinkcat," shouted the Vrouw Prinsloo, and was ordered to be silent.

"Do you acknowledge," went on the commandant, "that you sent to warn your wife and those with her to depart from the camp on the Bushman's River, because it was going to be attacked, charging them to keep the matter secret, and that afterwards both you and your Hottentot servant alone returned safely from Zululand, where all those who went with you lie dead?"

"I acknowledge," I answered, "that I wrote to tell my wife to come to this place where I had been building houses, as you see, and to bring with her any of our companions who cared to trek here, or, failing that, to go alone. This I did because Dingaan had told me, whether in jest or in earnest I did not know, that he had given orders that my said wife should be kidnapped, as he desired to make her one of his women, having thought her beautiful when he saw her. Also what I did was done with the knowledge and by the wish of the late Governor Retief, as can be shown by his writing on my letter. I acknowledge also that I escaped when all my brothers were killed as did the Hottentot Hans, and if you wish to know I will tell you how we escaped and why."

The commandant made a further note, then he said:

"Let the witness Hernan Pereira be called and sworn."

This was done and he was ordered to tell his tale.

As may be imagined, it was a long tale, and one that had evidently been prepared with great care. I will only set down its blackest falsehoods. He assured the court that he had no enmity against me and had never attempted to kill me or do me any harm, although it was true that his heart felt sore because, against her father's will, I had stolen away the affection of his betrothed, who was now my wife. He said that he had stopped in Zululand because he knew that I should marry her as soon as she came of age, and it was too great pain for him to see this done. He said that while he was there, before the arrival of the commission, Dingaan and some of his captains had told him that I had again and again urged him, Dingaan, to kill the Boers because they were traitors to the Sovereign of England, but that he, Dingaan, had refused to do so. He said that when Retief came up with the commission he tried to warn him against me, but that Retief would not listen, being infatuated with me as many others were, and he looked towards the Prinsloos.

Then came the worst of all. He said that while he was engaged in mending some guns for Dingaan in one of his private huts, he overheard a conversation between myself and Dingaan which took place outside the hut, I, of course, not knowing that he was within. The substance of this conversation was that I again urged Dingaan to kill the Boers and afterwards to send an impi to massacre their wives and families. Only I asked him to give me time to get away a girl whom I had married from among them, and with her a few of my own friends whom I wished should be spared, as I intended to become a kind of chief over them, and if he would grant it me, to hold all the land of Natal under his rule and the protection of the English. To these proposals Dingaan answered that " they seemed wise and good, and that he would think them over very carefully."

Pereira said further that coming out of the hut after Dingaan had gone away he reproached me bitterly for my wickedness, and announced that he would warn the Boers, which he did subsequently by word of mouth and in writing. That thereon I caused him to be detained by the Zulus while I went to Retief and told him some false story about him, Pereira, which caused Retief to drive him out of his camp and give orders that none of the Boers should so much as speak to him. That then he did the only thing he could. Going to his uncle, Henri Marais, he told him, not all the truth, but that he had learnt for certain that his daughter Marie was in dreadful danger of her life because of some intended attack of the Zulus, and that all the Boers among whom she dwelt were also in danger of their lives.

Therefore he suggested to Henri Marais that as the General Retief was besotted and would not listen to his story, the best thing they could do was to ride away and warn the Boers. This then they did secretly, without the knowledge of Retief, but being delayed upon their journey by one accident and another, which he set out in detail, they only reached the Bushman's River too late, after the massacre had taken place. Subsequently, as the commandant knew, hearing a rumour that Marie Marais and other Boers had trekked to this place before the slaughter, they came here and learned that they had done so upon a

warning sent to them by Allan Quatermain, whereon they returned and communicated the news to the surviving Boers at
Bushman's River.

That was all he had to say.

Then, as I reserved my cross-examination until I heard all
the evidence against me, Henri Marais was sworn and corroborated his nephew's testimony on many points as to my relations
to his daughter, his objection to my marriage to her because I
was an Englishman whom he disliked and mistrusted, and so
forth. He added further that it was true Pereira had told him
he had sure information that Marie and the Boers were in danger
from an attack upon them which had been arranged between
Allan Quatermain and Dingaan; that he also had written to
Retief and tried to speak to him but was refused a hearing.
Thereon he had ridden away from Umgungundhlovu to try to
save his daughter and warn the Boers. That was all he had to
say.

As there was no further witnesses for the prosecution I cross-
examined these two at full length, but absolutely without results,
since every vital question that I asked was met with a direct
negative.

Then I called my witnesses, Marie, whose evidence they
refused to hear on the ground that she was my wife and prejudiced, the Vrouw Prinsloo and her family, and the Meyers.
One and all told a true story of my relations with Hernan Pereira,
Henri Marais, and Dingaan, so far as they knew them.

After this, as the commandant declined to take the evidence of
Hans because he was a Hottentot and my servant, I addressed
the court, relating exactly what had taken place between me and
Dingaan, and how I and Hans came to escape on our second
visit to his kraal. I pointed out also that unhappily for myself
I could not prove my words, since Dingaan was not available
as a witness, and all the others were dead. Further, I produced
my letter to Marie, which was endorsed by Retief, and the letter
to Retief signed by Marais and Pereira which remained in my
possession.

By the time that I had finished my speech the sun was setting
and everyone was tired out. I was ordered to withdraw under
guard, while the court consulted, which it did for a long

while. Then I was called forward again and the commandant said :

" Allan Quatermain, after prayer to God we have considered this case to the best of our judgment and ability. On the one hand we note that you are an Englishman, a member of a race which hates and has always oppressed our people, and that it was to your interest to get rid of two of them with whom you had quarrelled. The evidence of Henri Marais and Hernan Pereira, which we cannot disbelieve, shows that you were wicked enough, either in order to do this, or because of your malice against the Boer people, to plot their destruction with a savage. The result is that some seven hundred men, women, and children have lost their lives in a very cruel manner, whereas you, your servant, your wife and your friends have alone escaped unharmed. For such a crime as this a hundred deaths could not pay ; indeed, God alone can give to it its just punishment, and to Him it is our duty to send you to be judged. We condemn you to be shot as a traitor and a murderer, and may He have mercy on your soul."

At these dreadful words Marie fell to the ground fainting and a pause ensued while she was carried off to the Prinsloos' house, whither the vrouw followed to attend her. Then the commandant went on :

" Still, although we have thus passed judgment on you ; because you are an Englishman against whom it might be said that we had prejudices, and because you have had no opportunity of preparing a defence, and no witnesses to the facts, since all those whom you say you could have called are dead, we think it right that this unanimous sentence of ours should be confirmed by a general court of the emigrant Boers. Therefore to-morrow morning you will be taken with us to the Bushman's River camp, where the case will be settled, and, if necessary, execution done in accordance with the verdict of the generals and veld-cornets of that camp. Meanwhile you will be kept in custody in your own house. Now have you anything to say against this sentence ? "

" Yes, this," I answered, " that although you do not know it, it is an unjust sentence, built up on the lies of one who has always been my enemy, and of a man whose brain is rotten. I never betrayed the Boers. If anyone betrayed them it was Hernan Pereira himself, who, as I proved to the General Retief, had been praying Dingaan to kill me, and whom Retief threatened to put upon his trial for this very crime, for which reason and no other Pereira fled from the kraal, taking his tool Henri Marais with him. You have asked God to judge me. Well, I ask God to judge him and Henri Marais also, and I know He will in one way or another. As for me, I am ready to die, as I have been for months while serving the cause of you Boers. Shoot me now if you will, and make an end. But I tell you that if I escape your hands I will not suffer this treatment to go unpunished. I will lay my case before the rulers of my people, and if necessary before my Queen, yes, if I have to travel to London to do it, and you Boers shall learn that you cannot condemn an innocent Englishman upon false testimony and not pay the price. I tell you that price shall be great if I live, and if I die it shall be greater still."

Now these words, very foolish words, I admit, which being young and inexperienced I spoke in my British pride, I could see made a great impression upon my judges. They believed, to be fair to them, that they had passed a just sentence. Blinded by prejudice and falsehood, and maddened by the dreadful losses their people had suffered during the past few days at the hands of a devilish savage, they believed that I was the instigator of those losses, one who ought to die. Indeed, all, or nearly all the Boers were persuaded that Dingaan was urged to this massacre by the counsels of Englishmen. The mere fact of my own and my servant's miraculous escape, when all my companions had perished, proved my guilt to them without the evidence of Pereira, which, being no lawyers, they thought sufficient to justify their verdict.

· Still, they had an uneasy suspicion that this evidence was not conclusive, and might indeed be rejected *in toto* by a more competent court upon various grounds. Also they knew themselves to be rebels who had no legal right to form a court, and feared the power of the long arm of England, from which for a little while they had escaped. If I were allowed to tell my tale to the Parliament in London, what might not happen to them, they wondered—to them who had ventured to pass sentence of death upon a subject of the Queen of Great Britain? Might not this turn the scale against them? Might not Britain arise in wrath and crush them, these men who dared to invoke her forms of law in order to kill her citizen? Those, as I learned afterwards, were the thoughts that passed through their minds.

Also another thought passed through their minds—that if the sentence were executed at once, a dead man cannot appeal, and that here I had no friends to take up my cause and avenge me. But of all this they said nothing. Only at a sign I was marched away to my little house and imprisoned under guard.

Now I propose to tell the rest of the history of these tragic events as they happened, although some of them did not come to my knowledge till the morrow or afterwards, for I think this will be the more simple and the easier plan.

XXI

THE INNOCENT BLOOD

AFTER I had been taken away it seems that the court summoned Hernan Pereira and Henri Marais to accompany them to a lonely spot at a distance, where they thought that their deliberations would not be overheard. In this, however, they were mistaken, having forgotten the fox-like cunning of the Hottentot, Hans. Hans had heard me sentenced, and probably enough, feared that he who also had committed the crime of escaping from Dingaan, might be called on to share that sentence. Also he wished to know the secret counsel of these Boers, whose language, of course, he understood as well as he did his own.

So making a circuit up the hillside, he crept towards them on his belly, as a snake creeps, wriggling in and out between the tufts of last year's dead grass, which grew here in plenty, without so much as moving their tops. At length he lay still in the centre of a bush that grew behind a stone not five paces from where they were talking, whence he listened intently to every word that passed their lips.

This was the substance of their talk; that for the reasons I have already mentioned it would be best that I should die at once. Sentence, said the commandant, had been passed, and could not be rescinded, since even if it were, their offence would remain as heavy in the eyes of the English authorities. But if they took me to their main camp to be retried by their great council, possibly that sentence might be rescinded and they be left individually and collectively to atone for what they had done. Also they knew that I was very clever and might escape in some other way to bring the English, or possibly the Zulus, upon them, since they felt convinced that Dingaan and I were working together for their destruction, and that while I had breath in my body I should never cease my efforts to be avenged.

When it was found that they were all of one mind in this matter, the question arose : What should be done ? Somebody suggested that I should be shot at once, but the commandant pointed out that such a deed, worked at night, would look like murder, especially as it violated the terms of their verdict.

Then another suggestion was made: that I should be brought out of my house just before the dawn on pretence that it was time to ride ; that then I should be given the opportunity of escape and instantly shot down. Or it might be pretended that I had tried to escape, with a like result. Who, they urged, was to know in that half-light whether I had or had not actually attempted to run for my life, or to threaten their lives, circumstances under which the law said it was justifiable to shoot a prisoner already formally condemned to death?

To this black counsel they all agreed, being so terribly afraid of a poor English lad whose existence, although most of them did not know this, was to be taken from him upon false evidence. But then arose another question: By whose hand should the thing be done? Not one of them, it would seem, was anxious to fulfil this bloody office; indeed, they one and all refused to do so. A proposal was put forward that some of their native servants should be forced to serve as executioners ; but when this had been vetoed by the general sense of the court, their counsels came to a deadlock.

Then, after a whispered conference, the commandant spoke some dreadful words.

" Hernando Pereira and Henri Marais," he said, " it is on your evidence that this young man has been condemned. We believe that evidence, but if by one jot or one tittle it is false, then not justice, but a foul murder will have been committed and his innocent blood will be upon your heads for ever. Hernando Pereira and Henri Marais, the court appoints you to be the guards who will bring the prisoner out of his house tomorrow morning just when the sky begins to lighten. It is from *you* that he will try to escape, and *you* will prevent his escape by his death. Then you must join us where we shall be waiting for you and report the execution."

When Henri Marais heard this he exclaimed :

" I swear by God that I cannot do it. Is it right or natural that a man should be forced to kill his own son-in-law ? "

" You could bear evidence against your own son-in-law, Henri Marais," answered the stern-faced commandant. "Why then cannot you kill with your rifle one whom you have already helped to kill with your tongue ? "

" I will not, I cannot ! " said Marais, tearing at his beard. But the commandant only answered coldly :

" You have the orders of the court, and if you choose to disobey them we shall begin to believe that you have sworn falsely. Then you and your nephew will also appear before the great council when the Englishman is tried again. Still, it matters nothing to us whether you or Hernando Pereira shall fire the shot. See you to it, as the Jews said to Judas who had betrayed the innocent Lord."

Then he paused and went on, addressing Pereira :

" Do you also refuse, Hernando Pereira ? Remember before you answer that if you do refuse we shall draw our own conclusions. Remember, too, that the evidence which you have given, showing that this wicked Englishman plotted and caused the deaths of our brothers and of our wives and children, which we believe to be true evidence, shall be weighed and investigated word by word before the great council."

" To give evidence is one thing, and to shoot the traitor and murderer another," said Pereira. Then he added with an oath, or so vowed Hans: " Yet why should I, who know all this villain's guilt, refuse to carry out the sentence of the law on him ? Have no fear, Commandant, the accursed Allan Quatermain shall not succeed in his attempt to escape tomorrow before the dawn."

" So be it," said the commandant. " Now do all you who have heard those words take note of them."

Then Hans, seeing that the council was about to break up, and fearing lest he should be caught and killed, slipped away by the same road that he had come. His thought was to warn me, but this he could not do because of the guards. So he went to the Prinsloos, and finding the vrouw alone with Marie, who had recovered her mind, told them everything that he had heard.

As he said, Marie knelt down and prayed, or thought for a long while, then rose and spoke.

" Tante," she said to the vrouw, " one thing is clear, that Allan will be murdered at the dawn ; now if he is hidden away he may escape."

" But where and how can we hide him," asked the vrouw, " seeing that the place is guarded ? "

" Tante," said Marie again, " at the back of your house is an old cattle kraal made by Kaffirs, and in that cattle kraal, as I have seen, there are mealie-pits where those Kaffirs stored their grain. Now I suggest that we should put my husband into one of those mealie-pits and cover it over. There the Boers might not find him, however close they searched."

" That is a good idea," said the vrouw ; "but how in the name of God are we to get Allan out of a guarded house into a mealie-pit ? "

" Tante, I have a right to go to my husband's house, and there I will go. Afterwards, too, I shall have the right to leave his house before he is taken away. Well, he might leave it in my place, *as me*, and you and Hans might help him. Then in the morning the Boers would come to search the house and find no one except me."

" That is all very pretty," answered the vrouw ; " but do you think, my niece, that those accursed vultures will go away until they have picked Allan's bones? Not they, for too much hangs on it. They will know that he cannot be far off, and slink about the place until they have found him in his mealie-hole, or until he comes out. It is blood they are after, thanks to your cousin Hernan, the liar, and blood they will have for their own safety's sake. Never will they go away from here until they see Allan lying dead upon the ground."

Now, according to Hans, Marie thought again very deeply. Then she answered:

"There is a great risk, tante; but we must take it. Send your husband to chat with those guards, and give him a bottle of spirits. I will talk with Hans here and see what can be arranged."

So Marie went aside with Hans, as he told me afterwards, and asked him if he knew of any medicine that made people sleep for a long while without waking. He answered, Yes; all the coloured people had plenty of such medicine. Without doubt he could get some from the Kaffirs who dwelt upon the place, or if not he could dig the roots of a plant that he had seen growing near by which would serve the purpose. So she sent him to procure this stuff. Afterwards she spoke to the Vrouw Prinsloo, saying:

"My plan is that Allan should escape from our house disguised as myself. But as I know well that he will not run away while he has his senses, seeing that to do so in his mind would be to confess his guilt, I propose to take his senses from him by means of a drugged drink. Then I propose that you and Hans should carry him into the shadow of this house, and when no one is looking, to the old grain-pit that lies but a few yards away, covering the mouth of it with dead grass. There he will remain till the Boers grow tired of searching for him and ride away. Or if it should chance that they find him, he will be no worse off than he was before."

"A good plan enough, Marie, though not one that Allan would have anything to do with if he kept his wits," answered the vrouw, "seeing that he was always a man for facing things out, although so young in years. Still, we will try to save him in spite of himself from the claws of that stinkcat Pereira, whom may God curse, and his tool, your father. As you say, at the worst no harm will be done even if they find him, as probably they will, seeing that they will not leave this place without blood."

Such then was the trick which Marie arranged with the Vrouw Prinsloo. Or rather, I should say, seemed to arrange, since she told her nothing of her real mind, she who knew that the vrouw was right and that for their own sakes, as well as because they believed it to be justice, the Boers would never leave that place until they saw blood running on the grass.

This, oh! this was Marie's true and dreadful plan—*to give her life for mine!* She was sure that once he had slain his victim, Hernan Pereira would not stop to make examination of the corpse. He would ride away, hounded by his guilty conscience, and meanwhile I could escape.

She never thought the thing out in all its details, she who was maddened with terror and had no time. She only felt her way from step to step, dimly seeing my deliverance at the end of the journey. Marie told the Vrouw Prinsloo nothing, except that she proposed to drug me if I would not go undrugged. Then the vrouw must hide me as best she could, in the grain-pit or elsewhere, or, if I had my senses about me, let me hide myself. Afterwards she, Marie, would face the Boers and tell them to find me if they wanted me.

The vrouw answered that she had now thought of a better plan. It was that she should arrange with her husband and son and the Meyers, all of whom loved me, that they should rescue me, or if need be, kill or disable Pereira before he could shoot me.

Marie replied that this was good if it could be done, and the vrouw went out to find her husband and the other men. Presently, however, she returned with a long face, saying that the commandant had them all under guard. It seemed that it had occurred to him, or more probably to Pereira, that the Prinsloos and the Meyers, who looked on me as a brother, might attempt some rescue, or make themselves formidable in other ways. Therefore, as a matter of precaution, they had been put under arrest and their arms taken from them as mine had been. What the commandant said, however, was that he took these somewhat high-handed measures in order to be sure that they, the

Prinsloos and the Meyers, should be ready on the following morning to ride with him and the prisoner to the main camp, where the great council might wish to interrogate them.

One concession, however, the vrouw had won from the commandant, who, knowing what was about to happen to me, had not, I suppose, the heart to refuse. It was that my wife and she might visit me and give me food on the stipulation that they both left the house where I was confined by ten o'clock that night.

So it came to this, that if anything was to be done, these two women and a Hottentot must do it, since they could hope for no help in their plans. Here I should add that the vrouw told Marie in Hans's presence that she had thought of attacking the commandant as to this matter of my proposed shooting by Pereira. On reflection, however, she refrained for two reasons, first because she feared lest she might only make matters worse and rob me of my sole helpers, and secondly for fear lest she should bring about the death of Hans, to whom the story would certainly be traced.

As he was the solitary witness to the plot, it seemed to her that he would scarcely be allowed to escape to repeat it far and wide. Especially was this so, as the unexplained death of a Hottentot, suspected of treachery like his master, was not a matter that would have been thought worth notice in those rough and bloody times. She may have been right, or she may have been wrong, but in weighing her decision it must always be borne in mind that she was, and until the end remained, in utter ignorance of Marie's heroic design to go to her death in place of me.

So the two women and the Hottentot proceeded to mature the plans which I have outlined. One other alternative, however, Hans did suggest. It was that they should try to drug the guards with some of the medicated drink that was meant for me, and that then Marie, I and he should slip away and get down to the river, there to hide in the reeds. Thence, perhaps, we might escape to Port Natal where lived Englishmen who would protect us.

Of course this idea was hopeless from the first. The moonlight was almost as bright as day, and the veld quite open for a long way round, so that we should certainly have been seen and recaptured, which of course would have meant instant death. Further, as it happened, the guards had been warned against touching liquor of any sort since it was thought probable that an attempt would be made to intoxicate them. Still the women determined to try this scheme if they could find a chance. At least it was a second string to their bow.

Meanwhile they made their preparations. Hans went away for a little and returned with a supply of his sleep-producing drug, though whether he got this from the Kaffirs or gathered it himself, I do not remember, if I ever heard. At any rate it was boiled up in water with which they made the coffee that I was to drink, though not in that which Marie proposed to drink with me, the strong taste and black hue of the coffee effectually hiding any flavour or colour that there might be in the herb. Also the vrouw cooked some food which she gave to Hans to carry. First, however, he went to investigate the old mealie-pit which was within a few paces of the back door of the Prinsloos' house. He reported that it would do well to hide a man in, especially as tall grass and bushes grew about its mouth.

Then the three of them started, and arriving at the door of my house, which was about a hundred yards away, were of course challenged by the sentries.

" Heeren," said Marie, " the commandant has given us leave to bring food to my husband, whom you guard within. Pray do not prevent us from entering."

" No," answered one of them gently enough, for he was touched with pity at her plight. " We have our orders to admit you, the Vrouw Prinsloo and the native servant, though why three of you should be needed to carry food to one man, I don't know. I should have thought that at such a time he would have preferred to be alone with his wife."

" The Vrouw Prinsloo wishes to ask my husband certain questions about his property here and what is to be done while he and her men are away at the main camp for the second trial, as I, whose heart is full of sorrow, have no head for such things. Also the Hottentot must have orders as to where he is to get a horse to ride with him, so pray let us pass, mynheer."

" Very good ; it is no affair of ours, Vrouw Quatermain—

Stay, I suppose that you have no arms under that long cloak of yours."

"Search me, if you will, mynheer," she answered, opening the cloak, whereon, after a quick glance, he nodded and bade them enter, saying :

"Mind, you are to come out by ten o'clock. You must not pass the night in that house, or we shall have the little Englishman oversleeping himself in the morning."

Then they entered and found me seated at a table preparing notes for my defence and setting down the heads of the facts of my relations with Pereira, Dingaan, and the late Commandant Retief.

Here I may state that my condition at the time was not one of fear, but rather of burning indignation. Indeed, I had not the slightest doubt but that when my case was retried before the great council, I should be able to establish my complete innocence of the abominable charges that had been brought against me. Therefore it came about that when Marie suggested that I should try to escape, I begged her almost roughly not to mention such a thing again.

"Run away !" I said. "Why, that would be to confess myself guilty, for only the guilty run away. What I want is to have all this business thrashed out and that devil Pereira exposed."

"But, Allan," said Marie, "how if you should never live to have it thrashed out ? How if you should be shot first ? " Then she rose, and having looked to see that the shutter-board was fast in the little window-place and the curtain that she had made of sacking drawn over it, returned and whispered : "Hans here has heard a horrible tale, Allan. Tell it to the baas, Hans."

So while Vrouw Prinsloo, in order to deceive any prying eyes if such by chance could see us, busied herself with lighting a fire on the hearth in the second room on which to warm the food, Hans told his story much as it has already been set out.

I listened to it with growing incredulity. The thing seemed to me impossible. Either Hans was deceived or lying, the latter probably, for well I knew the Hottentot powers of imagination. Or perhaps he was drunk ; indeed, he smelt of liquor, of which I was aware he could carry a great quantity without outward signs of intoxication.

"I cannot believe it," I said when he had finished. "Even if Pereira is such a fiend, as is possible, would Henri Marais, your father—who, at any rate, has always been a good and God-fearing man—consent to work such a crime upon his daughter's husband, though he does dislike him?"

"My father is not what he was, Allen," said Marie. "Sometimes I think that his brain has gone."

"He did not speak like a man whose brain has gone this afternoon," I replied. "But let us suppose that this tale is true, what is it that you wish me to do?"

"Allan, I wish you to dress up in my clothes and get away to a hiding-place which Hans and the vrouw know, leaving me here instead of you."

"Why, Marie?" I said. "Then you might get yourself shot in my place, always supposing that they mean to shoot me. Also I should certainly be caught and killed, as they would have a right to kill me for trying to escape in disguise. That is a mad plan, and I have a better. Vrouw Prinsloo, go straight to the commandant and tell him all this story. Or, if he will not listen to you, scream it out at the top of your voice so that everyone may hear, and then come back and tell us the result. Of one thing I am sure, that if you do this, even if there was any thought of my being shot tomorrow morning, it will be abandoned. You can refuse to say who told you the tale."

"Yes, please do that," muttered Hans, "else I know one who will be shot."

"Good, I will go," said the vrouw, and she went, the guards letting her pass after a few words which we could not hear.

Half an hour later she returned and called to us to open the door.

"Well?" I asked.

"Well," she said, "I have failed, nephew. Except those sentries outside the door, the commandant and all the Boers have ridden off, I know not where, taking our people with them."

"That's odd," I answered, "but I suppose they thought they had not enough grass for their horses, or Heaven knows what they thought. Stay now, I will do something," and opening the door, I called to the guards, honest fellows in their way, whom I had known in past times.

" Listen, friends," I said. " A tale has been brought to me that I am not to be taken to the big camp to have my case inquired of by the council, but am to be shot down in cold blood when I come out of this house tomorrow morning. Is that true ? "

" Allemachte, Englishman ! " answered one of them. " Do you take us for murderers ? Our orders are to lead you to the commandant wherever he may appoint, so have no fear that we shall shoot you like a Kaffir. Either you or they who told you such a story are mad."

" So I thought, friends," I answered. " But where is the commandant and where are the others ? The Vrouw Prinsloo here has been to see them, and reports that they are all gone."

" That is very likely," said the Boer. " There is a rumour that some of your Zulu brothers have come across the Tugela again to hunt us, which, if you want to know the truth, is why we visited this place. Well, the commandant has taken his men for a ride to see if he can meet them by this bright moonlight. Pity he could not take you, too, since you would have known so well where to find them, if they are there at all. Now please talk no more nonsense to us, which it makes us sick to hear, and don't think that you can slip away because we are only two, for you know our *roers* are loaded with slugs, and we have orders to use them."

" There," I said when I had shut the door, " now you have heard for yourselves. As I thought, there is nothing in this fine story, so I hope you are convinced."

Neither the vrouw nor Marie made any answer, and Hans also held his tongue. Yet, as I remembered afterwards, I saw a strange glance pass between the two women, who were not at all convinced, and, although I never dreamed of such a thing, had now determined to carry out their own desperate plan. But of this I repeat the vrouw and Hans only knew one half; the rest was locked in Marie's loving heart.

" Perhaps you are right, Allan," said the vrouw in the tone of one who gives way to an unreasonable child. " I hope so, and, at any rate, you can refuse to come out of the house to-morrow morning until you are quite sure. And now let us eat some supper, for we shall not make matters better by going hungry. Hans, bring the food."

So we ate, or made pretence to eat, and I, being thirsty, drank two cups of the black coffee dashed with spirit to serve as milk. After this I grew strangely sleepy. The last thing I remember was Marie looking at me with her beautiful eyes, that were full—ah! so full of tender love, and kissing me again and again, upon the lips.

I dreamed all sorts of dreams, rather pleasant dreams on the whole. Then I woke up by degrees to find myself in an earthen pit shaped like a bottle and having the remains of polished sides to it. It made me think of Joseph who was let down by his brethren into a well in the desert. Now, who on earth could have let me down into a well, especially as I had no brethren? Perhaps I was not really in a well. Perhaps this was a nightmare. Or I might be dead. I began to remember that there were certain good reasons why I should be dead. Only, only—why should they have buried me in woman's clothes, such as I seemed to wear?

And what was that noise that had wakened me?

It could not be the trump of doom, unless the trumping of doom went off like a double-barrelled gun.

I began to try to climb out of my hole, but as it was nine feet deep and bottle-shaped, which the light flowing in from the neck showed, I found this impossible. Just as I was giving up the attempt, a yellow face appeared in that neck, which looked to me like the face of Hans, and an arm was projected downwards.

" Jump, if you are awake, baas," said a voice—surely it was the voice of Hans—" and I will pull you out."

So I jumped, and caught the arm above the wrist. Then the owner of the arm pulled desperately, and the end of it was that I succeeded in gripping the edge of the bottle-like hole, and, with the help of the arm, in dragging myself out.

" Now, baas," said Hans, for it *was* Hans, " run, run before the Boers catch you."

" What Boers ? " I asked sleepily; " and how can I run with these things flapping about my legs ? "

Then I looked about me, and, although the dawn was only just breaking, began to recognise my surroundings. Surely this was the Prinsloos' house to my right, and that, faintly seen through the mist about a hundred paces away, was Marie's and my own. There seemed to be something going on yonder which excited my awakening curiosity. I could see figures moving in an unusual manner, and desired to know what they were doing. I began to walk towards them, and Hans, for his part, began to try to drag me in an opposite direction, uttering all sorts of gibberish, as to the necessity of my running away. But I would not be dragged; indeed, I struck at him, until at last, with an exclamation of despair, he let go of me and vanished.

So I went on alone. I came to my house, or what I thought resembled it, and there saw a figure lying on its face on the ground some ten or fifteen yards to the right of the doorway, and noted abstractedly that it was dressed in my clothes. The Vrouw Prinsloo, in her absurd night garments, was waddling towards the figure, and a little way off stood Hernan Pereira, apparently in the act of reloading a double-barrelled gun. Beyond, staring at him, stood the lantern-faced Henri Marais, pulling at his long beard with one hand and holding a rifle in the other. Behind were two saddled horses in the charge of a raw Kaffir, who looked on stupidly.

The Vrouw Prinsloo reached the body that lay upon the ground dressed in what resembled my clothes, and bending down her stout shape with an effort, turned it over. She glared into its face and then began to shriek.

" Come here, Henri Marais," she shrieked, " come, see what your beloved nephew has done ! You had a daughter who was all your life to you, Henri Marais. Well, come, look at her after your beloved nephew has finished his work with her ! "

Henri Marais advanced slowly like one who does not understand. He stood over the body on the ground, and looked down upon it through the morning mists.

Then suddenly he went mad. His broad hat fell from his head, and his long hair seemed to stand up. Also his beard grew big and bristled like the feathers of a bird in frosty weather. He turned on Hernan Pereira. " You devil ! " he shouted, and his voice sounded like the roar of a wild beast ; " you devil, you have murdered my daughter ! Because you could not get Marie for yourself, you have murdered her. Well, I will pay you back ! "

Without more ado he lifted his gun and fired straight at Hernan Pereira, who sank slowly to the ground and lay there groaning.

Just then I grew aware that horsemen were advancing upon us, a great number of horsemen, though whence they came at that time I did not know. One of these I recognised even in my half-drunken state, for he had impressed himself very vividly upon my mind. He was the dark-browed commandant who had tried and condemned me to death. He dismounted, and, staring at the two figures that lay upon the ground, said in a loud and terrible voice :

" What is this ? Who are these men, and why are they shot ? Explain, Henri Marais."

" Men ! " wailed Henri Marais, " they are not men. One is a woman—my only child ; and the other is a devil, who, being a devil, will not die. See ! he will not die. Give me another gun that I may make him die."

The commandant looked about him wildly, and his eye fell upon the Vrouw Prinsloo.

" What has chanced, vrouw ? " he asked.

" Only this," she replied in a voice of unnatural calm. " Your murderers whom you set on in the name of law and justice have made a mistake. You told them to murder Allan Quatermain for reasons of your own. Well, they have murdered his wife instead."

Now the commandant struck his hand upon his forehead and groaned, and I, half awakened at last, ran forward, shaking my fists and gibbering.

" Who is that ? " asked the commandant. " Is it a man or a woman ? "

" It is a man in woman's clothing ; it is Allan Quatermain," answered the vrouw, " whom we drugged and tried to hide from your butchers."

" He turned on Hernan Pereira . . . and his voice sounded
like the roar of a wild beast " (*See page* 268)

" God above us ! " exclaimed the commandant, " is this earth or hell ? "

Then the wounded Pereira raised himself upon one hand.

" I am dying," he cried ; " my life is bleeding away, but before I die I must speak. All that story I told against the Englishman is false. He never plotted with Dingaan against the Boers. It was I who plotted with Dingaan. Although I hated him because he found me out, I did not wish Retief and our people to be killed. But I did wish Allan Quatermain to be killed, because he had won her whom I loved, though, as it happened, all the others were slain, and he alone escaped. Then I came here and learned that Marie was his wife—yes, his wife indeed—and I grew mad with hate and jealousy. So I bore false witness against him, and, you fools, you believed me and ordered me to shoot him who is innocent before God and man. Then things went wrong. The woman tricked me again—for the last time. She dressed herself as the man, and in the dawnlight I was deceived. I killed her, her whom I love alone, and now her father, who loved her also, has killed me."

By this time I understood all, for my drugged brain had awakened at last. I ran to the brute upon the ground ; grotesque in my woman's garments all awry, I leaped on him and stamped out the last of his life. Then, standing over his dead body, I shook my fists and cried :

" Men, see what you have done. May God pay you back all you owe her and me ! "

They dismounted, they came round me, they protested, they even wept. And I, I raved at them upon the one side, while the mad Henri Marais raved upon the other ; and the Vrouw Prinsloo, waving her big arms, called down the curse of God and the blood of the innocent upon their heads and those of their children for ever.

Then I remember no more.

When I came to myself two weeks afterwards, for I had been very ill and in delirium, I was lying in the house of the Vrouw Prinsloo alone. The Boers had all gone, east and west and north and south, and the dead were long buried. They had taken Henri Marais with them, so I was told, dragging him away in a bullock cart, to which he was tied, for he was raving mad. Afterwards he became quieter, and, indeed, lived for years, walking about and asking all whom he met if they could lead him to Marie. But enough of him—poor man, poor man!

The tale which got about was that Pereira had murdered Marie out of jealousy, and been shot by her father. But there were so many tragic histories in those days of war and massacre that this particular one was soon quite forgotten, especially as those concerned in it for one reason and another did not talk overmuch of its details. Nor did I talk of it, since no vengeance could mend my broken heart.

They brought me a letter that had been found on Marie's breast, stained with her blood.

Here it is :

" MY HUSBAND,

" Thrice have you saved my life, and now it is my turn to save yours, for there is no other path. It may be that they will kill you afterwards, but if so, I shall be glad to have died first in order that I may be ready to greet you in the land beyond.

" I drugged you, Allan, then I cut off my hair and dressed myself in your clothes. The Vrouw Prinsloo, Hans and I set my garments upon you. They led you out as though you were fainting, and the guards, seeing me, whom they thought was you, standing in the doorway, let them pass without question.

" What may happen I do not know, for I write this after you are gone. I hope, however, that you will escape and lead some full and happy life, though I fear that its best moments will always be shadowed by memories of me. For I know you love me, Allan, and will always love me, as I shall always love you.

" The light is burning out—like mine—so farewell, farewell, farewell! All earthly stories come to an end at last, but at that end we shall meet again. Till then, adieu. Would that I could have done more for you, since to die for one who is loved with body, heart and soul is but a little thing. Still I have been your wife, Allan, and your wife I shall remain when the world is old. Heaven does not grow old, Allan, and there I shall greet you.

" The light is dead, but—oh !—in my heart another light arises !

" Your MARIE."

This was her letter.

I do not think there is anything more to be said.

Such is the history of my first love. Those who read it, if any ever do, will understand why I have never spoken of her before, and do not wish it to be known until I, too, am dead and have gone to join the great soul of Marie Marais.

ALLAN QUATERMAIN.

THE END